Risqué

BEAUTIFUL SINNER SERIES

ELENA M. REYES

SUMMARY

I'm the new KING of London, but it's her body I crave to CONQUER. Her enemies have become my own. Her body is my favorite toy.

We were never supposed to meet, but then there she was across the bar sitting beside my cousin's newest obsession. A small little beauty with a grin on her sweet lips and a low-cut top meant to tease—to destroy a man's self-control. She didn't see me, but I took in every sensual inch while placing a target on her head.

Our paths will cross, and she'll fight, but I'm a man of my convictions. My vow is unbreakable.

I'll be back for you, my Venus.

RISQUE
(Beautiful Sinner Series) Book 5
was written by Elena M. Reyes
Copyright 2021 ©Elena M. Reyes

Cover Design: T.E. Black Designs
Editor: Marti Lynch

Publication Date: August 30th 2021

Genre: FICTION/Romance/Erotica Suspense/Contemporary

ACKNOWLEDGMENTS

Before we get into RISQUE and its yumminess, I need to thank a few people that I adore:

K.I. Lynn, C.M. Steele, and Mary B. Moore: My girls. My chicas. My Boo's. You are a huge part of my life/success and I'm beyond blessed to have you as my peeps. Thank you from the bottom of my heart for being in my corner, for pushing me when I get stubborn, and for never letting me settle. You are such a huge part of my life and I'm thankful to have you in my corner. I love you.

Marti Lynch: I can never say THANK YOU enough! Seriously, you have the patience of a saint with me and always come through. You are the best editor and friend an author could ask for.

T.E. Black Designs: BEST. COVER. EVER. Seriously, I can't stop staring at my pretty. Thank you!

Michelle Myers: Babe, I legit can't thank you enough for the amount of work you did with me on this. You rode with me to the end, the long days, and made by baby so much better. Thank you for loving these characters and helping me become a better author. Love you!

Elena's Marked Girls: You guys keep me going and always give me a reason to smile. Thank you for everything. For your unconditional support and encouragement. Please know that I love you—that you mean everything to me.

Hubs and Kiddo: You are my heart. My entire world. Everything I do, I do it for you.

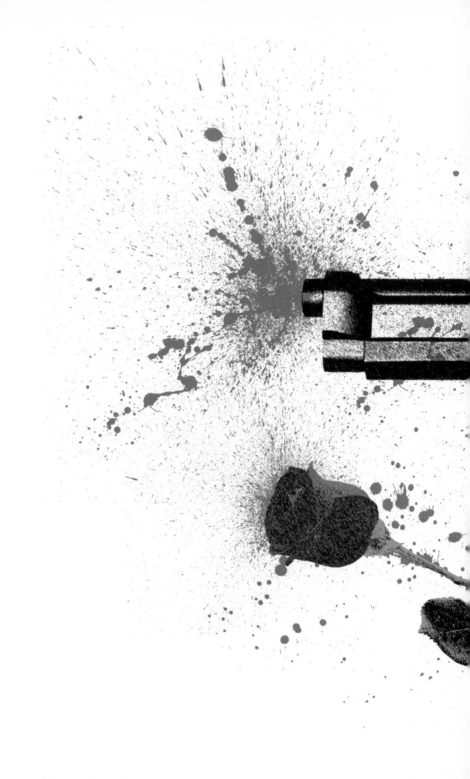

1
CALLUM

"**D**ISPOSE OF THE two separately."

"The two?" the man on his knees asks. These whimpered words slip through busted lips, the sound is amusing—a little whimsical—and I smile down at him. This is someone I've known my entire life, I grew up with the bloke, but greed is a dangerous disease and he let it consume him.

You don't steal from a Jameson.

You don't run from one either.

My family has a certain code we live by, and Jonathan Bryce broke every commandment.

Outside of his connection to me, he's no one of real importance, a normal man working a boring desk job with a wife who's pregnant and a dog who bares his teeth at him each time he walks through the door. The animal is a good judge of character. Can smell the bollocks that reek from this man's pores while he lies to his wife about where he's been and with whom.

He's useless, yet many overlook the shortcoming; the flat he lives in belongs to her, while the car he drives was a gift from me on his last birthday. His employment is another gift he didn't deserve then, and much less now as the family business isn't worth shit under his care.

Three simple responsibilities he couldn't provide for himself, and it stems from a gambling problem he refuses to accept.

Bryce loves football yet chooses the wrong team each bloody time, and as a mate, I've bailed him out more than a handful of times. Killed so he would be spared. I gave my protection because I felt bad for those he'd leave behind if a bookmaker took back a failed payment in blood.

He shared meals with the Jamesons.

He was allowed perks that weren't his to imbibe in.

And yet, he bit the hand that feeds.

Jonathan Bryce stole from me, and all for a night of basic sex with a whore's used pussy.

At the sight of my smirk, John pisses himself once again. *Disgusting.* "Please, Callum. It doesn't have to end like this, brother. Let me work this off. Or better yet, let me just call Mum. My family's good for it, and she'll wire you—"

His mouth snaps shut after kissing the two large rings on my fingers, the skin further tearing from the blow. "This is your mess, mate. Not theirs."

"Please." It's low. A cry. "It's not that big of a deal. Ezra was in on it. He—"

"No." Another plea sits heavily on his bloodied tongue, but I shake my head. He's afraid and has every reason to be. My friendship was an honest one, no strings attached on my end, but he abused the power it came with. I let him live in my shadow, and now I'll take away his right to breathe just the same. "You knew the consequences and took the risk anyway. Did you think someone loyal to the family, a hacker of all fucking things, wouldn't protect himself? I've seen the video. I heard every word that came out of your mouth."

His eyes drop to the ground, expression contrite. *Too late.* "I'm sorry."

"Lying to me will only make this worse."

"I don't want to die."

"And yet you've failed to give me a single reason why I should take pity, Jonathan."

"My unborn daughter." Bloody spittle lands on my trousers while I finger the edge of the blade in my hand. It slices the pad of my thumb, a few drops dripping down the metal and onto the handle while he watches, unmoving. Paralyzed. "She will need me."

"How sure are you about this?" I scratch my jaw. "What are you willing to bet?"

From the corner of my eye, I see one of the cleaners with me stop a few steps to my right with a familiar briefcase in hand. I'm not the only one who notices his presence, and I chuckle at the sight of Jonathan moving closer to me. An idiot move. *I'm the reaper. His executioner.* Jonathan's bloodied face tips up, his hands gripping my pant leg while tears roll down each cheek.

A true disappointment.

"She will need me."

"You can do better than that, arsehole."

For every action, there is an equal consequence you must accept and confront with pride. In my world, to hide, beg, or cry is a disrespect. More so than the offense that led you to your sentencing.

"I'm their sole provider. Neither would survive—"

Pursing my lips, I tilt my head to the side and give him a small sense of hope. As if I'm considering his idiocy—pretending for those few seconds that I don't know the kind of pathetic wanker he grew up to be. He's mistaken my friendship for something it's not, and even if he were family, I'd slit his throat just the same after a betrayal of any kind.

There's nothing above loyalty. Not even familial ties.

"Liar," I spit out through clenched teeth, and he stumbles back on his haunches, trying to crawl away but the stomp of my boot on his left knee stops him. Four times, and a scream rends the air; he's quick to grab the injured leg but stops when the tip of the knife in my right hand presses against his forehead, digging in just enough to bring blood to the surface of the small incision. "You're not worthy of the family you had, Jonathan. Melissa deserves better than you, and I'll make sure they're both taken care of. She'll never work two jobs again, nor will she continue to pay for your mistakes."

"If I don't return home, she'll call the cops. There's a file—" He trails off when the briefcase is opened and a second later a manila folder is tossed at his feet. He makes no move to grab it, but tears do fall when a few seconds later a dial tone fills the warm building I own a few hours outside of London. The area is all private farmland, almost two hundred acres of untouched property with a few buildings at the center that I use for personal storage. There's one road in and one out with security around the clock to take care of my cars, a few small planes, and my private collection of war memorabilia— weapons used throughout history to be exact, including a tank used during the Gulf War.

"That file?" The knife's tip digs in a little deeper.

His expression is one of disbelief—betrayal—but that soon turns to abject horror when his pregnant wife's voice comes through the line. "Is it done, Callum?"

"Not yet," I say before slicing down from forehead to cheek while puncturing his eyeball.

"Fuck!" His scream, full of anguish, makes pleasurable goose bumps rise across my flesh. The darkness within my soul is feeding off the echoes that surround us in the large, open space. The cut isn't deep enough to cause blindness, not that he'll be alive to enjoy the sights and sounds of life outside these walls, but enough to make him hiss in pain and tear up—each track down his cheek turns a reddish-brown as the dirt on his face mixes with his blood. "No more. I've learned my lesson."

"We have a request I must oblige." Maybe it's because of the cut or the realization that he's truly dispensable, but Jonathan's face drops and his shoulders slump. He's the poster child for someone who's disingenuously ashamed, yet either way, I pat his head like one would a dog and wag the knife in his face as one would a finger. "Someone needs to hear the verbal confirmation of your blessing."

"Are you taking the piss?" Her laugh is sardonic, completely ignoring his pain-filled yell, but I can still make out *her* tears. The anguish Jonathan has caused. "Do my words really matter?"

"Yes." Yet I'm not the one she's asking. Her question is directed to the piece of shit on his knees crying like a git. "Give me your vote."

She takes a deep breath, and I plunge the blade of my knife from one cheek to the other and leave it there while her husband whimpers. Paints the ground red with his blood one drop at a time, the sprinkling reminding me of one of those designs made by a macabre artist I admire from Seattle. "I've been a widow since the day after we said *I do*. It's time to recoup my full freedom."

"No!" Jonathan yells out without thinking, ripping the flesh on each cheek apart. His mouth fills with blood, it rolls down his neck and onto the dirty collar of the light pink polo he's wearing. "Love, please. Please don't abandon me. You're my—"

"I'm tired of bailing you out," she says lowly, the words full of so much hurt, and for the first time, I see true repentance on his face. *Too late.* "Your family's legacy is gone because of your selfishness, you bloody bastard. The dealerships are under insolvency proceedings, the houses are being sold to pay back the money you stole, and all while your mum had a heart attack at the care home after finding out what you did. While you were busy shagging..." She chokes on a sob, the pain raw, and if I had a better conscience, I'd forgive him for her. But I don't. I won't. "She's been in a coma while you were busy bending over a woman that isn't the one you promised to love and cherish."

"I'm sorry." His split lip wobbles, his entire frame shaking. "I'm so fucking sorry."

"No. You're not."

"Melissa, I know I've hurt you. That I've—"

"Wasted enough years of my life." The woman on the other end takes in a deep breath, the silence looming from the line before a painful sigh escapes her. "I can't do this anymore, and neither can your mum. You can go in peace knowing we'll be better off."

"I'll make this right. Just please—"

"You're only sorry you were caught, Jonathan. Goodbye." The dial tone follows, and the sorrowful scream that leaves him shakes his entire frame. And I'm humanitarian enough to give him a second to come to terms with his reality. His death sentence was handed out by the same person to whom he tied his life to, and then proceeded to hurt by breaking each of those sacred vows.

And while I'm not a man who believes in love or spending my life with one woman, I respect those who do. I respect those vows. I've seen in my life what a good woman can do for a man in my aunt and uncle's relationship, my own parents not being the best example, but *those* two made it work. She was his true right hand before he stepped down and Casper took over as the head of our family.

Classy and poised—nothing like the women that cross my path.

They want an easy fuck with the hopes of taming my cock and bank account. To become a Jameson.

I fuck and leave. No strings attached. No commitment.

Pussy doesn't rule my life. I scratch the itch when the need arises and that's as far as it goes.

"Call her back." It's no more than a whisper, but I hear, and I also don't respond. "Call her!"

My hand extends out, palm side up while my eyes hold his. His anger is rising, and I find the false bravado amusing to an extent. It also doesn't last long as a second later my favorite toy is placed in my hand by the cleaner just slightly behind me.

The heavy leather feels good in my palm, centers me, and I breathe in deeply while letting its coiled length fall to the ground. The slapping sound isn't muted, and the subtle hint of a *clink* makes

Jonathan's ire lose all strength, going from hot to a shivering form sitting atop his own mess.

He knows what this is. He was with me when I acquired the specially made whip.

"Vest off."

"I'll leave the country. I'll disappear."

"Shirt. Off," I spit out from between clenched teeth, and the guard who's been standing at the ready to help dispose of Jonathan comes forward. Within seconds, he rips the bloody garment from Jonathan's body, the fabric digging into his skin and my old friend hisses, feebly attempting to push my employee's hands away. But then again, he's always been a weak man. Once done, the guard looks at me, and I nod in appreciation. "Stand back."

"Yes, sir."

My thumb rubs against the handle, feeling the small button there, but I refrain from pressing it.

Instead, I take two steps back while dragging the thick leather against the harsh concrete, my eyes on the man I once called family. There are cuts and bruises, the holes on his cheek are a nasty color already, and his chest bears the brunt of an earlier kick to his sternum.

"Don't. Come on, mate...not—" He doesn't get to finish as my wrist flicks forward and the first lash lands across his upper torso, the skin there welting and in some spots ripping. *And this was a soft strike.* No real force was applied. The second and third are much the same, but now his abused body crawls away from me—he drags himself toward a door to the left he'll never make it to.

I follow at a leisurely pace.

For each step forward, I bring down the whip with precise strikes across his slim build: back, legs, and even the pads of his feet, all while ignoring his sad attempts at swaying my emotions. His tears and pleas mean jack shit to me; it's his blood I am after.

"No more. I've learned my lesson."

Each slash slowly releases his life's essence. Each pays one drop at a time for each pound he stole.

"You held a gun to the head of a Jameson employee." Another direct hit, this one down over the center of his spine, and he arches, a silent scream catching in his throat a second before losing control of his bodily function, once more. Jonathan throws up, the bile liquid escaping from both his mouth and the tear on each cheek. *Disgusting.* "You threatened his mum and twelve-year-old sister. You told him you'd put a bullet between the eyes of a minor if he didn't transfer half a million pounds into an offshore account in the Cayman Islands. Am I lying?"

"No." Jonathan's trembling, arms giving up as he falls forward. He's face down and mumbling, fingernails digging into the concrete, and that only serves to break each to the flesh. The meaty stumps leave tracks across the floor as he fails to escape.

His words—the low mutterings—reach my ears, and I know what they are. What they represent.

I let him pray.

Honor the one thing he grew up with; what his mum wouldn't forgive me for if I interrupted. They are devout Catholics, and I'm granting him mercy by letting him speak to his maker one final time.

After a few minutes, a shuddering breath escapes him. "Will you forgive me?"

"Already did."

"Will you end me, then?"

"Almost." Bending my knees, I lower my body beside his and place a hand on his shoulder, squeezing it, something I've done over a million times. "But before I do, I need you to answer one thing." His barely perceptible nod is agreement enough. "Why?"

Jonathan swallows hard, fat tears rolling down the corner of his untouched eye. "The truth?"

"Anything but, and I'll make your last breath excruciating."

His response is quick and just as bloody idiotic as I thought it'd be.

"Because I never thought you'd kill someone who's been like a brother to you."

"And that was your biggest mistake." My hand grips the back of his neck and I pull him up, forcing him into a painful kneeling position at my feet. Then I take a step back and the whip falls over Jonathan's left shoulder. Just lies there as I walk around him and say my own silent goodbye. *I'll see you again someday.* Stopping behind him, I bend and put my mouth near his ear while gripping the leather end hanging against his body. One end in each hand. "Your cockiness landed you here; I'd kill my own father if he betrayed the family."

His mouth opens, lips beginning to move but then snapping shut as I press the button on the handle. At once, two-inch blades—surgically sharp pieces of steel—pop out, and I pull them tight to his neck.

"No!" Bryce thrashes and tries to pull the whip away, but my grip is unmoving. Instead, I embed them deeper—each blade piercing his skin and cutting through as if it were butter. "Have mercy. Don't kill me like this!"

"All debt will be erased and your family protected." Those are my last words before I give one hard pull across his flesh and the blades slides through, sawing down to the bone without pause. His head falls back, and horrified vacant eyes stare back at me.

One second, you're here.

The next you're not.

A reality for those who let greed overtake their common sense.

A Jameson always collects.

2

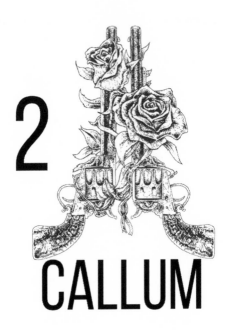

CALLUM

THE BLOOD ON my hands is beginning to dry—cracking between my fingers with each flex of my hand on the steering wheel. The flakes, these minuscule fragments of what used to be Jonathan, are almost undetectable to the eye, but I see them fall onto my trousers and then the carpet of my Mercedes AMG G63 as I rush through nighttime traffic on my way to the family's pub.

Casper's waiting on me while the two men disposing of Jonathan's head and body take a more scenic route. That was his final penance. No funeral. No recognition. What remains of him is being disposed of in two pieces and in separate locations.

Stepping on the gas, I hit ninety miles an hour while my body thrums with endorphins. Killing is my high. The moment a person takes their last breath is unforgettable—feels almost as good as a warm cunt choking my cock.

It's a beautiful sensation that both calms and winds you up. My muscles are tense, yet my reactions are languid and fluid—almost serene as everything around me blurs into colorful lights and sounds. Picking up the lit cigarette laced with cannabis from my ashtray, I bring it to my lips and take in a deep inhale. I hold the smoke in my lungs and for a moment, I close my eyes and exhale slowly while the car maintains its course, opening only when the car gives a small beep alerting me to an object being too close to my right.

The vehicle is an older model BMW from the early nineties and has two arseholes revving up beside me unlike the rest of the calm traffic around us. Not these two, though. They're shouting while nearly hanging out the vehicle, waving hands to draw my attention, and I take in another deep drag instead. The wrapping paper burns quickly, the reddish glow almost touching my lips before I lower my window and toss it in their direction.

"You fucking wanker!" the driver shouts while his mate's mouth is open, yet no words come out. Especially after I flick on the lights so he can see me. His reaction is instantaneous: fear. The heady reaction brings a grin to my lips.

My mug is known. My reputation is all true.

However, the arsehole behind the wheel is slower, and it takes the backseat passenger forcing his face to stop moving for it to click. Then he pales while I simply stare, unmoving, not giving a flying fuck about ramming my car into anything or anyone.

They wanted my attention, and now they have it.

His eyes widen and the car swerves; a harsh yank to the right, away from me, causes two other cars to slam on the brakes. There's a lot of honking as I pass them while the idiots car stops in the middle of the road. *Pussies.*

From there, it takes me another ten minutes to reach the semi-empty parking lot, and I pull into my private spot. At this time of night, the place is closed to the public, but not those in our business. At night is when the dark souls roam and degenerate deals are made while someone does a line or two and a pretty girl entertains their boss.

The latter is always part of the visiting party's group. A mistress.

Never one of ours. We don't traffic or whore out.

We also don't touch.

It's the two rules my aunt demanded from her husband while he was the head of our family, and we've followed the same path out of respect.

When I walk in, though, the place is quiet except for the low riffs of a guitar playing—an old rock song—filling the space. Two tables are occupied with men that work for the family, and at the very back, a transporter from Ukraine is nursing an amber-colored drink. Just him. No associates and I raise a brow in question at our head guard, Jeffrey, while tossing him the keys to my car.

They know to clean and erase every trace of Bryce.

The shrug of his shoulders is barely perceptible, but I've known him long enough to read every subtle change or twitch. I flick my eyes to the visitor once more and then meet his eyes, and he nods at the silent command. *Watch him.*

I don't bother to acknowledge anyone else and walk through the clean, empty kitchen. The private door to Casper's office is open, and filtering through is the sound of music and chatter that sounds American. And I'm right as I stop at the entrance and my eyes focus on the screen.

We don't acknowledge each other. His eyes and mine are watching—struck by the same scene.

Two women, but it's one that stands out. Motherfuck, I can't look away.

My heart rate spikes up and a lick of heat flows through my veins, igniting every molecule in my over six-foot frame. I'm hard— furiously throbbing. *Who the fuck is she?*

The brunette is sitting with another woman, one I recognize as Casper's newest obsession and what's keeping him focused after the death of his mum. It was a senseless assassination that burns, and had he not found *her*—his end goal—London would be bathed in blood.

My own hands twitch to end her murderer's life.

The women are similar in height and hair color, but that's where the similarities die. No. Aurora Conte would never measure up to the reincarnation of Venus sitting at what looks like an American sports bar and sipping a pink drink with a sexy smile on her lips.

"Who?" This leaves me on a low growl, a rumbling that builds deep in my chest, and my cousin's eyes flick to mine for a brief second. In them, I find mirth and a bit of cockiness, a better demeanor than the pain-filled eyes of the last month. Moreover, whatever he sees in my face is enough to pull a low chuckle from him, and had he not been family, I would've given him a bunch of fives. *Arse.* "Answer me."

"Aren't you hostile tonight?"

"It's been a testy evening," I hear myself answer, but my attention is on the beauty on his screen. She's laughing now, head thrown back, while her tits shake in a low-cut top meant to tease—to destroy a man's self-control. "Name, and who's following?"

"Her name is Aliana Rubens—" If he said anything after, it doesn't matter. Not when said beauty stands from her chair and raises both hands, shaking her hips to the Latin beat playing in the background. Moreover, everything in my world stops. Nothing moves but her. Nothing exists but her gyrating form with arms up high, fingering her soft, long waves before dipping low.

Then back up again.

And I enjoy it, eyes traversing her short stature while taking in the flair of her hips in a pair of distressed jeans that seem to have been tailored for each sinuous curve. They sit low. Almost dangerously so, and I take account of every face in the background glancing her way. Some women, some men, and it doesn't matter if it's out of lust or envy; my hand itches to put a bullet between each pair of eyes.

Is this what jealousy feels like? Not that it makes much sense.

I don't know her. I'm a danger to her.

The sound of wood splintering registers a second later. I feel a few pieces of the now broken door trim embedded into my skin and then the few drops of blood that follow, and yet, I'm struck by her.

Watching her dance is foreplay.

Decadent. Sinful.

Another harsh jerk of my cock, and I feel the beads of pre-come at the tip roll down my engorged head. It's been a while for me since I've wanted a woman, and this one has my attention with a ferocity I've never experienced before. Never like this.

Another drop rolls down my length and it feels like a caress, like the tip of a soft tongue laving my heated flesh, and I bite down on my bottom lip to keep in the hiss fighting to slip through. Not that my cousin is paying attention to me—his eyes are on the woman he's claimed as his.

"Sit." His voice catches me off guard a minute later, a bottle of whiskey now on the table with two tumblers sitting atop his desk. When he got them, I have no idea, nor do I give a bloody fuck. I take the offered seat and drink, pouring him one as well before refocusing on the screen. Both women are standing and shimmying, laughing over God knows what, while my mind runs through different scenarios.

Because I will meet her.

Tomorrow. A few days from now.

She doesn't know I'm watching, but I'm taking in every sensual inch while placing a target on her head.

We have a meeting with Malcolm soon. I could...Aliana Rubens?

"Rubens?"

"Yeah." Casper nods, scratching his jaw covered with two days' worth of stubble. "Oldest out of three and the only girl."

"Who is she related to? The name is familiar."

"Why?"

My eyes snap to his, and my glare only makes the arse smirk. "That doesn't concern you, mate. Don't cross that line."

"Oi. Just giving you the same shit you give me."

"And yet you tell me to piss off just the same." Bringing the glass to my lips, I knock back its contents and pour another three fingers' worth. "Am I lying?"

"Negative."

"Then answer my questions. Who is she related to? Who's watching them?"

He clicks something on his mobile and the screen freezes, both girls' glasses mid-clink. Eyes on mine, Casper levels me with a serious look, and I meet his stare. We know each other, and the only time I back off is on business matters, but only if I agree. If he's wrong, he's wrong, and I don't hold back.

"She's not an easy lay."

"Answer me."

"Governor Rubens."

"Huh." I don't say anything more. That piece of shit isn't what he tells the American public, and I find it amusing. Always have. He's dirtier than some of the men he swears to prosecute and fails to each term. "Aren't we a few weeks from election season in the States?"

"They might be."

"Interesting."

"How so?"

"Because there's nothing a monster fears more than the devil pulling his strings." If he wants to ask, he doesn't. He has his secrets and I have mine; things that don't involve our business, and this is one of those instances.

He's crooked. Very dirty.

"And Alexander is there. He's my eyes."

"Good. He's loyal." Standing, I pull out my mobile and send a message to a good acquaintance of mine overseas. He'll have what I need. "Keep him there."

"I am." Pressing the play button, Casper's eyes turn back to Aurora. "Did you finish what you needed to tonight? Everything cleaned?"

"Yes." Aliana decides at that moment to press a quick kiss to Aurora's lips, and my groan isn't quiet. Neither is Casper's and I choose to leave, but not before drinking up the gorgeous doll on the screen a final time. *I want to bite her. Fucking mark her skin.* "Do we have anything pending stateside? I'll volunteer to attend."

I should be asking about the compromised wire. How Malcolm plans to make amends.

If we've had news on the cockroach hiding from us after killing my aunt—his mum.

Once again, I'm too struck by her to do anything but watch. My cock is hard for her—throbbing—while the coquettish little thing is ignorant of the dangerous web she's been caught in.

"Unless things change, two weeks. Malcolm's dealing with his family now."

Motherfuck, the tits on this goddess. "I'll be taking a few days off right after."

"Is that a request?"

"No." At my chuckle, he raises a brow, but I'm not deterred. He may be my boss, but I'm not afraid. I'm just as much of an arsehole. A Jameson. "That's a notice of intent without guilt."

"Aye. Are you staying or coming back for that time off?"

"Undecided." A lie, yet it's the answer I give before stepping out of the office and heading toward Jeffrey to collect my car. I don't care if they've had enough time to clean or not, there's something more important than a few drops of blood on a rug.

Our paths will cross and she'll fight, but I'm a man of my convictions.

My vow is unbreakable.

I'll be back for you, my Venus.

"Your allure is a mystery I will taste."

3
Aliana

L EAVING MY BEST friend with her father shouldn't be something to worry about, and yet it nags at me because they aren't the norm when it comes to paternal figures. With them, there were never any kissed scraped knees or congratulations for winning a spelling bee. Nada. Nothing but an icy indifference and a demand you give even if it breaks a piece of you each time.

Because we are commodities. Useful once at a certain age.

Mr. Cancio wants her to take over for him as the head of their dynasty, while mine wants total control of my life, my future, and the set of skills I acquired to survive in his world.

My best friend might not understand to what degree I sympathize with her dilemma, but I do. Better than she even knows herself, because being the child of a powerful man is a nightmare even if you don't carry his last name. That's her blessing, and one I wish were mine as well.

I am her in a lot of ways while privately worse off, because what I've done makes me everything she's not:

Dirty. A criminal.

Shaking off the negative thoughts, I walk past a man who looks at me from head to toe with a gleam in his eyes I'm all too familiar with. There's a seediness to his persona. The greed-fueled aura of a man ruled by darkness, and this isn't the first time I bump into him.

He works for Aurora's father. No one important, just a guard, and he's doing a poor job of watching this door while her father's right hand talks on the phone farther down the sidewalk.

"Evening, Miss Rubens," the guard says while giving me a half bow, eyes on my body the entire time. Not my face, but chest and then lower, causing me to shudder in disgust. I don't address him, and this causes the jerk to chuckle. "Did your parents teach you not to speak to strangers? Or did a cat catch your tongue?"

"You work for Cancio." My response is cold and flat. That of a woman who finds him beneath her standing, and one I've perfected over the years. The governor's daughter always conducts herself differently:

I can never entertain a man like him or anyone that isn't approved of by my parents.

The authoritative head of the house and his silent, submissive wife.

She does what he says, and I'm forced to do the same.

My sole reprieve from under his thumb is working at the Conte House, and it's because to the public, I'm the perfect daughter. Charitable. Humble. Hardworking. Between running the public relations part of the women's home and then teaching the computer literacy program three days a week, it doesn't leave much time to get into trouble. Add to that my college classes and breathing, some days are hard.

Not that anyone in my family cares. I'm a pawn the governor moves at his will.

"I know who your father is, sweetheart."

"Everyone does." Just as Aurora's father promised, a car pulls up to take me home then, and I'm thankful. "If you'll excuse me..."

He moves as if to open my door but pauses with his hand on the handle. His face is close to mine, breath on my cheek, and I cringe. "Does he know she's taking over?"

"Please move."

"How will it look to his constituents to have his daughter running around the city with a future mob boss?"

My eyes narrow, I meet his cocky grin with an icy glare. "My life is none of your business, and trust me, Cancio would agree that neither is his daughter's. Don't threaten me again."

"Will he hurt you?" he asks instead, his stare focused on my mouth now. "I could protect—"

Pig. But he isn't the first, nor will he be the last, to flirt or be pushy. Not in our world.

"And are you going to be there for me?" I'm watching him now from beneath long lashes, relaxing my previously stiff form. Men like him like that. To see a woman back down, but little does he know that they're nothing more than puppets against a quick smile or the thought of an easy lay. Pathetic, really. "Will you defend me?"

The guard licks his lips. "Yes."

"Should I bring that up while my father and your employer play a round of golf before Mr. Cancio heads back to Boston? Or what about at dinner tomorrow night over the first course?" This time, my sarcasm isn't missed and his eyes narrow, hand shooting out to grip my arm. I step out of reach, though, just as Cancio's right hand begins to walk our way. Another man that makes me feel uncomfortable. Something just isn't right about him. "Please move."

"You'll learn your—"

"Is there a problem, Santis?"

"No, Dominic. Just getting the door for Miss Rubens." There's no missing the hard grip he has on the handle nor the tightness in Santis's jaw, but he follows through and opens it for me before stepping aside. I don't wait and slip inside, closing the door before either tries to engage me again.

And yet, I don't miss the angry scowl on both their faces.

One looking toward the Town Car. The other watching him.

"Your parents' house or your apartment, Miss Rubens?" a voice I know asks, and at once, I let out the breath I didn't realize I'd been holding, my body semi-sinking back into the seat. Pierro has worked for the Cancio family for a long time—if Aurora's father is in town, so is he—and is the only person that my best friend will hug without a second thought. He's old, charming, and always respectful. He also engages the locks immediately. "Are you okay? Did they say something—"

"I'm fine, and my house, please." My smile is genuine, but I can't entirely remove the stiffness in my body. There's no hiding it, but thankfully he just nods while looking at me through the rearview mirror. "It's late, and I have an early morning tomorrow."

"As you wish." Pierro pulls off from the curb, but I can still feel Santis's eyes on me. Something about him puts me on edge more than Mr. Cancio or his right-hand man. "There are some chocolates back there, by the way. Your and Miss Conte's favorite."

"Have I ever told you that you're my favorite person, Pierro?"

"A time or two, and each involves chocolates."

"Just speaking the truth," I sing off-key, making the man chuckle while I find the offered treats near the opposite door. *Come to Momma.* They're from a shop back in Boston that does the best sweets in my opinion, and this box, their signature collection, is to die for. Grabbing a piece of dark chocolate with hazelnuts and a hint of orange, I pop it in my mouth and groan. Everything—all the stress I tend to carry—evaporates. My eyes close and the city becomes quiet; nothing matters. "I needed this."

"There's also a bottle of water in the pocket behind my seat."

Opening my eyes, I find the offered and reach for it. It's a little cooler than room temperature and I twist the cap, taking a small sip before grabbing another treat from the box. "You are a lifesaver and the best man to ever live."

"If only the missus thought so..."

I laugh at his reply, ignoring the vibrations coming from my wristlet. "Trust me, she does. It's just smarter to keep you humble."

"Women," he mutters, but his shoulders shake with amusement. "There's not much traffic tonight so we should reach your home soon. Do you need to stop somewhere before we do?"

"No. All I want right now is my bed." Pierro doesn't say anything else, taking the left turn at the light and then driving straight toward the area I live in. Just like Aurora, my home is in the Lincoln Park area and just a few blocks away from hers in a townhome community that my parents approve of solely because a few stuck-up acquaintances have children that live in the area.

My phone vibrates but I don't bother to look. There's only one person who'd contact me right now, and I'm sure he'll do so again once I'm safely inside. *I'm going to leave Chicago one day soon.* A throat clears then and I snap into focus, not having realized I'd zoned out. We're parked outside my place, the dark green door lit up while a large box from my favorite chip company sits atop the mat.

"Are you sure you're okay, Aliana?"

"I'm sure." My eyes meet his through the rearview, and while I can see he doesn't believe me, Pierro doesn't pry. Instead, he gets out and opens my door while offering a hand to help me out, which I take, gripping it while grabbing his gift with my empty one. Once outside, I give him a smile and place a chaste kiss on his cheek. "Thank you."

"I'll be in town until Mr. Cancio leaves. If you need anything, please let me know."

"Tell your wife that if I were older, I'd steal you away."

At my words, his grin widens and a small touch of pink stretches across his cheeks. "I'm the lucky one, Miss Rubens."

"And we'll agree to disagree." With one last smile, I leave him at the curb and take the small set of stairs that lead to my front door, pausing only long enough to grab the box and input my code before ducking inside. I'm smiling as I drop my wristlet, snack package, and my thin sweater before reaching for another small morsel of delight while my home phone begins to ring.

The generic landline's ringtone blares through my quiet home four times before the red light of the recorder signals my doom. Only two people have this number, and both reside in the same house while carrying the same last name: one as a control mechanism and the other because she follows his orders. Even if it means hurting her child.

They're both selfish; how they communicate with me when it's not a social call.

I know what it means. I dread what they'll ask of me.

Dropping the box of chocolates on the entry table, I toe off my shoes and then put my hair up in a high ponytail. *Not yet.* My kitchen is just to the left of the townhome's entrance past an arched entryway, and I walk to my fridge, grabbing the opened bottle of wine in there. It's still three-quarters full, and after popping the topper, I begin to pour myself what's left inside a huge glass Aurora gave me as a gag gift last year.

Am I taking my time in answering? Yes.

Will I get crap for it? Another yes.

"Screw it," I whisper before chugging the contents of the glass, not stopping to breathe until the last sweet drops sit on my tongue. The crisp note of fruit is refreshing, and so is the added warmth that sweeps my short frame as it mixes with my earlier drinks create a quick buzz that makes me smile. "Liquid courage for the win."

And no sooner had the last words passed my lips than there's a sudden pounding on my door. It's a firm knock, harder than needed, and I walk over, opening it without looking through the peephole.

"Why the fuck aren't you answering your phone, Aliana?"

"I just got home. Literally."

"Not good enough."

"Hello to you too, Father," I say, not that he acknowledges or even gives me a smile. Instead, he walks past me and looks at the empty glass with disdain. He also doesn't comment on the hint of annoyance in my tone. "Please, take a seat. Would you like anything?"

He does sit, crossing one leg at the knee while watching me, expression blank. "You know why I'm here."

"Couldn't this have waited until tomorrow's dinner?"

"No." It's hard—so hard—but I nod and take the chair opposite. I mimic him. "The buyer is waiting, and I need this resolved before the campaign for re-election kicks off at the end of the month. You'll be leaving soon."

"I have a job and my schooling. Getting up and disappearing on a whim isn't responsible."

"Neither is a political figure's daughter being best friends with a mafia princess and soon-to-be mafia boss."

"What?" My voice comes out shaky, my palms becoming sweaty. "Why would you say something like—"

"Do you really think of me as an idiot?" That's rhetorical, and I keep my lips shut because truthfully, I want to call him so much worse. My father is the kind of criminal that considers himself above others—untouchable. It's what all the men in my family believe, from the youngest adult to the oldest—it's a man's world, while it's the woman's place to dirty her hands for them. A life where public image is more important than the love or well-being of your child. "Cancio is in town and came to see me earlier today. He's donating a hefty sum to my re-election fund, so I turn a blind eye to his daughter's future endeavors..." Dad scratches his jaw, a dark gleam in his eyes "...and I agreed, with a catch."

A sinking feeling hits me, my earlier dinner threatening to make a reappearance. "A catch?"

"There are two things I need from him."

"Money?"

"Very astute of you." He uncrosses his leg and switches to the other. "I will get a monthly cut of all his illegal activity taking place in the state of Illinois."

"And?"

"I'm interested in doing business with someone he knows but has a dislike for me."

"Interested how?" Something isn't right. *God help me.*

"As a suitable husband for you."

"Husband." The word is thick on my tongue. Makes my skin crawl. "No. I'll refuse."

"Mateo hasn't agreed to that stipulation yet, but he will," my father says as if I hadn't spoken. "It'll be beneficial for us all. Someone to keep you in place."

"You can't do this. I'll never accept whoever this ass—" My face snaps to the side, the hard sting burning my cheek while he simply sits back. I taste blood in my mouth while heat scorches, throbs in time with my heart, and I swallow back my cry of pain. That would only make it worse. *Te odio. Hate you with every fiber of my being.*

"Watch your mouth, mi hija. You know the consequences of going against me."

Cradling my cheek, I bite back my retort because it's always the same. He threatens me with hurting my mother and younger siblings, and even though she deserves no pity from me, Diego Jr. and Sebastian will always have my protection. "Understood."

"Good," he says, softer this time, and I don't trust the tone. "You will do as you're told and go where I send you. No more arguing."

"Okay."

"Tell Aurora you're needed for a family emergency and plan to be gone for a few days."

"Anything else?" I want him gone. Loathe him.

"The information on the artifact will be sent to you via courier in a few days. Study it and prepare, Aliana; I won't allow a fuck-up on your behalf. That small statue is worth half a billion on the black market, and my buyer is desperate."

"So much so that you'd put my freedom in jeopardy?"

"So much so that I'd sell you if the offer had enough zeroes attached." With that, he stands and takes the few steps separating us, and before I can escape, his fingers grip my chin hard and tilt my face up. "You will not fail me, Daughter. Don't force me to hurt you."

Without waiting for a reply, my father walks out, and I finally let the tears fall. This is the shame I carry—the burden that no one knows about. And my biggest fear of all is that someday I'll be caught and live the rest of my life behind bars because no one will believe me.

4
CALLUM

Aliana Camila Rubens...

HER NAME IS the first thing I see after waking up.

It's on the screen of my mobile forty-eight hours after my eyes landed on her, causing my cock to swell and my stomach to clench. There's something about the little beauty that piques my interest, makes my body thrum with a heated excitement I've never encountered before...

Hunter versus prey.

Swiping a finger across the screen, I open the folder with a grin. I feel no shame while reading each line slowly, memorizing every detail about a slip of a woman I've yet to meet face to face. And yet, that doesn't diminish my interest in the little goddess.

Instead, it makes the yearning to see her again burn just a little brighter. Hotter.

Then again, it's her face that's accompanied me the last two days without pause. No matter where I've been and how much blood is on my hands, it's her I think about and what I'll do once she's in my grasp.

I want to hear her moans.

Watch her fall apart.

Feel her walls clench and milk my cock.

"What is it about you, Miss Rubens?" I ask myself before turning the page, but then pause and close my eyes while gripping my hard dick lazily with my unoccupied hand. I don't wank, just close my fist tight as I replay the way she danced while the people with her egged her on. Coquettish with the right hint of mischief that I find utterly sexy.

The mobile vibrates in my hand and my eyes snap open, Casper's name flashing across the top. We're meeting in a few hours, and I think I know what he'll ask of me. I know the chess-like moves he's starting to make within the organization. *I can almost understand him, too, but is it enough?*

Refocusing on the picture at the top, I'm starting to think his reasoning is indeed enough. It's one of Aliana with two other women at a beach, dressed in nothing but a pair of extremely distressed cutoffs and a bikini top, smiling at the camera. Her skin is sun-kissed, no makeup on her sweet face, and hair wavy from the salt water.

"*Motherfuck*," I hiss out from clenched teeth, stroking down once and then twisting my wrist—tightening my hold further on the upward motion, and pausing. *One. Two. Three.* Then again, each piece of her I take in is a pump of my hand—my balls tighten, and I throb. Hurt.

Then stop.

I let myself twitch, a bead of pre-come rolling from the tip and onto my fingers as I bite my bottom lip.

There's an innocence to her that I find attractive, but it's the heat hidden underneath that draws me in. Even here, in a picture showing a relaxing outing with her mates, I see that *more*.

It's there. It calls to my own darkness.

My eyes take in the supple hips, how the button at her waistband is undone and exposing a hint of light green that matches the color of her swim top. The two minuscule triangles hold in enough to be decent, but not enough to calm the sudden lick of jealousy that snaps through me.

Each swell spills out at the sides and center; she's a lot more than a handful. Another harsh jerk forces my hips to pump. I fuck my hand as I make out the two beaded tips through the thin fabric, vowing to find out who was with her that day and kill any man who was present.

Kray was astute enough to send his female cousin out on this outing; they sent me separate emails pertaining to what they found. She took these photos—sent one where she's faking a selfie and Aliana can be seen in the background—while he pulled the background information.

Because for her I find myself being a possessive arsehole. It's sexist, and I have no shame.

No excuse. Not embarrassed over the fact either.

I want to be the only one that sees her like this. To enjoy her beauty.

My eyes roam lower, and I groan as a tiny jewel catches the sun's rays right at her belly button. It's small, highlighting her flat, toned stomach and the skin I want to mark. My teeth ache with an overwhelming desire to bite her.

She's bloody perfect. My cock swells in my hold and I jerk my wrist, taking myself to the edge before slowing down. There's something at her hip, showing just above the waist of those blasted shorts that causes every muscle in my body to tense. There's more to it, but the angle she stands at blocks my view and this both angers and excites.

"Christ." I know she's marked—the dark contrast highlighting the edge of a tattoo—and the lightest touch to my engorged head, feather-light across the slit, is enough to pull the come from my balls.

Two long ropes shoot from the tip, coating my abdomen while the rest dribbles down my fingers and palm.

If this is how I react to a picture, I'm fucked.

Truly. Utterly. Fucked.

"This is how obsession starts," I mutter to myself, releasing myself and then tracing a come-soaked finger across the picture where her lips are. "We'll be meeting soon, Miss Rubens. Really soon."

Another twitch, and I close my eyes with a grin.

What she brings out of me makes no sense. My reactions aren't me, and yet I need more. To be closer. To feel those curious eyes on mine.

Maybe then the desire will wane, and I'll fuck her out of my system. One and done.

Lies.

Letting out a slow breath, I wipe my hand on the blanket near me and focus on the electronic file next, turning to the page with her personal information. Line by line, I memorize each stat for later use as any good stalker would.

Age: 21
Height: 5ft 3in
Weight: 125 lbs.
Blood Type: O Negative
Lives: Lincoln Park
Mobile Number: XXX-7174
Nationality: Spaniard and American

THERE ARE OTHER DETAILS THAT I ALSO TAKE NOTE OF.

Aliana works with Aurora at the women's shelter—teaches too—and even with a heavy work week, she still attends the uni there, keeping a 90% overall. *Beauty and brains.* That's a heady cocktail that most men can't handle, but I'm above the rest. A woman should be both and never forced into one box to satisfy the needs of anyone around her. My aunt taught us this, God rest her soul, and it's also a lesson my mother failed at.

My mother's purpose in life is to travel and shop while pretending the money she spends isn't dripping in blood.

A note toward the bottom of the page makes me pause, and it's a unified concern by her professors over unaccounted absences without a note to excuse each—something the uni she attends is sweeping under the rug.

"Where are you going, Aliana?" *Or why?* The dates seem to all surround the latter part of the last two years, between July and October with one short trip over the New Year holiday. They are abrupt with no pattern, and it doesn't sit well in my gut. "What are you hiding?"

My informant attached a class schedule, and her days off coincide with my arrival in the states. *Perfect.*

There are a few other things about her family, but when we reach her father, his clean file makes me laugh. I know him. I've dealt with him once in the past while exchanging a beneficial favor, and the politicians in that family are sexist arses with no loyalty shared.

"How can she come from that rubbish?" This leaves me with more questions than answers, but I have to push it back until we land in America. It's the only way I'll concentrate, but it doesn't stop me from sending a message to the bloke that gathered the information.

Eyes on her at all times. ~Callum J.

A quick line, he responds to without pause no matter the time difference.

While the information on her was good, there's a gnawing feeling —demanding I dig deeper, see past what others want me to see. Knowing who her father is, it leaves a bitter taste in my mouth.

A man willing to prostitute women in exchange for donations isn't someone I trust.

A family led by misogynistic men, wankers with no real back-bone, is one I'm repulsed by.

She doesn't belong there, and no matter how much this makes no sense and I don't understand this sudden obsession, I'm not fighting it. The only thing I do understand right now—what's been brewing since Casper spoke her name—is that I don't want him to taint her.

"YOU OKAY?" CASPER ASKS, COMING TO STAND BESIDE ME WHILE our men and Malcolm's load a truck full of cocaine and stolen merchandise a few days later. Two days earlier than the original meet up, but it was opportune when the moment arose, and we were already in the US. My cousin has already tasted the product and accepted the generous donation. We're even now, could leave, but have been asked to remain and bear witness to the owner of Asher Holdings disciplining those involved. "You've been too quiet."

Casper's eyes and mine are on the men and one woman kneeling a few feet away. Some are crying, writhing, while some remain as still as statues, trying to keep themselves out of anyone's line of sight. *Motherfucking pussies.*

Malcolm is a mean son of a bitch when necessary, and I respect him for that. His beliefs align with mine: loyalty above everything.

You don't see.

You don't hear.

And you sure as fuck don't speak.

A lesson learned by his cousin who is now missing a tongue.

"Yes." We both know I'm taking some time off; I just haven't told him where I'm going. Not yet. To him, I'm either heading back home or slipping away while no one notices and it's best he leaves it at that. "Just enjoying the show."

There's a different kind of energy flowing through me, licking at my spine as the time draws near. I'm here as a witness and then gone, my evening to be occupied by a pretty little brunette that has no idea the devil exists. That I've laid a claim on her.

Because I'm back in Chicago.

Because I want a taste of every sensual inch of Aliana Rubens's small frame.

And I'm also not blind to Casper's own distractions. He hasn't asked me to take over yet—is still holding back, but the time will come. The wanker also knows I'll accept without hesitation. With honor.

"Still taking a small holiday?"

Momentarily, my eyes shift to him, and I arch a brow in question. "I am."

"Enjoy the time off."

"You do the same."

"I will." Casper squeezes my shoulder, a smirk on his face. "See you in a few days." He leaves after that, walking over to where Malcolm stands with a neutral expression on his face. No pity. No emotions. It's why the Jamesons and the bloke have become more than a business transaction over the years: he understands and lives by the same cold code.

They exchange words, not that I pay attention as I meet the eyes of the woman whimpering. She's afraid. Pale. *What did she touch to end up here?*

Two bullets dislodge from a gun, and I look toward the man holding this meeting. He's enraged but keeps the devil within on a tight leash, and yet I see the bloodlust. The desire to slowly kill each one of those he considers traitors.

The men—his guards who had been wearing hoods a minute ago —slumped over, a bullet to the neck and chest respectively. They tip toward the hysterical woman, and she subtly attempts to move closer to me until I remove the light sweatshirt I'm wearing so she can see the two Ruger's I have underneath in a leather holster around each shoulder.

I smile as the little glimmer of hope in her eyes dies. She

wouldn't be here unless she's directly involved with our sabotaged wire transfer.

Blood pours from the dead guards' wounds, the cold concrete soaking up their life's essence while my cousin and Malcolm face the others on the floor.

The latter tosses something on the ground, and the younger of the two men kneeling gets paler. Shakes harder while Malcolm's cold eyes stare him down, unwavering, as he crouches to his level.

"If you ever lay a finger on her again..." Casper holds up his hand and motions for us to move. Jeffrey doesn't hesitate to follow orders while I watch just long enough for the butt of Malcolm's gun to break the bloke's hand before winking at the crying woman and exiting myself.

Just beside the loading area, I find the trucks with our men already behind the wheel. Jeffrey takes the one in the middle while I take the front, exiting the warehouse in relative silence while heading toward the port to secure storage before we move the electronics to a cargo ship heading to South America.

It takes a few hours, but we get it done. The hot equipment has already been sold and paid for, and I'm negotiating another shipment through emails with the buyer.

The mobile in my pocket vibrates again, the third message from the man watching Aliana. It's her location, a picture I requested, and status—I'll only check once I'm inside my rental while these men head home to London.

"That's all of it," Jeffrey says, bringing a small towel to his face to wipe his forehead. "*Christ*, all this moving around has me feeling like a roast."

"It's a pretty warm evening." Another of the men hands me a bottle of water. I grab it with a nod of *thanks* and take a sip. "Sweep for anything left undone and head to the airstrip. The plane will be ready when you are."

"What about you?" Jeffrey's expression holds confusion. And he's not being nosy; I've known him long enough to see the wheels turning—calculating how he could be of assistance. "Do you need me to stay? You know I'm here for whatever has to be done."

A smirk spreads across my face, my hand gripping his shoulder and giving it a squeeze. "Not necessary. This is a solo mission, but there is one thing I'll need."

"Personal?"

"Extremely."

"Done, and please enjoy your time off, Mr. Jameson."

5

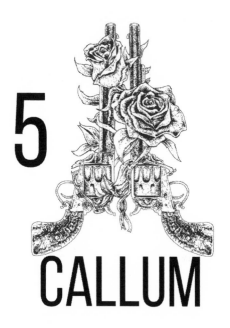

CALLUM

THE MOMENT I step outside the elevator and onto the rooftop lounge a few hours later, I'm met with a familiar scene from around the world. No matter the country, it's all the same. Bodies grinding, pulsing beats, the heated stares of strangers as you walk by, and then come the subtle whispers: *Who is that?*

Men and women.

They all look at me, not realizing that my hands will forever be stained with blood—a badge I wear proudly. I'm a killer. A criminal. And I've hurt many for the personal gain of myself and those who share my last name.

And yet, it's the over six-foot frame with dirty blond hair up in a small bun and light greenish eyes they focus on. It's the tattoos and the black designer trousers and long-sleeved vest I changed into along with the accent that lures them in. Because no one believes me to be anything but a businessman upon first impression, they don't see the devil within until close enough for me to execute without empathy.

A commoner walking down the street or inside a pub having a drink wouldn't think I'd easily burn them all alive if they crossed me. A costly mistake. If more people were aware of their surroundings, fewer innocents would die.

"Well, aren't you handsome." A woman in her mid-twenties with too much lip-gloss and mascara steps into my path. She's overly done from head to toe, the light pink in her bleached hair a bit nauseating, but it's the hand on my arm I'm repulsed by. "Where have you been hiding—"

Before she can finish, I've gripped her wrist, turned it just a bit, and removed it from my body. "Not interested."

"But—"

"Don't make me repeat myself, Miss." There's an air of arrogance to her, a slick remark sitting on her tongue, but she's smart enough to read the warning in my eyes. Without another word, she turns and walks away, her posture stiff while I search for my Venus.

The mobile in my pocket vibrates then and I pull it out, reading the text from Aliana's guard.

She's at the bar with a few more people now. One male in particular seems interested. ~Kray

There are two bars in this place; I studied the layout he sent me earlier and I turn my head toward the smaller one. It's full. All men. A stag party judging by the stupid matching outfits and the one guy's tie with the word *groom* down the center.

The next one is on the other side of the roof, and the closer I get, the same sensation rushes through my veins. It's almost like I'm back inside Casper's office at the pub back home, watching—unable to fight this pull. It's tangible, this buzzing heat that forces me closer.

With each step, it's hotter.

A shiver rushes down my spine.

And it's when I spot a familiar head of dark hair that my cock swells to near the point of pain. Because there she is, the object of my lust, and the pictures I've received of her out and about until I came to Chicago didn't do her justice.

"Motherfuck," I hiss out through clenched teeth, unable to understand my reaction. How I'm unable to look away...

This delicate little morsel is a heady temptation. I memorize every delicate inch of her short frame, pausing to enjoy the swell of her breasts in a black sweater vest and then gaze lower, to the lithe thighs in a minuscule plaid skirt. Simply put, this woman is stunning and the more she ignores my heated stare, the more I'm intrigued.

A sudden presence beside me forces my hand to the gun at my waistband without taking my eyes off her, but his chuckle makes me pause. "It's me."

The cool metal is soothing in my grip, eases a bit of the heat snapping at my flesh, but I let go and readjust my jacket. "Never sneak up on me, mate."

"Understood."

"Good," I say, busy taking in how small she is—a delicate little goddess that I yearn to touch. Taste. Corrupt. "Who are the men?"

I could give a fuck about the women. Those two are insignificant to me.

"Those two..." from the corner of my eye I see him pointing in the general direction of two men beside the laughing girls "... are boyfriends of her classmates. This one, though, is not part of their group. He's crashing their outing, and Miss Rubens wasn't too pleased to see him. At least, the icy glare she sent him gave that impression."

"Hmmm." An amber-colored drink is offered by him and I take it, bringing it to my lips while I take account of the bodies around us. There are two guards on this floor, and they're not employed by the lounge. Big men with subtle earpieces and overly crisp suits, are out of the norm for a place filled with a college-age crowd. "They need to leave."

"By their own free will?"

"Doesn't matter to me." Taking another sip, I let this one settle on my tongue as the heady wooden notes calm me. I could empty my magazine in the arsehole's body, a tempting idea, but Aliana's first impression of me won't be tarnished by his dead body at her feet.

She can meet the demon within another night.

"There's a woman he likes to see—"

"Bring her," I answer without pause and beside me, he's nodding.

"She's already here. Has been for the last fifteen minutes."

"Is she under your employ?"

"No, but we're familiar with each other. This is all her doing."

"And those two?" I point toward the two blokes that don't belong here.

"The bodyguards are with her." *Why the protection to come see this arse?*

The woman in question—a tall, leggy blonde—walks by us, winking at Kray before strutting toward the bar. Her smile is wide, completely fake, as she wraps herself around the git while saying hello to everyone else.

He's pissed, while the smile on Aliana's face holds relief.

"You know what I'm going to ask for. I want everything on them." For a moment, I glance at Kray and find him watching the scene with anger. Jealousy burns in his dark eyes. "Are you okay?"

At six foot five and two hundred and forty pounds, he's a wall, Kray Timmons is an ex-MMA fighter turned private investigator due to his connections with me. I saved his little brother's life; the sixteen-year-old was caught at the wrong place, wrong time, and at the center of a dispute he had no business in.

So instead of taking his stepfather's words and pinning the kid with stealing and selling for his personal gain, I strangled his mother's handler until he confessed. I also let the brothers decide his fate and then made the body disappear.

Kray's loyalty has been infallible since then, and after breaking his leg in his last match a year ago, he became my eyes and ears here. My employee.

Because while Casper is the head of the beast, I'm the body.

A body that strikes to protect.

"Yes." It's a bit terse, but the look I give him is enough for his expression to quickly turn apologetic. He's angry with the woman hugging the arsehole that came to see Aliana. "It's not the first time I've seen him around, and I know one of the rat holes he crawls out from. You'll have it by tomorrow."

However, the scowl is back when he turns to watch them leave. The men in suits move in closer to the pair, and his clenched hands are proof of a history I give no fucks about as long as it doesn't interfere.

"Thank you," I say with a nod before walking toward the bar, my eyes set on her. I'm taking in her smooth tan skin, how the LED lighting bounces off her flesh while highlighting the sinful body she's swaying. There's a drink in her hand while she dances, nearly giggling as the unwanted arse is led away by the woman Timmons knows with the guards a few steps behind.

Who is she to Kray? But more importantly, who is this wanker to Aliana?

A question for another time as those gorgeous eyes meet mine from across the room, and pause. There's surprise in those sweet orbs and a small grin on her lips, but what I find bloody mouthwatering is the hint of pink that quickly blooms across her cheeks.

Her eyes roam my face and then lower, and I like the way they feel. Like a fucking delicious sweep of a finger down my skin, but I break the stare as I pause just beside her on an empty stool. Aliana watches me while the bartender comes over, a man who winks and smiles a little too wide. He's also older than everyone in this place.

"What can I get you?"

"Whiskey on the rocks." At my accent, there's a low gasp from my right. *Do you like accents, love?*

"Any preference?"

"Macallan. Twenty-five if you have it."

"Right away." He turns to grab a glass when the scent of peaches and vanilla infiltrates my senses. It's soft, fresh, and my cock throbs behind the zipper of my trousers. As the man pours my drink, I feel her eyes on me. And it's so motherfucking hard, but I bite back a smirk and instead keep watch through the mirror behind the bar. She's oblivious, and her curiosity in me is honest. "Here you go."

"Thanks, mate." Sliding a fifty across the bar, I turn to leave when I hear her.

"Is it any good?" *Motherfuck*, that sweet little voice is delicious. I turn toward her. "Yes."

"Seems harsh to me." She shrugs, a small smile curling at the corner of her lips, and I want to lick the gloss off. "Plus, it smells awful."

"Let me guess..." I tilt my head toward the half-empty glass in her hand "...you like your drinks sweet?"

"Don't be judgy." Her glare is playful, and I enjoy the way she leans a little closer. How perky her tits look in the cashmere sweater. "I'm more of a citrus-with-a-hint-of-sweetness kind of girl."

"I'll be sure to keep that in mind."

"You do that."

"Saucy little thing, aren't you?"

She rolls her eyes at that and holds a dainty hand out toward me. "I'm Aliana, by the way."

"Aliana." It leaves me on a low rumble as I taste her name on my tongue. Softly, I grab her hand, moving a little closer before lifting it to my lips. I kiss her knuckles, her middle finger, and then turn it slightly to place my lips at her pulse point. My eyes never leave hers, cataloging every reaction, and I'm pleased by Aliana's soft gasp as her stare becomes slightly hooded. *Good girl.* "A pleasure to meet you, beautiful."

"Are you going to deny me your name?" She doesn't take her hand back. Doesn't chastise me for taking a few liberties. "Or do you want me to play the guessing game?"

"Ali?" One of the women she's with calls her name, but Miss Rubens doesn't acknowledge her past the minute shake of her head. I can feel her friends' stare, their curiosity, but more than that, I love her reluctance to break this little tit for tat. "We're heading to the dance floor. Will you be okay?"

Her concern for Aliana is the only reason I don't dismiss her myself.

"I'm fine. Text you in a bit."

"If you're—"

"I am." A hint of annoyance flashes across her expression, but it's soon replaced by a smirk matching my own. "Go have fun with your boyfriend. I'll be here."

"Okay." The four walk away while I take another sip of my drink, an action the beauty next to me watches, and when her small, pink tongue darts out to lick her bottom lip, I offer her a taste.

"Drink."

"Name first."

I chuckle at her demand, amused by the way her hand goes to her slightly cocked right hip. "Bossy too?"

"I can be," Aliana says, and the serious demeanor she tries to hold on to crumbles as a low giggle follows. "It's about the only thing I learned from my dad that's useful."

There's no missing the hint of animosity in her tone. It's quick, and evaporates the second the words slip past those plump lips.

"I'm sure you've learned a lot more than that."

"And I need you to quit stalling and tell me your name."

"Take a drink, and I will."

"Fine." She tries to take the glass from me, but I shake my head and tip it against her lips. They part, just a small opening, and she take a tiny sip. Not even a third of a shot, but I don't comment as I'm fascinated by the way she savors the warm notes of smoke and dried fruits before swallowing. "That's actually pretty good."

"I know." And because I can't stop my impulses when it comes to this woman, I lick the bloody rim where her lips touched. There's just the slightest bit of saliva there, and I hold back a groan at the small taste. "Perfect amount of heat to sweet with an earthy tone."

"Agreed." Her answer is a bit huskier. Her eyes, which I didn't notice until now, have small flecks of green within those brown orbs and seem a little darker. "It exceeded my expectations."

"One more." Taking a step closer, I offer her the last bit in the glass while leaning down until my lips are just against her ear. There's a shiver that runs through her body, goose bumps rise and spread while a groan reverberates through my chest. Sinful fucking woman. For a second or two, we remain still, just the rise and fall of our chests until I give her what she wants. "My name is Callum Jameson, my Venus. At your service."

6

Aliana

Four hours ago...

"**Y**OU'RE LATE." Those are the first words to come out of my father's mouth the moment I enter their formal living room the Saturday after his last visit. No warmth. No asking how I've been since they'd canceled the last family dinner without a single explanation. "Where have you been?"

"In traffic." My reply is just as short, and his lips thin, but before he can respond, my mother walks back into the room with another woman right behind her. My cousin's wife. They're dressed in a similar fashion, conservative black dresses with delicate strands of pearl around their necks. There's also the matching updos, for my mother a tight bun high on her head while the other prefers it at the base. They're the epitome of Stepford wives, and the tray holding two drinks in my mother's hand finishes the ensemble.

Without acknowledging me, she walks over to Dad and hands him his drink. "Dinner will be served soon, dear."

43

"Thank you, Ada. Please set the table." He demands every meal to be catered to him: cooked, plated, and nearly fed to him.

"Of course. I'll be right back." As she speaks, my cousin's wife, Alicia, makes eye contact with me, and her disdain drips from every pore. I'm dressed in a simple pair of dress pants and a company shirt, having come from a meeting with a potential donor for the Conte House. And while normally Aurora handles these setups, I took over the pet project as it's the class I teach that would benefit the most.

"Do you have something to say, Alicia?"

"No."

"Then please refrain from looking at me in that manner or I'll be enticed to—"

"Why can't you ever act like the young lady I raised you to be?" My mom steps closer to Alicia, almost shielding her, and I chuckle. But what can I expect from her? She's used me as much as my father exploits me. My stealing has procured them both enough money to retire and buy more than one private island, while I don't get a dime. *She's just as guilty.*

A chuckle escapes me while my chest tightens. Not that I'll ever show them. "You raised me?"

"Of course, I—"

"Liars never make it into Heaven."

Her gasp is as fake as the tears that brim in her eyes. "How dare you speak to me like that."

"Because a fact doesn't change no matter how you plan to twist it. It always unfurls."

Alicia's husband, Jorge, walks into the room then. His face is tight, and his eyes are narrowed while the heavy scent of tobacco infiltrates the room. "Prima, watch your mouth or I'll be forced to knock it closed."

"Silence!" My father's sharp tone cuts through my cousin's threat, leaving it hanging mid-air without any weight to it. There's the anger in his eyes that catches me off guard. *Since when do you defend me?* "You don't threaten my daughter, Jorge. Know your place inside my home; you touch her, and I'll return the favor to your wife."

Both he and Alicia tense, faces becoming ashen. My cousin moves closer to her as if to act like a shield. "Uncle, how can you—"

"You don't threaten another man's property."

And there it is.

A word that cuts deep.

Destroys every bit of hope that for once, he'd be there for me.

Breathe in. Breathe out. Just eat and leave. A mantra I play on loop, forcing my emotions to the furthest recess of my mind where my heart can't dominate. Instead, ice fills my veins, and my expression mirrors the emotionless pit I become to survive near these people.

Because they're not my family. Never will be.

"My apologies, Tio. Won't happen again."

"Good." For a few minutes, everyone stands in place, unmoving, unblinking, until my father takes a sip of his drink and waves his hand in the air. The other occupants let out a quick sigh while I remain still; I don't trust them. "Please set the table and have our meal served in twenty minutes."

"Yes, dear," Mom says, voice meek while her hand grips Alicia firmly. As if worried for her. "We'll get to it right away."

They move toward the archways leading out and I follow, but the throat clearing makes me pause. My head turns in his direction, and his amused eyes are focused on me. "Not you."

"Okay." I acquiesce with a neutral expression, knowing what's coming and the small bit of leverage I have at the moment. He needs me, and without my help, they'd never pull off what he hopes to accomplish. "I'll stay, but he leaves."

"You're pushing it today, cousin. You don't have a say—"

Dad holds up a hand, and Jorge stops mid rant. "He'll leave."

"You can't be serious! She's in no position to demand anything."

"Am I not?" I arch a bitch brow and dare him to say something to piss his precious uncle off. *Wimp.* "You also forget I'm his daughter. Ruthlessness runs in our blood."

"Uncle Diego, do you hear her? How can you just sit there and not correct her behavior?"

"Like this." Before my cousin can move back, my father stands to his full height—towers over him while bringing down the not empty tumbler on his face. The sickening crunch is as loud as my gasp; the blood that now pours from the wound on my cousin's nose is disgusting. Dad hits him three times before stepping back, holding out the now-cracked glass for me to take. I do so, moving close and then retaking the few steps separating us quickly, while my father offers Jorge a handkerchief. "That's the last warning for tonight. Go home, son. I make the decisions here, not you, nor do you have any leverage over me. Keep that in mind, and this little incident won't happen again. Understood?"

"Yes."

"Good. Go eat and head home."

Holding the bridge of his nose with the fabric, he turns and does as asked, but not before sending me a hateful glare. His disdain for me is no secret nor is it a sweat off my brow. Jorge looks to my father for approval, wants to be his child, and has tried to one-up me all my life.

He has a seat at the city council.

He has an Ivy league education.

He does as he is told without question.

He's a sexist jerk that follows my father's ideology to a T.

"Take a seat, mi hija." Picking my battles is prudent. I won a small battle against the others, but not the war. So I do; I pick the chair furthest from him and sit with my head held high and shoulders straight. This makes him chuckle. "You are a lot like me. So stubborn."

"And yet, I'm the one risking everything."

"For the family, we all make certain sacrifices." His words pull a scoff from me which he ignores, choosing instead to stand and come sit beside me. "Name your price."

"W-what?"

"What do you want? I won't give you this opportunity again."

"My freedom."

"At the moment, I have to decline that request. You get one more." My stomach sinks; I knew he wouldn't give me the chance to back out. But what truly guts me is the menacing glint in his eyes, the victory smile on his lips. "Especially now that I've been offered something too beneficial in exchange for your hand in marriage."

My world stops.

All sound vanishes for a while. I have no idea how long, but I come back to the chanting of the word *no* over and over again. It's hoarse, so full of despair, and it takes me even longer to realize the person speaking is me.

There's wetness on my cheeks. My breathing is labored.

"Don't do this to me. This isn't the 1800s where women were traded for cattle," I manage to choke out while bringing my hand to my chest. I press down hard as if hoping to squash the sensation there. It's automatic, the distress and pain, and my breathing becomes labored.

"Breathe."

"You can't—"

"Breathe, dammit!" But I can't. Just the thought, thinking that I'd be trapped for the rest of my life—that my plans to move overseas in the next two years would vanish—caused my throat to close up. My body shakes. My vision blurs. "Last warning. Get a hold of yourself."

"Please." That's all I get out as his hand wraps around my throat and squeezes, forcing me from my panic and punching straight into fear. There's a difference in the two, a teetering edge that slams you back into reality where you can breathe but are being blocked not by your nervous system but by a physical presence.

"Calm yourself."

"Dad, stop."

"Are you ready to quit being childish?" My chest burns, the limited air he's allowing only reigniting the panic within me. I'm fighting it, trying to stay alert, but the tighter he holds me, the more it grows. Dad's face comes closer, his eyes staring straight into my wide ones. "I'm willing to listen to your reasoning, but you better have a very compelling reason as to why I shouldn't force this on you. Nod if you understand." I do, minute, but the movement is there. "We can shelve this conversation for now, but we will revisit. I'm only allowing you this respite because I need your head in the game and the artifact in my hands within the next ten days. Now, ask me for a favor, and I'll grant it."

He releases his hold and I cough, bringing a hand up to the tender skin. "What are you allowing?"

This is another way he controls me. I'm told what to ask for, but if I want to get out of the country and never return, I need him to think I'm being complacent. *After this job, I'll disappear. Maybe the Cancio family can hide me.*

"Money or a personal favor."

"Personal favor, then." I don't want his money. My response is immediate, though my tone is scratchy and my chest is still heaving.

"Ask."

"My brothers remain untouchable." Another cough leaves me and he stands, walking toward the water carafe atop the table next to the seat he'd occupied earlier. With the glass in his hand, Dad walks to me and holds it to my lips, urging me to drink. Begrudgingly I do, and with each second that passes, my body further calms. Not fully, but enough to control my panic. "Promise me. Not so much as a blemish on them."

Dad is pensive as he sits back in the chair beside me. He rubs his chin, eyes on mine, but then nods in agreement. "Done, until they turn eighteen or ask to be a part of my office."

They're twelve and fourteen now, which gives me a few years to breathe. That, and they're his golden children. His heirs. Their political careers are already set in stone, while neither care for the limelight.

Once they turn sixteen, I can take them with me.

"Then you have yourself a deal. I'll bring it back."

"I never had a doubt." His chuckle is loud, shakes him a bit. "Now, let's go eat. I'm sure your mother is wondering what's taking so long. She lives for these dinners."

"Can I go home instead? I'm not hungry."

"Sorry, kid." The fake remorse is another slap in the face, but I swallow it back. I just need to get through this and leave. I'll begin planning once I'm home. "Family dinners are sacred, and you know this."

"Of course." With a heavy sigh, I stand and make my way toward the entryway, and I'm almost through it when he speaks again. It's not what I'm expecting and not a single piece of me believes him, but the man knows how to hit low.

"Aliana, you might not believe me, but I do love you. You are my daughter."

"I know you do, in a very self-serving way," I whisper under my breath. Tears brim my eyes, but I blink them away before looking back from over my shoulder. "You just love money and power more."

Present...

I'M FROZEN. UNABLE TO SO MUCH AS BLINK WHILE HE PULLS BACK to stand at his full height.

Christ, out of all the men to flirt with. This isn't good.

Because I know him. Know men like him and those that he surrounds himself with.

Just like my father, Aurora's father, and plenty of other power-hungry jerks who step on others while maintaining full control of everyone and everything around them.

And yet, I'm not scared. I should be, but the feelings he's bringing to life are anything but. It also doesn't help that I've been drinking since leaving my parent's house after a disastrous dinner. I've been here for a while—after being home just long enough to shower/change and call two friends to meet me here. This now my personal area, rented by me with no plans of calling it a night any time soon.

My inhibitions are low. My desire to control any aspect of my life is a wrecking-ball-sized force I'm not willing to subdue tonight.

Not after being pushed into a panic attack.

Not after being choked into complacency.

But instead of pulling away, I take a step closer. I also find my fingers curling in the material of his shirt, stretching it, and all the while he watches with an expression that makes my cheeks heat up while he blindly places his glass on the bar top behind us.

It's want and amusement with just the right amount of cockiness.

This isn't an average man; I should leave.

My father would kill me if he knew I was here flirting with this man, the second-in-command to a family that has transatlantic criminal ties from here to London.

This I know for a fact. Because there's a fundamental survival instinct that a lot of people forfeit in their ignorant bliss, yet I don't.

I watch. I listen. I remember.

I want to lick each tattoo, starting from his neck and moving lower.

The blush spreads, skin tingling from my face to the top of my breasts.

He's dangerous. Turn around and go.

However, a low whimper escapes me instead when Callum cups my cheek with a gentle squeeze, his touch lighting me from within. "You are truly beautiful."

His accent alone incinerates any reason I have to leave.

His tone, that gravelly cadence, makes my thighs clench while the lace material covering my mound clings to my labia.

Dios mio, he's got trouble written all over him.

"Thank you," I say, voice low as unpleasant thoughts drifts across my processors: I'm a pickup. Just another woman in a bar with a random stranger, and I need to view it as he does. Like two people meeting and having fun. Nothing more. Nothing less. And yet, as I'm busy tracing a circle around his stomach, ignoring the way the muscles there clench while pursing my lips, I feel bothered by the thought. *Why does it taste so bitter? What is wrong with me?*

"Now, is that the best pick-up line you have?"

Why am I even asking him this? He does not matter.

We will never be anything past what I'm allowing tonight.

Better yet, how strong were those drinks? Did Lynne order an extra shot for each?

7

CALLUM

I CAN ALMOST make out the thoughts swirling in her pretty little head. Her expressions are honest and open while being tinged with a heady hint of anger.

And the latter is something I find attractive on her.

It brings out a bit of the dormant claws I wish to feel break my skin. The sign of each aggressive thought is there in her body language. How she stiffens, pulls herself subconsciously a little closer while gripping—digging the blunt fingernails into my abdomen—while her lips curl up a little around the corner.

Bloody adorable.

Then, she ruins me when they turn into a pout.

She's Venus in human form. Perfection.

"Fucking delicious," I mutter low, not that she hears me either way. Aliana's thoughts are yo-yoing back and forth, at war with each other, but it's her fear of *what they would say* that is of no importance to me.

Fuck her father. Fuck what anyone thinks.

All I need is her smile and to watch that mouth wrap around my cock, and in that order. The rest we can figure out because this pull between us—the way my entire being is held captive by her—is something I won't deny myself.

I want all of her. Every bloody inch.

Because every part of this short, full-of-sass beauty calls to the part of me that's more beast than human. I'm a man who thirsts for blood, who tortures those who have done me or mine wrong, and that protective instinct is burning me alive with her proximity.

She has no idea of the target I'm placing on her head. Of the claim, but she will.

"Not even close, Miss."

"So that was—" Aliana's eyes narrow while releasing my dress shirt as if to step back, but I lay my hand over hers, trapping it there.

"Stop."

"Listen, Callum..." she begins and then trails off.

The way she says my name. *Motherfuck.*

A heated hiss escapes me, my entire body coiling tight in plea-sure, and I bite down on my bottom lip to not scare her. There's a rumbling building in my chest, a growl I'm fighting back, but the now heavy-lidded eyes staring at me are my undoing.

"Say it again." Not a question, but a demand through gritted teeth. My need is too overwhelming to ask nicely.

"Say what?" *Lord help this girl because once I have her...* Espe-cially with the way those dark eyes are watching me, a dangerous gaze that caresses my skin. She looks down, stopping at my Adam's apple, and licks her bottom lip with a slow sweep. Lower, and she bites the plump flesh while admiring my chest, belt, and then the thick bulge in my trousers.

Her gaze stops there, and a soft gasp escapes.

I flex behind the zipper of my trousers, fucking painful jerks as pre-come dribbles from the tip, staining my pants. An action she sees, and again her thighs move, clench for me.

Fucking temptress.

But before she can further test my control, I grip her waist and lift, holding her against me for a few seconds. Chest to chest. Her lips are a few centimeters from my own; my need to taste them is near perverse, but I don't. Not yet. Instead, I sit her down on the barstool I watched her occupy a short while ago.

Automatically her thighs spread for me, the fingers in my dress shirt tugging me closer. I step between them without pause, forcing them wider so my hips are cradled just an inch or two from her wetness.

I feel her heat through my trousers, though.

I have the perfect view of that sinful skirt pushed up, exposing the gusset of her underwear with the plump flesh of her pussy spilling out of the sides. There's a little bit of sheen on her flesh, her wetness, and I throw my head back with a groan.

This woman was made to tempt me. Chest expanding, I take in a deep breath and let it out slowly. Then again, and again, but nothing calms me. Instead, I'm lit with an unsatiated desire to lay Heaven down at her dainty feet before the demon inside breaks her apart with pleasure.

"Christ." Aliana's call for divine help is almost amusing. *Almost,* because no deity or man could pull me away, and as my eyes meet hers again a second later, I think that sinks in for her. I don't need to voice it. Not with the hunger in my eyes, nor the way my hands shake while tightening my hold on her hips. "Are you okay?"

Am I? Not in the motherfucking slightest.

My control is slipping, but I'm not questioning it.

"Say my name," I utter instead of answering her. Her chest rises, a slow, shuddering breath leaving her, and there's a low mumble of *fuck me* she thinks I don't hear but I do. For a few seconds, Aliana doesn't say anything. Her eyes are on mine, and the longer they meet, hers darken, the dark brown with hints of green disappear and eyelids drop to watch me from beneath long lashes. She's attracted to me, and it fills me with heat. Excitement. A want for more that's foreign. "Say. It."

"Callum," Aliana whispers, those supple lips molding over each letter, and I shiver—slam my body against hers while a hand moves to her back protectively. And having her like this, nearly wrapped around me, cements that need to not let go. "Callum, maybe we should—"

I cut her off with a soft, chaste kiss to her mouth. It's quick, but enough to pull a harsh flex of my hips against her heat. Her moan is low but throaty, and every molecule in my body throbs for her. Right fucking there; I feel her heat, a bit of wetness, and I want more.

To fuck and take and gorge, but not here.

A final thrust is all I give myself before pulling back, gripping her hand in mine before yanking her from the stool. Aliana stumbles right into me, a small yelp escaping before I have her turned around and facing the crowded lounge with her back to my front. No space between us as I pull the hem of her skirt back to cover what is mine. My lips are at the crown of her head.

"Will you do me the honor of a dance, love?" I say low, leaving a trail of kisses until I reach her temple. There I pause and breathe her in, pulling the sweet fragrance of peaches into my lungs. This calms me—I'm hard as fuck—while it ignites a fire at the same time. "I'll be on my best behavior *tonight*. Promise."

"What if that isn't what I want?" She's watching her friends dance not far from us. They're laughing, not an ounce of coordination between them, and oblivious to our observation. They forgot about her the moment whatever rapid-hand-movement-meets-booty-dropping routine they learned on a social media app began. "What if, for the first time in my life, I want to forget and be me?"

Be me.

Two words, and they stop me dead.

Be me.

Be me.

"You can always be yourself with me." *Something is dodgy.* The more the words turn in my mind, the more bloody scenarios become conclusions, and they all have to do with her father. Has he abused her? Or anyone in her family, for that matter?

I'd fucking skin them alive and feed them to my pet a piece at a time.

From what I can see, she doesn't have marks on her, but that means jack shit when things can be hidden underneath makeup or clothing. My hands twitch on her hips, the urge to strip her bare and check every inch is unbearable, but I grit my teeth and walk us toward the dancing crowd.

The music tonight is a mixture of the island beats with heavy bass, and I wrap an arm around her midsection, pulling her in closer. She's short even with heels on, and my cock nestles just above the curve of her arse, so I lift her off the ground and settle myself where I belong.

Her body is my home.

Motherfuck, I feel it deep within.

It's been there since I found myself entranced by a simple video, enamored by the mere sight of her.

A rightness that makes no sense and that I'm powerless to stop. *What is it about you that makes me want to bring the world to its knees in worship of you?*

More so when her hips begin to grind against me.

Aliana doesn't complain about being manhandled or how hard I am behind her. Instead, she works those thick hips harder. Even in my tight hold, she manages to massage my cock behind the zipper of my trousers for the next thirty minutes. Not once did she step away from me or demand to be put down.

She feels good. Too good.

One song flows into another, a dancehall rhythm taking over the crowd, and the girl in my arms loses all inhibitions. Back arching, she circles her hips, winding slowly with a little bounce against my thick length.

Had we been sitting down, she'd be riding my cock.

This little move is one I'll revisit. Bare. Sweaty. No barriers.

"You're playing a dangerous game tonight, Miss Rubens," I hiss between clenched teeth when her arms wrap around my neck and she fists the hair at the back of my head. She tugs and I feel it down to my balls, holding me prisoner to her every breath.

But then she stops.

Her hips cease all movement.

Craning her head back to look at me, she arches a brow. A little apprehension in her expression. "How do you know my last name? I didn't tell you."

Lowering my lips to her forehead, I kiss her there. "I know everything about you, love. You can thank my cousin for that."

"But why?"

"Because I'm very attracted to you." *Can't get you out of my head.*

"We just met." Aliana's eyebrows furrow in the most adorable way while a pout forms across that tempting mouth when I place her back on her feet. She doesn't like it and neither do I, but this is a conversation that is best had in private. "Where are we going?"

"I'm taking you home."

"Who says I want to go to your house?" Cheeky little thing.

"Never claimed you did." I nuzzle her temple. *Smells so sweet.* "That's why I'm driving to yours."

"How?" Aliana's fucking adorable as she rambles question after question. I also don't miss the fact she never said no.

My smirk turns cocky when I look back at her. I'm walking us toward the elevator, her small hand in my rough one. "With my car."

"Smartass." Smacking my arm, she rolls her eyes but keeps up. I'm gauging her body language, and so far she's at ease, making this easier than I expected. "I meant you don't know where I live. How can you take me home?"

"Because a Jameson always does his homework."

"What does that even mean, Callum?"

"Let me get you home, and I promise to explain." With a tug, I'm looking at her again after pressing the down button. "Any objection?"

"I shouldn't trust you."

"No, you shouldn't. And that's something we'll discuss after."

"Then why do I feel so comfortable with you?" The vulnerability in those words causes my heart to squeeze. "I'm not scared when you sound like a stalker."

"That's because I'd never hurt you. I can't." The door dings and I release her hand, stepping inside while giving her a choice. To choose to come with me. Warm brown eyes flicker between me and the crowd behind her then back again, before taking my offering. Soft, warm skin skims my palm while small fingers entwine with mine; one small pull, and she's in front of me as the doors close.

I press the ground button and she moves back, leaning against the wall, our hands disconnecting. Not liking the separation, I take my position in front of her while those plump lips spread into a sweet, wide smile. "You gave me a choice."

Not what I'm expecting, and I frown. "Of course, I did. You wouldn't have gotten far—want you too much—but I'd gain your trust and then all of you."

"Good answer," she says before fisting my shirt's collar and pulling my lips down to hers.

She ruined me since the first contact. With the tease of her desperation to feel me.

Her fate is now intertwined with mine.

There's no bloody going back.

8
Aliana

I T'S IMPULSIVE, AND crazy, and God knows I'm being irresponsible, but I had to. He gave me the one thing that no one ever does: a choice. The human right to pick and accept versus being given an ultimatum with the venom lacing of a threat.

I'm in charge of my time.

Of what I do.

"Fuck." It's a rumbled groan that rises from deep within his chest and vibrates against my mouth in the most erotic way. It's sinful, feels so good, and I can't stop myself from flicking his top lip and then bottom with the tip of my tongue.

They're so soft. Plump.

"Callum." It leaves me on a whimper he swallows, his tongue slipping inside my mouth to caress mine. Soft, then ardent, and then the way he's kissing me can only be described as famished. A hunger that matches my own, lit up like a match and I'm pushed back, his body caging me in.

One hand cups my face while the palm of the other slams against the metal wall, the sound of his raw hunger causing my pussy to clench. This kiss is everything you read about in books; a soul-destroying moment that exposes a weakness you didn't have before.

This is bad. So irresponsible.

A little voice says in the back of my head, and yet, I can't pull away. Just can't.

I'm not someone who sleeps around, much less right after meeting a man, but he makes me want to break every rule. To live. To be free.

"So sweet. Too good for me," he groans, right hand tilting my head slightly to his liking—angling me—before deepening the kiss. This is so much more and everything all at once. There's no fighting for dominance; Callum takes while I'm powerless against him—his touch—and holding on while I'm devoured like the sweetest treat.

Each groan pulls a shiver. Each curse is a rush of wetness where my need for him grows with every passing second.

Behind us, I hear the elevator ping and then its doors open, yet it's the throat clearing that brings us into the present.

"We should go." I'm boneless. Breathing hard. Helplessly watching his Adam's apple bob; the large dragon wrapped around his throat mesmerizes me with its haunting beauty. The style is beautiful; heavy on the black and grey, but it's the hints of color that create a striking piece.

Much like the ones lower. Ones, I hunger to discover.

"I know." Callum pecks me again, dragging his teeth over my bottom lip before turning around to glare at the person interrupting. "Move."

His tone is hard, a warning hiss for an impending strike if the person doesn't follow his demand. The two men, no older than twenty-five, do so quickly, shooting each other nervous looks while I'm being pulled out.

Not that Callum pays them any attention; instead, he's on his phone. "I'm exiting," is all he says before hanging up. The doorman sees us coming and quickly holds open the door, bidding us a good night right before we step through.

"You as well," we answer in unison, and I can't help but giggle. This night has been one giant rollercoaster, and I feel like a hot mess, but I can't deny that he makes me feel alive. That the sour mood I'd been in earlier tonight—the hopelessness I've been fighting—isn't heavy anymore. It's just not there.

Instead, I feel light and carefree.

I'm a woman making her own decisions no matter how dangerous they are.

A sleek sports car stops in front of us before we make it to the curb and a man steps out, tossing the keys at Callum. "I'll be off to the airport."

"See you soon." That's the extent of their conversation before I'm being picked up and placed inside of the car as if I were a doll. And once again, I don't protest his manhandling. *Why don't I protest this?* His large hand grips my seatbelt and buckles me in, and the clench of my thighs is answer enough.

This is sexy. I'm attracted to this behavior.

Attracted to what he's making me feel and what he represents: the ultimate flip-off to my family.

Or maybe, this is all because of him. A man with a bad reputation that's well deserved, yet with me is attentive. Almost soft. Contra-dictory.

I feel powerful next to him.

"You okay there, love? Need anything?" My face turns toward the driver's side where Callum is already behind the wheel and looking at me with a gentle smile. "I'll even make an exception and pick up some takeaway for you if you'd like."

"Takeaway? Exception?" I ask even though I know what he means. It's his reaction that I'm after, and I bite back a grin at the way his nose scrunches up. "Don't like greasy food and tasty calo-ries?" Callum shudders, and it's the cutest thing. His disgust is clear to see and this time I can't fight my mirth, letting out a giggle. "Mr. Jameson, are you a food snob? Is that it?"

"Takeaway is how we say fast food, Miss Rubens." His mock glare only serves to amuse me further. "And to answer the latter, no. Not a food snob per se."

"Then?"

"I'm used to cooking all my meals, outside of family gatherings or businesses we own." His honesty is a bit unnerving, but I get it. In his life, trust is something not given freely. "But I'd make an exception for you. No questions asked."

Again, he gives me a choice. Placing my hand atop of his on the gear shift, I give it a small squeeze and leave it there. "Not needed, but thank you."

"Never thank me for trying to please you."

Those words hang heavy in the air, filling me with a sense of ease that thrills me. I'm comfortable with him, although it makes no sense.

I shouldn't be.

He's the kind of man I avoid.

Like Santis.

Like Giannis Martin tonight. He showed up without being invited —after I turned down his offer to go on a date two days ago—as if I was there for him. He's like all the others in my life; pushy, meddlesome, and thinks he knows what's best for me without asking for my input on my wants or needs.

An idiot I, unfortunately, see at school while moving from class to class and sometimes when I'm forced to play the dutiful daughter at events where family presence is necessary for my father's political career. He's the son of a lobbyist—my father knows his family—and is as self-righteous as our fathers.

My parents approve of his interest, while I say no...

Find you a suitable husband.

A suitable husband.

Dad couldn't be talking about him?

No. Just no. I'd rather—

"What's wrong?" Callum's voice cuts through my thoughts, his warm fingers now intertwined with mine. They're warm, a little rough but soothing at the same time. "You seemed upset."

"I'm okay," I say, but he doesn't buy it. It's there in the tick of his jaw and furrow of his brows. "Just thinking about some family drama. Promise, nothing exciting."

He wouldn't care either way; this is a one-time thing. However, ruining the mood—these calm yet thrilling butterflies that have overtaken me since our eyes met—is unacceptable to my peace of mind.

"Are you sure?"

"Yes." Then I remember something else and I'm smiling, leaning a little closer as if to whisper a secret. "But your family dynamic is one I'm curious about. How do you know me?"

"My cousin." Our fingers flex, shifting the car into another gear. He switches lanes, driving around a five-mile-below-the-speed-limit van and punches the accelerator. The action pushes me back into my seat, adrenaline spiking as the city lights become a blur. *Did he hit 90?* "Relax. I've never been in an accident."

"Have you ever heard of cops? They'll pull you over and—"

"You're bloody sinful when you care."

"I don't."

My response is quick, earning me a throaty chuckle that ends in a smirk. He hit me with a twofer. "Of course, but to assuage you, we won't be pulled over."

"Why are you so sure?"

"It's a secret, love." I'm trying not to get excited over the term. Brits use it all the time and so do a lot of other countries, but I can't stop the way my heart rate picks up.

"That's not going to work here."

"No?" Callum asks, turning onto the expressway. "Care to elaborate?"

Slick bastard. "What does your cousin have to do with me?

You're the first Jameson I've met, and you've now mentioned him twice."

"You know who I am." Not a question, and I nod. From my reaction when he told me his name, he knows I knew. There are a few families that span the globe who are notorious, and being the friend of a mafia princess—no matter how much Aurora hates it—does come with perks. As does being the daughter of a state governor; you know who to avoid at all costs. "How informed are you?"

"I'm a governor's daughter. It's drilled into my head to stay away from criminals, and your family does business here." It's not meant to be an insult, just the truth, and he nods for me to continue while that dangerous smirk remains in place. "Should your name not be on that list?"

"It belongs at the top."

"But that doesn't explain much."

"It does when my cousin is close to your best friend."

"Aurora?"

"Yes." The next exit is mine, and he gets off, driving straight before making a left, then a right. We're less than three minutes away. "They met in London."

"That little hoochie! He's who has her flustered and with her head in the clouds?"

"Casper would enjoy knowing that."

"But you won't spill."

"Is that so?" he says, brow raised and head tilted to the side. "How can you be so sure I won't tell?"

"Do you want to lose my trust?" The words are out of my mouth before I realize. I'm not even sure why I phrased it that way, but the sudden seriousness in his expression makes me pause. There's a hidden emotion there that I can't decipher, almost as if my words hit him deep, but instead of voicing his thoughts, he just pulls up in front of my little driveway. Shifting the gear shift to park, he lets the engine idle while his body turns toward mine. Well, as much as the car allows.

The man is the literal definition of tall, has a dark aura with dirty blond hair and eyes the color of a gem. A mixture of green with a hint of light blue. He's dangerous and exciting and maybe some regret if you let him break your heart.

One time. No emotions.

"I'd never do anything to make you not trust me. You have my word."

"Can I shoot you if you do?"

Jesus, help me. He grins this time, no cockiness, and his eyes crinkle just a bit at the corners. So boyish. "I'd let you empty an entire clip in me."

Those words don't sit well with me. No part of me wishes him harm.

"Don't say things like that."

"Why?"

"Just don't." For some reason, my heart clenches at just the mere thought. "Not again."

"Okay." Bringing a large hand to my face, he cups my jaw and slides his thumb over the edge of my mouth. "And I promise to keep my lips sealed."

"For now..."

"Until you say I can give him shit over it."

"Thank you." Then, because I can't help myself, I push his hand away just so I can smack his arm in excitement. This little nugget of gossip is too good. *I'm going to mess with her.* "Can't believe Roe's been hiding this from me. She's going to regret not telling me."

"Why?" His mirth is clear.

"Because I'm going to pick at it." Shrugging nonchalantly, I unbuckle myself as does he. "I'm going to annoy her with the sex-fest they had since she's keeping her lips sealed about the man's identity. Don't worry, I won't divulge what I know, but I will be pesky about it."

"Aurora must have her reasons."

"And I have mine." Turning in my seat to match his stare, I go back to being serious. Arms crossed over my chest, I narrow my eyes. "Which brings us back to how you know so much about me, Mr. Jameson? You know my name, address, and I don't believe in coincidences. You knew I was there tonight."

"I did." No shame or denying. "But I've already answered your question. I found you through Casper."

"I'm going to need a little more of an explanation here."

"We have eyes and ears in the states, and you just so happened to be in the frame when Casper was checking in on her."

"He's having her followed?"

"Protected."

"That's an invasion of—"

"His mother was killed while out shopping not long ago, Aliana." For a second, his voice breaks and the fresh pain is written across his expression. So unguarded. Open. Not at all what I am used to from the males in my family. "This is protocol, Venus. Everyone is guarded."

And it's that palpable sadness that stops whatever rebuttal sat on my tongue. I'm also not going to question the nickname.

"Okay."

He snorts. "That easy?"

"Not really, but it's been a long day and I would rather not end it in an argument."

"Noted." Unbuckling his seatbelt, Callum exits and rounds the car, stopping at my door. He's fast to open it, holding a hand out for me to take. Which I do, letting his warm fingers pull me out and walk me up the stairs to the front door.

Stepping past him once we reach the entrance, I reach for my keys when a hand on my arm stops me. His touch is gentle yet firm, and then I'm being turned into his chest with one soft yank. I don't stumble. I give in, and when his lips slam into mine once again tonight, the low moan that escapes me is full of need.

They are firm and plush, and there's a hint of the drink he'd been sipping on; a heady concoction that I want more of and I take it, angling my head a bit, I return the kiss hungrily. A little sloppy with nips across his entire mouth before intertwining his tongue with mine.

My body feels as if struck by electricity.

My core clenches.

And I whine pathetically when he pulls back only to peck my chin, cheek, and lastly my forehead.

"Before you head inside, I need you to know this isn't a game for me."

"Uh huh." Breathing hard, I lick my bottom lip to catch a little bit of his saliva there. "Sure."

"I'll be back in the morning. Be ready by nine."

"If you say so."

"Bloody adorable." Callum's right hand grabs the back of my neck, his forehead pressing against my own. "I'm trying to behave here, Miss Rubens. Get inside, lock the door, and be ready for me at nine. We have a date."

"A date?" I ask, my mind still foggy from his kiss. His touch. His everything.

"Yes." Then his warmth is gone, and I'm left wanting it back. He's watching, waiting, and once my racing heart calms, I step inside my home and don't look back. *Why didn't he come inside? Did I misread things?*

Because he can't be serious.

We're not going on a date.

A thought that bothers me as I change clothes, brush my teeth, and then settle beneath my covers. Was I a game to him? Or worse, does he know my father?

"I can't see him again." *He'd ruin my plans to leave.*

9
CALLUM

I 'VE BEEN THROBBING since I left her on that unworthy doorstep.

Hard. Skin taut. Balls heavy and nothing will appease my hunger until she's pinned beneath me.

It's why after four hours of restless sleep, of imagining those pouty lips wrapped around my girth, sucking me in deep, that I made plans and got dressed. I promised a date and I will deliver, but while she sleeps, I watch her door while intermittently reading the notes Kray had on Giannis Martin and his connections to Aliana.

Most of it was rubbish. Things that I already knew, but I am intrigued by a pattern of unaccounted disappearances a few times a week. Same days. No deviation on the hours.

I also take account of Kray's neglect to add the woman Giannis left with inside this docket.

Which leaves me with two bloody conclusions…

"He's either being protective or she's covering her tracks."

Which one doesn't matter. Before I get on a plane to London, he will atone for this oversight.

For now, I send Ezra an email with what I have on Giannis and ask him to cross check and then return my focus to the neighborhood's occupants. To each of Aliana's neighbors: an old lady three doors down, a couple to her right, a group of college kids, an empty townhouse, and then a man across the street who only comes and never stays longer than one night here and there.

No rhyme or reason.

No frontal picture of his face, as if he knows where the cameras are and avoids those angles.

But it's enough for me to deduce that the owner knows her. There's no other reason as to why someone would buy an expensive home under a fake alias and corporation as proof of income unless you're hiding your tracks. There's only a handful of criminals in this city worth a shit, and they all stay far away from the Jameson hold or Asher's nose.

Could one of them be bold enough to make this move and try pushing their product? Yes.

Has anything been attempted since they purchased this property? No.

Which leaves me to think someone is spying on her. But who, though?

An ex.

A family member.

Someone that shows up unannounced to an outing.

There's a vibration coming from my mobile alerting me to a text. Picking it up, I swipe my thumb across the screen.

I'm a few feet from your vehicle with the breakfast you requested. ~Kray

Tossing my mobile aside, I exit a few seconds later and watch the large man carrying my breakfast approach. In his hands is a bag with baked goods and a tray with a cuppa for me, and whatever sweet concoction with a dash of coffee Aliana drinks. They're from a place near her school that she likes, a local bakery, and I know the gesture will be appreciated. I'm not hiding anything from her. She'll know I pulled a background check and that every single moment cataloged from her birth to the current date is accessible to me.

"You know, Jameson. This isn't in my job description," Kray says while I place the items on the roof of my rental. "I'm not a gopher."

"Yet you offered this morning, mate." Grabbing my cup, I take a sip of the breakfast tea: no sugar, splash of milk. My eyes are already back on her door from the driveway of my recently purchased empty townhome next to hers. Because money talks, walks, and has everyone bending over to take it up the arse if enough zeroes are attached. This purchase took me less time to accomplish than ordering at a restaurant. "Uber Eats would've worked just fine."

"So unappreciative, Jameson," he snorts, but then his amusement dies. "I don't think you'll like what I found, by the way. There's more to this than what I thought."

"So, the missing information I requested was a mistake?"

"I need a few more days for her. Please."

"Are you asking me as a mate or as the person paying you to do this?" He's quick to try and answer, but I shake my head causing him to pause. "Think before you speak, Timmons. One is a favor, the other an admittance to neglect and I'm giving you the option here to save your own arse."

"As my friend, Callum," Kray says the moment I'm done. No hesitation. "She's not a threat, I promise. We have history."

"Three days."

"Thank you."

"Your loyalty thus far has earned you the benefit of the doubt, don't disappoint me." That's the only warning I'll give him, and he knows it. If Aliana's hurt due to his idiocy, I'll kill them both. The threat hangs heavy in the air, yet he places a hand over his heart in acceptance of my terms. "Now, what did you find? Is it about the property with the phantom owner behind me?"

"Yes."

"Well?"

"Last night I pulled a few strings and traced the dummy company back to its owner, and you know him." My reply is a wave of the hand for him to keep going. I have a woman to wake up and feed. "It's Malcolm Asher."

Interesting, yet I'm not buying it. Something reeks of rubbish in this equation.

"Do you have the paperwork with you?"

"Yes."

"And you're sure he's the owner?"

"Not one bit."

My eyes leave her door and focus on him. The bloke's never lied to me yet. "What are your suspicions?"

"Someone's using his name to cover up whatever they're up to."

"Agreed." I scratch my jaw, my mind running through possibilities, planning how to rid Aliana of this arsehole that's too close for comfort. Either you're here for her, or you can involve her in the *wrong place, wrong time* scenario, which I don't appreciate. "A dead man walking."

"How deep do I go?"

"Until I have a name. No matter the cost."

Kray nods, mobile in hand as he shoots off a series of texts. "I'll have everything I find to you by tonight. No excuses."

"Good." The alarm on my mobile goes off then: it's ten a.m. and Miss Rubens needs a reminder to get dressed. I've already let her sleep an extra hour. "Expect a call from me."

"WHERE ARE WE GOING AGAIN?" ALIANA ASKS FROM BESIDE ME between sips of my cuppa—the same cup of tea she teased me about since I didn't make it myself. *Such a bratty little thing.* More so when she just called me a pampered punk after I explained that a guard inspected our order.

Miss Rubens is the only person walking this earth that could get away with calling me that.

I'd shoot my own father if he'd made the same joke. Casper too.

But with her, I laugh and let it go. Love it, actually. The temptation. The foreplay.

I also let her steal my drink after she finished her sugar rush in a cup before walking out the door. The sinful little number she's wearing today had a lot to do with that decision.

A white bodysuit with a plunging neckline, and a pair of jeans that accentuate her hips and arse, while on her feet she has on a pair of nude wedge sandals. Her body is on full display, each bloody curve highlighted while my eyes keep coming back to the two little beads poking through her top. She isn't wearing a bra; her perky tits tempt me to nip each peak as they bounce in time with the car.

With each dip in the road, they strain against the cotton keeping them from me.

Each time I press the brake, a little more skin comes into view.

Motherfucking goddess of seduction.

"You'll know when we get there, sweetheart. Be patient."

"Patience is overrated." Her huff is cute, as is the way she licks her bottom lip to catch a drop of tea. "Besides, what if I'm under-dressed? Or I'm wearing the wrong kind of shoes?"

"I wouldn't let you be uncomfortable, Miss Rubens. I'm prepared for all situations." It's the third time today I've said those words, the first time being seconds after she opened the door in nothing but a tank top and sleep shorts, looking rumpled and warm.

"Whatever it is, I'm not buying, nor do I care about saving the world at this time of day. Please come back during my non-sleep and on non-weekend hours."

"Good morning to you too, love." At my greeting, her head snapped up and a second later the door was slammed in my face. *From inside, I could hear her grumbling and a few noises that made*

no sense, but I still found so attractive. What are you doing to me, Venus? *"Open the door, Aliana. We're going to be late, and I brought food."*

"Food?" she asks, voice low. Almost too low to hear, but I catch it and bite back a chuckle. I've never felt so relaxed around someone before. Not like this. *"Does the order come with any form of caffeine?"*

"It might."

"I need a yes or no answer, Mr. Jameson."

"You'll have to open the door and see for yourself, Miss Rubens."

"Not really." From the other side of the door, there's a snicker and even that sound makes my cock twitch. "That's what peepholes and my Ring camera are for."

"True. You could..."

"Why is there a but *in that pause?"*

"Because it's on you if the drink which you desire turns cold." I've never seen someone open a door so fast. A second later, she was tapping her small foot and holding a hand out with an expectant face. "Good morning, Miss Rubens. Ready to try this again?"

"My coffee, please."

"So polite." There's a flash of annoyance in her eyes, but that's dashed the second I hand over her cup and the bag of baked goods. Then, she's all smiles and stepping aside so I can enter while she swallows half the contents in the cup in one go. "I'll close the door."

"Sure," she says, but her attention is on the bag as she pulls out an orange and cranberry scone. For a few minutes, Aliana just looks at it before lifting her eyes to mine. "How did you know?"

"I have my ways."

"You were serious, weren't you? You've been watching me?"

"Yes, on both accounts." Closing the distance between us, I step beside her at the breakfast bar. "So eat, take a shower, and dress however you see fit. I'm taking you out, and there's no getting out of it."

"Who says?" The question loses all merit when a small smile curls at the edge of her lips.

"Me."

"Me who?"

"The man your mother warned you to avoid at all costs."

"We're here," I say, turning off the ignition after parking in the designated spot. It's an undisclosed building about a fifty-minute drive from Aliana's home; it's all red brick with one large glass door and the letter R above it in bright white neon. There's no one outside and only a car at the furthest end occupies the lot, but I send a quick text ahead of exiting. "Ready?"

"Is this where you kill people?" she asks as soon as I open her door, extending a hand for her to take. *Christ. This woman amuses me.* Aliana undoes her seatbelt and grabs my hand, letting me tug her out while looking around and seeing how isolated we are. The area we're in is affluent, private, and holds a business or two with a morally grey clientele. This building in particular is owned by a chef and is a private test kitchen, and he's been gracious enough to host us for a minimal fee. "Because if that's the case, I'm out. I've watched way too many CSI shows and know that buildings like this, isolated and empty, scream danger."

And yet, she walks beside me. There's a bit of trust there.

"First rule…" throwing an arm over her shoulders, I tug her with me to the boot of the car "… never believe your kidnapper or the person assaulting you. They'd never tell you the truth."

Not that I'm going to let anyone get close enough.

I'm going to enjoy dismembering anyone who touches a hair on her head.

My eyes go to the side of her neck on the left where a finger-sized bruise sits just below her ear, and I breathe in deeply and fight to find my calm and not demand answers—a name to engrave on the bullet they'll meet soon enough. *I will find out. They will pay in blood.*

But I don't voice my vow, dry swallowing the building ire at its sight. This is our first date, and I won't ruin it.

Then, there are her words about being free and having a choice. Her appreciation of me considering her wants or needs.

All this is starting to paint a picture full of utter shit I don't like, one I need to verify before I make her bury someone she cares for by mistake.

"So what do you suggest, then?"

"I'm going to give you one of my guns and teach you how to shoot. I never want you to be defenseless."

"Really?" The excitement in her voice is endearing. "I've always wanted to learn, but my father's a bit chauvinistic in that regard."

"I'm not him." Unlocking the trunk, I grab a zip-up hoodie and close it.

"I see that." Aliana clears her throat, looking down at my hand holding the sweatshirt. "Are you cold?"

"No, love." Bringing my lips to just below her ear, I kiss the fragrant skin there, exhaling roughly when she rewards me with a sweet sigh. "This is just in case you get cold in there. We'll be here a while, and I want you to be comfortable."

"What is in there?"

"Our first date." Goose bumps rise, a shiver of sensitivity across her processors when I nip her neck. I pull Aliana closer, walk toward the entrance with her body nestled against mine.

There's a man standing there now; he's in a chef's jacket and greeting us with a polite smile. "Welcome to Casa de Reyes, Mr. Jameson. We're delighted to have you both with us today."

"Holy shit." Aliana's whispered curse makes me laugh, while the chef and owner of this place bites the inside of his cheek to hold his own amusement in. "You brought me here to—"

"Yes, sweet girl. Today we will learn how to cook paella."

10
Aliana

I 'M IN SHOCK.

Happy.

Swooning a little bit.

Just a smidge, but there's no stopping my reactions—the way my heart palpitates and body vibrates with excitement—with this surprise. It's sweet and thoughtful, and Lord help me, I'm wanting to throw myself at him and kiss those lips that are spread into a boyish grin.

He knows he did good. *He makes me forget the ugly. He makes me feel safe.*

I know I shouldn't be here. That he's the type of man—powerful like my father—I told myself I'd never so much as entertain, but I'm being pulled in by an uncontrollable hurricane and stepping away feels unnatural. Every instinct in my body, my heart and mind, agree that he's the epitome of danger, yet so much more beneath the expensive clothes and the gun he's not concealing in his car.

What is it about you, Callum? Why can't I say no?

Maybe it's because there's something special about someone taking the time to see you. To know your likes and dislikes—even if I know he's pulled information on me, I'm still touched. Being of Spaniard heritage is the only thing I have in common with my family on my father's side. They originally came to the US from the Northern area of Menorca. Fornells is a beautiful fishing village known for its lobster stew and glorious sunsets; I'd been a few times as a kid while my grandparents were alive, but now my father would rather focus on being seen in extravagant places—another social media attention-grabbing photo—than going to visit his parent's grave.

I'm proud of where my family is from.

Turning, I move to stand in front of him and rise to the tips of my toes. "This is very thoughtful, Mr. Jameson." My arms go around his neck, pulling him down just enough that I reach his chin with my lips. I breathe in his masculine scent: earthy and natural with just a hint of spice that most cedar-based colognes carry. *Smells so good.* "Some might even say sweet."

"I aim to please." His voice is husky, a low rumble that causes my walls to give an involuntary clench.

"You did."

"Always, my...*bloody fuck*," he hisses from between clenching teeth, his hands back on my hips with a tight hold. I'm biting his chin and then his jaw. "You're dangerous."

"I'm appreciative."

"And I'm thankful." Before I can nip his chin again, I'm turned to face the front of the building with his strong front against my back. His legs move mine forward, his hard length rubbing against my cheeks makes me blush.

It's impossible not to feel him; the bulge behind that zipper is thick and long. Has been hard every time I look down.

Why doesn't this bother me with him?

Anyone else I would've punched.

I have broken two noses before for much less.

"Welcome, welcome." Chef Reyes steps aside, his thick mustache twitching beneath his smile as we pass the entrance. "We've set up a small tapas selection for your enjoyment while we begin to prep. Is that all right?"

"Of course. Please lead the way," Callum answers after looking down at me and I nod. To be honest, I'm so excited about this. Paella is a dish I love but is scary to make. Especially when anything less than authentic is an insult to the country. I don't want a derivative or a likeness, no.

His warm hand is on the small of my back urging me forward, and I follow the chef up a spiral set of stairs near the middle of the first floor. The space is light and airy, all white furniture and walls with a splash of color from the few art pieces hanging on the painted brick.

The second floor is completely different, and it takes my breath away.

This floor is open with a wall of floor-to-ceiling windows that showcase the lake just a little beyond the end of this lot. There's a large terrace attached; it goes from one side to the other with one table near the center that is set for two.

"This is beautiful." There's no mistaking the excitement in my voice, and I turn my head toward Callum when he chuckles. "Don't poke fun. I really love this."

"I find you utterly adorable, Venus."

There's that name again.

Venus: the goddess of love, beauty, prosperity, fertility, and victory.

He's said it a few times now and I've chosen to ignore it, but the questions keep mounting the more time I spend with him. Callum Jameson is an enigma of a man, and the reputation that precedes him isn't matching up with the thoughtful and affectionate male who seems hell-bent on spending time with me.

Is that how he sees me? But more importantly, do I want him to?

"Venus?" I ask with an arched brow, trying to calm my racing heart down. *How can he unnerve me so easily?* My emotions are all over the place: confusion, to happiness, to unnerved, to this attraction that's palpable and dangerous. "Or is that what you call all—"

"Don't." Callum's tone is harsh, and I try to step away but he grips my hip before I can. My eyes dart around toward Chef Reyes, but he's nowhere to be seen and I find myself a little nervous. *Would he hurt me?* "I'd shoot myself before I ever laid an angry hand on you."

"What?" It leaves me on a shaky whisper and I lick my lips, but that soon turns into a low moan. His hand on my hip is squeezing gently and pulling me a little closer while the other cups my cheek softly, almost reverently, and I rub my face against his palm. This is instinctual. Everything about the way I am with him feels that way: effortless. "What is all this?"

"A man spoiling his goddess. Simple as." Lowering his face, Callum tilts my chin up and brushes his lips across my mouth. Once. Twice. Then he bites down on the plump flesh of my bottom one before pulling back. "Can I do that, beautiful? Can I indulge you while cooking some good food and hopefully getting you a little drunk?"

I can't stop the laugh that bubbles out at that. *Cheeky bastard.* "I'm not a lightweight, I'll have you know. I'm really good friends with tequila, vodka, and rum."

"So, what you're saying is you're a lush, love?" He's fighting a smirk, and I have the sudden urge to flick his forehead. "That I'll need to lock my liquor cabinet in the future?"

"Who says I'll go anywhere near your cabinet?"

"You will." With one small peck to my lips, he guides me toward the large open kitchen where an island with two high-back barstools awaits us. Callum pulls one out for me to sit, and when I do, comfortably leaning back, he places his mouth against my ear. Each exhale is warm. The feeling of him against me is divine. "I call you my Venus because I've never seen such an honest beauty before, Miss Rubens. You're a little treasure. The literal definition of femininity and grace; what a man needs to conquer his demons."

His explanation brings goose bumps to my skin, a feverish shiver that flows through every limb while my heart gives a harsh thump inside my chest. Those words. *Christ*, he'll never know how much they mean to me. "Callum, I—"

"Shhh." I'm silenced by his thumb on my lips. "Let's shelve that conversation for later. For now, let's cook, eat, and enjoy the day out here. Nod if you agree." When I do as he asks, he moves back and then takes a seat next to mine. There's a bottle of white wine there that's chilled along with a small selection of covered tapas. "Thirsty?"

"Yes."

"Good girl." He pours me a glass first, sliding it closer, and waits for my approval. It's light and crisp, the fruity hint of apricots and lemon simply delicious. "Do you like this one? Or would you prefer something a little bolder?"

"Bolder is best saved for the after. Don't you think?"

"As you wish." Pouring himself a glass, he takes a few sips before setting it down and then uncovering the plates in front of us. There's one with what looks to be Manchego cheese and serrano ham with a few olives, the other has small meatballs, and the last is something called patatas brava, which I love. The potatoes are cut in cubes, fried, and then covered in a spicy cream sauce that I've tried to replicate but just can't ever get right. "Please, dig in. We'll be starting prep work here in the next thirty minutes or so."

"You're going to cut vegetables and proteins?"

Callum shrugs. "I told you before, I'm responsible for a lot of my meals."

"You seriously cook?"

"I do." Picking up a piece of bread, he sops up a bit of the ragu with the meatballs and pops it into his mouth. "My favorite's Indian food. I've got a mate I went to school with, and his family is from

Jaipur. His mum taught me a few dishes, and I'm quite good; I can even make my own naan bread."

"Impressive." There are small plates in front of us and I grab two, sliding one over to him. "Fill yours, and let's sit outside. That view is spectacular, and I'm interested in hearing more about this cooking of yours. I'm a sucker for a well-made butter chicken or biryani."

"I'm going to enjoy spoiling you, sweet girl."

"You better." The words are out of my mouth before I can stop them. Idiotic. Irresponsible.

Because this, whatever we are, can't go past today. Not when I'm being forced to put my safety in danger and steal for my father's gain. Not when my family would never accept this.

They'd rather see me miserable than in the protective arms of a man that will destroy them.

They need me to be compliant and not untouchable. *Dad will go back on his word and hurt my brothers.*

I know my expression changed after that, but I'm glad Callum doesn't question it. He simply presses a button I hadn't noticed atop the counter and two women dressed in all black, like you see at restaurants, come over and take our food outside. They disappear just as fast as they appear, not that I have time to complain as I'm being picked up and carried outside only to be situated on his lap after the slick bastard settles in a chair.

"Eat, Aliana."

"Say please." My voice is low but he hears, and a chuckle meets my ears a few seconds later.

"Please."

"Thank you." Turning my head, I kiss his cheek. We sit like that for a while quietly, eating and sipping while watching the serene lake and the few birds that fly over it. Well, I ate all the potatoes while he gave me a look that screamed, *Are you seriously not going to share?* I stab the last two pieces with my fork and then raise it to his lips. "Would you like a bite?"

His eyes become hooded, and the thickness beneath my ass gives a hard jerk. And I won't deny that I gyrate just a bit, teasing him further, and the harsh hiss that escapes him is worth it.

The proof of his desire is raw and palpable.

I caused that sound. I made him throb.

For *me*. Because he wants *me*.

"Careful, sweetheart." His voice is deeper, accent more pronounced. "I'm trying to behave, but you're making it very hard on this hungry chap. Don't complain after if I bite."

"And how often do you *bite*?" I ask, because curiosity is a nagging whore. I've thought about it, how often he gets around, and the idea of him with another woman doesn't sit well with me. And while I'm not a virgin, self-love and a one-time mistake makes me a little self-conscious. "Because I'm squeaky clean and a solo type of gal. Have been for a while."

"Not as often as you might think, and I've had months with the company of my hand." He shrugs. "This type of life isn't easy, Aliana. Most women see me as a conquest with a thick wallet."

"I could care less about your money."

"I know. It's one of the things I enjoy about you."

"That I'm cheap?"

"No." A bark of laughter escapes him, shakes his shoulders. "It's how at ease I am with you. There are no pretenses with you."

"Well, a little nibble never hurt anyone. Just for future reference." Again, the words spill out before I can stop them.

"You're trouble, my Venus."

Every cell in my body vibrates when he calls me that, but this time, the meaning behind it sets my heart into a palpitating cadence I can't control. Then, there's the goose bumps and the embarrassing sigh that wants to escape, and almost does when a throat clears, and we both look toward the intruder.

"We're ready to begin when you are, Mr. Jameson," Chef Reyes says, staring straight ahead instead, giving us privacy. "Everything has been set out per your wishes, and your aprons are at each station."

"Cheers."

When the chef walks away after nodding, I flick my eyes back to Callum who's busy staring at me. Heat blooms across my cheeks, but I ignore it and raise a brow. "Cheers?"

"It's a universal answer, love. It can mean just about anything."

"Good to know."

"Why?"

"Mind your business, Mr. Jameson. A woman has to have some secrets." Jumping off his lap, I fix my top a bit and walk inside, his heavy footfalls following close behind. Almost touching. The heat from his body licks at mine. *I'm playing with fire. So stupid.* "Now, where do you want me?"

He sidles up next to me, his arm brushing against mine. I shiver, and he smirks. "That's a bloody dangerous question."

"Am I at the veggie station or the protein?" It comes out a little breathless, and I cross my arms to cover up the way my nipples pebbled—how tight each bud is. "By the way, can I—"

"Vegetables, and yes." Voice gruff, he leans over and picks up the hoodie he's brought for me from a little further down the counter. The other people, the chef and now one assistant, are not far from us, waiting. Both males. Undoing the zipper, Callum walks behind me and places the sweater over my shoulders, turning me around to face him so I can slip an arm into each sleeve. Eyes hungry, he looks at each hard tip and then swipes his tongue over his bottom lip. "No one sees those but me."

"Very possessive of you, don't you think?"

"You have no idea." Before I can protest, he dips down and steals a harsh, yet quick kiss before pulling the zipper halfway up. "You look simply mouthwatering in my clothes."

I laugh at that. Dear God, I'm swimming in his hooded sweat-shirt. Looks more like a no-shape dress, almost a winter-style muumuu on me. "I'm sure I look smashing."

"More than." Callum stands to his full height and places a hand on my shoulder, turning me around to face the others. "We're ready to begin."

And that's what we do. For the next thirty minutes, we watch and then follow instructions, each working with one of the cooks. I'm with Chef Reyes, while Callum works with a guy who seems scared of his own shadow. It's quite amusing, really.

"Good job, Miss Rubens. You're a natural in the kitchen." We finished prepping the vegetables, bringing them over to the large paellera where Callum was busily browning the rabbit and chicken, all the seafood set aside for now.

At the chef's praise, I smile. "My abuela taught me everything I know. Best cook in the area she lived in while alive."

"Really? Que parte de España?" he asks, his Spanish accent becoming thicker, smile widening. "I'm from Valencia myself."

"Fornell's in Menorca."

"What a small world."

"It is." We stop near the hot pan, placing the tray down with all our diced vegetables. "You ready to get out of my way, Mr. Jameson? You're taking too long."

"Brat." One by one, he pulls out the meat and places it in a large glass dish while handing over a metal spoon the likes of which I've seen before. My paternal grandmother had a few and never used anything else while cooking. This was her all-in-one kitchen multi-tool. "Now I'm hungry. Hurry up and feed me, woman."

His playfulness makes me laugh while the other two men hide their chuckles behind a sip of wine. We've gone through a few bottles now and I'm a tiny bit tipsy, but I've never had so much fun.

No pretenses. No pushiness.

And while the chef instructs, I take over the cooking and put the rest of the dish together with Callum at my side. Handing me items. Giving me a sip or three from his own glass. By the time we finish, I am relaxed, hungry, and more than ready to be alone with him.

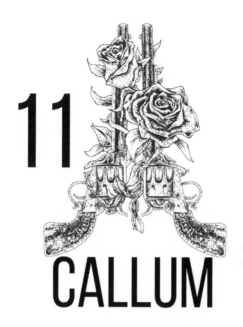

11

CALLUM

"I'M SORRY IF I ruined the rest of your plans," she says from beside me, head resting on my shoulder as I drive back to her place after having spent the rest of the afternoon sitting out on the large balcony at R's eating and drinking. Just being while watching the sun rise to its highest peak and then begin to set.

And while it's still somewhat early, only a little past seven, we're heading back to her home for something she likes to call Netflix and only chill. *She's bloody adorable.*

Aliana likes to pretend she's not as affected by me as I am her, a lie she's feeding herself to not feel so out of control, but the truth is there's no denying that she's my perfect catastrophe while I'm hers.

Something brought us together, and I'm no longer questioning my sanity. Not after the last twenty-four hours in her presence. She calms the demon within me. He's a playful beast for her.

"To be honest, I much prefer your idea." At my words, she sighs and nods. There are so many questions floating around that beautiful head. So many doubts, but I plan to shut them all down. This is right.

We are right. "Anything you want to watch in particular? Any sweets or nibbles we need to pick up?"

"Sweets or nibbles?" Her lips quirk. She's loving the accent, the differences in her English to mine. "You mean junk food?"

"Aye."

"You're Irish now? Or a pirate?"

The road is empty near her home, and I press the brake before attacking, digging my fingers into her sides. Loud giggles fill the inside of my rental, her hands trying to fight me off and failing. "You love taking the piss, love? You think yourself a comedian now?"

"Oh God," she yells out, trying to push me back, but I don't stop. Those two words cause me to throb, fucking jerk behind the zipper of my trousers while she's unaware of the cruel punishment she's submitted me to. I want her crying out beneath me, to hear her beg God for mercy while I give her none. "Please....please!"

"Apologize, love."

"No!" My fingers dig in deeper, especially when I discover that right above her hips makes her squeal. I focus on that area until tears run down her flushed cheeks and the word *sorry* becomes a mantra. "No more."

"Then don't be cheeky." Her warm eyes narrow at my wink, but she settles back when I put the car in drive and continue toward her house. "And to answer your question, I use it from time to time. When the family votes, *aye* means yes."

"Gotcha." Still out of breath, Aliana reaches over and flicks my ear hard. "You're still a jerk for that, by the way."

"My apologies." I'm anything but.

"Not good enough." Arms crossed over her chest, I look over to catch her lips pursed in thought. *Fuck, I want to bite them.* "You'll need to make it up to me."

I swallow hard, forcing my eyes back to the road. "Name it, and it's yours." It takes her all of two seconds to snort then fight to contain her amusement. "How painful is this going to be, Miss Rubens? Can I buy my way out?"

"No, and excruciating."

"What if I—"

"No."

"No?" Pulling into her driveway, I put the car in park and cut the engine. "Are you sure you want to say no to me?"

"Positive." Her gorgeous brown eyes sparkle in the dark, the little bit of streetlight streaming in through her side bringing out their warmth. "You will head inside, eat what I give you, and not a single complaint."

"Are you giving me orders, love?"

"Yes." No hesitation, but what I enjoy the most is the look of surprise on her face. The shock, yet she doesn't waiver or cower from me, and I'd sit through a hundred corny movies to see the silly grin on her face all day.

"As you wish. Do your worst." *Someday I'll repay you for this with my tongue between those thighs.*

───────────

I LEAVE HER PRIMLY ASLEEP ON HER BED—AFTER BEING CARRIED— before we reach the midway point of *The Little Mermaid*. She was snoring a bit, stretched out on the couch she slowly overtook while I played with her hair. The soft strands felt like silk on my fingertips, but it's the satisfied groans that had beads of pre-come falling from the tip of my cock and rolling down the length.

Unlocking the front door to the townhome beside Aliana's, I walk over to the Ziploc box sitting atop the kitchen island. It's there along with a thick manila envelope, a cheeky welcome basket that makes me snort, and the instructions to change the front-door pass-code to my temporary residence.

Kray's been in and out all day, the security app on my cell alerting me each time he entered, allowing the furniture company access to set up the few things purchased. Couch, dining table, and a king-sized bed are all I need. My plans don't account for staying long, but this place will come in handy and when you have the money, anything is accessible within the timeframe you allow.

Pulling out the set of keys I took from Aliana, I remove the one I need and slip it inside a small plastic bag. Timmons is already at the door per my instructions silently waiting, and I toss the item his way.

He catches it, giving me a nod. "This will take thirty at the most. The shop is a little far."

"No worries. I'll be here."

"Will you be needing me after?"

"No." I know what he wants, and she should be easy for him to locate. "Handle what you need to. I'll call you when I'm ready to discuss her protection detail."

"Will do. My phone is always on if you need me." He leaves, the door closing behind him, and I'm already at the fridge, grabbing a cold lager and popping the top. The first sip is refreshing, almost enough to cool the simmering heat left behind from her skin on mine.

It doesn't, though.

I'm starting to think nothing will.

There's a TV in the living room and I turn it on, switching over to the app with the feed I'll need, which leads me to the Airplay setting on my iPhone. I left three gifts inside her home, an invasion of privacy I don't regret.

Her words, the genuine reactions every time I give her a choice, don't sit well with me. It nags—like a slowly penetrating blade—piercing my skin until a wound appears that will not close.

If someone is hurting her, I will kill them.

Without a second thought. No empathy.

My beautiful girl deserves to smile more. I've claimed her. There's no going back.

I'm a man of my word and convictions; Aliana Rubens is mine and will be.

"She'll catch up soon enough." Placing the bottle down atop the granite, I open the file and read. It only takes a few lines for things to begin clicking into place, and my vision turns red. Anger burns through me just as a light across the street turns on, bringing a smile to my lips.

A man should never hunt when he's unprepared. Being comfortable makes you weak.

And while I want to empty a clip in his head, I have better plans for Mr. Martin.

His shadow moves across the window while my lights go out. He sits where I can make out his body, and I can easily shoot him from here without him noticing the man taking in his every move.

I have a silencer. I have enough bullets to repaint the inside of that home with his blood.

"Your time is almost up."

MALCOLM AND JAVIER ARE WAITING FOR ME AT THE FRONT DOOR OF the Asher estate when I enter his driveway. It's a little after one in the morning and past the customary visiting hour, but this matter couldn't wait. Not when my concerns for Aliana continue to grow, and after this visit, I have one more person to see.

I also can't show up at Asher Holdings with the feds looking into our moves.

Casper and I aren't "here." There are no tracks leading to our entry or exit.

They're both looking a little haggard with a few specks of blood on their clothes, but the identical business-like grins on their faces say they know why I'm here. Truth is, though, they don't. They'd never guess the trouble I'll bring to their doorstep if I'm pushed the wrong way.

Friendships won't matter this time.

With a nod and no words exchanged, we walk inside and straight to his home office, and I understand why when I catch a glimpse of a woman laughing down the opposite hall with Mariah. She's young, reminds me a bit of Aurora, but I know she's not.

My cousin hasn't let his girl out of his sight since we parted ways.

"Callum, it's good to see you," Malcolm says after Javi closes the door, extending a hand for me to shake. "I didn't know you were still in town. Everything okay?"

"Oi, mate..." I roll my eyes before pulling him in for a hug. "...take that formal crap and shove it."

"I'll take note and add it to his file," Javier says from behind me, moving to sit in a chair across from Asher's desk. "Doubt he'd listen, though."

"You two are a pain."

"A needed one," I counter, and then pull back to sit in the other unoccupied seat. The amusement drops from my face the moment I sit and the other two men take notice, mimicking my body language. "I'm heading back to London soon, but I have something pressing to take care of first."

"I see." Malcolm walks to the bar inside his home office, lifting up a crystal decanter with what I'm sure is gin. "Drink first or after?"

"First, but not that shit." At my response, he laughs, presenting me with a bottle of whiskey from the shelf beneath, and I nod. "Better, and bring it over."

"Shot or?"

"Better go with the full bottle just in case."

"That bad?" Malcolm's brows furrow, he casts a quick hard glance at Javi.

I shrug. The way this conversation will go depends on his answer. "Not per se."

"Are you here to discuss the financial issue we—"

"No."

That surprises Malcolm, his head tilts to the side while he scratches his chin. "Then?"

"I'm here to discuss your business agreement with Diego Rubens and Rigo Martin."

"You know I don't discuss banking between clients." He places the bottle down with two empty tumblers, one for myself, and the other for Javier, before taking a seat. His expression gives nothing away. "That's against the NDA we both sign."

"I could give a bloody fuck about money right now."

Malcolm doesn't react to the anger in my tone. "What's going on, Callum? What did they do?"

"My apologies." I take in a deep breath and calm myself. He's considered family, and I need to remember that before I do something I can't take back. At least, not until I know how deep he's involved. "But Malcolm, I need the truth from you. I need your word."

He nods. "Ask me what you must."

"Do you or do you not own a townhome in the Lincoln area across the street from Rubens's daughter?"

"No." No hesitation. His posture is calm.

"I believe you, but…" grabbing the whiskey, I pour three fingers' worth for myself and Javier. "…why is it traced back to you?"

Like a light being switched on, he's furious. His anger runs as hot as mine. "Please explain."

"A bullshit corporation was set up with your name as the sole owner. They purchased a home where one of my men is monitoring someone under my protection."

"Who's under your protection?"

I raise my glass in appreciation before taking a deep sip. "The governor's daughter."

Understanding flashes across his eyes, but he keeps a controlled expression. I see it, though. There's anger in the twitch of his jaw and the tense way in which he grips his drink, one he throws back before placing the glass down with care. "Is she okay?"

"Yes."

Javier gets up then, walking over to a cabinet behind us, and opens the bottom drawer. Without a word, he walks back and places a single sheet of paper down in front of me.

"I had no knowledge they'd done this, and I apologize for my ignorance on this issue."

"My anger isn't directed at you, but her safety is my main concern." Both men nod in understanding, they also share another look. "My belief is that either the governor is behind this or Martin, and while the end game is still unknown, it won't be for much longer.

"How serious are you about this subject?"

"Enough for me to consider putting a bullet between your eyes had I thought you to be involved."

His lips twitch with a smirk. "Fair enough. I'd do the same."

"So, you understand I'll do whatever needs to be done."

"Yes." Nodding toward the face-down sheet of paper, he taps the wooden desktop. "Rubens banks with me, and the other man hasn't stepped foot in any of my banking institutions in a year at least. Cleared everything, moved it offshore, and has been laying low from my understanding."

"Why low?"

"He owes someone a lot of money."

"Who?" I ask. There's no one in the city that moves higher quantities than my family, even with our headquarters out of the country.

"A loan shark with a hard-on for taking over, but he's made no move yet. Casper knows this; they've had words in the past."

The name comes to mind at once, and I also recall the way I personally killed the right hand to their boss. "The Gaspar family?"

"That's the one."

Hmmm. "Not too surprised. Those wankers are too hardheaded for their own good."

"They are. They've also been warned, so do what you must."

"Aye." For a moment he's quiet, while my mind is running a hundred miles a minute. There's more here than meets the eye, and I don't trust any of the players. Gaspar and Rubens shouldn't be on speaking terms, much less, after the latter used his father once as a piggyback bust to claim victory over his opponent when he came into office.

"I move all of Rubens's money, you know." Malcolm's voice pulls me out of my thoughts, but those words make me smile. "All of it."

"With stipulations, I presume?"

"Plenty, and I believe a few here have been broken. Thank you for bringing it to my attention."

"Of course." Throwing the rest of the spirit back, I place my tumbler down and relax a bit, leg crossed at the knee. "I'll respect your NDA, but I want the rest. Addresses, mobiles, where they eat and shit. We both know you have this information., Malcolm."

"Already in front of you."

I don't turn the sheet over, but I do grab it and after folding the paper, I place it inside the right pocket of my trousers. "Cheers. It's much appreciated."

"If you need any assistance—"

"I know." There's an understanding between us; a man must protect at all costs what's his. Malcolm has done so with his woman. My cousin will shift his life for his, a conversation I know is coming.

"But there is one request I ask you to adhere to for my assistance on the matter."

"This is your playground, not mine. The guest is always courteous to the host."

"Rigo Martin is mine to deal with."

"As long as you understand the others are solely at my mercy."

"Understood."

"Good." *This isn't the first time I've dealt with greedy politicians with White House or Parliament dreams.*

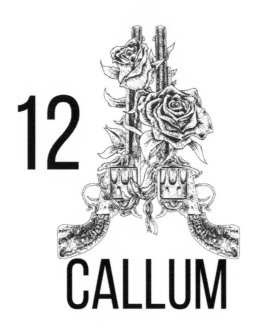

12
CALLUM

"**W**HAT THE FUCK?" Giannis wakes up sputtering, the ice-cold water running down his front while he startles on the chair he'd fallen asleep on. *Two p.m. and taking a nap, fucking waste of sperm.* He's not strapped down. He's untouched so far, completely unaware of the man sitting across from him in a plastic chair with a folded table to his right. My Ruger with a silencer is visible on the table; it's all black and heavy, with a full magazine. Each bullet has his name on it, but the discharge will all depend on him. "This shit isn't funny!"

"No. None of this is amusing to me." At my response, his eyes fully open and focus on me. His blue eyes widen, and his mouth drops open while consecutive bouts of shivers begin. "Who are you?"

"The bloody boogie man." Lifting my hand, I tap the small table and he flinches. He's a small bloke. No real muscle. No balls. "And I'm here to either kill you or watch you become my bitch."

"I haven't done anything. Please—"

"Speak when spoken to and we'll get along..." he exhales before I'm done "...for now." Immediately, he scrambles back, falling off the arm of the chair. Not that he gets far as Kray steps into his line of sight. "If it's money you want, my father has more than enough to pay you twice over even if the ass refuses to pay his debts." The last parts were mumbled, but I hear him loud and clear. *Rigo owes money, but I wonder how many times this git has been threatened because of him.* "Call him and demand a high amount. Just don't kill me."

"Who is Aliana Rubens to you, Mr. Martin?" At her name, he becomes paler. Sweat begins to bead on his forehead, his chest rising and falling rapidly. His mouth opens and closes, but no words come out. "Speak up, Giannis. I asked you a question."

Martin swallows hard, his shaking a little worse now. "You're a Gaspar?" My eyes meet Kray's for a second; he immediately pulls out his mobile and steps outside. The man on the floor lets out a whimper, and I look at him again. His fear is heady, but more than that, he's confused. "Dad has an agreement with your boss. And I only moved here because it's a nice neigh—"

"No. I'm not."

His low *shit* almost makes me smile. Almost. "W-who are you?"

"Callum Jameson."

"Oh fuck."

"Answer my earlier question, you arse." Leaning forward, I let my hands hang between my legs. "How do you know Aliana Rubens?"

"Our fathers." Giannis is shaking, a small pool of wetness now on the front of his joggers. *Disgusting.* "We grew up together. Our families have run in the same social circles since we were in middle school."

"And?"

"A-And they always expected us to be close."

Fucking choir boy is testing my patience with his stuttering. Before he can scream, I grab my gun and dislodge two bullets to the right of his head. They break through the drywall and wood beneath, leaving circular openings where a bit of sunlight filters through. "This is your last warning. The full story, or the next time I fire it will be aimed at your knee. Understood?"

"Yes."

I place the gun down. "Carry on."

Giannis licks his dry lips, swallowing hard while trying to control the uncontrollable twitching of his body. "Before I start, I'm begging you not to hurt her. She's been pulled in every direction all her life and doesn't deserve to end up in the middle of the crap her family pulls."

"Agreed."

"You do?" The cracking of his voice is amusing, yet I don't answer. Instead, I wave a hand for him to continue. I'll be heading back to London soon, but before I step foot on the plane, protection for her needs to be in place. "Because men like you don't—"

"Be very careful how you finish that sentence."

"I mean no disrespect, Mr. Jameson," he says, eyeing the gun without blinking. "Please know that, but with the type of men who seem to follow us or show up randomly at our fathers offices, we can't trust anyone. It's an expectation that scares the fuck out of me."

"The men?"

"The Gaspar family."

Again, that family. Two different people that mention them.

Twice that I'm made aware of how little respect they have for our territory if they're harassing people here.

"This is the last time I'll ask you this, kid. I want the full story." Giannis takes in a deep breath and then lets it out slowly. He looks to be giving himself a mental pep talk, one that is taking too long. "The clock is ticking."

"We met in school after our fathers became close. Dinners, fundraisers, even the occasional BBQ while they talked politics and money with the donors at these functions. And because we were stuck there, we hung out. Nothing more. Our parents saw that, though, and a passing hello became a forced conversation or *you two don't move from here* while they socialized. It just became our thing."

"Keep going." My hand closest to the gun twitches, and he shrinks back. His fear overwhelms the room in a way that soothes the need within me to spill his blood. "And get to the point. My patience only lasts but so long."

"They wanted us together at first." *At first?* "Her father wants my father's connections while my father wanted an insider to push his employer's agenda, and through marriage they'd forge the bond. No one asked if we so much as tolerated each other; we were not given a choice."

That word again: choice. *What else have they taken from you, beautiful?*

"Why at first?"

"Because I don't see her that way, and our fathers made a very costly mistake."

"What way? What bloody mistake?"

"The latter is more important than how I see her." He stands to retake his seat, watching me as he does and then leans back. He looks knackered, nothing like the cocky arse inside the lounge a few days ago. "Because this involves money my father owes the Gaspar family while Mr. Rubens incarcerated their old boss. The Gaspars want blood and retribution, and right now, I'm here to watch out for her. She may think I'm an asshole, but I stay close to try and dissuade them as much as I can. My father still has hope that she'll be the one."

Then it clicks.

"You made the fake corporation to buy this place?" He nods in answer, head down and not meeting my eyes. "On your own?" Another barely visible nod. "Why the fuck would you cross a man like Malcolm Asher? Did you really believe no one would notice?"

"Because I fear for her safety more than mine." Those words immediately calm the raging ire flowing through my veins. I'm looking at him differently, putting together puzzle pieces that will ultimately rain blood down on the streets of this city. "And without many choices, I picked one of two names they will not cross. It's all I could do to help."

"Asher and who else?" I ask when he doesn't divulge, and only when another bullet dislodges, this time near his sock-clad feet, does he look up. A horror-filled expression overtakes his features, yet there's a hint of determination in his eyes that I admire. Most men wouldn't meet my stare head on unless it's for someone they care about. "Why are you so protective?"

"Asher and the Jamesons. They want no problems with you." Tears brim in his eyes then, and he gives me a forced smile. "I'm a shithead most of the time and can be very self-absorbed, but I don't want her hurt. And while I don't see her in a romantic light—I just can't—I'm begging you not to hurt her."

"You have my word that I won't."

He lets out a ragged breath. "Thank you, Mr. Jameson."

"What are you not telling me?"

That makes him pause, a small bit of blush staining his cheeks. "The reason I'm not attracted to Aliana is because I'm in love with someone else. I see her more like a cousin or annoying sibling when she's being hardheaded, but nothing romantic." At my raised brow, he lets out a small chuckle, but it's done out of nervousness. "I have a boyfriend, sir. I'm in love with my soulmate."

And just like that, he's been born again.

I won't kill him if he's telling the truth.

At least not today. He can be of use. He's going to become my eyes and ears on the inside.

"Meeting the day after tomorrow," Casper says the moment I answer my mobile after exiting the townhome where Giannis has been hiding. It's a little late, just after six in the evening, and my girl is finally home from work. I left him to get himself sorted; he's to expect my call within the next twenty-four hours to come clean to Aliana. Because what he said, and my own conclusions have left a bitter taste in my mouth; my little Venus being anything but happy doesn't sit well with me. Fucking infuriates me, and I've accepted the fact that I'll kill to protect her. May the universe have mercy on anyone who makes her so much as frown. "We have a lead."

"Time and place." My plan has always been to catch a very late flight out. I'm not leaving without a taste of her natural sweetness.

"Early afternoon and my home."

"I'll be back in London by—"

"You're still in Chicago?" His surprised tone any other day would've had me giving him shit, but I'm not in the mood. Right now, he's not my boss or cousin and being polite isn't on my list of priorities.

For the most part, we never go completely off the grid, the locators on our mobiles always stay active, but this once, I didn't follow protocol. I want no one near her until things are settled between us.

"Yes."

"In Lincoln or a few states down south, Callum?" *Tosser.*

"That doesn't concern you, mate." His response to my dry retort is a snort. *Bastard knows exactly where I am now.* "Are you heading home tonight or tomorrow?"

"Tomorrow."

"Fancy catching a flight home together? I feel like we have a conversation pending."

"We do," Casper says. For a beat, the silence stretches between us. Changes are coming and it's inevitable, and while I'm not angry at him for wanting what he does, no more waiting. My own immediate plans have changed, and I have Aliana to account for in the equation now. "The plane will be ready to take off a little after midnight."

"I'll be there."

"Be safe."

"But not too much," I finish for him before hanging up, pocketing my mobile and then pressing her doorbell. There's a bit of movement from inside, what sounds like something falling before a rush of feet stops on the other side of this door.

And fuck me if I don't feel those warm eyes watching me through the peephole.

There's just something about her. This connection doesn't break or wilt, and the more I'm blessed by her presence, the more I crave it. Want to devour and then cuddle, taking her with me everywhere I go.

Things need to get settled first. A reminder that sits like acid on my tongue.

I owe it to my family to avenge my aunt's death. I can't bring her into the middle of a blood-filled hurricane, my world, until I guarantee our enemies are dead.

My wife will fear no one. "Fuck me," I mumble, surprised by that last train of thought, but I'm not opposed to it. No fear. No questions. No second thoughts. "My beautiful little Venus."

Cock hard, I reach down and adjust it, but not quick enough as my grip tightens to just shy of pain. I hear her. This beautiful little hiccupping breath through the camera's speaker, and I was wrong; she's watching me through the Ring app like a naughty girl. I'm also sure Aliana has no idea she's pressed the talk button on her screen.

"Open the door, Miss Rubens." Another sound. This one a low, an almost indiscernible sigh, and I groan. No shame. I want her to hear me. Know that I hunger for every single inch of her. "I'm here to claim the morning kiss I didn't get this morning."

"Kiss?" The tiny whimper makes me bite my lip. "Who said I owe you a kiss?"

"I do."

"That's very demanding of you even if I'm not opposed to it."

"Not going to deny that I can be a dictating bastard, Venus. Now open up." The lock disengages, but Aliana doesn't open the door.

Instead, I hear the shuffle of her feet walking away through the speaker of her alarm. "So be it."

I have her door open and locked within a few seconds, my heavy footfalls following the path to her bedroom. I'm not going to waste my time searching for her; she's either there or will come to me.

The half-open door lets me see inside the dark room. And there is the object of my obsession; Aliana is on her bed atop the strewn covers with an arm thrown over her eyes. Her chest rises and falls rapidly, each sinuous curve highlighted by the last streams of daylight coming between the window drapes where one small bit where it's parted, and I'm bloody thankful for that ray.

My mouth waters, eyes devouring the glimpse of skin beneath the threadbare light pink lounge set she's wearing. Just a tank top and shorts, nothing over the top, yet minuscule and tight. *Christ, she's beautiful. Looks so warm and comfortable.*

"Are you going to take that kiss now?" Aliana says without looking at me, tone breathy. *She wants it just as much.* A heady real-ization that makes my cock swell to the point of pain.

"I will." Not saying anything else, I slip through the opening and then close the door, leaning against to simply watch. For a minute or two, silence turns into heavy breathing while her lithe body squirms under my gaze. Her nipples pebble. Her thighs press together. "Just let me enjoy you like this a little more."

A shiver runs through her at my words, and a stuttering breath gets caught in her chest. "Okay."

"Good girl." In the dark with limited lighting, I take her in. My eyes have adjusted, loving the softness—how natural her position is without a single ounce of tension in it. From her small toes with a light purple coloring on them to the lush curve of her hip, I memo-rize each dip. From her tiny waist to the ample swell of her chest, I take count of each area I plan to kiss before heading back to London.

Pushing off the wall, I walk across the room and pause at her bed with a knee atop the mattress. It dips under my weight, the movement causing her to tense. She's not afraid. This, that reaction, is all anticipation.

A want that mirrors mine. *My girl.*

My plan was to get on the plane tomorrow with her juices still drying on my lips, but I'm not going to turn this gift away. Now, she'll be my dinner and then breakfast with the potential to become a snack at any given moment until I walk out of her home.

"Callum, I'm—"

"Can I touch you?" I'm not a man that asks for permission in any other area of my life, but I want hers. Crave it.

"*Fuck,*" she mutters under her breath, but I hear. I also don't miss the way her tiny hand reaches out for me, and I want her to grab me. To pull me closer. "Please."

"Please what, gorgeous. Tell me."

Fingers wrap around mine, skin so soft, and she gives a tiny tug while meeting my hungry gaze. "Lay with me."

Without a word, I do as she asks and crawl in beside her. On my side, my face next to hers, I close my eyes and inhale deeply. Motherfuck, she smells bloody good: sweet and all woman with just a faint hint of peaches that lingers all around her.

"Are you tired, sweetheart," I say, skimming a finger of my free hand from her elbow to shoulder. She shivers, moves a little closer, and I bite back a grin. Instead, I focus on the feel of her near while I continue my exploration. I'm keeping my touch innocent; I hunger for her consent.

She's not a woman to throw herself at a man or a one-time deal for me. No.

I want her again and again and again. The ferocity in which I crave this small woman is near painful, and only the taste of her on my tongue will satiate the beast within that demands I make her mine.

Because this is what being in her mere presence brings forth. A yearning.

She's driving me fucking insane.

Her head turns in my direction, a bashful grin stretched across her lips. There's also a slight blush at the apple of her cheeks that I find delicious. "Not at all."

"You sure? You seem ready for an after-work nap."

"My shower was relaxing." Slim fingers twitch, her grip tightening. "I feel peaceful."

"That's good." *Motherfuck,* a throaty little mewl escapes when I skim my fingers across her collarbones. "But you still haven't answered my question, love. Do you want my touch, or is this too soon for you?"

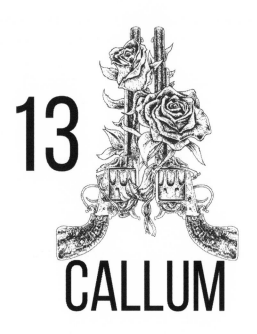

13

CALLUM

"I WANT IT."

"That's my good girl." The fingers on her collarbone travel lower, just to the edge of her top, and slip beneath the soft fabric. Not low, but just under the trim while my eyes watch her every reaction. Those sweet brown eyes close for a brief second, her lips parting on a sigh while a lovely vibration runs through every limb. "Thank you for the honor."

"Christ, I love your accent," she whines after a minute or two, not liking my standstill position on her skin. "It's quickly becoming a weakness."

"Is it, now?" My lips are at her temple, leaving tiny open-mouthed kisses on my way to her neck, inhaling deep to brand my lungs with her scent. I pause at her ear, though, nipping the sensitive flesh there, and enjoy the sight of goose bumps rising—the way her body arches into my touch. "Even coming from a bastard who has no right to want something so pure."

"You're not a bastard."

My rough exhale against her neck makes her whimper. "I've done things with these hands, Aliana." With a painful slowness, I caress the swell of her right breast and then the left. Once, twice—moving lower with each pass. "I've worn my enemies' blood with pride, my Venus, and yet, nothing would give me more pleasure than a single taste of the sweetness between your thighs. The need is near maddening."

"I feel this..." she trails off, but there's no fear in her eyes. No disgust. If anything, they become darker. Heavy-lidded. "Callum, this is—"

"Did that make you change your mind?" I know she hasn't. It's there in the way she keeps her hold on my other hand tight. How she's making sure there isn't a single inch of space between her side and my body. "Do you want me to move?"

"No," she hisses out; the urgency in her tone would shock anyone else, but not me. Not when I understand it. Not when I feel it too—just as much if not more—and have accepted whatever consequences come from this.

I'll take on the world just to feel her like this. To have her laid out like the perfect meal.

This between us is fast and unpredictable, but palpable and real. And I want it.

All of it. Her.

"Then relax for me, sweetheart. Let me make you feel good."

"Please, Callum. I dreamed of you last night and—" I cut her off, taking her lips in a hungry kiss while positioning myself to hover above her. Her thigh's part, lifting a bit to urge me closer while I maintain my distance. I'm not going to fuck her today. I'd never do that to her when I'm getting on a plane tomorrow night; she'll be safer here until things settle down in London.

Then, I'm going to bring her home.

I'm going to make her my queen.

She releases a little mewl from the back of her throat, so much like the one a short while ago by her front door, and I can't control the rumbled groan that builds in my chest. It's deep and almost angry, spilling between her lips when I press mine a little harder. I take her mouth with every bit of the passion that's been building since the day I saw her on Casper's screen, while a hand slips beneath her head to grip long, soft tresses. The tighter my hold, the more she arches into me, swiping her tongue across mine in a sensual cadence that I throb to.

My cock jerks, seeking out her warmth, and fuck me—I want to take. To leave her a dirty mess, but not today. Today will be about her.

Next time...

I'll be selfish.

Pulling my mouth from hers, I sit back and grip the bottom of her top, nearly ripping it in my haste to take it off. Her tits spill out, giving a small jiggle from the movement while the fabric lands somewhere on the floor. They're perky. More than a handful of perfection that sit high on her chest while the pebbled tips tighten further under my heated gaze.

I don't touch them for now, turning my focus to the next offending obstacle: her shorts.

I'm rough in my need to see all of her. The fabric gives a small groan, splitting on the right side while my hands drag them down shapely thighs and off the end of her feet where they'll lay in tatters.

"Son of a bitch," I hiss out, the sight of her bare and so wet is almost too much. It brings forth a haze of lust I can't control. Every molecule in my DNA throbs within me; I'm hard while my mouth salivates—desires to catch the drops of wetness sliding from her tiny entrance and down toward her arse. "I'm going to taste you, sweet girl," I groan, licking my bottom lip while flicking my eyes from her cunt to her sultry brown eyes. "Not a single inch of you will be left untouched. You will never forget the feel of my tongue or the bite of my teeth. How hard I made you come."

"Callum, please. Please touch me." Her cry settles on the tip of my cock like a shock of electricity, and I give in. My mouth brutally reclaims hers. Teeth clashing, tongues intertwining, but it's the sting of her teeth embedding into my bottom lip that breaks the last of my resolve.

I pull back, gripping her neck while I trace a path down her chest with my tongue. Loving the skin, leaving little indents of my teeth until I reach her right nipple and nuzzle it. It's soft; the perfect little dusky rose bead against my skin, but it feels better between my lips.

Suckling, I squeeze her left breast, weigh it in my palm before pinching the tip. It throbs under the harsh treatment, but my girl only moans, thighs trying to pull me in against her slick heat.

Aliana flushes, the tantalizing pink growing from her cheeks to the swell of each breast, and I smirk against her warm flesh.

Releasing her, I move across from one tip to the other. Bite. Lick. Sucking hard enough to sting before pulling back. "How sensitive are you, my Venus?" Not that I give her a chance to answer, testing her limits myself with one sharp smack to the slope of each breast, catching her nipples.

And the immediate scream that follows isn't of pain, but of need. Of want.

Her muscles lock, a hiss catching between small teeth before beads of sweat begin to spread. I lick the path from her sternum to belly button, savoring each salty drop before tugging at the small piercing there with my teeth.

Aliana hisses, while I smirk. "Something wrong, Miss Rubens?"

"Yes."

"Then speak." Another bite, this time on the area between her abdomen and mound. There I pause, resting my chin while she squirms. Trembles for me. And while she gathers her thoughts, vocalizes her needs, I begin to trace the lines of a beautiful tattoo adorning the space/skin from hip to just below her breast with a tip of a finger.

It's a black and grey vine curving along her skin, its thorns embedding in her flesh while roses bloom where each puncture would be. They grow from the representation of blood, hers, giving life to each flower that grows in the same color. Vibrant reds in different tones, yet striking against her lightly tanned complexion.

"Enchanting." I follow my digit with my lips and tongue, tracing from the top to bottom and then nipping her hip. Her scent is so sweet, decadent, and I inhale deeply. "You're a treasure worth savoring, Aliana. Worshipping."

A gasp escapes her, hips rising off the bed. An offering. A silent demand to touch where she needs me most.

My eyes leave hers. Slowly, I take in her hard nipples, the contracting of her flat stomach, and then the way her hands clench at her sides, gripping the sheet tight. The fine mist of her sweat, wetness, and that mind-fucking smell of peaches is all around me. Enhanced. Drowning me.

But nothing. Not a bloody thing compares to the pink of her cunt and the wetness that clings to her bare lips when I settle right over it. My breathing is hard, every muscle tight.

Aliana whines, the sound almost angry before slim fingers grip my hair. She pulls, forcing my eyes from her pussy to her face. "No more waiting. I need—"

"Only me," I growl before my lips graze her clit. The soft touch makes her shake, nearly pulling my hair from its root, but I pay no mind. She could leave bald spots for all I care. All that matters is the softness, her natural scent, and the hungriness in which I lick her from tiny entrance to clit, sucking the small bundle of nerves between my teeth as a deep groan reverberates through every inch of me.

One taste. A barely there touch.

I'm gone.

I feel like an animal salivating over its prey, and I feast on her like one too.

Nothing about the way I eat her cunt is gentle or sweet; I give into every baser instinct.

"Oh God. So good." Her moan is like lightning to my senses. It settles over my flesh and spreads before snapping against the tip of my hardness. I can feel each bead of pre-come as it stains my trousers with each jerk against the fabric. No underpants. Nothing but a single piece of clothing is keeping me from her slick heat.

"Never...good...more."

Each word is a choked breath, her hips rolling against my mouth in search of more. And I give it to her because it's my duty to do so. With the flat of my tongue, I part her lips and catch the rush of wetness that seeps from her entrance in a nirvanic rivulet.

"Son of a bitch," I snarl against her swollen flesh, my tongue working her harder. I'm lost to her taste while slipping a finger inside to the first knuckle. *Christ,* she's tight. Her walls are snug around my digit, clenching to pull me in deeper, but I don't.

I keep my strokes shallow. Just caressing her entrance.

However, my lips suck her clit harshly, and I'm rewarded with the shaking of her thighs on either side of my head while her back arches off the mattress. Her hands are no longer in my hair but gripping her breasts, squeezing the firm globes while undulating against me.

My finger slips in deeper and then out, alternating between the suckling of her clit and labia. Her juices coat my mouth and chin, her tight walls begging for my cock while I finger fuck her with precise pumps that rub against that beautiful little patch of rough flesh that swells with each touch.

"Come for me, Venus. Feed me what is mine."

"I'm close." Aliana pinches her nipples, but it's not hard enough. Not how I would.

I push them off her tits. "Hands up and don't move them, love."

"Callum, please. Just...oh *fuck!*" she screams out as I squeeze a nipple, pulling on the tip while my teeth scrape across her trembling bundle. It throbs, swells against my harsh licks and alternate sucks— her wetness seeping onto my wrist, but it's the next time I bury two fingers deep and press against her spot that she loses control.

Aliana's muscles contract, orgasm slamming into her with force as her eyes roll back and mouth drops open, but no sound comes out.

Instead, I'm rewarded with the sight of her lost in pleasure and her natural saccharine sweetness on my tongue.

I don't stop eating her until she calms and a satiated smile curves her lips. And even then, I take a few more licks before crawling up her body while leaving tiny kisses on her exposed, sensitive skin. Lip caught between her teeth, Aliana welcomes me and then moves without hesitation to cuddle into my chest when I lie facing up. My arms go around her, my lips at the crown of her head, and I find myself wanting this for more than today.

Yes, we need to talk and discuss our relationship.

Yes, she needs to meet the people I'm leaving to watch over her.

However, what I do is close my eyes and relax with her tucked in close. We'll get up in a minute or twenty, I'll order in dinner for us, but first I need her like this, so supple and warm and letting out a content sigh each time my hands rub up and down her back.

It further cements that we aren't done. Not having this is something my male instincts rebel against.

If Casper doesn't speak up, I will.

He needs to be here with Aurora, and I need my Venus home in London and standing to my right.

14
CALLUM

"**A**RE YOU BEING honest right now?" Aliana asks, eyes narrowed while darting between myself and the man beside me and opposite of her the following afternoon. We've been sitting in her living room for thirty minutes now—she'd gone in to work for just a half day—and it's been six hours since I woke her up with my face between her thighs. I'd licked every drop of her sweetness, made her coffee with a bagel, and then told her I'd be leaving tonight. The immediate sadness that flashed through those lovely orbs cut me deep. I don't want to leave her, but the sooner I go, the sooner I'm back to escort her home.

Because she belongs with me. She's my better half.

The Martin kid swallows hard. "I am."

"Jesus, Giannis. Why didn't you say anything before?" It's not lost on me that she hasn't given Kray more than a passing glance, not the least bit affronted by his presence in her home, at least, that's because she doesn't know he'll be her shadow while I'm gone. *That's a conversation best had in private. I'm not taking no for an answer.* However, the kid she's known since middle school—*he's* another matter. That's her focus. There's confusion, a bit of anger, and now sadness. "For crap's sake, we've known each other for years, and it would've made things easier between us. At the least, I wouldn't have been so rude to you."

"I'm not blaming you for that. I was pushy."

"But still."

"It's not that I didn't, Ali. I just couldn't." Giannis flicks a quick look toward a sitting Kray who's listening with a neutral expression. The bloke already sent me an email this morning with the header: *Her name is Lindsey Blackheart,* but I haven't cared to open it. His reactions right now are speaking louder than words on a screen. "Too many factors stood in the way. People who asked me to keep it quiet; one of them being a good friend and the other my father—"

"He knows?"

"That I'm gay?" She nods and he shrugs, body language showing heavy exhaustion. "They *all* do."

"What a mess." That's it. She hasn't yelled or ranted. Instead, she's looked at me for confirmation, and my nod seems to be enough each time. Aliana grabs her can of pop and sits back in her large accent chair, taking a few sips, while the matching one is occupied by Kray. He's on his mobile checking the addresses I gave him for Rubens and the Martin family, but when Giannis confessed, I didn't miss the sudden drop in his tense posture. Not in surprise, but as if this is a confirmation he needed. *Interesting indeed.* "Wait a minute. Time-out." The adorable girl even holds her hand up in the universal sign for stop. "What about the chick from the other night? The one you went home with?"

Thank you, gorgeous. But then again, I wasn't going to ask. I'm a person who watches, lets those around him hang themselves, and these two are protective over the woman but for different reasons.

"Umm." Giannis rubs the back of his neck, ears turning pink

while Kray pauses and looks up. His eyes are hard on the git, silently demanding that Martin tell the truth. "About her..."

"Speak up, bloke. Don't dig yourself a hole you won't get out of."

It's not a suggestion, but a demand he adheres to. Giannis takes in a deep breath and lets it out slowly. "Lindsey knows my boyfriend. They're cousins, actually, and she's around to help buffer for us. He was one of the men that came in with her to the bar; they all work together."

A loud, boisterous laugh pulls our attention toward the guard. He's smiling, slapping his knee while sitting forward in the green velvet chair with gold trim that's not large enough to contain him properly. *Dwarfs my perfect girl, though.* "That woman is a genius little troublemaker."

"Oi. You okay there, mate?" Had this meeting been formal, two lashes from my whip would've reprimanded his outburst. Kray sobers immediately at my harsh glare, but his relief at their non-intimate connection is noticeable. *She's his.* "Is there something you want to share with the rest of us?"

"Please forgive my interruption."

I nod. "Carry on, Giannis. Finish explaining."

"Dwayne is my everything." Hands in front of him, he wrings them together nervously. "We've been together for eight months now, and we met through her. By pure divine luck, to be honest, I caught a flat and she happened to be driving down the road. Lindsey offered to help, and then called him when she realized her kit wasn't in the trunk."

"So, he changed your tire?" Aliana is smiling now, a genuine, silly grin, and my chest clenches at the gorgeous sight. "That's how he swept you off your feet?"

"And gave me his number."

"You meet up with Lindsey and her cousin outside the city limits every Monday, Wednesday, and on the weekends. Correct?" Kray interjects, and Giannis blushes a bit but doesn't deny it. "I could've helped her. She had no need to lie."

"The better question is why did they pull you out of the bar?" All eyes turn toward my girl, and I'm proud of her for being observant. The answer to her question is the one that matters. "What was the urgency, because she was adamant on you leaving."

"Your cousin was in the building with his newest flavor of the month. I cut them off in the elevator before they made it upstairs." The rosiness in her cheeks disappears at his words and she becomes pallid, eyes wide. "We cut off Jorge and invited him to join us at another club. He didn't see or know you were there."

"Thank you." Her voice is shaky, uncertain. "This is such a clusterfuck."

"This is my truth, Ali. What I'm doing to help—"

"Giannis, what do you...no." She's shaking her head from side to side. "No. You can't get involved."

"I already am." They share a look I don't miss, nor can I ignore the heavy implication.

"Venus," I say, pulling her attention toward me, hating the worry in her expression. "What is going on with your family?"

"Don't ask me that." Head shaking from side to side, she stands and walks into her kitchen. The other two remain seated, but stand once I point at the door. In the background, I hear the slam of kitchen cabinets and a muffled curse that worries me.

"Get out. I'll see you before I leave with instructions."

"I'll be near. My brother has a baseball game tonight." Kray steps beside me, carefully placing a hand on my shoulder. It's a friendly gesture. "Are we okay? Everything he said is true and can be found in the email I sent you. I love her and don't want to see her get hurt."

"We are." That's the only reason I'm calm. I'm doing the same for Aliana. "But fuck up again, and I won't be so forgiving. Don't make me doubt you."

"Thank you."

Timmons walks out without another word, and I turn my face

toward the other man. He's running a rough hand down his face, eyes shifting toward the kitchen. "Something you want to say?"

"My family's having dinner tonight, but I can get out if you—"

I level him with a hard stare; it's not friendly. "You will go and pretend nothing has changed. Understood?"

"Yes."

"You will also be spending more time across the street until I return." There's no doubt in my mind that he's aware of what's going on with her, but I'm going to give her the chance to be honest with me. To trust me before I act out of reflex and not fact.

"Okay."

"I expect a report every night when I call. No exceptions."

"Yes, sir."

"Good. Now leave." The front door hasn't fully closed when I enter her kitchen, leaning against the doorframe to watch her. She's wiping down cabinet doors while muttering under her breath, ignoring my presence. "Talk to me, love. What upset you?"

Venus doesn't pause in her cleaning but tilts her head to let me know she heard me. "Too much at once. This is all so overwhelming."

"I can understand that, but—"

"Why is there a *but* in there?"

"Look at me." She doesn't, and I push off the wall to walk over, taking the dishrag from her hand and settling that, and bottle atop the counter. There's a small whine of protest and I get a dirty look when she looks up, but at least I have her full attention. "Much better."

"You're not going to let this go?"

"No." A single tug to her arm and she's standing upright, both hands on her hips. I lift her small frame, loving the way she immediately wraps those pretty thighs around my waist. She's so warm and soft, melts into me, and I walk us back toward the bedroom.

Her bed is still unmade. The room still holds a small hint of her earlier release.

Lying us down in the center, I remove her top and mine, rolling onto my back before pulling her in close. I need to feel her skin to skin. Aliana doesn't complain, her willing body burrowing closer until half her lithe curves cover my harsher planes. It's perfection.

To feel her like this is my version of heaven.

We don't talk. I have a feeling she needs this. To just enjoy the silence, and I'll be whatever she needs, whenever it's needed, until I have her full trust.

That's not to be mistaken with sainthood. My moves in the shadows will always be dark.

"I know you mean well," is the first thing she says after a while. Her fingers are busy tracing the lines of the Jameson name across my abdomen in Old English and leaving behind a trail of heat over every inch she touches. It's maddening, but at the same time absolutely fascinating how enraptured I become in her presence. "So please understand when I ask that you give me time. We just met, Callum. Literally. I'm still trying to wrap my head around you and this..." pushing off my chest, she points a finger between myself and her "...attraction I don't understand and can't help. My life is complicated enough as is, and all I need is time to assimilate you, Giannis, and the meathead you have lingering around like a guard."

The teasing tone and sassy grin on her makes me chuckle. "Caught on to that, did you?"

"Hard not to." Aliana snorts, then rolls her eyes. "The guy is a fridge."

"So dramatic."

"So is avoiding an admittance," she counters, and I roll us over, my body pinning hers to the mattress. "Hey! No fair."

Running my nose against hers, I nip her top lip. "I'll give you time, Venus, but he stays. I'll be gone a little bit, but I need eyes and ears here to make sure you're okay. That's not up for negotiation."

"You're being extra." Even her huff is cute. "We just met, and a security detail should come after a three-month relationship, not the first weekend."

Not a no. Not denying that we are more than a passing hookup.

"Three days was my limit." I run the pad of my fingers down her side and to the edge of her tights, slipping a finger beneath the waist to feel the warmth of her skin there. "I need you safe. My world is dangerous, sweetheart, and I can't take chances where you're concerned."

"Part time." Voice low. A bit husky. "Actually, more like a trial basis, and I choose the events he's allowed to come to."

"Full time, and you don't complain."

"Three times a week, and I'll FaceTime you on the other days to give you a day-by-day breakdown. It'll be boring, I must warn you. I'm not that interesting between work and school." She arches her back, pressing her chest against my mouth. Goose bumps rise across her skin and her thighs cradle mine, my trouser-covered-cock against her yoga-pant-covered heat. "I'll even throw in the occasional picture."

"Naughty?" I growl, flexing against her once. The thin lace bralette she's wearing is black and covers nothing. Her nipples are hard, her flesh spilling out. "Are you trying to bribe me, Miss Rubens?"

"It can be if you agree to my terms." Her attempt at distracting me is charming, but all it does is make me want her even more. To be around every second of her day.

"Love, I was going to demand that either way." I lick a path from one pebbled tip to the other, lightly biting on the right one. "I'll give you time, but my sanity needs this. Agree."

"Not fair."

"Nothing in life worth a damn ever is." This time I blow across the tender flesh, my hands moving lower to the waistband of her bottoms. They're easy to remove, more so when she whines and lifts her hips when I tease her nipples, but once they're off, I pause. It's easy to become lost in her body, but Aliana needs to understand what I'm asking of her.

"Why'd you stop?"

"When I walk out of here tomorrow, I'm no longer the man you have at your mercy, Aliana. I'm a murderer. A criminal." It's the truth, and I won't lie to her. I'm exposing myself so she sees that I'm serious, that she can trust me. "I'm going home to London to help my cousin kill every single man involved in the murder of my aunt. I'm going home to make changes, eliminate every single threat, and then I'll be bringing you home. You, my stubborn beauty, are important to me and I want you safe. So can you please do this for me? Don't give them a tough time, and let me know if something is wrong."

Tears brim in her eyes, and she nods. "After my trip."

"What trip?"

"Give me this, and I'll accept this without further argument."

"What trip?"

Lifting a hand, she cups my face and brings it to hers. Lays a tiny peck across my lips. "Trust in me the same way you're asking me to trust you."

"Okay." This time I kiss her, dragging my teeth across her bottom lip. "Will you be safe?"

"It's a family retreat. I promise to be careful while vacationing."

"Aye."

"Thank you." Relief sweeps across her expression, but I'm not letting this go. I'll find out what she's hiding soon enough, but Kray will remain on duty, just not out in the open. At least, until she gets back. "I appreciate it."

"Then show me, my Venus."

"How," she moans low, a keening sound as I drag my lips down the column of her throat and to the valley between her breasts. I lick and suck the skin there, the lovely shade of bruising complementing her tanned skin tone. "What can I do to show my—"

"Feed me." A grunt. My chest rumbles as I hold back my need to dominate and own. To demand she be honest and then take her away from whatever problems she has. Because I know they are there; the clues laid out so far create a picture that would lead to the destruction of her family, but before I make her an orphan, I need concrete proof.

I'd hate to be wrong and eradicate someone she loves. "I need you to shimmy out of your knickers, arch your back, then spread your pussy lips and present me my meal."

"Oh *fuck*."

"Soon, Aliana. I'll claim you soon, but today I want to taste your pleasure."

15
Aliana

I 'M AN IDIOT. Completely and utterly moronic, but smiling like the hussy this man is turning me into. *If only I could say no.* But I can't, and every time those piercing, gem-like eyes ask me for something or need an answer, I end up agreeing while letting down every single one of my walls.

Dios mio, ayudame. This position I've put myself in will cost me. I know it will.

My father will never allow this, but I also can't stop the small bloom of hope taking place in my chest, burrowing deep and holding on for dear life after Callum shared his plans.

He wants to take me home. To London.

Somewhere far from Chicago and all that I know, but with him I'd do so happily and without a second thought, knowing this could blow up in my face in so many tragic ways.

That man is the perfect heartbreak waiting to happen.

He'd tear me apart, something I'm no longer able to stop if he walked away.

I already care too much.

So much can go wrong.

What about returning to Spain?

That had been my original plan, but after hearing his, it doesn't hold the same appeal.

Nothing else does. And perhaps I'll feel differently tomorrow, but in the afterglow of his touch, I want to follow him. Because a part of me, the scared and disillusioned fragment of my soul, wants it —craves his words to be true.

Which makes no sense. But then again, nothing of the last few days does.

"How did I let myself get caught up in such a mess?" I want to feel whole again. I want to trust him. "Things that sound too good to be true usually are." My low muttering is accompanied by a hiss, my thigh muscles protesting as I stand on the tips of my toes to grab a glass from the cupboard. This is the aftereffect of being kept on my back, legs spread wide while he worshipped me for hours.

Mouth. Fingers. But never his cock.

And damn him, I wanted the latter. Begged for it, but Callum denied my request each time.

"Oh God," I moan, body thrumming as the aftershocks of my last orgasm still ring through me. Not that the man between my thighs cares. If anything, the last two weren't enough. Another long lick with the flat of his tongue and I close my eyes, fighting instincts that contradict each other. Push him away. Pull him closer. More. Stop. "Callum, come here. Please, just come up here."

"No." A growl, the vibrations of the simple word running through me like a live current. From the tip of my toes to the last strand of hair on my head, I feel it. Pulsing. Pushing me. "Need you to give me another, Venus. One more."

"Too much."

"Never bloody enough."

Back arching, I scream as his teeth scrape over my throbbing clit.

It hurts a bit; a painful pleasure seizes every nerve ending and lights me on fire. "Please. Please, I need to feel you inside me...son of a—"

"I'll never fuck you and leave, Aliana." *He bites my thigh, teeth digging in. This shuts me up. My mouth is open in a silent scream, body shaking as another orgasm is ripped from me with nothing more than a harsh nip. With my flesh between his teeth, his hooded eyes watch me come apart, his cheek nuzzling my tender pussy as uncontrollable tremors rock me. I pulse. I cry a bit, but then my breath gets caught in my throat and nothing matters more than the sight of this man gripping his cock.* "Please tell me you understand."

"Callum, I—"

Muscles straining, he braces himself with one arm on the mattress, his body leaning over mine. "Answer me, Venus. Tell me you understand," *he hisses, teeth gritted tight as he jerks off at the juncture of my thighs. He's thick, the head almost angry while his pace is punishing.*

I've lost all ability to speak. I'm lost to the perfect picture of masculinity he paints.

I'm following each movement hungrily, my core clenching involuntarily, and another rough spasm shakes me. "Fuck me."

Pace quickening, Callum's eyes travel from my wet core to my eyes. "Beautiful." *His stare is hooded, so hungry. Those gem-colored eyes stay on mine as the first rope of warm come lands across my labia and clit, dripping down to my ass and then the sheets. They don't waver when the next two make a mess of my mound and stomach. Instead, they darken even more as he rubs the tip against my skin, spreading his release all over me.*

I'm a mess. My pussy still throbs.

"Why?"

"Tell me you understand why I denied us both what we need?" *he counters, and I want to tell him that I do, but that would be a lie. Rejection suddenly floods me, and I look away, my eyes tearing up for a different reason.* Maybe I'm being too desperate? *"Stop that."*

Callum's hovering over me now, lips almost touching mine as I meet his hard stare. He's a total contradiction to the man that watched me come a minute ago and then marked me with his release. I try to move away, to slide out from beneath him, but his weight drops, and I find myself pinned to the bed.

"Please move."

"No." Two warm hands cup my face and hold me so I can't look away. "Don't shut me out, Aliana."

"It's okay."

"No, baby. It's not." With a pained groan, he lowers his mouth to mine and kisses me slowly. So tenderly. The way Callum takes my lips this time is what every woman dreams of, and I didn't know I've been missing for so long. It's raw, shakes me to the core, and the taste of my release on his sweet lips quickly becomes something I'll crave until the day I die. It's the tangible proof of his hunger for me. A peck and then nibble to my bottom lip and he pulls back, smiling down at me. "Never think that I'm rejecting you, love. I couldn't, but I am postponing the inevitable when in a few hours I'll be gone. There's no way I'd be able to leave if I do, and taking you back with me until our enemies are removed; I can't put you in danger like that. So please, sweetheart. Be patient. Wait for me."

Wait for me.

He said those same words a few days ago when he walked out after a final kiss and the exchange of our phone numbers. Formally, anyway. I know he's had mine since pulling information on me, and it doesn't bother me in the least.

The sudden hard knock on my front door pulls me back into the present and away from the memory of his touch. They're not pounding, but the noise is loud, and I cautiously make my way over.

I'm not expecting anyone.

Standing up onto the tips of my toes, I look through the peephole and find a man I've never seen before standing on the other side. He's tall, his face impassive, and in his hand is some sort of envelope.

I don't open the door. Instead, I take quiet steps back until I'm back in the kitchen and can grab my cell.

With shaky fingers, I press the security camera app and go to live feed. His retreating form is what I find, and the envelope is no longer in his hand.

"What the hell?" For the next ten minutes I keep watch through my phone, not moving from my spot until I'm sure no one is outside, and then I rush to check the outside of my door. With each step closer, dread fills my stomach and my nerves pick up. And I'm right in doing so, because there lying atop my floor mat is a padded manila casing with my name written across the front in a penmanship I'd know anywhere.

Moreover, my suspicions are confirmed when I open it and read the first page.

This slice of reality slams into me with a vengeance. Brutally. Unforgiving.

There's no future with Callum. There's no reason to entertain him or any offer he makes when this is my life.

I'm a puppet on a string.

How can I withhold this from him and my newly appointed guard long term while keeping my father happy and at bay?

I can't juggle this.

I can't live multiple lives.

You leave in seventy-two hours. Disappoint me, and you know the price.

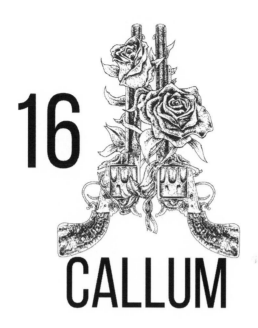

16

CALLUM

"WE'RE BEHIND SCHEDULE."

Casper's head snaps in my direction at the sound of my voice, a shitty grin on his face. He has a small carry-on over his left shoulder and a large love bite on the left side of his neck. Our plane is ready, the pilot is on standby, but we won't be getting on it until much later. *I'm not leaving this up to him.* "By four minutes, you arse. If I'm late, it's acceptable."

Pushing off the wall beside the door he walked through, I clap his shoulder. "To me, it's not."

At once, his amusement drops and the bag in his hand is tossed to a male crew member standing at the ready to assist a few feet away. The lad catches it, rushing away to stow it while Kray's car pulls up and idles.

Before we leave the States, there are two personal messages I'll be delivering.

"What's wrong?" This is the head of the family I know and have trusted all my life.

"Gaspar."

"What the fuck did that cunt do? Is he pushing product here?"

"Worse." Tilting my head in Kray's direction, I motion for him to follow me. We don't talk while we walk, and when the door closes and the SUV drives off the private airstrip, I look over. "I'm going to ask you a series of questions, and I want your honest answer, Casper. Not as my boss, but as my family. Can you set your ego aside and do that?"

"What the fuck?" An angry hiss. "Of course, I can."

"Good." Turning my head, I lean forward and tap the back of Kray's seat. "Pull up to the end of the road and step outside."

"Understood," Timmons says, following my instructions and stopping near a small cluster of trees and then exits, holding his mobile up to let me know he'll wait for my text to come back.

When his back is a few feet away, Casper clears his throat. "Talk to me. What's going on?"

"Are you moving to Chicago?"

For a few beats he's quiet, his face unreadable, but a nod follows. "Yes. For a little bit, at least."

"Fuck does that mean? When were you going to tell me?" My tone comes out a bit accusatory, although I'm not mad—more like annoyed with his current lack of communication. We've always had each other's backs, I respect him, and having to deduce clues and decipher his head space shouldn't be how we work. Because even if he moves to Japan or the South Pole, we're family. He will always be a Jameson. "What are you planning?"

"I want Boston." No further explanation. Just throws that out.

It's also not something I saw coming, and I scrunch my nose in question. He's never expressed a need to take over another state in the US. "Now isn't the time for riddles, cousin. Speak up."

"You sound like a boss."

"That's because I am." I'm not going to pussyfoot around this subject anymore.

"I haven't stepped down."

"You will."

His reply to that is a smirk and another nod. Acceptance. "Gem's father wants her to take over Boston, and she will. By my side."

"Are you with her for—"

"You fucking taking the piss?" Callum says, his tone acerbic. "I love that woman."

"Good."

"Good?"

"Yes, good. I'd hate to break that ugly mug of yours for being a cunt."

Usually, something like that would make him laugh or flip me off, but instead, his eyes narrow and lips thin. "Since when do you care who I see or don't? Or if I'm using—"

"You hurt Aurora, and that affects Aliana." Shrugging, I begin to undo the button of my right sleeve and roll it up to my elbow, then repeat with the other. "I won't allow that."

It clicks where I've been, and his hand comes up to scratch his jaw. The tosser hasn't shaved in days, it seems. "My offer is to help her. She can take it or leave it, but I'd still move here for her."

"You don't think she'll relocate to the U.K.?"

"Not when the Conte House is here. She'd never abandon her mother's legacy."

"She'd still be leaving Chicago." *Aliana didn't reject my desire to move across the ocean with me. My Venus smiled, more than likely unaware of the act, but she did, and that's all that matters.*

"We're talking from a few states away to across the ocean. It'd be easier to relocate the office here and just expand locations, something I know she wants to do."

"That's very true." My mobile buzzes in my trouser pocket, but I ignore it for now. "Think she'll turn down his offer?"

"No. She won't." Casper closes his eyes and leans his head back. A small frown on his face. "That woman has a huge, yet fragile heart, and it bites her in the arse at times. This is one of those instances, and her father is close to having her cave."

"You think he'll go for it?"

The smirk is back as he shrugs while looking at me through slits. "Fucker has no choice."

At that, I throw my head back and laugh. He means it. He'd kill him if he had to for Aurora. Sobering a bit, I hold a fist out for him, which he bumps with his. It's a gesture we've always done over the years right before celebrating or eliminating an enemy. "When do you want to make the announcement? Our clientele needs to be informed of the change in management, Casper. I'm not you, and things will run a bit differently."

"They all know and have dealt with you in the past."

"You still had the final call. Not anymore."

He's pensive for a moment, a flash of pain crossing his features. "As soon as I've burned Mum's killer alive."

"Aye." That's more than fair. I would've insisted on it. "Now, as for our visit—"

"Gaspar's meeting with Rubens, isn't he?"

"He is."

"Personal or business, Callum?"

"Personal."

"Then let's go ruin their night, boss."

———

The leader of the Gaspar family is sitting in a booth inside of a seedy strip club across town. He's unaware, body relaxed, while a dancer gyrates atop the table like a perverse buffet. Men sit and watch, point and make lewd gestures, while ignoring the three men walking inside and taking over a table near theirs.

Then again, it's dark in here with the harsh strobe light high-lighting specific areas: the stage, and two high, circular platforms that have a pole at the center and are only big enough to hold two people at the most. Then, there's the tobacco smoke and the lines of blow in plain sight.

Most of the men here surround the stage, tipping the girls, while a few sit to the side with a dancer on their lap and with wandering hands.

My eyes shift around the room, and I find a few more of his men spread throughout, not really paying attention. They're busy celebrating something, the ends of their noses powdery white while their pupils are blown wide. Stumbling. Laughing. Fucking twats.

All out in the open, no fucks given. However, their unprofessionalism works in my favor.

"Spread them cheeks, sweetheart. Show me how loose you are for me?" Flavio says, his stubby finger running up the young woman's leg while she dances with her eyes closed. The smile on her face is fake, forced, and highlighted by the mirror above where they sit, but none seem to care. They ignore. *Sick fucks.*

I point to the emergency exit near the restrooms and Kray stands, quickly taking position and blocking with his weapon drawn. The bouncers here won't be an issue. We've already taken care of them, knocked unconscious by the front door and then dragged off to the side of the building.

"I can handle those by the stage," Casper says. In his hands are two loaded Rugers like mine, but his are from a limited addition line. Mine are all black, the silencer matching the murdered-out powder coat finish. "You ready?"

"Always." We share a look and wait. Watch as those around us become more inebriated, uncoordinated, while laughing at the implication of their boss's words. His hands are higher up the dancer's thighs, almost to her core when the first shots are fired. Then, there is chaos.

Blood splashes the front of a waitress at the center of the room, and the man she'd been serving while pushing his hands away is dead upon impact: neck wound with a head thrown back by the force. Her scream is the first to rend the air, but quickly a symphony of fear overtakes the room as panic and confusion—the flight or fight instinct—takes over and like roaches, bodies begin to scatter.

Many fall, pushing against each other as they fight to get out while the second and third bullet rips through the wall near Flavio's head. His men stand, eyes darting around the room while missing the two men standing a few feet away with their guns drawn.

They're too high. Too unprepared. Yelling at each other while their unfocused eyes dart around the room in search of the threat. Not once do they look at us; they glance over and then focus on the other side of the stage as if the perpetrator is using the elevated platform as coverage.

Having men like these is a costly mistake for someone who is hell-bent on making enemies. Because in this world, you never let your guard down. You don't stop questioning every single person that walks into the room you occupy, and you never get plastered while on the job. Losing the awareness of your surroundings is dangerous: a death sentence.

A lesson this family needs to learn.

From his place by the emergency exit, Kray fires three consecutive times, and more bodies fall. The women huddled against a wall all cry, shaking, but he raises the gun to his lips and taps it once. *Silence.*

They quiet down, still whimpering a bit, but calm down enough to walk when he steps aside and lets them scramble out the door.

"The fuck!" Flavio screams, shoving the poor scared woman and table out of the way, knocking her hard onto the ground while those around him crowd in a protective way. Casper shoots again, hits one of the enforcers in the knee, tripping him, and the man's sheer size alone knocks the two beside him to the ground. "Fire back! Find who's shooting!"

Six left.

"Bloody idiots," my cousin sneers, lip curling in disgust while I aim at the arm of Gaspar's right-hand man. I'd studied his profile earlier today, a young wannabe playboy related to the man I killed last time we had words. I killed the last right hand arsehole, and I'll prove just how easily I can do so again. "It's insulting to the human species."

"Agreed." Another shot, this one to the opposite arm. He falls back on impact, yelling some form of a curse that makes no sense when I step forward. "Oi. Your men are too slow, mate. You're bloody sitting ducks."

"Who the fuck are you?"

"Callum, what are you doing here?" Flavio, and some bloke who's too green in the gills, speak in unison. One with fear. One with cockiness.

The latter of the two slumps over with a bullet to his head before I respond, my silencer muting the sound. "Muzzle your pets, Gaspar. My patience is running thin tonight."

A flash of fear crosses his face, but he schools his features quickly. "Is Casper aware of the trouble you're causing tonight? There are codes in place, Jameson. You're starting a conflict between our—"

"Silence." Casper steps in beside me, his face impassive. "I'm not his boss. Callum makes his own calls."

You can see the confusion on his face and the utter look of loss on what's left of his men. Their expression says it all.

No one else is here. The music, a heavy-based beat, plays in the background while the lights continue to highlight how easily we ruined their night. How easy they are to kill.

"Sit, Flavio." I point my gun to the area he'd been enjoying himself in before. The dancer he'd been touching is on the ground, though. She's not unconscious but is shaking in fear, and I look over at Kray. "Get her cleaned up and out."

"Yes, sir." Without another word, he walks over and kneels next to the woman. He says something and she nods, quickly gripping his hand, and then stands on trembling legs.

"Tip her."

"Callum, this is—"

"Tip her, or I shoot you. Your choice."

Flavio nods, lips in a tight line while pulling out a wad of cash. He tosses a hundred-dollar bill at the floor by her feet. "Here."

"All of it, and if you toss it, I'll make you pick it up with your teeth. She's not a dog."

"It's okay, sir," the woman says, looking toward Gaspar with that forced grin back in place. "He doesn't owe me anything."

Ignoring her, I tilt my head to the side with the barrel of my gun pointing at the same man I've already shot twice. His second-in-command is bleeding, gritting his teeth as the pain begins to settle and his body shakes. "All. Of. It." Flavio heeds my warning as Casper grabs two chairs from a nearby table and brings them over. One for me. One for him. The large stack of bills is exchanged under my watch and then Kray takes her away, walking her to the back to collect her things and then out the front door. "Now sit."

Cautiously, one of the men with him rights the table and then steps back.

"Callum, what's the meaning of this?" Flavio asks, his anger and embarrassment is palpable. He feels disrespected in front of his men, something that no boss can ever allow. Once you show weakness, no one will follow you. "You're in my territory and I can—"

"Can what, mate? What the fuck can you do?" I take my seat casually, and Casper does the same. He's quiet, while I enjoy watching the maggot not worth a shit try and keep his composure.

It won't work. Gaspar will make a mistake.

His men will pay the price.

He takes in a deep breath and sits across from us, hands atop the old table. "Why are you here?"

"Because you seem to need a reminder on how this business works. On how to stay in your lane." Someone scoffs as Kray reenters the room and walks toward me, the woman now gone. My guard hears it, head snapping to the side with a gun against the man's temple before the already injured git could react. "What's your deal with Rubens?"

Flavio swallows hard, throat bobbing harshly, but recovers

quickly, expression neutral, while those around him are anything but. "I don't know what you're talking about."

"Are you sure you want to take that route, lad? My patience is bloody thin as it is."

"I haven't done anything to warrant this level of disrespect, Jameson. You're in my home, my country, and...son of a bitch!" he yells out, hand gripping his ear where my bullet took out a small chunk. Blood seeps through his fingers, the left side of his clothing now ruined.

"Watch it, Flavio. I'd hate to think you truly meant that insult." One of his men twitches, his hand moving toward his belt, but before he can take his next intake of air, Casper's gun remedies his idiocy. He's not dead, but a bullet to the abdomen can do a lot of damage and if not treated immediately, it'd become irreparable. "And you wouldn't be stupid enough to do so. Would you?"

"No." Voice low, he looks at the men beside him. Not one of them is fit for the job, in my opinion, but I'm almost embarrassed for him. I'd feel bad had he not been stupid enough to be intertwined with Rubens's and Aliana's safety.

People like him have no word. No code.

He's an animal that needs to come to heel or be put down for his insubordination.

"Last time we met, Flavio, do you remember what I said to you before walking out the door?"

"That you'd kill my—"

"Louder," I hiss out, my own weapon on the table. My finger is on the trigger as it lays on its side, its muzzle pointing at his heart. "What did I tell you before walking out?"

"That you'd kill my men and then force me to eat them before ending my pathetic life."

"And yet you try to gain territory when we've been generous." My eyes scan the room, finding product on nearly every table. A waste. The color is also off; it's cheap and cut wrong. Shaking my head, I level him with a hard look. "You try to befriend a politician to what end? What is he offering?"

"Nothing. It's a monetary—"

"The truth, arsehole."

"A truce."

"A truce?" I ask while Casper scoffs beside me. "Fuck do you have to gain from that?"

"Immunity." Flavio's explanation sounds plausible, and any other day I'd give him the benefit of the doubt, but Giannis wouldn't be so afraid if it were that simple. The way his hands shake is also telling. *Wanker is scared.* "We'd be left to do business without harassment or possible jail time in the future if caught mid-transaction. Just that. Nothing else."

"Bullshit." There's only one man left in his circle that hasn't spilled blood, and I bring the count down to zero before his next blink. All of the men sitting or surrounding their boss have now paid for his greed. They groan, some trembling where they stand at the ready to die for Flavio. Admirable, but he's not deserving of their loyalty. "But I'm going to let it slide…" Flavio exhales roughly while the man now on the floor cries out in pain "…for now."

"I swear it's the truth."

"And I don't give a flying fuck either way."

"Callum, Casper…this hostility between us isn't necessary. I can talk to Rubens; we can all prosper from my alliance. Think about it."

"There's nothing for me to think about, Gaspar." Sitting forward, I level him with a hard stare. He's sweating; the fear pours out of him. "You will stop whatever it is that you have with Rubens and Martin. No more meetings. No more threats."

"Listen, Callum. I don't know what the problem is, but you can't—"

"I can and will." Lifting my right hand, I empty every bullet left in the wall just two inches from Flavio's head. The gun in my left hand still has ammo, and he sees the intent. The next time my Ruger discharges, the target is his skull. "The next time I visit over this, I'm going to burn you each alive and then feed your cooked meat to my pet; I'll ship him over from his cushy home in one of my London properties just for this meal. This is your only warning, Flavio. Stay away from the Rubens and Martin family. All of them. Understood?"

He nods. "Yes."

"Any Gaspar found to be trespassing my order will be put down. Understood?"

"Yes."

"You don't speak to their families, employees, or the person who makes their coffee at the local deli. Not so much as a bloody nod in their direction." My eyes shift to all the men one by one, not moving onto the next until they nod. "Heed my warning. I won't hesitate to kill you."

17

Aliana

"WE DESERVE A gold medal after the last few days," I say, sighing as the warm water of the pedicure bowl pulses with massaging jets. We're in pamper mode today—activated and unreachable while taking a much-needed break. It's been a week now since both men left, since my father canceled my trip again—no notice or explanation, just a text telling me to hold off until further notice. It's also been seven days since all hell broke loose and we got an influx of women that left us scrambling to accommodate and protect, leaving me no time to wonder why the sudden change in plans.

Two of the new residents had a drug addiction, while the other three were running from abusive men that had no qualms about threatening us, but one took it the extra mile. That one didn't care, charging in with a weapon drawn while trying to intimidate by looking to hurt us or the building his ex was seeking sanctuary inside of.

The visit lasted a few minutes at the most, tense seconds where

Aurora pulled out her gun while I doused his face with pepper spray before he could shoot, or worse.

"Bring her out," the man screams; a tall jerk with twitchy movements and the nauseating scent of garbage all around him. He's unkempt. His expression is of pure rage while holding an old pistol in his grip. Arm down and shaking, he stormed inside, scaring the two assistants helping with the dietary changes needed for a seven-year-old with a peanut allergy. "Where is my wife?"

"Sir, you need to put your weapon away, or we will be obligated to call the police." Aurora moves in front of the two shaking women while I gently push them toward the office. We've gone over drills with the staff and those who live here, practice these at least once a month, but when fear kicks in, you can't predict how a person will react. "Put it away, and we'll go to my office and speak calmly—"

"Shut the fuck up, bitch. Bring me my wife, or I'll shoot every single one of you."

"Last warning," Aurora says, tone neutral while her hand opens the drawer of the desk right beside her. The man looks down at it, but before he can see her reach for her weapon, I push a high stack of papers onto the ground; it flutters in the space between us and him. It's just enough of a distraction for Aurora to grab her gun and aim at his chest, while the other women lock the door to her office. "You didn't listen. This is private property, and I want you out."

"I'm not leaving without her. I'd rather burn this entire place to the ground."

"Get out," I hiss, while Aurora clicks the safety off. The man's eyes flash with fear, but soon that's gone. That miniscule second reasserts his careless way of thinking, and it also gives me a chance to pull out the pepper spray I keep on myself, finger ready to dress down.

"No." He takes a step forward in my direction, but I'm already spraying. I empty the bottle, focusing on his left eye that is partially uncovered through spread fingers, and then step back.

"You whore!" the man screams, stumbling back and falling as

the papers cause him to slide. His body crashes hard, the gun slipping out of his hand and ending against the opposite wall. "The fuck is this shit? It burns!"

"That was a warning, sir. Get up, and get out." No sooner do those words pass through Aurora's lips than we hear police sirens. They are close. The office is at the front of the compound, not far from the parking lot and main road. The closer they get, the more he panics and scrambles to get up, only to fall once more, hitting his face this time as he's having a hard time keeping his eyes open. "And we will be pressing charges. See you in court."

With difficulty, he pushes himself up and stands. He's facing us, but not really focused. "I'll be back. This isn't the end, and my slut of a wife will pay for this."

After that, he left, body stumbling into the wall beside the door before managing to exit, still screaming, insulting us, and then not a single trace left for the cops to find.

None of our cameras caught sight of him past the front door. He disappeared.

No blood. No body. Nada.

These occurrences aren't really the norm with us. Most men don't want cops involved or looking their way and approach the women in a softer manner. Some fall for the fake repentance, some don't, but we defend ourselves either way. This also makes me think that Aurora's still being watched.

Or is it me?

Callum gave me his word—that he'd respect my wishes for a few weeks, but did he?

But more importantly, I'm not upset if he hasn't. The last seven days while stressful, have been pleasant in a way I'm not used to. My father has left me alone since that text, and no more harassing crap from Giannis as I know the truth and our friendship grows. Instead, I'm coming and going with more ease, and I don't want to go back to the way it was before.

"Amen, chica." Aurora cranes her neck back and closes her eyes.

"I was seconds away from turning to a life of heavy drinking and a full-time hermit career."

At that I snort, ignoring the vibrations inside of my pants pocket. It's a little after three in the afternoon and I know it's Callum, but I don't want to draw attention to myself. If she hasn't told me about Casper, then I'm keeping Callum a secret.

Besides, it's kind of fun. The secret messages and the naughty phone calls. The picture of him shirtless and joggers pushed below mid-thigh while he gripped his cock; a picture now forever inside a private folder locked under a passcode.

"Aye." It slips out, and my cheeks burn. *What the hell?* "I hear ya."

"You a pirate now?" A spa worker comes over with another mimosa on a tray and we each take one, smiling at the girl. When she leaves, my best friend looks over with a raised brow. "Have you been watching *Pirates of the Caribbean* again? Your obsession with the male actors in those movies is highly—"

"Shut it, and guilty."

"You look guilty."

"So do you, bestie." I waggle my brows. "I'm still waiting for the play by play of lover boy's trip here. When are you going to spill?"

"I already did." She rolls her eyes, and I want to flick her forehead. "You know he came, and we spent a few days together. We went out on dates, ate, and there was plenty of the good stuff I'm not sharing about."

"How can I live vicariously through you if you deny me the juicy details?"

"How about you tell me about Giannis instead? Is he still following you around like a lost puppy?"

Immediately, I want to defend him—correct her—but that wouldn't help the low profile we've decided to maintain. Giannis came to me after Callum left and we talked; he explained himself and the situation fully, and I'm so grateful to have him in my corner.

I've also seen pictures of him with the boyfriend. The goofy smiles they both wear when together, and if I can help make things easier on him, then why not? We are two people stuck in a tough position and deserve a break. To be happy.

"You know it. I'm almost tempted to say *yes* just to get it over with." The lie feels wrong, but I can't tell her what's going on. The less people involved, the better, and besides, if her father plans to help mine in finding me a "suitable" husband, things will be out in the open soon enough.

Do I want to be responsible for another fight between them? No.

Do I want to kill the glow that surrounds her amid a Casper Jameson romance? No.

So, while the nail technicians come over and we hand them the chosen colors, I giggle. While they scrub, file, and then massage our feet, I do what I do best and pretend nothing is wrong.

She's oblivious, but I'm not mad because hiding my truth is what I've been taught to do. Someday she'll know, and she'll be mad at me for not asking for help, but until then, I want to enjoy the peace and quiet.

"I'd pay good money to see the look on his face if you do. He'd probably pee his pants." She laughs, pulling out her phone after it pings in her small bag. Her eyes brighten while reading a text. Smile wide and cheeks with just a hint of pink, she quickly begins to write back, oblivious to my movements.

Because I check my cellphone too, a small smile fighting to curl at the edge of my lips. I don't, though, biting it back even though my heart is racing, and my skin breaks out in goose bumps.

I miss you, my Venus. ~Callum J.

Five words. So simple and yet, I feel each one down to my bones. They make me happy. Make me want to giggle and be all high-pitched squeals, but I can't.

Aurora has enough on her plate, the mess with her father and his demands for her to take over weighing heavy on her shoulders. I also don't know how she'd feel about me seeing Casper's cousin. Would it bother her?

I'm keeping so much from her already.

I hope that on the day all my truths come out, she forgives me.

"Clean sheets and shaved legs for the win." I sigh, snuggling deeper into the bed after another long day. Yeah, we took a break in the afternoon, but that was cut short mid-lunch when the receptionist at the Conte House called with an urgent new case. This one came with a police escort and two signed court orders that say her ex-boyfriend isn't allowed within a hundred feet of her and their son. No excuses.

That led to more paperwork, room placement, and then a long meeting with them while Aurora explained the ins and outs—rules—while I worked in a curricular activity for both. Schooling for the twelve-year-old, job training for her, and then medical and mental health visits for both.

I'm not sure the extent of what they've gone through, but one look into her empty eyes spoke louder than the screams of a thousand angry souls. And while I usually handle the public relations side of the house and the few classes I teach a week, I sat down and helped a tired Aurora with what I could before walking out the front doors a little after seven p.m.

I'm hungry, but too tired to make anything.

I'm sleepy, yet awake and wanting something. Him.

I miss him.

Grabbing my phone from the nightstand, I open our last text exchange and read them. His last reply was over twenty-four hours ago, a corny joke that made me laugh until my eyes watered. It involved a bike, being tired, and the mother of a dad joke delivery that morphed into a catastrophe of comedic genius.

His timing killed me. I'd been running late, rushing to my car when it came through, and I laughed so hard my phone slipped and skidded across the ground, earning itself a nice scratch across the screen.

You should be arrested for this joke. ~Venus

I changed my handle to his nickname before hitting send. Couldn't help myself.

Before I'm able to place the device down, though, it rings, and I'm surprised. It's so late in London. Pressing the green button, I smile as a tired-looking Callum smirks back at me.

"I'll have you know I'm very funny. Have been approached several times to run my own big network special."

"Is that so?"

"Aye." At my snort, he rolls his eyes and then sighs. His finger traces across the screen. "You're so beautiful, Venus."

My cheeks heat up, and my heart races. That same fluttering energy fills my stomach, and it's like he's here all over again. "Thank you."

"You look so soft and warm, love. Are you in bed?" That's when I notice he's in an office of some sort; a large screen hangs behind him while a half empty bottle of dark liquor sits just to his right. "Let me see you."

"I am," I say, sitting up against my pillows. My back arches a bit as I situate myself, and the thin cotton of my shirt stretches—exposes just how hard my nipples are. The mere sound of his voice does wicked things to me; I'm wet and achy with that growing need he incites. Just like when he was here. When I had his touch, his mouth on my skin. "How do you want me?"

"Don't tease me, sweetheart." His groan is loud, and I shiver. "It's been a long day, and I'm nowhere near done. Take pity on a lad and show me a little skin."

"Have you missed me?" At my counter, he gives me a lecherous look. "PG-13 miss me, not rated MA, Mr. Jameson."

"I have. More than you could ever imagine." There's amusement in his tone, but it's the heated look that makes me simper. A low, keening mewl escapes my lips, my skin breaking out in goose bumps while he watches. Licks his lips. "And you...did you miss me? My touch?"

"Both." It's my truth, and his expression softens a bit. *A sweet hunger.* He's older than me, in his late twenties, but the boyish looks and the way his gaze sweeps across the screen should be considered illegal. "Has anyone told you you're quite charming? It's nearly impossible to not be drawn to you."

"And you're simply captivating." Callum pours himself a drink, grabbing a glass from somewhere within arm's reach while not standing from his seat. It's a few fingers' worth, no ice or soda to mix. "I can't stop thinking about you, Aliana." He takes a sip and holds it. Savors it. "All day. All night."

"I'm stuck in the same cycle." Because I am. Morning, noon, and night; this man is on my mind and refusing to give me a single moment of reprieve from the promises he made. "Yet you're far, and I'm here."

"This separation is temporary."

"What do you consider temporary?" I pull the phone further from my face and tilt it, giving him a better view of my body from my mouth to the edge of my panties. Then a little lower, where I shimmy my bedsheet down to lay over my mid thighs, pausing at the juncture where he can see me. There's no hiding the small patch of wetness there nor the small lift of my hips. His groans fuel me, make me want to be bolder, but I want the answer to my question more. Not keeping the focus there for long, I pull it back, drag the camera view up slowly until he can see my eyes again. "I'm still waiting for your answer, sir."

"You're a naughty little thing."

"And you do this to me."

"Everything I told you was true." Callum lets out a rough breath then. The desire is still there, but I'm transfixed by his gem-like stare that's so honest and open. "I want your home to be London, Aliana. Beside me." Before I can answer, though, someone comes into the room after knocking once; their words aren't clear, and after Callum nods, you can hear the door close. His face is tense now, a complete contradiction from the man who a minute ago confessed to missing me. Wanting me with him. "My apologies, love. Casper's looking for me."

"Is everything okay? Is this about your aunt?"

His head bows slightly in affirmation. "It will be soon."

He's going out to work. To possibly kill.

"You need to go, don't you." Not a question and he nods, knocking back what's left of his drink. Whatever he's about to do isn't something I want the details on, but I worry. It builds, creates this uncomfortable feeling in my chest that begins to eat at me. I'm in too deep and care too much. *Diosito, please watch out for him.* "I need you safe, Callum. Promise me you will not get hurt."

"You have my word." For a second, neither of us speak. We watch until there's another knock and he sighs, the sound heavy, and it settles across my body like a warm blanket. It's a sound of remorse and need, and I feel the heaviness in my bones. *I don't judge you. I can't.* "You're embedded deep, Venus. So motherfucking deep, and I don't want it to change because every part of me needs you."

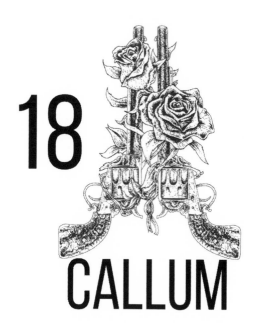

18

CALLUM

"**H**IJO DE PUTA, I'm going to...*fuck!*" Felix De La Vega screams two weeks later, the gun he'd been clutching— hand shaking while reality sets in—is now on the floor. One bullet from my Ruger, that's all it takes, and I chuckle at his idiotic expression.

Fear and loss; he reeks of it. *Pathetic cunt.*

He's a nobody. A bloody middleman that made himself available to my aunt's killer by facilitating a hitman while gaining a pretty penny for the connection. His hands are tinged with her blood, and we have plans for him.

"Oi, my apologies, bro. My finger slipped."

Casper chuckles a few steps from me; his amusement rivals mine. "I'm going to start calling you *butterfingers*."

"I'm not that bad." I shrug, not the least bit repentant for the slip. If it were up to me, I'd do worse, but being a patient killer has its benefits. No one can say I'm anything but thoughtful and accommodating, and I take repayment in their screams shortly after.

While he prays, I'll peel his skin back.

While he cries, I'll feed it to him.

"You only have a few seconds left, Felix." Casper's mood changes then, his body language aggressive—from relaxed to a volcanic rush of ire that makes the man bleeding from the hole in his hand shake. He eyes my cousin, the tick in his jaw more pronounced now with each beat of the clock.

"Who are you?" Felix screams, but we all see his intent. The man's a runner, taking a few steps back and turning his hip toward the halls behind him. His Ocean City home in New Jersey is big, has plenty of places to hide, but he won't get far. "What do you want?"

"Your head on my mantle." At Casper's words, he takes off as bullets rain through the house from each of our guns. A door slams closed, and I pull out my empty clip, replacing it with a full magazine.

"Don't shoot to kill. We have a deal."

"We do, Callum." Green eyes meet mine; the silent promise is all I need. Because we might be bastards—arseholes—but we've never taken back our word. There's always been a certain level of respect between us, even when he was the boss, and I trust him with my life. "Watch the exits. I'll be back with a gift."

With that he takes off upstairs while Archie, one of our new guards and a close friend to Jeffrey, heads toward the back.

My gait is slow toward the front of the home.

Two things stick out the moment I cross his threshold: the area is quiet, and it's warm. Sun high and no clouds, I turn my face from right to left and pick up no movement. No police sirens. No one walking down the street and no passing cars.

From the open door I can make out a bit of shouting, the heated, hushed words of desperation, but it's the sound of a gun going off that makes me smile.

Then again.

Two, and I cock my head to the side. Immediately, Felix's screams fill the silent afternoon with a pain-filled cadence that I quite enjoy. Loud, full of misery, but most importantly, it gets closer. And closer.

Their feet are heavy on the stairs, his whimpers rending the air until both stop at the foyer.

Casper's eyes meet mine. So much anger in them. So much pain. "He's being gracious and accepting our offer to ride with."

"What a courteous tosser." The man in question groans, his body landing at my feet after a small push from my cousin. He has a bullet wound to his knee and hand while a few bruises are beginning to form on his face. *Casper went easy on him.* "Do you need anything before we go?"

"Please don't do this. I'll…I'll tell you everything." His wounds are bleeding, but the flow isn't excessive. Not enough to need any wrappings.

Crouching to his level, I tap the muzzle of my gun on his lips. Push the dark metal past his lips just a bit, not even past his teeth, and Felix gags. A few tears spill down his dirty cheeks. "Oh, I know you'll talk, Mr. De La Vega. And I'm going to enjoy every bloody scream as you tell it."

That's the last thing he hears; I pull out the gun and whip him across the face with it. His unconscious form topples over, blood covering his face as Archie comes around the corner, rushing over and dragging him to our vehicle. De La Vega is put in the trunk while we exit the property without another word.

It's time to play.

———

"WAKE UP, ARSEHOLE," I GROWL OUT, LANDING A SWIFT KICK TO Felix's midsection. He's tied up, hands up on a high water pipe with his feet dangling just a smidge off the ground inside of a borrowed property not too far from Felix's home. We've let him sleep for the last five hours, gave him time to calm down after the small panic attack at his house. It's almost funny how quickly a person can go from *do you know who I am* to *please don't hurt me.*

In that time, while he slumbered, we've gone through every last connection he has in the US and back in the Dominican Republic. His ex-wife has been notified of his death; his money transferred to her account along with the two properties he's purposely screwed her out of.

How can a man vow to love a woman, marry her, and then leave her with kids for another?

How can a man abandon his children and leave them to live in squalor while his whore travels the world on money that belongs to their mum?

That's why he's here now.

Greed. Cockiness. Stupidity.

Felix groans, his body swaying a bit from the blow. "W-what's going...*fuck*!" he screams, the next blow from my boot landing on his ribs. It's hard enough to crack a rib, and the way he tries to fold into the pain is a good sign of just that, but this is just the beginning.

He dodged up. Touched a woman that to the Jameson's was sacred.

"The next time I strike, I'll use my knife. Wake up." Casper tosses a sleek blade in my direction, and I catch it, a butterfly version, and flip it open. The clean metal glints in the sunlight filtering through the glass panels used to make up the building's roof. "You have five seconds to open your eyes."

They snap open at once, and he winces from the earlier strike across his face. The area is swollen and a nasty shade of purple. He tries to move his head back, away from me, but I don't take it personally as I'm sure it has something to do with the cold tip running down his cheek. From temple to jaw, I leave a shallow cut that brims red, but only a few small drops fall.

There's fear in his eyes. Petrified with a good mixture of horror that seeps from the cunt's every pore. *Pathetic.*

"Nice of you to join us," I say as I embed the very tip into his skin, just an inch. "Now, are you ready to play?"

"Who are you?" He's asking me, yet his eyes are on Casper; I look over at the latter and find him sitting atop a few boxes. His posture seems relaxed, but I know better. Can read him like no one else, and I'm not the least bit surprised to find Casper's gun on his thigh and his finger on the trigger.

"Oi."

"Callum."

"We made a deal to play nice." As I say this, I push in another inch of my blade. "We need him to talk."

"Agreed." Casper shoots him once, on his thigh this time. "Please ignore me."

"Thank you." With my attention back on Felix, I pull the knife out and wipe the bloody metal across his bare chest before dropping it. I'll be going a different route today. "I'm ready for that story now. Why did you do it?"

"You're Callum Jameson?"

"I am."

"And he's Casper Jameson." Not a question, but I nod in confirmation. "Dios mio ayudame. Que hice."

"You helped an innocent woman die. You have his mum's blood on your hands." Leaning closer so we're at eye level, I pat his bloody cheek. "God will not save you, De La Vega. He's gifted you to us; we are your penance."

Tears flow down his cheeks, body shaking, but I stand back and let him have his moment.

I take a seat next to Casper and accept the cold bottle of water Archie offers me. "Thanks, mate." He doesn't reply, just gives a subtle nod, and retakes his position. "Any news on the wanker?"

"Ezra's working on it. Last known location was in South America, but I know he's not there now. No man running would be stupid enough to stay in one place for long."

"Caribbean or—"

"We already know he lives there, but don't know which island yet. My guess is one not too far from the US."

Nodding, I empty half the bottle in two deep pulls. "That gives us a few choices, starting with those closest to Florida."

"It does."

He gives me a pensive look, and I raise a brow. "Something you want to say?"

"You okay, Callum?" His question catches me off guard and I frown, not getting it. "You've been a bit quiet lately. Since Chicago."

"I'm fine."

"Are you? Is there something I need to know?"

"I'm fine." I make a move to stand, but Casper puts a hand on my forearm, and I pause. Look down at him. "Bro, I promise I'm okay. Trust me...nothing I can't handle."

"Mum would be proud of you," he says instead of prying further, and a knot forms in my throat. For as much shit as we give each other, we know the other, and his mother was like my own. She was there when my mum decided that vacationing—or for my father, work—was more important than raising me. And while I don't hold anything against them, my loyalty lies with Casper's parents.

His mum's passing hit me hard. Still hurts.

And just like her son, I've made a private vow to avenge her death.

The doorbell rings suddenly, making me pause inside my aunt's kitchen, the sound loud—seems to reverberate throughout every square inch of their massive estate. My aunt is out in the shops picking up an order while my uncle's footsteps walk toward the front door.

No one from the house's security team rang. No one's expected to drop by, either.

"Wait two minutes before opening," I call out to my uncle, knowing he heard by the two taps on the wall closest to him. It's not too loud, not enough to be heard by whoever's waiting by the front

door, but it does give me a moment. Opening the drawer beside the fridge, I grab the Glock inside and head toward the French doors.

This exit leads to the garden, and past that is a swimming pool and a small cottage my aunt claims as her woman cave. *I'm quick to rush around the side of the home, keeping alert for any movement, but there's none when I reach the front.*

What I find is one of our guards, his face pained and eyes red-rimmed. A sinking feeling settles over me, my heart clenching, but I manage to walk over and use the key code to unlock the door.

Then it's the four of us, my father, who'd been inside his brother's office, joining us. He's the reason my aunt went out alone today, needing to discuss some half-arsed crap or other that will never go anywhere. His brother's no longer in charge, and Casper feels like I do; we don't live in the past—this family is run by young blood and new ways.

Dad's eyes meet mine then, and his expression mirrors; something isn't right. It's a heavy cloaking aura that suffocates, and I shift to look at the man. "Speak."

"I'm so sorry, Mr. Jameson. So sorry." He's not speaking to me or Dad. His eyes are on my uncle, and when it clicks, the world beneath his feet disappears. I've never seen a strong man crumble like this before.

It's heartbreaking.

This has nothing to do with Casper. The wanker is off with Aurora, and had something happened, the call would've come via Jeffrey or Ezra. That leaves one other person. Motherfuck. No. *At once, my chest squeezes painfully tight, and my eyes close. This can't be happening.*

Words fail me. I can't voice the questions running through my head.

My uncle's legs give out and a fist comes up to his mouth, body shaking as a sob catches in his throat. "Where's my wife?" How he manages to ask this, I have no clue, but he does. Voice cracking, he stumbles toward the guard and grips the man's long-sleeved vest.

One tug, and he's face to face with Jameson senior, with his glare—eyes red while his body language is pleading. "Where is she? What happened?"

"I'm so sorry, sir. Mrs. Jameson's vehicle was attacked, and she's been taken to the A&E with multiple gunshot wounds."

"Get the car," my father shouts, moving to help his brother close the door and walk down the few steps onto the circular drive. I'm on autopilot. I can't get past the feelings coursing through my veins. This is something I've never experienced before: fear. A choking, bloody helplessness.

Not for me, but for her. Her husband. Her son.

And I vow to do what I must to keep my family standing no matter what the future brings.

I'm pulled from the memory by a choking cough. Bloody spittle flies out of Felix's mouth, landing on the cold concrete below his feet.

He looks tired, his wounds a nasty red.

"Something you want to say?" I ask, looking toward Archie and giving him the signal to drop the lever. He does so. De La Vega's body drops to the ground and his ankle turns at an awkward angle. It's dislocated, and the accompanying scream is almost as satisfying as Aliana's taste. Almost. "Speak."

"We can come to an agreement." Gritting his teeth, he twists in pain while finding a position to sit in. Sweat beads at his brow, and his chest heaves. "Please. I can help you."

"How can you help us?"

"I can tell you what I know."

"And what is that?"

"I'm the one who—"

"How well do you know Mauricio Hernandez?"

"In passing." Felix swallows hard, his hands fisting on his lap. "I know someone he does, and vice versa."

"Is that true, Casper?" I ask, feigning stupidity. Even before picking up this sack of shit, we knew of his involvement and how well he knows the hitman.

"Negative. Not what he said earlier."

"So I'm dealing with a liar, then?"

"Aye."

"All right." Turning my face toward my cousin, I point toward the black bag near him. "Toss that my way…" he does, and I catch it with one hand "…And Archie, we'll be needing the bench now. Go ahead and set it up near the back."

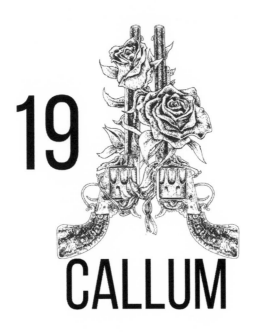

19

CALLUM

"WHAT ARE YOU going to do to me?" Felix asks, his body dragging backwards, and I make no move to follow him. He *will* come. He *will* accept his judgment. "Please, let's be reasonable. We can work something out."

"Come here."

"Callum—"

"If any of us have to grab you, it will be worse." Taking the item out of the black bag, I test the weight in my hand and check the leather used. It's not like mine back home. No. This one doesn't have the added touch of a madman, but it'll inflict plenty of pain.

One snap of my wrist and it unfurls, the whip snapping against the dirty concrete. The sound is loud, meant to spike his fear, and Felix throws up. Hunching over, he empties his stomach and I scrunch up my nose. *Disgusting.*

"Would you like me to fetch him, Mr. Jameson?" Archie asks, coming back inside. He wipes his brow and eyes the man with a mixture of pity for the lad and ire. Every person in our organization, from the tenured to the newest guard, has felt the death of Aunt Penelope. "Ezra called to make sure we are on schedule, and he's waiting for the signal."

"He worries a lot." Casper's traded the gun in his lap for one of his Karambits. "Send him a message with new airport ETA. An extra two hours today should be enough."

"Yes, sir."

Turning back to the man on his arse, I see he's still trying to crab crawl back and failing. His dodged-up knee, thigh, and hand are an impediment he can't escape. "Last chance, De La Vega." A warning he doesn't heed, and I flick my eyes to an eager Casper. "You get two shots."

"How magnanimous of you."

"I try, you arse."

The wanker doesn't answer; he's too busy looking at the man. For a few minutes neither moves, my cousin waiting, and when Felix whimpers, the Karambit breaks through the air and slices a clean cut across his left shoulder before landing on the ground.

Because that's the beauty of that knife: it's bloody sharp. The skin parts, the flesh having given way, and what's left is a deep gash that bleeds at a high rate.

"That's one." I'm admiring his work, ignoring the way Felix screams and writhes before picking up the knife. It's in his grip, but the twat doesn't know how to place his fingers, much less how to angle the blade for a more accurate slice.

"All I'm going to take."

"You sure?"

"Positive."

Blood loss is a bitch and Felix is beginning to show a bit of fatigue, the Karambit slipping through his loose grip. He's bled quite a bit from each wound, and when he attempts to stand with his unin-jured hand extending the knife out, it doesn't last. Instead, he stum-bles, and Archie comes back in time to grab him.

Felix thrashes, tries to fight back, but is quickly outmaneuvered and taken to a deviant little section Casper's acquaintance keeps here. Every apparatus back here is for discipline, to keep the recipient in place, and I chose the bench to start.

His body's bare except for the pair of boxers we've left on him. His feet are stepping on an array of broken glass that's kept inside of a built-in wooden box for added punishment.

He shuffles, tries to push the shards aside to save the bottom of his feet, but the first strike of my whip remedies that. It slices through the air, connecting with his back while leaving a sharp welt behind that quickly blisters.

"Fuck!" he screams, fighting his bonds, back arching yet the limited space keeps him in place. The blubbering starts at once, and it's disappointing. "Don't. I'll do…no!"

The second lash strikes from his right shoulder to the middle of his spine, this one breaking the skin, and the surrounding flesh turns red. "Why did you do it?"

"No more."

"Why did you do it?" I ask again, gifting him the third and fourth before delivering the fifth over the back of his thigh. The sounds coming from the man's throat are horror-filled and full of pain, loud and a little soothing to me. "If I have to ask again, I'm going to play the eye removal game. Count each strike across your face until I hit the orb at just the right angle to make you lose it. Your choice."

"I'll talk," leaves him on a pathetic whimper.

"Then do so." This time, the whip's tip hits his injured shoulder. "Convince me you're worth one more day."

"Mauricio is in the Caribbean but moves around a lot. He has homes in Jamaica, Puerto Rico, Dominican Republic, and Cuba. There's also Guatemala, Honduras, and Belize. That's just to name a few." He swallows hard, his teeth chattering as the pain peaks. "H-he's been a hitman since his early twenties and is smart, too smart to get caught easily."

"When did you meet, and where?"

"I need water." Each word is spoken between clenching teeth, but the way his body shakes is an indicator that he's breaking. He'll either pass out or lose control of his bodily functions. "My throat."

And to keep him alert, I flick my wrist and the leather snaps across his right flank. "Answer the question, lad. Don't test my patience."

His head nods, legs shaking. "We met in Miami while I was on vacation. He was close to a trafficker there."

"Who?"

"The Villegas, but they're all dead. Killed by the reigning family now: the De Leon's."

"Okay." Tilting my head toward Archie, I signal to the bottle at his feet. It's hot, has been sitting in the sun all day prior to this, but it's water. "Hold it up to his lips." Archie does so, and when that first sip lands on his tongue, Felix gags. He tries to reject it, but I nod, and Archie lets the entire one-liter tip and pour onto his mouth or face. "Thank you."

"Of course, sir."

"Felix, thank you for the information so far."

"I'll do anything."

"I'm sure you would, but finish answering my earlier question. Why?"

From the corner of my eye, I catch Casper move closer. In his hand, he has his favorite toy once more. He's worse than I am with my whip. "Go ahead."

Quietly, he gets behind Felix and waits. The man is unaware, or maybe he isn't. Doesn't matter as a few tense seconds later, he begins to speak. "They offered me a lot of money to do so. More than Mauricio and I have ever been offered for one job, and we took it without pause."

"How much was your cut?" I ask, placing the whip down just long enough to take my vest off and crack my neck.

"Half a million."

"And that was worth a woman's life?"

"It was never supposed to be his mama. His father or uncle, but not his mother."

"Then why protect Mauricio Hernandez?" Casper's voice tone is cold. His muscles flex, coiling as if he were an animal ready to strike. "Answer me."

"I didn't—"

"Liar," my cousin snaps, gripping the back of Felix's head, hair in a tight grip while he digs the tip of his Karambit down his back in a long and straight line. Then, he creates a half circle on the top of the line, the corners touching and turning his mark into a large letter 'P'—his mother's initial. "You hid him. You bought his plane ticket out and brought in others to help him escape our wrath."

"N-no. I-I swear...I-I didn't."

My cousin lets him go and steps back. "Enjoy yourself."

"Thanks, brother." A tsking sound escapes me while Felix blubbers and begs. His cries and pleas fall on deaf ears. "Liars never make it into the kingdom of heaven."

I show no more mercy.

We knew his moves, motives, and connections.

We just wanted him to voice it out loud. To be a man and admit it.

This time as the whip's leather snaps against his back, I don't pause or let him breathe. Each strike is brutal, cutting and breaking flesh as his life's essence splatters after each precise lash. Some lands on my skin, some on the ground and the equipment within. There's no counting or spoken words inside the room as his screams of pure agony go from loud to unintelligible blubbers—from begging to silence as he loses consciousness and Felix's body goes limp.

He's a mess. Broken. Bloodied.

The last two from my whip land at the back of his head, and when it bounces, just a slight rebound that leaves behind a thick welt on the shaved bottom half of his skull, I step back.

It's a disgusting scene to most. The torn flesh and rivulets of red that flow down and to the ground, creating a puddle at his feet.

To me, though, it's poetic. He deserves so much more, but I know this isn't enough for my cousin, and I have a gift of my own.

I turn my gaze to Archie. "Get him cleaned up and as stable as possible before we leave."

"Leave? Where are you—"

"Alexander's on his way to finish this, cousin." His smile widens and nods in approval. Alexander is Aurora's bodyguard for a reason, and it's his brutality that's kept him under our employ for so long. He has no boundaries nor empathy, and he'll give De La Vega an ending he deserves. "And don't worry about Gem. I moved someone there already, and Archie will be in charge until Alexander returns."

"Thank you."

"None needed." Walking to him, I clasp his shoulder and squeeze. "Just don't forget to videotape it. We've got plans for it."

"We do?"

"We do."

CASPER NEVER ASKED ME WHY I TOOK OFF OR WHERE I WAS OFF TO, but I do send a text when I land.

Twenty-four hours. ~Callum J.

His response is just as fast, and nothing more than *okay* before I pocket my mobile. I'm turning my locator off, but the device will stay on until I'm back in the air and across international waters just in case something goes wrong.

No one but Ezra knows where I'm at or why, but he'll erase every proof of our—my—being on US soil before sending a second plane for my private use. I'd left Casper with the other. The government doesn't need that kind of information, not while investigating that bullshit wire fraud case, and Malcolm helped by letting me use his private jet and airstrip to land in Chicago after cleaning off Felix's filth in the meantime.

He's also moved our money again. Every cent. Something that gives security to our suppliers back home.

The tarmac is empty when I arrive, except for Kray who waits outside his large SUV. Once I'm close, he pushes off and holds out a hand. "Good to have you back," he says, and I take it, shaking it quickly before tilting my head toward the car.

It's been a few weeks since I've seen Aliana. A day feels like too many, and although she understands that duty binds me this once, I need to see her. The daily reports that Giannis turns in are shit in comparison to being near her.

They don't fill that void, this ever-growing need that I can't contain.

"Aliana's home tonight. It's been a busy time at the center, and she seems exhausted." This I knew; Giannis has told me as much. Seems the last few weeks they've had an influx at the Conte House, and she's been working late to help Aurora. "Is there anywhere you want to stop first, or…?"

"Straight to her house."

"Done." After a minute, he begins to thump his fingers on the steering wheel, and I know why. I'm waiting for what I know is coming. Kray settles after a minute, exhaling roughly. "I'm sorry, Callum. I let you down."

"Am I angry? Yes," I say, resting my head back with eyes closed. "However, they were at work. They take risks every day to help women in need, and I understand that. You stepped in and removed him the moment you realized what was happening."

Kray chuckles and I raise a brow. "Miss Rubens emptied a can of mase on his face. Direct hit."

"That's my girl."

"I was on my way in when he ran out and into me. Those women are exemplary—tough."

"But…"

"It won't happen again. I'm working on an idea to have someone on the inside."

"Smart. Let me know when you have the specifics."

We don't talk the rest of the way. With each turn the vehicle takes and the closer to her home we get, my body thrums. It's a different kind of energy. Just as pleasurable as taking a life, but with the memory of her taste still lingering in my mind, I'm throbbing.

Hungry. Pulsing.

A heady feeling that almost compares to taking a life, and yet, this one is more. It's everything.

The street where her townhome sits looms close, and I notice Giannis outside when I pull up. He doesn't say anything when I exit, but simply nods and then gets into a vehicle with a man I recognize as his better half. They drive away, and Kray does the same.

I want no one around.

No interruptions.

There are twenty-four hours between this trip and my return to England, and I just want her.

I'm at her door before both cars turn right at the stop sign down the street, my fist pounding on her door. Five hard knocks, and nothing. No sound. But when I raise my fist once more, I hear that melodic voice.

"I'm coming!" my Venus yells, her feet stomping toward the door before yanking it open. "Giannis, for the love of God, I just want a quiet night and—" Aliana stops abruptly after I clear my throat. She's in a cute romper set with a towel wrapped in her hair, a warm flush covering her peach scented skin, and staring at me with wide eyes and plush lips in the perfect shape of an "O."

"I've missed you too, love."

20

Aliana

H E'S HERE , and it feels like I can breathe again—like what's been missing since he left has been returned and the world feels a little calmer. Safer. For me, at least.

I've been left to my own devices since he left, and I've wondered if he has something to do with it. *Do they know about him?* My family has been quiet; even Dad's campaign manager has excused me from any of his recent events—a first, and I appreciate it heavily. He's not in full-swing campaigning yet, just a brief base-run affair for the people who only care about money and the status quo.

Those men whose wives get younger every three years.

Those men that spend millions of taxpayer money to front their travel expenses and dirty secrets inside of hotel rooms.

Because I've seen things. Hear things.

My father has never hidden his cheating or how beneath him he feels the female species is.

"What are you—" I'm unable to finish as his lips meet mine and I find myself being pushed inside, the door slamming behind us. His groan reverberates through me like a sinful caress. His touch sears my skin, and I want to bleed for him.

But that's what he does. I go from nothing to everything right before the floor is swept out from beneath my feet each time he's near.

"I needed this," he growls against my lips, body forcing mine deeper into my apartment. Callum doesn't pause or say anything else. He's on a mission, and I won't stop him. Can't, because it's been obvious for the past few days that I've *missed* this too.

He's deep under my skin.

Strong fingers grip the back of my towel and he pulls, forcing my newly cut strands to sweep across my shoulders. This makes him pause, and I become nervous when he closes his eyes and then buries his head in my neck. *Does he hate it?*

"Fuck, Aliana." Callum's groan brings goose bumps across my skin, the heat of his breath on my skin making me shiver. He's breathing hard, holding me close while his lips sweep across softly. "I'm almost afraid to look, beautiful. I don't think I'll survive it."

"It'll grow back. A few months and it'll be like...*shit!*" I yelp, suddenly airborne as he stalks toward the back of my house where my bedroom and bathroom are with my body over his shoulder. A warm hand holds me in place with a firm grip on the back of my bare thigh—squeezing and caressing between steps. "What are you doing?"

"Proving a point." Callum doesn't turn toward my room. Instead, he enters the large bathroom and sets me down in front of the vanity. I'm turned, our eyes meeting in the mirror while he runs his fingers down my slightly curled, dark locks. The strands are still humid, barely towel dry, and the look on his face is of a man transfixed —mesmerized.

"Beautiful." Voice low and gravelly, Callum pushes one piece behind my ear and then twirls another. "How is it possible for one woman to be this stunning. I loved your long hair, my Venus, but this little shoulder length cut frames your face in the most sinful way. It's fun and sweet, and the only thing I want to do is bend you over this sink and bury myself deep. So deep that you'll spend the next few weeks feeling me every time you so much as inhale."

"You like it?" It's breathy, my body thrumming at his words.

"I fucking love." Pressing his back against mine, he lets me feel just how much he does. How hard he is for me, and every cell in my body vibrates for him. "You look so sweet and tempting, Miss Rubens. Like the perfect little doll."

"A doll?"

"Aye." From behind, he kisses the crown of my head and then lower until placing his lips at my temple. "Every inch of you is perfection, Aliana. How can you ever question that?" Then, he inhales deep and groans, his hands gripping the edge of my sleep top before slowly lifting it up. My stomach is exposed, the soft cotton stopping just below my breasts. "Your curves are decadent, while your scent is enough to bring any man to his knees. So sweet."

"Callum, I—"

I'm cut off with a quick nip to my ear. "Just listen, baby girl. Let me tell you what I see."

"Okay."

"Good girl." Callum steps back just enough to pull my top over my head and then he's back, skin on skin, my back to his chest. "When I look at you, Venus, I see a future I'd never wanted before. I see holidays all over the world. I see candlelit dinners." Strong fingers undo the delicate bow at my waist before pushing my bottoms down. They fall to my feet, leaving me bare to his eyes. No underwear. No barriers. There's lust in those eyes when they meet mine again, but something else pushes forward—an emotion that I don't understand but find myself wanting to. "I see a woman who's sweet and pure with a body I want to worship for years to come. You, my perfect girl, are a gift I plan to cherish, and you have a heart I'll nurture. You deserve the world, Aliana, and I'll give it to you. I'll help you see what everyone else does when they look at you."

"And what's that?" I whisper shakily, my eyes misting. "How do others see me?"

"A smart, gorgeous, and goal-oriented young woman that doesn't need a man to give her value, but when she allows one to stand beside her, he'll be the envy of every bloody bastard alive. They see a woman full of so much love and loyalty. They see a woman who deserves to have the world bow at her feet, and one day, I plan to make that a reality."

"Thank you." Those words fill my heart and warm my soul. To have someone like him see me like this... *Jesus*. With him, I feel like someone and not a commodity. "That means a lot."

"That's not enough for how special you are." Placing one last kiss, this time on my cheek, he steps back and holds out a hand. "Come take a shower with me."

I just took one and the proof still lingers in my hair, but I place my palm in his and let him lead me toward the shower where he turns the lever and waits a second for it to heat. Within seconds, a little steam begins to rise and he checks how hot, humming in the back of his throat when he approves.

Then he leads me in, body behind mine. I'm under the spray while he fingers the wet strands, pushing them back so the ends all meet at the center. His warmth rivals the water, his hands massaging my back and then spreading out.

"That feels good."

"And you are my heaven. My calm." Callum reaches for my bottle of shampoo and adds a generous amount to his palm. He rubs them together, creates a little lather, and then runs those talented fingers across my hair and scalp. From the very top to the last strand, he washes it slowly and with firm strokes that feel so good.

I'm lax. Had I not been leaning against him, I'm sure my body would be slumped against a wall. As it is, my legs feel weak and when he gives a gentle push so I'm standing directly under the rain shower attachment, I pull him with me. Reaching back, I grip his hip and keep him close, give a subtle gyration against the hardness digging into my lower back.

"Behave, love. Let me take care of you." A recurring theme. Each time it's about me, but I want to touch him too. To make him feel what I do, but when I try, I'm rebuffed by strong hands and my peach shower gel that he uses to rub my chest. From shoulders to breasts and back again, he massages my skin with firm strokes and then quick smacks to the tip of each tit. My nipples are hard, and each slap borders on pleasurable pain. "And trust me, Aliana, I'm doing this for selfish reasons. All I want is to touch you. To feel you bend under my fingertips."

"Feel the same," I whimper, the keening sound a mixture of frustration and bliss.

Hands wandering lower, he washes my midsection. Pays extra attention to my tattoo and piercing, fingering the new belly-button ring I bought with a jewel in the same tone as his eyes. If he's put it together, he doesn't say, but when Callum gives the metal a small tug, I push back harder. Grind myself against his cock; a torture, since I want to feel him stretch me.

To make me his.

"Do you dream of me every night?" One of his large hands cups my core, and I stop all movement. Whine in his hold. "Do you make this pretty little cunt come with my name on your sweet lips?"

"Yes." Another truth I can't deny. These last few days, no matter how tired I am, he's the last thing I see when I close my eyes, and not coming is an impossibility. "I touch myself to thoughts of you. To the memory of your mouth between my thighs."

"Motherfuck, love." A single digit parts my labia, the proof of my desire coating its tip. It's not the water, but him. All because of him. The eyes, tattoos, and raw hunger that possesses me even when he's not here. I'm powerless. "Such a good girl. All soaked for me. Ready for me."

The heel of his palm massages my clit, touch firm, and I moan. Loud and drawn out, the quickness in which he slips two fingers inside and pumps them savagely leaving me teetering on the edge before I can regain rational thought. I'm on the tips of my toes, hands on the wall now while he curves over my back, pumping two fingers deep and then pulling them out.

In and out. In and out.

Then they're gone, and I'm left gasping—groaning as my walls clench in need of him.

"Turn around."

"I can't move."

"You will." There's a sound that greets my ears above the water and my entire frame pauses. It's skin on skin, repetitive, and my mouth waters. My core throbs. "Turn for me."

"Please."

Faster. He's groaning low. "Now," Callum grits out and I force myself to function. Will myself to confirm my suspicions and seeing this specimen of a man pumping his cock into a tight fist is enough to break me. My knees buckle. I kneel before him and take the head between my lips and moan. He's warm and hard and the heady *fuck* that escapes in that deep voice is sinful. Worth the discomfort of the tiles digging into my knees.

I move his hand aside and take in another inch. Then another, bobbing my head along his thick length before pulling back with a string of spit connecting us. "Are you going to *behave* now and let me touch you? Let me feel your weight on my tongue?"

"You have sixty seconds."

"And what happens after," I ask right before flicking the tip with my tongue. "Will you punish me?"

"Fifty."

"That's not fair."

"Fifty-two."

With my eyes on his, I take him down to the back of my throat and swallow. His eyes narrow, hands clenching at his sides while I flick the tip of my tongue against the base of his length once, twice, and then pull back. This time, though, I pause at the engorged head and suck, hollowing my cheeks until I get what I want.

"Fuck, love. You have such a pretty little mouth," he growls. The sound is deep and reverberates through his chest, and I feel it all the way down to my core. My walls pulse—they grip at nothing. I want him. "Lips stretched. Full of me."

"More."

"You want more?" One of his large hands grips the back of my head, fisting the wet strands there. "Want me to fuck you?"

"Please."

"Then take what I give you." His hips snap forward and he strokes deep, not stopping until my lips touch the base and then he stays there, savoring the feel of my throat choking him. Callum groans deeply, shivers, and then pulls out and in. With each pump, the dark look in his eyes is hot. Exhilarating, and I let out a long moan at the sight. "You like this, don't you? To be used by me?"

All I can do is nod. Suck harder.

I'm not a virgin. I'm not someone who sleeps around or needs a man to get off.

But this, him...*he* brings out my inner whore.

I want to please him. Watch him lose control.

"Give me all of you, Callum."

For some reason, those words snap him back and he pulls out abruptly. The look on his face is feral, aroused and angry, but before I can ask *what's wrong*, I'm up, feet off the ground.

He's holding my weight and core right over his hard cock, labia against the heated flesh. My wetness coats him, my right thigh lifting a bit to open myself up a little more before closing.

I trap him against me, my thighs tightening.

This also reminds me of the night we met, how he lifted my body off the ground and held me while I gyrated against him, my ass to his thickness. Now it's my slick flesh that rubs him. *He feels so good.*

"All I wanted was to hold you all night. To rest, because I'm tired, Venus. So tired," he says, voice deep and low. Almost a growl.

"I've missed my girl. Missed her smile. Her fresh peach scent." And I no longer argue those words. *He's right. I'm his.* With one hand, he grips my right asscheek, flexing his cock between my lips and they part, spreading to let him slide through. From clit to entrance and then poking out from the curve of my cheeks, I feel him. I'm nearly overwhelmed by his size and girth; I know he'll stretch me to the point of pain. Because Callum is bigger than my one rebellious mistake and the toys I have inside the drawer beside my bed. "Since I left, all I could think of was coming back to you. To have you beside me again."

"Me too." I'd leave with him today if he asked. No hesitation.

"But more than that, I hate that all I get is a few hours before I'm back on a plane."

"It's more than I thought I'd get," I whisper back, the heated rush of lust receding a bit. It still lingers in the background, simmering, but it's his sincerity that takes the forefront. To hear him, to experience his need, is heavenly. This between us isn't easy. Hell, my circumstances are a mess, but I'll wait. Find a way to be with him. *I was leaving for Europe soon anyway. That alone is a sign.* "We knew it wouldn't be an overnight fix, Callum. I'm willing to wait."

"I know, but the guilt still sits heavy with me. It's a feeling I'm not used to."

"Why guilt? You've done nothing wrong."

"That's the thing; I should be here. Always with you." His lips slant over mine the moment the last words slip through his plump lips. This kiss is less hurried and more worshipping, a slow overtaking of my senses, and I can't stop the gentle roll of my hips. Cock hard and tight against my slick pussy, I do it again and again, earning a hiss that I taste.

It's need and lust and an emotion that I'm not ready to decipher. The implication alone would be the end of me.

So instead, I give in and close the world out. I kiss him back just as eagerly, entwining our tongues and savoring a taste uniquely his. There's a hint of whiskey and smoke, but not cigarette. This is earthier. Attractive. Drawing back, I bite his lips, dragging my teeth down the abused flesh.

His grip on me tightens, and I cry out as pleasure spreads through my body. That small jerk, how the thick flesh drags across my clit, has me gasping for breath. I'm wound tight. I'm in need, and he knows this.

Revels in it.

"That's my Venus. Work me between those soft lips..." his exhale is rough, his touch a bit savage the next time I circle my hips "...I want to feel you come on me. I want to watch you lose control."

"Oh God," I whimper, picking up speed—rubbing my sensitive flesh over the hard flesh. It's all I can do with the limited movement he allows, and I press harder. Hump a little faster, my movements jerky and uncoordinated, but the rush of pleasure right within my grasp is all I can focus on.

It's right there.

He thrusts against me, and my eyes roll back.

Another pump and my fingernails dig into his shoulders, breaking the skin, and I use the anchor as leverage and bear down. I feel every ridge and vein, how he throbs and then his desperation to come undone.

"Motherfuck, baby girl. That's it...fucking feel you."

"Come with me." Eyes on his, I bite down hard on his chin. Gem-like eyes blaze at the move, and his cock slides across my pussy angrily before the resounding smack over my left asscheek makes me freeze. Pain blooms over my flesh, sharp and wicked, but then I'm coming hard and nothing else matters but the euphoria burning through my veins.

I hear his grunt in the background, feel the second spank, but it only serves to prolong my pleasure.

I'm jittery and breathless and dirty. I'm tender and achy and watching him the same way he's looking at me.

In awe.

In salvation.

In need.

His cock jerks between my thighs and his come coats my skin, running down my leg and then mixing with the water below us. It's a glorious feeling. We are right together.

After a few minutes, I let my eyes close and rest my head in the crook of his neck. My body is lax, and the exhaustion of the last few days hits me hard.

Callum cleans us up as best he can because I refuse to let him go. Instead, he lifts me higher and wraps my legs around his waist, gaining the room needed to wash me gently. He doesn't linger in the bathroom. My droopy body knows we are moving, and I feel the warmth of a towel across my back before he whispers, "Rest, I got you."

And I do. I'm out before we make it to the bed.

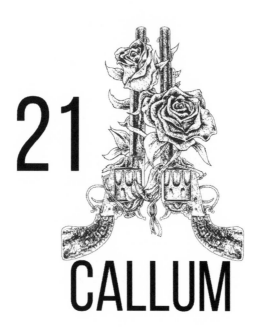

21

CALLUM

"I NEED YOU to wake up, sweetheart," I whisper in her ear, the clock on her bedside table reading six in the morning. I'll be leaving soon. My flight's scheduled for eight, but I want to spend a little more time with her.

Last night was amazing. Each time I'm near her brings me a sense of calm and happiness I've never experienced before. Yet, it also brings a level of guilt that eats at me like an infectious wound.

Leaving her doesn't sit right with me. I don't like the separation.

Aliana stirs but doesn't open her eyes. If anything, she tries to burrow in deeper, and I chuckle. She's bloody adorable—this beautiful little doll that I wish I could carry with me everywhere. I find myself being obsessive with her—wondering how she is and if she's eating or sleeping enough, something the bags under her eyes last night showed me she wasn't.

Giannis and Kray have explained that the Conte House has been busy, more so than normal, and long days have sometimes become longer nights. I'm also aware of the man that threatened to shoot the girls, and he's currently on his way to my plane after being held a couple of weeks in isolation.

He's been fed. He's been given one bathroom break a day.

I've been the model host.

"Baby, I need you to open those warm eyes for me."

"Don't wanna." She's pouting against my skin, lifting the sheet higher to attempt to hide. One second, she's half over me, leg across my hip, but on her next intake of breath, Aliana's on her back. I'm hovering, my hips cradled between her thighs—her lack of startling is an indicator that she's been playing possum the whole time, and I arch a brow. "Don't give me that look. You're warm and cozy."

"Every time it gets harder to leave."

"What time is your flight?" she asks, but her expressions are so unguarded. Open. I notice each: the sadness that flashes, and then the fake smile as if nothing bothers her. Her bravery and the hint of pain that's always there, lingering, even when she's laughing. *I'm going to uncover your every secret, my Venus. I want to take the weight you carry and make it mine.* "Do you need me to take you?"

"The only thing I want is to spend a few extra minutes with you."

"Okay." Aliana stretches, her naked flesh so bloody soft and sweet. She opens her arms, telling me without words to lower myself, and I do, covering her small form with my larger one. My lips are against her neck, taking her scent into my lungs and tattooing its genetic makeup on my DNA. "God, I need this too."

"Soon, sweetheart. Soon you'll be with me in London."

"You mean that? You want me to move across—"

Pulling back just enough so she can see my face, I stare into her eyes. That slight hesitation in her question—voice—shouldn't be there. "If I could take you today, I would without a single hesitation. But I will. We've taken care of everyone but the man who shot her. I left Casper yesterday to handle the facilitator to come be with you, but I do have to go home now and handle work. We're so close, baby. Just please be patient with me."

"I could never fault you for what's happening."

"Thank you." Retaking my place on her neck, I place a chaste kiss there. "By the way, when's your family holiday?"

"You remember that?"

"I do."

She hums for a second, her fingernails scraping down my back. I don't miss the way she tenses, but I'm not going to call her out on it. Not today. "Dad hasn't said anything yet, but I think in a week or two."

"You sure?" She's hiding something, and I will find out what.

"I'll ask and get back to you. Just give me a few days."

"Aye, love." The rhythmic way she touches me is soothing. Almost lulls me, and I go to move and lie beside her, keep from crushing her, but Aliana makes a noise of complaint in the back of her throat. "I just want you to be comfortable."

"I already am." She pulls me closer; her leg hooks mine behind the knee to keep me in place. Silence fills the room after that. We just lay while the early morning rays filter into the room, and my second alarm goes off. This is a text, the ringtone belonging to Kray, and it means he's waiting outside. "Already?"

"Unfortunately, yes."

"Hey, Callum?" she asks, but I don't move from my place at the crook of her neck. Instead, I close my eyes and nod, drowning myself in her warmth for another minute. "When will I see you again?"

"Soon."

"Can I get a timeframe?"

"I'd like to have that second date in two weeks, Miss Rubens. Do you accept?"

"Aye." Her attempt at my accent is atrocious, yet lovely.

She has me by the balls and doesn't even know it.

WE ARRIVE AT THE AIRSTRIP TWO HOURS BEHIND SCHEDULE, BUT fuck it, I couldn't leave her yet. Not when she was all warm and sweet and clinging to me while her mouth lied. Aliana says she's okay, understanding and unaffected, but I see her.

All of her.

But it's not just our situation. Something or someone here upsets her.

We need to talk. ~Callum J.

Pocketing my mobile after messaging Giannis, I exit the vehicle to an already waiting Kray while ignoring the responding buzz of a message. He's become someone I trust, reliable, and soon enough he'll have a decision to make.

"Thank you for the change of clothes and accessories, mate." I'm pulling the Glock provided out of the small case it came with and checking the magazine. It pops out and in easily enough, but I'm not one for deviate from my norm and my Ruger is predictable. Its accuracy is unparalleled, something not needed right now. "I'll leave the latter for you to dispose of."

"Will do."

"You can also bring her on."

The look of surprise on his face is almost comical. "What? How—"

"The Jamesons are good at what they do, my friend. We have eyes and ears everywhere." The meaning behind those words dawns on him and he nods, accepting that a life around my family means no privacy. We take no chances. "I won't hide who she is or what from Aliana, but Lindsey could keep close during the day without drawing too much attention. I'll video call you this week to discuss further, but I agree with it so far."

"Thank you, Callum." He steps back, and I walk toward the jet where a man waits for me. On his knees and on the left—away from the stairs—the arsehole that tried to hurt Aurora and Aliana at work waits while the flight crew looks straight ahead. "I'll personally handle this cleanup. No one will get this close to her again."

"You make sure of that."

From pilot to attendant, they stand side by side and I don't pause to acknowledge anyone.

I pull the trigger. And again.

Bullet after bullet empties into the man's head, and he drops sideways as the gun meets the tarmac.

"No one threatens Aliana."

"Yes, sir."

No one moves as I enter the plane and sit.

No one talks to me as they finish prep and then take off.

"GOOD TO HAVE YOU BACK, SIR," JEFFREY SAYS, GREETING ME AT the family's private airstrip. His hand's outstretched at the bottom of the jet's steps, a cuppa in his other from my favorite shop. It's for me, and after a quick shake, I take a hearty sip. "Miss Langley sends her regards."

"Cheers, mate."

"There's also a bag of biscuits in the car."

I nod, smiling. That woman is something else. "Did the old bat flirt?"

"Of course. It's what she does at the ripe old age of eighty." His laugh is loud, catching the attention of the flight crew beginning their clean-up procedure. "Says it keeps her young."

"As long as she makes me this, I give no bloody fucks." I make my way toward the black Lincoln he's driving but notice he's not behind me. "Something wrong?"

"Did you not bring a bag?"

"Casper has it. I had a secondary stop to make."

"Understood." That's what I like about Jeffrey. He doesn't pry. Doesn't meddle, and it also shows me Ezra continues to be loyal. He's the only one that knew of my stop in Chicago, although the reasons elude him too. "By the way, your father and uncle are at Sr.'s home. They're both living there now."

"Since when?"

"About a week ago."

"Interesting."

"Your mum doesn't think so." He's not being disrespectful. That's a warning of the situation I could be walking in to.

"How bad?" My tea is getting cool, and I drink half the contents in a few deep sips. "She still around?"

"Yes, sir."

"Great." I walk toward his vehicle and slide into the passenger side, Jeffrey just a few steps behind me. Once inside, he's quick to put the already running car in drive and exit the airstrip. "Head to my uncle's house first and then take the rest of the day off. I want no one inside, just leave two guards on the grounds, and we'll talk tomorrow."

"As you wish." Traffic isn't too bad today, just a few slow drivers that don't understand the *move the fuck over* policies of the road, but within thirty minutes, we're pulling into the long driveway where sure enough, my father's car is present. Jeffrey parks behind him, car idling. "What time do you need me tomorrow?"

"Ten."

"Here?"

I shake my head, hand on the door handle. "My penthouse over-looking Parliament. We have a lot to discuss."

"Of course, Callum. And if you need me—"

"Take the day off, mate. You never stop."

He laughs at that, his age showing in the crinkles around his eyes. "Old habits."

"Old being the operative word," I deadpan before getting out and closing the door, his laughter following me up the steps to a grand manor that seems cold and empty now. My aunt's flowers haven't been taken care of and the wreath at the door is faded and old, something she'd never allow if alive. "She'd be pissed at the sight of this."

The front door is unlocked, and I step inside, listening for noise. And it doesn't take me long to find the two old men whose ruckus makes my ears bleed. They're in the kitchen and arguing about something—more than likely politics—and sharing a bottle of whiskey without any glasses.

"Oi, isn't this a sight."

"My son returns." Dad stands, then sits, a little on the wobbly side. "Where have you been?"

"None of your business." Looking at the man beside him, I walk over and squeeze his shoulder. "You okay, old man?"

"Day at a time."

"That's all you can do." Grabbing the bottle, I walk over to the sink and pour it down the drain. "But this isn't going to help. You need food, a shower, and then we need to talk."

"My son made up his mind?"

"He did." There's a pod in the coffee maker and I press the start button, grabbing two cups from the cabinet above the machine. And while it brews, I grab the fresh bagels and cream cheese, popping the bread into the toaster. "Where's the house staff? Why are you two having a liquor-filled breakfast?"

Casper's dad nods, scratching at his unshaven jaw. "She'll be good for him. Has given him purpose."

"The staff?"

"Gave them the week off. It's been a loud one."

"What the bloody hell are you two going on about?" Dad asks, but I pay him no mind. Our dynamic has always been strained—like associates rather than father and son. "Who will be good for who? Who is *she*?"

"My son is taking over Boston, and my nephew is now the head if this family."

"Since when? Why am I just finding out now?"

"Because you have no say." Both turn to look at me, one with pride and my father with surprise. "That conversation was between Casper and me, the two who matter." The ceramic mug in my hand shatters upon sudden impact, the shards flying through the air and across the quartz counter. A piece slices across my knuckles, the blood pooling beneath my fingers. "We ran this syndicate for the last five years. We bathed London in the blood of our enemies while you spent your time between golf games and drinking with members of the house."

In the background, I hear the toaster pop and the coffee machine beep, but fuck it all—I couldn't care less. What this arse has implied won't be swept under the rug. Fuck him. Not this time.

"Callum, I think we should—"

"Stop protecting him from me," I seethe, flicking my heated gaze to my uncle. "You always step in, saving him from hearing the shit he doesn't want to hear. He was a horrible father, a messy right hand to you, and always unable to admit his wrongs. He's as bad as Mum, but at least her excuse is being absent and not just the self-centered nature neither grew out of."

My uncle tries to interject again, but Dad holds his hands up. "Let it be. He's right." There's no hiding the surprise on my face at that. He's not a man to ever admit his wrongs. "I've been an arse all these years, have missed a lot, but let me be clear here, son. Not once have I doubted you or implied that you're not capable of running this family. On the contrary. I know you'll do better than those before you."

I relax my stance and take the offered towel from his brother. "Then what did you mean?"

"I'm a member of this family, Callum. That's what I meant." Dad walks over and puts a hand on my shoulder, his expression softer than I've ever seen. "I'd like to be kept up to date, not shoved aside. That's it."

"Fair enough."

"You also need to know one more thing, lad." When I don't answer, he gives me a sad smile. "I've never...not once, doubted you or what you're capable of. You've always been bloody brilliant and responsible, you excel where I lack, and I'm proud of you."

"Thank you."

"Don't. I'm a shit parent, if you don't already know this."

"Speaking of parent," I say, changing the subject. That, and I need to move this along and get my hand stitched up. "Where is she?"

"At the house, fuming." Dad lets out a loud, long sigh. The sound heavy and full of exhaustion. "It's over. I've given her the divorce papers."

Motherfuck. "Great. I'm sure she'll call me to complain soon enough."

"And I apologize for that ahead of time."

22

Aliana

"SOCKS. I NEED SOCKS," I grumble under my breath, heading toward my small laundry room. I've done nothing but wash, fold, and arrange for the last two days—since getting the news— and my closet has never been so clean. I'm not a neat freak or anal over what goes where, but right now, I rival professional organizers. "Socks. Must get socks."

This is a coping mechanism, a way to distract myself from the inevitable. I know this. I'm not unaware of my faults and the role I play in this mess.

I'm leaving.

I'm doing this, even though every fiber of my being hates it.

I've lied to my friend. I have no choice but to lie to him, a phone call I'm dreading.

"Today." I'll call him today and just get this over with.

In a small way, I find reprieve in our long-distance relationship. The weeks without him near have made the lies a little easier to say

—the phone calls and video-chats hide more than just a person's true feelings. He didn't see my reaction after having no contact with my family for months. He didn't see how physically sick I became after the instructions were delivered.

A knock on the door of my small office at the women's home makes me look up from the new software I'm thinking of adding to our budget. It's nothing fancy or difficult to navigate, but definitely one you need if looking to land any office job.

"Can I help you?" *The man standing there looks vaguely familiar, but I can't pinpoint him.*

"Miss Rubens?" *he asks, voice rough as if he's smoked his entire life.*

"That's me." *Discreetly, I bring a hand to my waist and the new bottle of pepper spray there. It's a new brand and promises near blindness upon contact.* "And again. How can I help you?"

In his hand he holds a stapled sheet of paper and envelope. "I'm here to deliver this. Can you please sign for me?"

"Sure." *I'm not expecting anything, and he just doesn't fit the bill of a courier. This man is in a cheap suit and is wearing too much cheap cologne. His hair is slicked back and face unshaven.* "What is it?"

"It's from Governor Rubens's office." *Five words that ruin my day. My stomach plummets and hands begin to sweat as he brings the envelope over.*

I thought he was leaving me alone. I thought I was free.

Hastily, I sign my name, the man leaves, and I'm stuck with the manila bomb sitting atop the desk.

Just get it over with. *Tearing into the package, I'm greeted by the sight of airplane tickets, a fake itinerary, and a note that says:*

My beautiful daughter,

You work too hard and deserve a break.
There's more to life than the hustle and bustle of an office or

school, Aliana. Please accept this early birthday present from your mother and no complaining, sweetheart. It's done, and we've booked you an all-inclusive package with six days of fun in the sun and relaxation.

You leave in five days!

Have fun,

Your, loving parents.

But worse than that is the picture I find folded within the itinerary of my father with an arm thrown over my brother's shoulders. A knot forms in my throat. This is a silent threat. The picture depicts a loving family, a dad and his two boys, but I see the evil in his eyes. I take in the way my brothers are tense and...

The ringing of my cell in another room pulls me from those depressive thoughts—how easily they use and manipulate me while always saving face for the public. To an outsider, they seem like loving, caring, and generous parents. Doting and sweet, but I know better, and my father does everything in a way that saves his own behind.

He'll gamble mine, but never his. He'll hurt them to make me bend.

Rushing out, I toss my basket atop the dryer. It's Aurora's ringtone and I manage to pick up on the fourth ring, slightly out of breath and stomach in knots. "Yolo!" I half wheeze, half chuckle. "You back to the land of the living?"

"I am," she laughs, whatever music she'd been listening to dimming down a bit. She's been a bit under the weather the last few days, not coming into the Conte House. Thank God it's been manageable, the women who've been there the longest stepping up to help the newbies acclimate to the rules and daily routine.

Everyone has a chore or job: from cooking, to cleaning, to

daycare, and that has nothing to do with the classes we offer. And while most don't like the tight structure at first, they love it soon enough when it cements bonds with those around them. Friendships. Understanding.

They no longer feel alone or misunderstood.

"I'll be back in the office tomorrow. We need to go over the new class schedule before you leave, and that software you mentioned. Sorry about that, by the way. This bug came out of nowhere."

"Only you would apologize for being sick."

"Shut up." Roe snorts, then smacks her lips as if tasting something sour. "God, this stuff is awful."

"What are you eating?"

"Drinking." A groan of disgust comes through the line. A little gagging. "Kombucha is just not for me. Dear Lord, just say no."

"Who told you to put that in your mouth?" I've had that experience. That's one of those drinks that you either love or hate, and there is no in between. I get that the benefits outweigh the taste, but I'm a chicken and avoid it at all costs. "You should know better."

"Just a friend." The way she says *friend* makes me smirk. *Why are you hiding him, doofus?*

"Does this 'friend' have a name?"

"The person does, but my lips are sealed."

"Why is that?" A text comes in, the small device in my hand vibrating. I pull back to look, and a smile stretches across my lips.

We're going on a vacation soon. Just you and me. ~Callum J.

I'm not thinking of Aurora when I begin to type, ignoring her voice in the background.

Where to? Somewhere sunny and with a private beach I can skinny dip in? ~Venus

A few moments after I hit send, two things happen at the same time...

Aurora's face greets me through the FaceTime setting, switching over without me knowing.

Callum texts back, and I open it like an idiot, face flaming red when I'm greeted by a glistening-from-the-shower, thick cock.

My mouth waters. Her eyes narrow.

"You're hiding something," Roe sings, arching a brow from her kitchen, the phone propped up against something. But more importantly, that look is daring me to deny her. Funny, she says I'm a dog with a bone when I want to know something, and yet, I've left her alone. *I've been too busy losing myself in Callum.* "Spill."

"No, I'm not."

"Yes, you are."

Matching her stare, I mock-glare. "So, what does that make you?"

"Too nosy for her own good when I've been a shitty friend lately." Her voice is contrite and face sheepish—sad. It's not what I expected either, nor is it right. She has no reason to feel like this. Not at all.

"Stop it, chica," I say, flicking the camera as if it were her head. "You've done nothing to feel like that. We've been busy and life is a hormonal bitch at the moment, but a shitty friend you are not."

"Feels that way."

"Then so am I, if you look at it from that perspective. I should be burned at the stake."

Aurora rolls her eyes. "Always need to one up me. So extra."

"Who else will keep you in check?" Taking the device with me, I make my way back to the laundry room and lean it against the large detergent pod container. "But if you want to make it up to me..."

She snorts, the tightness around her eyes disappearing. "Lunch tomorrow?"

"Yup. I'm in the mood for Thai."

"Done." While I pull out my small load, she takes another sip of her fermented drink, grimacing after she swallows. "By the way, where are you guys going this time? Did the governor tell you, or does he just expect you to show up?"

"What do you think?"

"The latter."

"Word." With my hip, I close the dryer and walk out with her lying atop my clean ankle socks. "That's how the dependable man of the people always behaves. We are his sheep."

"He's so much like my father. Exhausting."

"How is dear Papa Cancio?" My luggage is atop the bed, empty, but there. I have my clothes all in piles and separated by types. *I'd rather go on vacation with Callum.* "Is he still expecting you to take over?"

"He is."

"And?" I ask, looking back at the screen to find her head tilted, studying me. "What?"

"You can't hide your emotions, Ali. Not from me."

"Why do you say that?" My voice comes out an octave higher. My hands are a little shaky and I dig them into the laundry, pretending to be looking for something.

"Maybe it's because in the span of this conversation, you've gone from smiling and blushing to sadness and then a one-eighty into irritation, only to turn back around and end at longing."

"You're seeing something that isn't there."

"Or something's going on with you." She taps her lips with her middle finger, and I can't help but snort. So immature, but it does help loosen a bit of my tension. "Something you don't want to share."

"Like you and mystery man?"

"Do you have one of your own? Because I know you, Rubens, and you're being weirder than normal."

"And if I do?" Better to give her something than continue evading. This way, she understands. "What if it's really new and I'm just feeling him out? What if he's knocked me on my butt, but I'm not ready for the intros and—"

My best friend holds up her hands. "I get it."

"Do you?"

"I do." For a beat, we're both silent but then she sighs, and I scrunch up my face in question. "I'm being an ass when you've been patient with me...aren't I? It's not like I'm sharing."

"No. You're not, but I'll be here when you're ready."

"And I'll do the same."

"Deal."

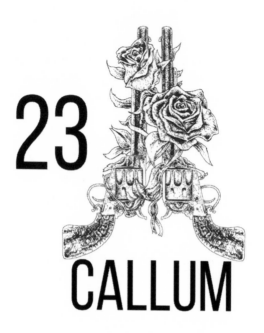

23

CALLUM

I T'S BEEN TWO months since I last touched her. Showed up unannounced and tasted her.

Sixty-one days since I've had to live off FaceTime and phone calls. Where I spend all day waiting for our nightly routine where I log into the cameras in her home and watch her sleep. My obsession knows no bounds. My need is near maddening.

Because since taking over, I've had one truth smack me in the face over and over. No matter where I am, who I'm dealing with, or while joining Casper on this search, I always have her on my mind.

Her place is beside me. She's my home, and I am hers.

It's one of the reasons I'd been so calm while flying into Cuban soil. We're here to put an end to the manhunt—I'm quiet and alert, talking only when necessary, and my bloodthirst is high.

The man inside is more than my aunt's killer; he's an obstacle that needs to be removed.

Where the fuck am I?

Let me go, cabron!

I'm going to kill you.

Mauricio Hernandez is a loud one, yelling and threatening from his place inside of the De Leon compound in Cuba. He's been here a few days now, a place where those who enter do not escape, and I admire the colonial facade and isolated structures.

No one to hear you for miles.

No one here will lift a finger against this family.

The doors are closed to the main area, and a quiet Casper opens them without pause.

Archie will stay outside with the De Leon guards, awaiting orders, while Ivan, the second-in-command and youngest son, walks beside me in silence. He's a lot like me in a way: easygoing until you touch one of ours. And the putrid twat inside did just that.

All the women in crime families are sacred. Untouchable, but to kill a mum?

That's an instant death sentence.

My nostrils flare as I step inside. The stench is rotten—disgusting —but it only makes the demon within me happy. Because I know the smells will match the almost corpse tied up and awaiting trial.

Bright lights turn on, and the noise level rises. Animals—large hogs—make their presence known within empty cells. Each door is open, the inhabitants quiet and watching now, while surrounding the lone figure at the center. I'm pleased with the hospitality he's been shown.

Dirt-caked blood on bruised skin, a dislocated shoulder taking the brunt of his weight from his restrained position.

For a second, I close my eyes and breathe in deeply. Ire pulses through my veins. Heat licks at my flesh.

I've come to accept a long time ago that I crave moments like this. I need the violence, but today it's more. It's personal while signaling a rebirth.

Casper's and mine. Two different paths, two syndicates to run, and yet, we'll always be intertwined by more than familial ties because of the women we love.

Because I do. It's been there the entire time.

No hiding. No denying. The moment she sassed me inside that lounge, she owned me.

Burn him alive if you must, Callum. Just take me away when you're done. ~Venus

Her text from this morning replays in my mind then, and I can almost hear Aliana's sweet voice utter her plea. Her need. *Something is off with her.* I notice it each time we talk now.

It's been that way since finding out she's going on holiday with her family. As if she hates the idea. No excitement. No funny quip or mention of the things she'll be doing while at some all-inclusive resort in Mexico.

Something that further cements she needs me as much as I breathe for her.

"I will, sweet girl." No one hears my words, and I open my eyes to meet Mauricio's.

He's dirty. Smells like utter shit. An old cunt with a big mouth.

"Who the fuck—"

"Evening," Casper says, tone even and calm. Mauricio's eyes turn to look at him, squinting due to the bright lights before looking at me again. He does this a few times. Back and forth before pausing on my cousin.

We're both dressed similarly; all black and wearing the damn suspenders I hate, but his mum thought they were dashing. And like him, I carry with me a piece of jewelry she had blessed when we were young—his by the Pope, and mine by a Buddhist monk.

He has a chain, while I have a bracelet with an attached medallion: a Greek warrior's helmet on the front.

"Who are you?" he asks again. "Why am I here?"

"Why *is* he here?" Casper repeats, looking back at me, then Ivan. His eyes hold a feral tint I'm sure reflected in my own, but we're not here for a quick death. Hernandez will hurt. Bleed. "The man's asking why he's here?"

"Poor lad," I answer in the same tone, my rage barely controlled as I walk over. In my hand, I have the package Ivan gave me when we arrived. "This is a horrible predicament to find yourself in."

Ivan steps into the light then, placing a chair in Mauricio's line of sight, then steps back. "It is."

"You!" the arsehole yells, fighting his restraints. His eyes are narrowed at Ivan. *So much hate.* "You were at the bar—"

"Yes. I was. And it was an interesting night, indeed. Many stories shared over a bottle of Havana Club. Do you remember that?" The doors to this room slam shut, locks engaging before Ivan hits the button at the center of the remote in his hand. At once, the lights dim making it easier for the piece of shit to get a better look. No more squinting. "Remember the story you shared of your recent time in London?"

"I don't remember."

"I'm going to give you a minute to go through your memories, Mr. Hernandez." Casper cracks his neck, then shakes out his arms. "Use your time wisely."

"You have the wrong man," he says without pause. His body glistens with sweat, more than when we came in. A natural reaction to fear; his choking is a pulsing wave permeating every inch of this personal jail. "I'm innocent."

The wanker gave himself away.

If you've done no wrong, there's no reason to defend yourself.

"I haven't accused you of anything yet, mate." Casper looks toward Ivan. "Have you?"

"Not at all."

"And you?"

My response is a snort. "I haven't said a word."

"See?" My cousin does a 360-degree turn, arms out wide. "No accusations. However, I do believe you have a story to tell us."

"I'm not him."

At that moment, Ivan turns, and I follow him toward the last cell. This one doesn't have an animal inhabitant but is full of useful items: a collection of knives in various sizes, ropes and chains, and two hospital beds that have seen better days. Both are rusted, and I'm not sure if the stains aren't blood.

We move the latter of the two farther back and pull out an old, creaky cart.

The laptop and camera on top of it are new, and it'll serve two purposes. We have a special movie-time feature, and my uncle deserves to watch his last moments.

This was too short notice for him to come.

"Motherfucker!" Mauricio suddenly yells out, and I smirk. *Fucker didn't wait.* Not that I blame him. This is his kill. "Stop! This is a mistake."

We stop with the cart a few feet from the now wounded arse, the blood coming from the back of his leg.

Casper's Karambit drips with blood.

The large swine squeal.

My eyes meet Ivan's and I nod. He's quick to press the button for the cells and they close, locking in all of the pigs but two.

Those two roam close. They're curious, the scent of blood creating a frenzy, and soon hunger will follow.

Because pigs can be cannibals. Cases have been reported of bodies being consumed, leaving only the bones behind.

"I'm going to ask you once more, Hernandez." Casper crosses his arms, his expression neutral. Yet, I notice the twitch of his fingers around the knife's handle. "Tell me the story you shared with my friend, here. Last chance."

"He's lying!" Mauricio's struggles intensify against his bonds, thrashing—shaking. "I was just at the bar celebrating my wedding anniversary."

"Really?" Ivan shakes his head, eyes hard on him from his position by the laptop. He's hooking everything up. "Because there was no one with you but the prostitute you bought for the night. And don't worry; I left her every single cent you had in your wallet back at the cheap hotel you were hiding in. Those two hundred thousand in cash will be used by her family and friends to survive and have a better life."

"You piece of shit. I will kill you!"

Ivan just stares. "That's a mighty big threat from an innocent man."

"Do you know who I am? I will...*fuck!*" My cousin strikes, this cut running from knee to mid-thigh. It's deep, bleeding heavily, and the floor beneath him soon has a puddle. This gets the animal's attention.

One gets curious. Snaps his teeth.

"Feel like telling me that story now? Come one, Mauricio. Let's reminisce."

His silence feels like a slap in the face. He's ignoring the man whose mum he killed. Denying his past instead of accepting his reality like a man. *Fucking pussy.*

"Maybe he just needs a little help getting there. Something to remember?" I walk over, my steps unhurried as I pick up a bottle of rum. It's open, half gone, but has enough left for me to get my point across. "Right, friend?"

Immediately his eyes widen, and he arches back, digging the rope into his wrists. "Don't. Please don't...I'll talk."

"So you do remember?" And like the arsehole I am, I pour a wee bit of the alcohol onto his leg. Not on the cut, but close enough that he screams like the twat he is.

"Don't do this."

"Do what?" A little more, this time a few drops slip onto the wound, and he cries out. Full-on blubbering mess. "Repeat that?"

"I'll tell you what you want to know. Just let me walk out of here alive—promise not to kill me."

"But first, let's start with a slide show. A beautiful message from a friend?" Casper nods in approval, while Ivan turns on the computer. The guest of honor is quiet, though, and I add another few drops over the last. "What do you think, Hernandez?"

"Yes."

The cart is moved closer, touching his body. Rust smears across his dirty flesh, a streak Casper follows with the tip of his blade. A shallow cut, but if you were to believe the sounds coming from Hernandez, you'd think we tore a limb off.

"Where are they?" Casper grits out, his lip curling over his teeth. I know he's hurting. All of this cuts deep.

His mum will never get to meet Aurora.

My aunt will never get to embarrass me in front of Aliana.

I point at the app, and he stalks over, pressing play before standing back. We all do.

Let him see how far our depravity goes. Let him see his friend, Felix Vega, take his last breath.

Because I was right in sending in Alexander when I did.

Mauricio should've never accepted the job. Neither should've.

Felix received a punishment—was tortured by one of the best in the business. Burns. Strikes. Cuts. Alexander is brutal, and he took pleasure in cutting the man's cock off an inch at a time. Then his balls. Slowly, bleeding him and then patching up enough to stave off his death before doing it again.

He broke his mind. His will to live.

And then when Felix takes the gun Casper gave him and pulls the trigger, blowing his brains out; it's all documented. It plays once and then again. Every brutal moment. Every scream reverberates inside the large room.

"I'm sorry."

That's my cue and I'm quick to flip from video to Skype, my uncle coming onto the screen a few seconds later. He nods at us, but no one speaks.

"So, you do know who I am?"

"Yes. I studied your picture and file for two weeks before the hit took place."

"Who sent you?" No answer. Mauricio's lips press tight.

That shit pisses me off, and I grab the bottle, jamming the nozzle into his thigh. Tip it over. "Answer him!"

Screams rend the air, the wail painful to the ear. It also riles up the animals. They bang against the cages, squeaking and grunting, while the two on the loose come closer.

They shuffle at the floor by his feet. They snap at the air.

Ivan pushes them back with a metal pole.

"This will only work for so long, Hernandez." Casper taps his cheek with a bloody hand. "Tell me their real names and not the bullshit Felix gave me."

"No one knows their real names, and I didn't care enough to ask."

"Tell me what you know. All of it."

"Nico and Antonella are the children of Giada Savino. These three hate Matteo Cancio for something that happened between their father and the Boston mob boss a very long time ago. They never told me what, but from what Felix said, it all started a year after Aurora, Cancio's daughter, was born."

We're not surprised by this. Aurora's family is somehow involved; they're the catalyst, while we're the combustion.

"Matteo wasn't in charge then."

"The father, Matteo Cancio Sr., was."

"Okay." Casper tosses his knife onto the cart while I hand over what's left the liquor bottle. He brings it to the injured man's lips. "Drink. It'll help."

"Just kill me."

"I will, but I need something first."

Mauricio takes the offered drink, swallowing a heavy shot. "You want to talk about your mother?"

"She wasn't your intended target." Not a question, and Hernandez nods. "Then why shoot an innocent woman?"

"They doubled the offer." Another shot, this time a wee bit falls into his wound, and he hisses. "Those are a bitch. Hurt like hell."

"That's the point." I take the bottle back from my cousin, pouring the rest onto the floor. "Now, about the money?"

"I was supposed to receive the other half a mil next week to an account I have in Guatemala City. The national bank doesn't ask questions and after slipping the manager a couple of bucks, he speeds the process up personally."

"What day next week?"

"Wednesday."

"Thank you for your cooperation." With that, Casper pulls out his gun and shoots him four times in the upper torso. Mauricio groans, eyes rolling back, and I use Casper's knife to cut him down.

He lands on the cold, hard floor with a thud. The sound and his blood draw the roaming swine closer, and closer, while we walk away.

Once at the exit, Ivan lets them all out.

Hungry, feral animals.

It doesn't take them long to attack, and his horror-filled screams are beautiful. A soothing balm to my soul.

His ending is justified.

A man without honor deserves to be pig food.

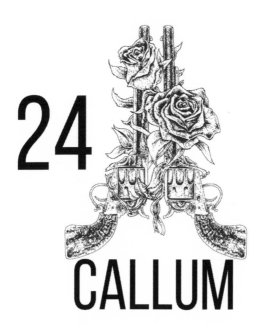

24

CALLUM

I'M FRESH OUT of the shower, towel drying my hair, when my mobile goes off. It rings twice and goes to voicemail, but within seconds someone's calling again. Walking to the dresser where I left it, I notice the screen is lit up with ten missed calls, eight texts, and three voicemails.

"What the fuck?" Unlocking the device, I scroll through the list and they're all from Giannis.

That puts me on alert, and I quickly log into the cameras in Aliana's home, finding her walking through the living room toward her room holding a laundry basket. She's talking to someone, laughing, but before I can turn the speakers on, Giannis's name flashes across my screen.

I press answer, and all I hear is a muttered, *finally*. "Callum? You there?"

"Yes." Tone annoyed, I snap at the interruption. My need to know who she's giggling with claws at me. "What's with the calls and messages?"

"I shouldn't be telling you this," he starts, voice a bit shaky, and I pause. He's not one to reach out outside of his reporting, and even then, I can tell he wants to get off the phone quickly. I intimidate him. "She's left me with no choice, though. Stubborn woman."

"Get to the point." Tossing the towel still in my hand and the one around my waist onto the bed, I grab the plain grey pajama bottoms and slip them on sans underwear. It's a warm night out, the windows are open, and a soft breeze comes in off the coast that isn't far from here. Between that and the ceiling fan above my head, I find it rather comfortable. "You're rambling is rather off-putting."

"Callum, before I begin, please know that I told her to tell you. I've been arguing with her over this for the last few days and—"

"What the bloody fuck is going on with Aliana?" My breathing is harsh, my grip on my mobile causing the plastic to strain. "Straight to the point. No more bullshit."

"Her father is sending her to Brazil on an errand by herself."

"Come again?" I must've heard wrong. Because that's not what my sweet Venus told me.

Two days ago...

Hey, you got a minute? ~Venus

Her text comes through while I'm sitting in on a meeting with our gun supplier, giving him the courtesy of knowing there's been a change in power. Not because we have to, but because he's worked with our family for a long time, and we consider him a friend. Or at least, his father was. This bloke I find to be an obnoxious twit with the personality of a potato.

In a meeting. What's up? ~Callum J.

Three dots appear on the screen and then disappear. Start up again and then nothing.

Are you okay? ~Callum J.

A throat clears and I look up, meeting Alfie's eyes. "Are you listening to me?"

His tone doesn't sit well with me, and I lean back, drumming my fingers on the table. "No. I'm not."

"And this is who you chose to take Casper's place?" he questions my uncle and father, that haughty arrogance coming through again, and I exhale roughly. It's been a busy few weeks between my stepping up while Casper searched and killed the man who shot his mum. I'm constantly traveling to where he is if I'm needed, and also dividing the men between who I will keep, and who will be moving abroad.

Most know what's going on, but the announcement's been pushed back for a reason.

I want to go through each person on our roster, from vendor to buyer to the fucking arse that delivers the morning paper.

My uncle vetted his people.

Casper vetted his crew.

I will decide mine.

Of the four people in the room, two move one hand beneath the table at his blatant disrespect while I look at the last message that came in.

I'm fine, just need to talk when you get a chance. ~Venus.

Give me ten. ~Callum J.

Placing my mobile face down atop the table, I meet my father's eyes and then look at the door. He gets it and stands, walking to it and then locks it while my uncle glares at the git. This makes Alfie nervous, and he shifts in his seat while the man beside him pales.

I feel for the bloke. He truly seems like he abhors his job.

"You're fired." At those two words, his head snaps in my direction, eyes wide. He tries to say something, to protest, but I hold a hand up. The same one that now holds my gun. "Our contract is now void, Mr. Buford."

"You can't do that," he gasps, looking toward the older men inside the room for support. There's none there, and Alfie swallows hard at the other weapons placed upon the table. "We've been in business for so long. Your cousin wouldn't agree—"

"It's my word you should concern yourself with." Relaxing back in my chair, I tsk. "Please hand me the folder to your right." Casper's father slides it across the table to me, his stare never wavering on the man who has no business being the head of a respected trafficking ring. When his father was alive, Sr. made sure to anticipate needs, adjust pricing to market demand, and compete with a quality rivaling that of the American and the British army.

This man is a joke.

Useless.

"Please think this through. No one can supply what I can."

"Wrong." I open the file and grab the top sheet, skimming down, and then passing it along.

"What's this?" Instead of answering, I point to it and wait. Alfie's eyes lower and read, face pinching tight while the paper in his hand crumbles. "How could you do this? We have an agreement—"

He doesn't get to finish. My finger's quicker than his reactions, and I shoot once, the bullet going through his arm and embedding itself into the wall behind him. "This has been a long time coming, in my opinion. You've relied too much on your father's legacy to keep up with the demands of loyal clients. The last three deliveries have been rubbish, your attitude obnoxious, and quite frankly, I can't see myself continuing this working relationship without slitting your throat."

"Callum, I—"

"It's Mr. Jameson to you." Pushing my chair back, I stand and lean over the table. "We're done, and as you can see," I hiss, hand slamming atop the new contract I signed yesterday with a Spaniard bloke who brings more to the table than guns. "I already made my decision. Leave with pride, or inside of a body bag. The choice is yours."

With that, I pick up my mobile and walk out of what is now my office. My father and uncle will see them out, while I have a more pressing matter to attend to. I press the number one on my mobile and her name flashes across the screen, ringing twice before her light breathing comes across the line.

The pub is not busy at the moment as I exit the establishment and pull out a joint. I light it up and take a deep drag, warming my lungs with the earthy smoke. It's soothing. My body calms.

"Talk to me, Venus. Everything okay?"

Whatever she hears in my voice makes her giggle, and fuck, I'm hard at once. Throb. "I'm fine, silly. Just have some news."

"Oh yeah? You coming to visit me?"

"I wish," she mutters low, but I hear. I also don't question it. "This is actually about our family vacation, Mr. Jameson. We have a date."

"When you call me Mr. Jameson…" reaching down, I adjust myself, squeezing a bit "…the only thing I want to do is bend you over my knee, love. I want to make that gorgeous arse a pretty shade of pink."

"Promise?"

"Naughty little thing."

My response makes her laugh again. The sound so sweet. "Behave. You're far away and my hand needs a break."

Fuck. That image is dangerous. For me. For her. *I'd break her.*

It's been too long since I've had her. Touched her.

"Tempting me—"

"We're heading to Bora Bora for a week," Aliana interrupts, her tone a bit nervous. The change in her lilt is minor, but almost as if she's embarrassed. *Cute.* "The entire Rubens family is going."

"You excited?" Another deep pull of my spliff, deeper inhale this time, and I hold it in for a few seconds before exhaling slowly. "Packed yet?"

"Sure."

Not the answer I'm expecting and my brows furrow. "Do you not want to go?"

"I do, but I'll miss you."

Present...

"Are you sure about this?" I ask Giannis.

"Yes." He lets out a grumbled groan. "I told her to tell you. To ask for help."

"What the fuck is going on?" When it comes to my Venus, I have no patience. I'm trying hard to remember that he came to me, that he's worried, but rationality isn't my strongest suit with those I consider mine. "Where is she now?"

"Please don't kill me, but I can't tell you. I've broken her trust enough with this call."

"Then why tell me?"

"Because no one else can protect her."

Exhaling, I run a tired hand across my face. "Get me her itinerary and include yourself on this trip. Do whatever the fuck you must, but where she goes, you go. Understood?"

"Already done. I convinced her father she needs help."

"Good." My tone is cold. Angry.

"Please don't be mad at her. This really is out of her hands...it's her story to tell."

"Too late." An email comes in and I pull the mobile away, checking. It's from Giannis with confirmed days, airfare, and the place booked for their stay. Ezra will change this. She'll go to my home there. "I'll take care of everything. Your job is to get on the plane with her and find alternative lodging for the days following your arrival; I'll cover the cost. She's mine to deal with."

25

Aliana

I HATE LYING TO HIM.

It eats at me. Makes me feel like utter crap, but I have no choice. Yet, as I land in Brazil with Giannis in the seat to my right, I wish it were Callum beside me. That I'd been strong enough to tell him what's going on, the threats and illegal deals I'm forced to be a part of.

"You can always call him," Giannis leans over and whispers before undoing his seatbelt. Those around us pay no mind, though, too busy opening the overhead compartments and grabbing their carry-on luggage. "He can help you, Ali. Hell, if you don't want to explain, I will. This is fucked up."

This is fucked up. I know. I've been repeating those same words for the last few years while trying to find an explanation for the way my father treats me. Uses me.

"He has enough on his plate. What they did to his aunt…" my voice trails off, the memory of his face—expression—while he asked me to accept the protection of the man he called Kray, broke my

203

heart. So much pain. His eyes, those beautiful, gem-like eyes, showed me in that moment the kind of man he truly is.

Caring. Passionate. Loyal.

Categories I'd never thought he'd be a part of. Because in my ignorance, I wrote him off the moment he introduced himself, and yet, walking away has been impossible. I can't.

Callum is everything the men in my family wish they could be, and so much more. His power doesn't dominate him. His money doesn't define him.

I'm falling for him. My truth. Undeniably.

"I'm screwed." Those two words, my tone, they say everything I can't. And weirdly enough, Giannis understands. He nods, making no move to stand as those around us disembark. And we don't, not until every person exits and the flight attendants congregate at the front.

He's first to stand and grab our bags. The two carry-on's we brought have just the basics while what we'll need for the job was shipped to the house the governor rented days ago. My father's been planning this for a while, longer than I suspect, and he'd given me enough freedom to mess with my head.

It doesn't take long to get off the plane or out of the airport. Giannis handled this part of the arrangements, renting us a fun convertible for our time in the country. Not that we'd get to enjoy any of it; we can't be seen or draw attention to ourselves, but the drive out to the private property in Rio will be amazing.

Maybe I can come with Callum one day.

"If he's around that long," I mutter low, grateful that Giannis is too busy hooking up the Bluetooth system to his phone. The last thing I want right now is another lecture. To be told I'm an idiot.

Because I am. I should've told him. Asked for his help.

"Are you hungry, Ali?" Giannis asks, pulling me back from my thoughts. "You haven't eaten much in the last few days."

"How would you know that?"

"That's a dumb question, and you know it."

"Shut it." And because I'm not ready to get into that conversation, the implications of him watching me because of Callum, I slap his shoulder with a giggle. "By the way, I can't believe our fathers bought the whole, *I'm trying to make sure she doesn't fuck up*, spiel you gave them. It was almost insulting how easily they gave in to you coming with me."

"Don't take it personally. They're both arseholes." His butchered British accent at the end makes me miss Callum. Even when cursing, he sounds so proper it's sexy. "My boyfriend, on the other hand..."

"Is he here?"

"Look behind you." And sure enough, there he is in a mid-sized SUV just one car behind ours. The tall man looks cramped behind the wheel, his posture stiff and aware, but more importantly, he is here for Giannis. In case anything goes wrong.

Why am I so jealous of that? Why didn't I just speak up when I had the chance?

I'm quiet and lost inside my head for the rest of the ride. I know my friend means well, that his attempts at pointing out landmarks and the beauty around us is an attempt at distracting me, but nothing works. The closer to the house we get, the gloomier I become.

My mood stinks. My body language is one of sulking.

And when we pull into the huge private beachfront property and Giannis parks, getting out to grab our bags and open the front door, I can't help but shed a tear. Then another. I'm quick to wipe them away, but the evidence is there for anyone who looks my way.

I shouldn't be here to steal an artifact for my father. I shouldn't be here and possibly go to jail if anything goes wrong.

But more importantly, Giannis isn't who I want with me if things get rough.

He's not who I trust blindly.

He's not Callum.

He's not the man I've fallen in love with.

THE NEXT DAY, I FEEL LIKE A ZOMBIE. I'M GOING THROUGH THE motions while the world around me moves—it shifts and carries on. Giannis tried to talk to me a few times, to get me out of this funk, but nothing works and after a while, he too gives up until it's time to go.

Which brings me to the present...

The outside of this building is intimidating and highly secured. There are guards everywhere: walking, posted, and a few snipers on the south end with their eyes on the main entrance. Their job is to not let anyone in or out, much less lose one of the pieces inside.

The official who runs this department is smart; the secretary of state or equivalent of, and his job is to keep certain items under lock and key. This could destroy the country's wealth, and the hold the government has over its citizens.

What my father's client wants with the artifact, I don't know, but its black-market price is exuberant. I've done my own research. I'm half tempted to run away with it and make a new life for myself, far from all I know.

No family. No restrictions.

What about Callum? "Focus," I grit out from between clenching teeth and Giannis looks over, nose scrunched up in question. "We need to focus. No mistakes."

"Got it."

The plans provided showed me three possible entry points, and I chose the heavily guarded one. Why? Because no one thinks you'll attempt a crime under the heavy watch of national police. Where the danger lies. A mistake many make, but I've learned over the years that the best way to hide is in plain sight while drawing innocent attention.

That's why I'm stumbling, giggling while walking by the back entrance with my sandals dangling from a finger and phone in the other hand. They see me but think nothing of the gringa taking pictures—selfies with an exaggerated pout and low-cut top.

Then, there's the man beside me in full military gear.

Their colors. Their medals on the breast pocket.

Some salute and he returns the gesture, giving two a nod before bending to lay a kiss below my ear. My giggles turn louder, I smack his chest, and I hear the chuckle from the guard closest to us.

To them, I'm just another tourist, drunk and out for a good time.

Like so many, we're curious and looking to live a little dangerously. Like so many, I'm letting my hair down, and they enjoy the show.

We walk past them after a few more pictures, him dragging me away with an arm tight around my waist until their attention goes back to the front. Straight ahead, where we left a present earlier.

The first small explosive goes off after ten minutes, and the heavy footfalls of soldiers are heard. They shout orders in Portuguese, and the snipers change positions, their scopes looking for the slightest movement in the general vicinity of the first bomb.

Not a real one, but the sound is loud and one I hate from every 4th of July celebration my father makes us attend. It doesn't have rays of colors light up the sky or the blinking of twinkling starburst. No, this one sounds like a machine gun, but ten times as loud.

The second goes off and someone shoots, a man on the ground talking through a walkie-talkie and demanding to know if those on the roof see anything.

This is when I enter through the unlocked door that three soldiers hovered by a few minutes ago.

Giannis is quiet beside me, his steps matching mine, and we duck behind another small building and keep to the shadows until the office I need comes into view. The keypad outside is the sole illumination after pressing the frequency blocker my father provided, a gift from the buyer to ensure our faces aren't seen.

Not that I trust it, but I warned him I'd talk if caught. If the equipment he gave fails, I'm not protecting anyone.

"Code?" I ask Giannis without looking over, my eyes on the device as I slip on gloves. "Five and counting."

He understands what I mean and follows suit, latex now covering his hands. The holiday-themed explosives are spread and the next two go off not far from the first, leaving us a short window before all is confirmed and they return to their post.

"1982." Voice low, he moves a little closer while I punch in the numbers. It pings green and the door disengages, the audible click loud, yet doesn't draw attention. "Get in."

"Hit the next explosive."

"Two minutes."

For someone who's never done this before, Giannis is a great help. I don't feel alone and breathe a little easier while scrambling the signal again, making sure we have no surprises inside. However, nothing takes the pressure off like seeing the jade statue inside of the glass containment, it's enclosure small and unprotected.

At least, I think so until a small red dot captures my attention. The minuscule circle glints off a metallic rim at the back, its beacon bouncing off and landing on the artifact's head.

"Second alarm?" he asks, stopping beside me.

"Yeah."

"Can you undo it?"

"This one has a remote. We just need to find it." How do I know? Because I've seen it before inside of Dad's office at the Thompson Center. The door to the left of his desk leads to a small room where they file and keep certain documents, things that the public doesn't need to see, and I was there the day it was installed.

Same small bead of light bouncing off metal. Same two wires poking out of a small hole, an open conduit, meant to deter if touched. The remote that turns it on or off is never far from the receiver, and as I turn my head and look around, I find a small stack of books that seem out of place.

A young adult series based on a vampiric love story doesn't seem like something the owner of this office reads. Nothing on his dossier —the fifty-page life story with everything from his breakfast routine, the seedy establishments he visits on the regular, or the three mistresses he keeps—hint at him being an avid romance reader.

Walking closer, I ignore Giannis's questioning look and stop in front of the books. To an outsider, they seem normal, the outside worn down from use. However, not so much when you're close. From my vantage point a few feet away, I can tell they're fake but painted to appear realistic.

"Bingo," I whisper, looking around to detect a secondary alarm, but after finding none, I pick up the small box and find exactly what I want below. The device is small, no bigger than a candy bar and with two buttons at the center.

"How did you—"

"Later," I cut him off, pressing the right circle while holding my breath. I'm going off of a memory here, what I overheard the installation company explain to a pompous governor who ignored his child being there, and when nothing goes off, I let out a rough exhale. "Christ, I'm going to need a lot of liquor tonight."

"You and me both, girl. This shit is heart attack inducing."

A whirling sound fills the room, a low buzz, before the display goes dark and the glass door unlocks. We look at each other, both smiling before rushing across the room and exchanging the pieces.

One jade, the other cheap ceramic painted green.

Within seconds we've made the switch and closed the display, re-engaging the lock. The remote is put back, the room given a quick glance over before we try to exit.

Try, because standing outside the room the moment Giannis peeks out is a man dressed in a soldier's uniform. He's tall, way over six feet, and the scowl on his face has me nearly stumbling back. He looks at us and the small backpack on my shoulder before stepping aside.

We don't move, though. Too scared.

"Leave before you are caught," he hisses, hand on his gun, and it's the heavy Spanish accent that makes the air catch in my throat. Not that I'm given much time to ask him anything; Giannis all but drags me from the room before I can ask who he is.

Did my father send him?

Why is he helping?

The man moves past us, his weapon drawn high while there seems to be a war zone not far from us. Many shouts, some gunfire, and all while the stranger walks us to the exit and tilts his head at the door.

"No one will follow you. Get out." That's the last thing he says before running back in the direction of the chaos, his large body disappearing behind a building. *What the hell was that?*

"You heard him. Let's go!"

I nod, my eyes meeting a scared Giannis. "Run."

26
Aliana

FOR THE LAST forty-eight hours, I've been on edge.

Worrying. Watching the news.

And nothing.

Not a single news story has broken out, nor has there been sight of the man who helped us escape.

He's the most predominant thought in my mind. Why did he help? Why not take it for himself?

That statue is worth a lot. By my research, more than the national debt of a small country.

So again, why help?

The only answer that makes sense is that my father hired him. Bought the soldier off to make sure we didn't screw up.

A knock at the door pulls my attention from those thoughts and I freeze, fear taking over, until I remember that Giannis went out with his boyfriend and left the key behind. Looking through the window beside the door, I catch sight of a white shirt and dark green shorts and smile. *Yup, Giannis.*

"You should've taken the key, doofus!" I call out, bare feet padding over the few remaining steps. The heavy door has a large metal handle on this side, and after turning the lock, I pull it open. My mouth opens as the man turns around and then I'm choking, nervousness settling in deep. "Callum?"

"Aliana."

One word, and I'm swallowing hard—chest rising rapidly while taking him in. From head to loafers, I watch him through wide eyes and trembling hands. I'm nervous, but happy, and at the same time a heated flash of fear runs down my veins and settles in my chest.

"How? What?" Not the most eloquent response, but my mind and heart have shut down. His presence hits me in the chest like a wrecking ball.

Oh, God. Does he know?

"Are you going to let me into my home, Venus?"

"Your what?" I wave a hand between us back and forth a few times before it drops, and I tilt my head to the side. I'm lost. So unsure of everything. And to make it worse, he's looking at me as if I'm the most amusing thing he's ever seen.

Hip jutting out, I put a hand there and narrow my eyes. Something isn't right.

Gem-colored orbs drop from my face to my hip; he bites his bottom lip. "You look beautiful, sweetheart."

"How did you find me?" I ask instead, although my cheeks stain pink.

Callum doesn't answer, but he does hold a finger up and turns it in a silent demand for me to twirl. When I don't move, he gives me a little grin. "Please."

The short, white cotton dress I'm wearing clings to me, molds to my every curve and when I turn for him, it rises just a little higher on my thighs. With a halter-style top, I didn't bother to wear a bra. A mistake now.

My breasts spill a little over the edge while my nipples are hard, pebbled tight and pushing against the soft fabric of the dress. His hooded eyes linger there for a minute before going lower and down the flat of my stomach to the width of my hips and then bare legs.

He even watches the way my white-painted toes wiggle against the travertine flooring with hunger.

How he watches me—devours me where I stand—makes me nervous. Fills me with anxiety, but more than that, it creates a palpable need in me. Those few seconds of silence make me shiver where I stand, and the thick outline of his cock becomes more pronounced. It jerks, and his name slips through my lips on a little moan.

Callum takes another step in my direction and lifts his hand to my cheek, cupping it while his thumb rubs my cheek. "I'd like to enter my home, please."

"Oh!" That snaps me out of it, and I scramble back, nearly tripping, and his hands shoot out to catch me. One hard yank, and I'm against his every muscle, can feel them move, holding me tight as his arm goes around my waist and I'm lifted off the ground. "What're you—"

"Let's head inside first."

"Okay." What else can I say when he's looking at me like I'm everything? Like he revolves around me, and it's more than likely wishful thinking on my part, but I indulge in the feeling and let him. I settle my head in the crook of his neck and breathe him in as the door closes behind us and his loafer-covered feet walk past the foyer and straight to the back deck with views of the ocean a short distance from the sliding glass door.

The view is pristine. His hold is the sweetest torture, but all I can focus on is the happiness seeing him brings.

My earlier concerns over getting caught are gone. I know he wouldn't let anything happen to me. *He'll protect us.*

Callum takes a seat at the edge of a large hammock while balancing me in his hold, hoisting me a little higher on his hip so he can lay back with my body over his. It's a little awkward at first, I'm gripping him hard and afraid we're going to fall, but a low *relax* and another short shift and I find myself nestled against his warm body.

We stay like that for a while.

Lying in silence with the soft breeze off the ocean flowing around us, my body slowly gives in to the fatigue that's been building since before this trip. I know we need to talk, all the questions I need to ask, but as his hand sweeps up and down my back and his lips press against my forehead, I close my eyes.

Each slow swing settles me. His earthy scent soothes me.

"You're in so much trouble, love." That's the last thing I hear before going under, but I'm too tired to fight the heavy blanket of sleep knocking me unconscious.

I'M PULLED FROM SLEEP BY THE SCENT OF FOOD. I DON'T KNOW what time it is or how I got on the hammock, until Callum's low timbre greets my ears from somewhere to my left. He's not beside me anymore and I peek out carefully, barely opening my eyes, but he sees.

Standing at the large outdoor kitchen and without a shirt is Callum with a phone between his ear and neck while holding a pair of grilling tongs. The sizzling of meat permeates the air with a delicious aroma, just like the view of him flipping what looks to be steak before stepping back.

Wide awake and biting my lip, I look away just long enough to catch the setting sun. *Jesus, how long was I asleep?* It was barely midday when Callum took me by surprise, but now it looks to be easily six in the evening.

"You've been out for a little over five hours," he says from beside the hammock, and I jump, almost falling down. Callum rights me, gripping my arm with one hand and the fabric with the other and pulls me in close. "Careful. The dismount can be tricky for a first timer."

"Thank you."

He nods, bending a bit at the knees once he's sure I won't fall. "Let me help you out."

"Please." Not because I can't get out by myself, but I want his touch. Crave it.

"Arm over my shoulder, love." I do as he asks and strong hands lift me out, turning with me in his hold to walk back toward the outdoor kitchen/dining area. The table there is set for two—plates and silverware with a small crystal vase holding a delicate white flower inside. I've seen that flower around the property; his garden is full of them.

His garden. His house.

He has to know.

"Thank you for letting me sleep for so long. I've been exhausted."

"I bet." There's a slight hardening to his eyes, but it doesn't last long and he doesn't elaborate. And I'm glad. I'm not ready to have the *who, what, when, and how the hell* conversation. "There's also a bit of selfishness in why I let you sleep for so long."

"There is?" I squeak a bit and he laughs, full on and loud before settling back with that smirk that does things to me. "Why?"

"Because I want you well rested tonight." The implication is there while the heat of his stare holds me captive, and all I can do is let out a shuddering breath. There's no fear or nerves, more of a building anticipation of what's to come, and for now, I'm pushing away all thoughts of the reasons we're both here.

I know we'll discuss it. That he's going to be mad.

But for now, I want to enjoy this because he might leave after knowing what I did.

Or did he send the man there to protect me? That thought strikes me like a lightning bolt where I sit and my head tilts, analyzing him from head to bare feet.

Would he do that? Does he care enough to?

Or, more importantly, how did he know? Because he does, of that I have no doubt now.

"How did—"

"Hungry?" he interrupts, and as if on cue, my stomach rumbles. I haven't eaten since yesterday morning, too nervous to do so. "I made a mixed grill churrasco for tonight with picanha, and some chicken in case you prefer that. The sides aren't extravagant: salad, sweet potato fries, fried banana, and cheese bread I picked up while you slept. There's a lady in a market a mile down the road that makes the best I've had."

"You went through a lot of trouble."

"I'm spoiling you tonight." *Tonight.* Tomorrow, I'm screwed. "Do I bring everything to the table, or do you prefer I serve you just what you want?"

"Let's bring it all over." Standing from the seat he placed me on, I walk over. My hands are shaking. My stomach is in knots. Callum notices right away and brings me in close with an arm around my waist when I reach the extravagant kitchen. It has everything from a grill to burners to a roaster, and that's just to cook; the fridge alone is larger than the one I have at home.

"Relax."

"I am." Lies.

"Aliana," he says lowly, an angry tinge to his tone that makes me freeze, "don't make a habit of lying to me. That's one of two offenses I won't forgive. You already used your freebie here, love. Understood?"

"Yes."

"Good girl." He kisses the crown of my head and then down to my temple, exhaling roughly against my skin. "Lying and cheating are my limits. I'd hate to look at you differently one day, when I know you are neither of those things. I'm not mad at you right now, but we will discuss why we're both in Brazil and it's not because we took a holiday."

"Okay."

I'm still tense and he loosens his hold, moving his face back so he can meet my eyes. "I'd never hurt you, nor will I take my anger at the situation out on you. This isn't your fault, but in the future, trust is key. You getting hurt is unacceptable to me."

"I'm sorry."

"I know." His expression relaxes, and so do I. "Now, let's eat. I'm not a fan of cold food."

"That makes two of us." And because karma deems this the perfect time to embarrass me, my stomach grumbles once again, causing him to let out a loud laugh. Like this, carefree and calm, he's simply the most handsome man I've ever seen.

"I CAN'T EAT ANOTHER BITE," I MOAN, PUSHING MY PLATE AWAY before picking up the glass of red wine he brought out with the bread. The taste is drier than something I'd pick for myself, but paired with the meal, it balances and leaves the pleasant taste of fruit and spice after each sip. "This was amazing."

"Glad you approve." Callum eats the last bite of fried banana and mimics my pose, relaxing in his seat. He's across from me, watching with a grin that hints at a sinful promise, and I squirm. Between the full stomach and three glasses of wine, I'm relaxed and aware.

Of his every inhale.

Of the way his fingers twitch atop the table.

"Dessert will have to wait, though."

"Who said anything about dessert?"

"I did." I remember the sweet treat on the kitchen island, waiting to be eaten. "I'm a huge sucker for a well-made flan."

"That's mine."

"You mean *ours*."

"No."

"Yes."

"So bratty," he grumbles, the mock glare only serving to make me laugh. However, that laugh turns into a shriek when he stands abruptly, chair flying back, and lunges in my direction.

I'm out of my seat just as fast and running, heart thumping harshly inside my chest with a devilish Brit at my heels.

The beach isn't far off the large deck, and I take the small staircase down, my feet sinking a bit when I hit the sand. At first I wobble, squeaking a bit, but right myself before he can touch me.

His fingers barely skim the back of my arm.

His breath warms the back of my neck.

"No!"

"Run, love." That hungry timbre causes my walls to clench, and my nipples to throb. "I love a good chase."

"Have fun trying!" I yell back, pushing my legs to go faster. My eyes are fixed on the water's edge; I'm going to dive in and swim a bit out but stop when my feet touch something soft.

Looking down, I'm standing on a large blanket surrounded by lit torches and a small speaker. The notes coming through it are soft, sounds like Bossa Nova, and I'm gasping—not understanding.

"Told you I'd catch you," Callum croons low, his arms wrapping around me from behind. "Now, I think you owe me a reward."

"Callum, what's—"

"Dance with me."

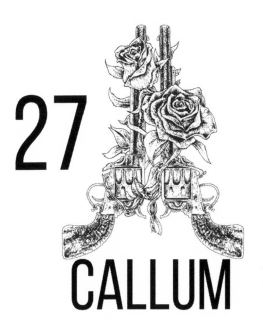

27
CALLUM

S HE'S SOFT IN my arms. Pliant and sweet, and I pull her in closer.

With her back to my front, I sway us in tune with the sensual cadence of the music playing. This feels good; having her lithe body move against me is a sinful experience that both sends you to heaven while condemning you to hell.

Heaven for her beautiful soul.

Hell for the wrath our world will face after we leave Brazil.

I've bloody condemned us both.

The music changes and a well-known song begins to play. It's the original version, the words sung in Portuguese about a beautiful girl walking by and I can't help but compare the woman in my arms to her.

Everyone she passes turns their head. You can't help but to feel enamored with her mere presence.

Twirling her about, I extend my arm all the way and then curl it back, this time bringing us chest to chest. I hold her closer. My face lowers to hers and I can't stop myself from skimming that mouth—from tasting the little keening sound that escapes her. "I need you, my Venus. Can I keep you?"

Not that she has much of a choice since I'll chase her to the ends of the earth if I have to. I'll spend my life convincing this treasure that the only man who can cherish her perfection is the man holding her.

Only me. Always me.

"Callum, I..." I don't hear anything else. Not after the breathy way she said my name and the subtle shift in her thighs, the rising pink on her cheeks at my question and all its implications.

How can such a simple request bring out the most delicious responses in her?

So decadent. So inviting.

It seals her fate and mine. There is no going back for either of us.

She's mine. In this life and every reincarnation, we're granted.

Fuck the past, her family, and the circumstances keeping us apart. The bad timing.

Whatever deity my Venus believes in screwed her with a man like me, but I'd never let her go. What we are—this insanity—I have no doubt that it'll always be.

This heat. The throbbing fucking yearning to always be near her is all-consuming—it dominates my senses—and nothing short of my cock buried deep within her tight walls will ever be enough. I crave the connection. I need her—just her.

No more waiting.

Cupping the back of her neck with one hand, I skim my lips up her throat, tipping her body back to gain better access. We don't stop swaying, touching, but her needy moan is my undoing when I nip her collarbone.

That sound is precious. I want more of it.

Standing us both upright, I lay my forehead against hers. "You haven't answered me, love."

"You already know my response," she whispers immediately, looking up at me from beneath long lashes.

"Do I?"

"Yes."

"Say it, Aliana. I need to hear the words."

"I'm yours."

Before she can take her next breath, my mouth slants over hers in a possessive kiss. This kiss isn't gentle. It can't be. Those two words have destroyed the last bit of sanity within me and bound my body at her feet.

I need to possess her just as she does me.

"Fuck, sweetheart. Can't get enough." Aliana's mouth parts on a moan at my confession while my grip on her neck tightens; I tilt her head back while my tongue slips inside and explores the unique taste that is solely hers. Madness grows within. My hunger is uncontrollable, and I revel in the little sounds she makes when I nip her plump lips or the breathy sigh when our tongues touch.

Everything about her was designed by God himself to bring a man like me to his knees. Her unexplainably divine taste sets every molecule of my DNA ablaze.

I'm hard. Throbbing.

Dragging my teeth down her plush bottom lip, I pull back. Her breathing matches mine, labored, and we wear matching grins. "Feel like taking a little dip with me?"

"Yeah."

"Good girl." One last bite to the abused flesh and I release her, taking a step while those hypnotizing brown eyes stay on me. She watches me toe off my shoes and then remove my vest top and shorts, letting them land somewhere beside me. I'm naked. Nothing covering my body, and I love the way she watches.

Hooded eyes. Lip caught between her teeth. Chest rising rapidly.

"Strip for me."

"W-what?" Her blush is endearing, but right now I want to explore the side of her that's equating me to her next meal, that hungry little minx I see beneath the surface but has never been given the chance to play. To be herself.

"You heard me, sweetheart." Turning my back to her, I move down toward the water. "Strip."

I don't wait for her. Instead, I step into the warm ocean behind my home in Rio and let the waves lap at my feet. There's shuffling behind me, a very low curse or two, but then she's standing beside me and reaching for my hand.

"I trust you." The words are spoken so low I almost miss them, and each syllable makes me feel a hundred feet tall. An arsehole like me doesn't deserve her, but I'll worship this woman like no one can or will ever get the chance to.

"And I promise to always be worthy of such a gift."

"Then show me, Callum. Show me what it means to be yours."

Without another word, I bring her hand to my lips and place a chaste kiss across every knuckle and tip of her fingers before walking us into the ocean. The waves are slow tonight, just a gentle rocking that moves—pushes us—against the current and the deeper we go, the closer to me she gets.

We wade through until the water laps across her hard nipples, the tight peaks highlighted by the moon.

"So fucking beautiful." Even in the moonlight, I can make out the light contrast of pink across her cheeks. "Don't be embarrassed, my Venus. You're above everything and everyone; the world will always bow at your feet."

"You make me feel that way." One tug and she's back against me, but this time with her legs around my waist. Her pussy is right against my thickness—she's rubbing herself. "Make me feel alive."

"I'm going to give you the world."

"All I need is you." Two warm hands cup my face, her lips hovering on mine. Her smile is sweet, but it's the glassiness in her eyes that makes me pause. I don't like it. Her tears cut me, but before I can ask, I'm silenced with a kiss that robs me of my senses. All I feel, hear, and understand is her. Her body. Her noises.

"Motherfuck, sweet girl."

"Always you," Aliana moans low, shifting in my hold. Her pussy slides against me, and on the second grind, her tiny entrance nuzzles the head of my cock. She's slick, and it's not the water. "I need you to know that…"

"Tell me."

"I love you."

Three words. Eight letters.

They undo me. They express so much and not enough.

Moving a hand to her hip, I keep her poised above me, the tip of my cock just within her entrance while fisting her shorter hair. The soft strands give me a good grip, and I tilt her head slightly.

Our eyes meet, green on soulful brown. "There are three things I need you to understand, Aliana. You agree, and I'll fuck you like the perfect doll you are." She nods, her bottom lip trembling, her hips trying to gyrate. "First; no more lies or secrets. Don't ever put yourself in danger like this again…*understood?*"

"Yes."

"Two; I need you with me."

She's nodding, yet her lips frown a bit. "I'll need a little time."

"Fair enough, but it will be soon."

"Really? You'll wait for me to settle everything?"

"Aye."

"Thank you," she breathes out, her legs around my waist flexing. That pretty little mouth smiling is dangerous for my sanity—showcases just how innocent she is. *My life now revolves around your happiness.* "It won't be long. Promise."

"Good girl."

"And number three?" Her tone is sweet, but I notice the subtle winding of her body. She tries to rub herself against my swollen head. *Or maybe she's the devil disguised in the one form meant to subdue me.* Aliana can go from angel to seductress without effort. As simple as breathing, and I'll reward her.

I want to hear her.

"And three…" I snap my hips and in one fluid motion bury myself deep. One thrust and we are flush, her cunt spasming around me while a throaty moan slips past parted lips. Wet. Fucking. Heat. She's tight and soft, and my cock swells to almost the point of pain. "*Christ,* I love you."

Her eyes close, a lone tear falling down her cheek. "Look at me."

"You…I—"

"Look at me, Aliana," I growl, pulling out slowly—dragging every ridge and inch against her pulsing walls. "Open those gorgeous eyes and see me." They open, hooded and full of desire. "There's my perfect girl." I drive back in and then out. And again, all while holding her stare. Our rhythm is slow, drawing out our pleasure. "The last thing I need you to know is that you've owned me since the night we met. You're an obsession, my need to breathe, and the one thing that's always right in my world. I love you, Miss Rubens. I'm yours."

"Oh God," her walls constrict, her hands finding purchase in my hair while I fuck her nice and slow. The water laps around us, her body so needy, and I make sure every stroke rubs her clit against my pelvis. "I've needed this. You."

"You have me."

"No. More." It's a whimper; she's thrashing in my hold now. "Love me fully and without holding back."

"Are you sure?"

"Please." Again she clenches, and I hiss, my fingers tightening on her hips, digging in hard enough to leave a small smattering of bruises behind visible in the morning. Another mark, and a rush of pleasure strikes down my spine. My next thrust is harder, forces her body out of the water. "*Fuck*, just like that. Callum, I need you to let go and make me whole."

I nip her lip for that, breathing hard. What she's offering is…*Christ.* "Our first time should—"

"Be what we both need. I won't break."

"I love you, beautiful."

"I love you, too."

No further words are exchanged as I carry her out of the water, her warm body wrapped around mine. Cock deep, I pause every few steps to bounce her a few times. Just to take the bloody edge off.

The blanket I'd put out for us to talk on is my target. The soft material will protect her from the sand below, because she's going to get exactly what she asked for. I want to claim her like an animal.

"Are you sure?" I ask a final time, and I receive another of her sweet grins while her hands wander across my shoulders and to the middle of my back where she sinks her nails in. It stings a bit, the cutting grip, but that only enhances the pleasure her pussy gives with each rhythmic pulse. I pull out, gritting my teeth as I try to fight back my natural impulse, that testosterone-fueled need to make her forget everything but me. My touch. My lips. My cock. "Say it. Tell me what you need."

"You. Only you."

"Fuck, baby girl," I growl, slamming back inside her tight cunt. She's gripping me, nearly choking my cock while goose bumps break out across her sun-kissed skin—while sweat and water drip down each muscled plane of my body as I fuck an imprint of my girth into her walls.

This perfect girl is my fantasy come to life. A distraction I welcome and crave; God himself couldn't pull me from tasting—chasing this piece of forbidden fruit served on a golden platter—and claiming her for myself.

She's beautiful and delicate; no taller than five foot one with raven locks and brown eyes with just a hint of green in the irises that watch me beneath long lashes. Those hooded orbs look at me with hunger—a starving need that pushes my own desire to a near manic state. Each thrust pushes her deeper into the blanket on the sand, the salty mist of the sea cooling our heated skin.

My Venus is too sweet for an arsehole like me. But fuck us both if I'm not riding her rougher than I should. Her cherry-red lips part, but no sound follows. Her chest rises rapidly while those sinful thighs around my waist tremble.

"You feel so good, love. Too good." At my words she cries out, her back arching and I take the invitation, wrapping my lips around her right nipple and nipping the budded flesh. It throbs against my tongue, her soft skin breaking out in goose bumps. "The perfect mixture of dirty and sweet."

I punctuate the last word with another hard thrust, but no matter the force, she follows my lead, grinding against me. Thrust for thrust. Bathing my cock in her juices, the wetness sliding from the tip to base and then down to my balls. I can feel each drip. I smell us, and the heady scent mixed with the soft ocean breeze is intoxicating.

There's no cooling the inferno this woman writhing against me has created.

There's no ignoring the curves pinned beneath me. How good she feels, and I'm powerless to stop or gather a single rational thought. Not a bloody one.

But then again, this is a problem of her making from the moment our eyes met.

"You wanted this. You wanted me," I hiss out, neck straining as another rush of wetness slides down my length. "Fuck, you dirty girl. I can feel how much you like this."

"Please." Lightning strikes somewhere behind us, and a light drizzle begins to fall from the sky, however, all I can give a single fuck about at this moment is her moans and the way she claws at my flesh. Trying to pull me closer. Rubbing her tits against my chest while the walls of her pussy massage my length. *Motherfuck*, she feels good. "Callum, I'm so close." Her whimper sends a shiver down my spine; I close my eyes as a rough groan rumbles up my chest. "Please...I need—"

"I know." It's the only thing I understand at the moment. Her need to come becomes one with her need for me, and together it creates a heady feeling I revel in. "Just feel me, gorgeous. Let go."

Those thighs cradling me tremble—tighten—and I respond with

another brutal snap of my hips before pulling back just enough so the bulbous tip rests against her tight entrance. From tiny hole to clit, I rub the length up and down her pussy twice, before sinking in to the hilt. Then again, I do this until she's angry and glaring, trying to keep me inside with the use of her legs.

Legs that now cross at the ankle at the base of my spine.

"Why are you—"

"Silence." Her heavy-lidded eyes widen, the warm brown irises focusing on me while small tremors rock her body. Not in fear, but want. In a desperation that makes me shiver. "We're going to play a quick game of questions, and for each honest answer I'll give you a reward."

"Are you insane?"

"Yes." And just because I need to watch those eyes roll back, I grab her hands and place them over her head while my hips punch forward. For the count of thirty seconds, I fuck her harder than I should, the sound of skin slapping merging with the night, and right when her mouth opens on a silent scream, I pull out. She's on the precipice, hanging between frustration and nirvana. "First question—"

"My father." Her chest heaves and eyes close. "I'm here because of my father and the money the statue is worth."

"Good girl." Leaning down, I kiss her mouth softly while grinding down against her clit. "Second question: why you?"

Aliana's back arches, hip fighting my hold. I'm keeping her on the edge, but not giving her what she needs. "He trained me to steal because I'm small enough to hide well."

Her response infuriates me, but I keep my ire in check. It's not directed at her, and she won't pay for the arsehole's idiocy. He'll pay with his life. Everyone involved will bleed at her feet.

"Third: why are you doing it?"

"Because he's threatening two people I love."

"Thank you," I growl out before pulling back, flipping her onto all fours, and burying myself deep. She screams at the sudden movement, but that quickly becomes a whimper when I grip her hair, curling the short strands around my fingers. Then, her arse rises higher as my other hand takes possession of her hip. I'm yanking her against me on every thrust, forcing my cock so deep she's clawing at the blanket while her cries fill the night. "I'm here now, Aliana."

"I trust you."

"And I'll live for you." Each punishing stroke brings her closer to the edge, but my beauty needs more. A little harder, and I lower my body over her—fuck her into the blanket with the shoreline a few feet away. "Come for me."

My hand slips between us, my cock pounding hard, but when a single digit grazes her clit, she tenses. From head to toe, she doesn't move, her breath caught in her throat.

I pump harder, feeling the plump globes of her arse jiggle while a low whine builds. Another harsh tremor overtakes her form and I take in the goose bumps on her skin and the glistening of sweat, the way her hair sticks to the side of her face.

She's never looked more beautiful. *Mine.*

"Baby, I—"

"Come for me." With my lips at her ear, I nuzzle just below as two fingers press on her trembling bundle of nerves. She curses, strains against me, but when my teeth clamp down on her neck and hold, she comes. Wave after wave passes through, and I feel her pleasure as if it were my own. Her walls milk me. Pull me in deeper. "Fuck, sweetheart. Your pussy feels so good."

"*God.*" It's a short gasp, she shudders and cries, her hips pumping against mine, but when she whispers a keening, *I love you* there's no holding back.

"Son of a bitch," I hiss and let go of her neck, my hips flush to her asscheeks. I'm held captive, unable to so much as breathe, while she pulls every last drop from my cock with nothing but the never-ending aftershocks of her own orgasm. "Just like that, Venus. You beautiful little treasure."

She doesn't respond. My girl looks so tired.

Instead, I cuddle up close while turning us slightly, my cock resting deep within her walls. We're a mess; sweaty and breathing hard but stay like that until her breathing evens out. And I close my eyes too, not to sleep but to enjoy her just like this.

No outside world.

No commitments.

No familial ties.

I need you home with me, Venus.

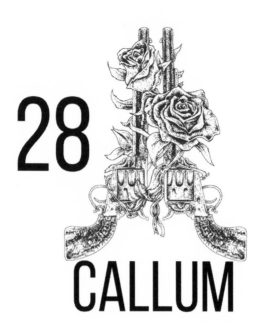

28

CALLUM

"**A**GAIN, ALIANA. Aim for the middle."

"It's harder than it looks," she grumbles two days later while staring at the target set up near the back of our property. *What's mine is hers.* Forty-eight hours where I kept her my prisoner, my personal toy—where I pulled orgasm after orgasm from her lithe body, and then licked every drop. Her pussy is the sweetest fruit, and I can't help but want more. All of her. "Quit laughing!"

"Breathe."

"You breathe." Her attitude is quite adorable, but she's too tense —afraid and avoiding the giant elephant in the room as if it were the plague reborn. I haven't asked about the theft after that first night; I've let her stew in her thoughts while silently letting her know I'm here when she's ready.

The tick of the clock is her enemy, though. Tomorrow we leave, and I'm adamant about two things with a bonus stipulation: I'm going to destroy her father, and she has a month to settle her affairs stateside while not complaining about the added security.

This isn't up for negotiation.

We ran through that road already: where I gave in, and it got her here.

So much could've gone wrong had Giannis not spoken to me. Moreover, had I not sent in Giannis's boyfriend and Kray, they would've been caught and dumped inside of a Brazilian jail cell where so much could've gone wrong before I'd been notified.

That piece of shit she calls *Dad*, wouldn't have done anything to help her. Of that, I am one hundred percent sure.

For his part, though, Mr. Martin kept his expression neutral when his boyfriend helped them get out unseen—or worse, arrested. Aliana didn't recognize him or Kray standing guard not too far from them while paid rioters distracted the military guards that night.

"Again."

"Why is it so easy on TV?" She squints her right eye, trying to focus. "What aren't you teaching me?"

I take a step forward, and she freezes.

Silly girl doesn't understand that I'm not mad at her. Never her.

My ire is directed at her father and his pig-shit schemes involving Aliana.

"Relax." Moving in behind her, I raise her arms a little higher and then anchor a hand at her hip, showing her how to keep a better center of gravity. Because while shooting is an art form, making the gun an extension of you is important. The more you tense up, the harder your reaction will be to the recoil.

There's a difference between locking your arms and being afraid.

"Easy for you to say," she complains, but lets me manipulate her into position. We stay like that for a few seconds, letting her get used to the weight and feel of the custom Glock in her hands. "Can you count me down?"

"Aye."

"Start at five."

"Five." She exhales roughly. "Four." She stretches her neck from side to side. "Three. Two." Aliana locks her arms and nods. "One."

Her finger on the trigger pulls, unloading the first and then second shot, each one missing the center target, but she does hit the paper. The next one moves into the man's torso, just barely hits his left side, but that shot is better than anything she's done today.

"Good. Now pay attention to that last shot, do you see how close you are to the chest area?

"Yeah."

"So what do you need to do to fix that?"

"Adjust my aim?"

"Are you asking me?"

"No." Her voice is firm, more secure, and I hide my smile behind a kiss to the back of her head. "I need to adjust and refocus."

"Correct." I drop my hold on her and take a few steps back. "You got this."

"I got this." Aliana tilts her head a bit to the side and shifts, a minute movement, before retaking the position I taught her. This time, I admire her posture and countdown to her next shot. It takes twenty-seven seconds for the finger on the trigger to jerk, firing off a shot that hits the target right at the center of his chest. "Oh my God!"

"Good girl." Her head snaps in my direction. The grin on her face is wide and holds so much pride. "That was an amazing shot, love."

"I did it." So much awe in her voice.

"You did."

"Again?" My answer to her question is a nod, and she turns, retaking her position, but this time for fun. She won her reward, and I waited patiently for her to finish—emptying the clip—before taking the gun and placing it on the ground.

I have her in my arms before my Venus can run, her legs around my waist and my mouth on hers before she can squeal.

The lightweight dress she's wearing gives me easy access, and so does the lack of knickers. Within seconds I have her back against a large tree, my swim shorts hanging mid-thigh, and my cock poised at her entrance.

She's wet. So slick.

I drag my teeth down her chin and to the base of her throat. "You did so good, my Venus. So proud of you."

"Thank you," she whimpers, arching back to give me better access. She's trying hard to move against me, but I keep her movements limited. There's no space between her body and mine. Not that I make her wait long; I quickly bury myself deep and reclaim her lips. "Baby."

That's her new thing. She's been calling me that since the first night, and I like it more than I should. It's quickly becoming an obsession; see how many times a day I can get her to call me that.

"Just feel me, sweetheart." My hips punch upward, bouncing her on my cock while I slip a hand behind her back to protect her from the bark. This is rough and fast, my punishing strokes not giving her a second of respite—bringing her to the edge quickly with one of her weaknesses.

She likes to be taken. To be manhandled and fucked rough, to be used for my pleasure.

A vicious circle.

I love to watch her break, apart and she enjoys my pleasure in the act.

"So tight, Venus. Precious little cunt," I growl, forcing myself deeper with each stroke. And she takes it with a smile, that sexy grin that tells me she's close and so fucking sensitive—her walls clenching.

Bringing a hand to her dress, I yank on the top and bare her breasts to me. They jiggle with each stroke, the tight tips a dusky rose that make my mouth water. Lowering my head, I suck one between my teeth and flick my tongue, timing each tease with my strokes before biting down.

"Oh my fuck!" she yells out suddenly, caught off guard by the sudden pleasurable pain. Her orgasm is hard and fast, striking me like lightning, and pulls the come from me without mercy.

"Bloody hell." Another deep stroke, and I hold myself deep inside her. I don't care if she gets pregnant. The bastard side of me wants that too. To have all of her. To see her grow round with my child.

Is it wrong? I give no fucks.

Is it too soon? Don't care.

Once that thought takes root, I see it behind closed lids. Again, I pull out and slam back in, and it's almost too much. *Christ.* The things she makes me want—all of this wasn't in the cards for me, but now I'd kill anyone who tries to break what God himself can't.

Slowly, I regain my composure. My breathing returns to normal, and I open my eyes to see her soft face smiling at me.

"Hi."

"Hello, love." Aliana's hair sticks to her, and I push it back, caressing the soft skin of her cheek. "Want to shoot some more or go relax in the pool?"

"How about we relax in the pool for a bit and later come back for another lesson?"

"You look like there's something else you want to say."

A lovely shade of pink grazes her cheeks. "There is."

"Go ahead, sweetheart. You can tell me anything."

Aliana takes in a deep breath and lets it out slowly, her shoulders straightening back. "I know I messed up by not coming to you, but I promise it won't happen again. Being with you makes me happy, Callum. Truly happy, and I don't want to lose this over a family that doesn't care about me."

"I'm not going anywhere, but I do appreciate those words." I peck her mouth softly. "Am I angry? Yes…" she goes to say something, but I nip her bottom lip and shake my head "…but not at you. What your father did is not something I'll let go of. I'm warning you now that he will face my wrath, but I do it because I love you. What he did is unforgivable."

"I'll accept whatever your terms are for going home, but I need time. There's my job and school and lastly, my biggest worry—"

"Your brothers?"

"Yes."

"Has he hurt them?"

"Once." Aliana's eyes gleam with unshed tears, and that hits me in the chest. *He'll pay for those tears.* "Dad closed them in the basement of the house for a week. They were ten and twelve at the time, and all because I refused to sneak into another politician's office and take a file he wanted."

My poor girl.

"I'll get them out of the country too."

At once, those brown eyes widen. "You will?"

"Aye."

"I'm so lucky to have met you, Callum. I'm so grateful—"

"Never thank me for taking care of what's mine, love. I'm honored to do so until my last breath."

"How about we grow old together instead?"

"You have my word." And then I kiss her, slow and sweet, while my cock hardens inside her soft heat.

"Again?" She giggles, yet I don't miss the clenching of her walls, or the slight flush traveling from her face to the top of her breasts.

"Always."

"THANK YOU FOR COMING TODAY," I SAY A WEEK AFTER BRAZIL, entering the room and taking my seat at the head of the table. It's weird in a way to have Casper to my right, but he's made up his mind and his sights are set on Boston with a feisty brunette currently giving him the cold shoulder. My father and his are also in on this meeting as is Archie, who'll be staying to work as my third-in-command. The job of my right is going to someone else, someone stateside at the moment. "I know this is short notice, but I'd like to set my plans in motion before the end of the month."

"No problem at all," Mauro Collado says, extending a hand from across the table. His grip is strong and expression neutral, not scared, but I notice the way he takes in the room. Everyone's position. "We are excited for this new venture."

"We?" Casper asks, brows furrowed.

"My brothers are also a part of the operation, Mr. Jameson." He chuckles a bit as if remembering something humorous. "I'm the brains, while they're a bit trigger happy."

"Good to know in case I ever need some hired assistance."

"They'd take it as an honor, Mr.—"

"Cut that out, mate. I'm Callum to you, and he's Casper."

"Understood. Gracias." He has a woman to his right, very serious and leaning toward him. I catch the glint of a ring on her hand. *She's the wife.* "The file, mi amor?" Without answering, she slides it over and he hands it to me.

At this point, it's all a formality to the people inside the room, but it doesn't change my plans.

"Do you have copies?"

"I'm sorry, I—"

"It's okay." Archie anticipates and holds a hand out to me; I pass the file and he rushes over to the copier inside the room. While he's there, I pour myself a cuppa and offer one to the others around the table. "Please, help yourselves."

"We need one of those." Collado takes the carafe and serves his wife and then himself, fixing each cup to their liking. Casper follows after, his like mine without sugar, and then sits back.

I can almost see the questions swirling in his head. He's looking at the new office inside of the three-story warehouse with construction workers just outside these doors outfitting the space. There will be a showroom, a testing facility, and then this floor which overlooks everything and will be used as office space.

One for myself.

The other for sales staff.

"You've been busy," my cousin says after a while, his smirk in place. "Holding out, too."

"Just a different perspective, is all."

"Here you go, sir." Archie places the main copy in front of me and then goes around the table handing one out to each person sitting around the conference table.

"Thanks, mate." Everyone but the Collados and I look at the contract. A few times, the three other Jameson heads snap up and look at me, their smiles growing wider the closer to the bottom they get. This isn't a complicated agreement; Mauro is the supplier while I'll distribute with a seventy/thirty split that suits us both. I'm going to showcase each piece and meet with different nations on a mass production end goal.

I take on the more dangerous side, so I take the heavier cut.

But more important than money, everything is done above board and legal.

No hiding. No small-time sales. No random searches.

I want it all.

I'm going to supply armies before they go to war. I'm going to play devil's advocate.

I'll design and he builds each piece; the new production location is being kept under wraps from the public and on a small private island off the coast of Spain.

"Are you shitting me?" That's the first thing Casper says after putting his copy down. He's sitting back, relaxed, but I see the interest. "That's quite an ambitious goal."

"Aye." I mimic his relaxed posture, bringing the cup to my lips for a sip. "But doable and very profitable while everything else stays the same. The drugs and hot electronics will continue to run through the UK via containers and into the Port of Miami, the latter of which will still be heading to Central and South America—our agreement with Thiago stands. The clientele he brings to the table is very valuable."

"And you've already contacted a British general?"

"I have. They're interested in what I have to offer after sending an email with the schematics and video demonstration."

"All in favor," Casper calls out, not that it matters as this is a done deal, but it's to prove a point.

All three Jamesons look at me with pride. "Aye."

I nod and then look over at Archie. "Please bring in the suitcase."

"Yes, sir."

"We are very happy to do business with you, Callum. We've brought you a gift to celebrate."

At Mauro's words, my eyes snap to his and I tilt my head. "I do enjoy gifts."

He laughs, and the others in the room follow suit. His wife, though, lifts up a large purse from beside her and pulls out a box. Nothing too big, but the wrapping is cheeky with a *Happy Birthday* theme. Mauro holds it out to me. "We, my family and I, hope you enjoy this."

"Thank you." Taking the box, I undo the wrapping and open the top. What lays inside, nestled within a soft piece of fabric, is a thing of beauty. The two guns inside are all black, heavy but when picked up and examined, the detail is on the powder coat finish. Desert Eagles with tiger stripes, the two tones of black—shiny and matte—working together flawlessly. "This is beautiful. How did you know?"

"That you like big cats?"

"Yes."

"You mentioned feeding a tiger the first time we talked, and I ran with the idea."

"I'm touched." Picking up one in each hand, I test their weight and grip. "Very sleek and comfortable. This is a fine piece."

"Aye," Casper agrees and holds his palm out. "I'm almost jealous."

"Wanker." Handing over one, I let my father and uncle check out the other. Archie walks in then with my own gift. He places the case in front of Mauro. "That's the agreed amount, and an extra ten percent to enjoy a weekend on us at the hotel I've booked in Monte Carlo."

"Thank you, Callum."

"Here's to a lucrative business venture, partner."

Aliana

"**Y**OU'RE LATE," my father greets, the second I step foot inside his office. That seems to be the way he breaks the ice each time we see each other, and yet, it's his instructions I've been following. After coming home from Brazil, leaving Callum, he refused to see me until now. *Just in case you're being followed*, he claimed over the phone while demanding I send him pictures of the statue beside a newspaper showing the current date.

That's how he's kept me for three weeks.

On edge. Always wondering.

And I've never been more thankful for the protection Callum put on me. For the man who comes to Chicago once a week to spend the day, to spoil me, while helping me sort through my priorities. So far, we have a few plans in place. My conversation with Aurora is coming soon, and he knows this one will be tough for me.

She's my best friend. My constant for so many years.

I'll be patient, but I'm not waiting six months, Aliana.

Kray and Giannis seem to always be around, but the one who's made the difference for me is Lindsey. We bumped into each other at my favorite breakfast spot before work, both picking up an order of coffee and an egg, bacon, and avocado sandwich.

"You know, a dash of hot sauce on that gives it a better kick than black pepper," I said, not realizing who she was. We were by the pickup counter, side by side, when she turned her head and gave me a bright smile. "You?"

"Me." Her shoulders shook a bit from giggling. "Hi, I'm the extra Mr. Jameson requested."

"You're a personal guard?"

"Among other things, and for the right person, yes."

My brows furrowed, not liking the implication. "What's that supposed to mean?"

"Just that you're important to Giannis, and he means everything to my cousin. Then, we have my personal headache that's your main security, Kray, and then his boss. That's three people watching out for you, and with good reason, I hear."

"I'm not useless."

"Not at all. I heard through the grapevine you have a decent shot, just needs some fine tuning." Lindsey placed her hand on my shoulder, giving it a light squeeze. "Just to stay limber, of course."

The thought of going to a range and shooting made me grin, but then it dropped. Callum took my Glock after each lesson and didn't hand it over before we left. "I don't have my—"

"That's because I have it. Mr. Jameson had a last-minute adjustment made to it."

"You're serious?"

"As a heart attack."

"That would be amazing. I didn't think I'd enjoy it as much, but once I broke through the mental fog, it all clicked." Unwrapping my sandwich, I grabbed the homemade chili pepper sauce and put on more than I should. And while I didn't usually eat super spicy, this one was like crack for me. "That, and I like knowing I can protect myself. Precautions never hurt."

"Agreed." Lindsey wiggled her fingers and I handed over the bottle, smirking when she poured more than me. *"What about today after work? I know a place that's open late."*

"Sounds good."

"Good. Then let's go."

I arched a brow. "Go where?"

"To the Conte House, silly. I'm the new self-defense class instructor." At my perplexed look, she shrugged. *"The old instructor was paid handsomely to take a sabbatical so I could step in. I 'work' for the same company."*

"Well, shit."

"Exactly. So let's go." Packing her items back inside a brown bag, she nodded at my sandwich. *"Can't be late on my first day."*

"How have you been, daughter? Had a good vacation?" Dad's voice snaps me back from the memory, and it's hard, but I hold in my glare, focusing just past his head so he doesn't see the hatred that brews within me. Because I do; I hate him. "Did you take any pictures? The place I booked was..."

My attention isn't on his words. Instead, I take in the dark room with the moon glinting through the floor-to-ceiling windows. The sole source of light is coming from a desk lamp near a turned-off computer and his cigar.

There's a small sitting area behind me and to the left, while the wall right across has built-in shelves filled to the brim with books he's never probably heard of. A bar with the kind of alcohol he drinks is there, too, the glasses cleaned three times a day by his personal assistant.

"...are you listening to me?" His terse tone pulls my attention to him, and I meet his eyes for the first time since stepping inside the room. He looks tired and stressed, hair mussed, and tie undone while sweat dots his forehead. "I asked you a question."

"Repeat, please."

"I said, did you run into any problems?" Exasperated, he levels me with a glare. "Giannis wasn't very forthcoming on your time in Brazil."

"Does it matter?"

At my counter, my father slams a hand atop his desk. "Cut the fucking attitude, kid. When I ask a question, I expect an answer. Keep testing me. You know the consequences better than anyone."

"That's not necessary." Another voice, male, fills the room, and my head snaps to the dark corner of the sitting area. With little to no lighting, it's hard to make out the tall form sitting there, but the light at the end of a cigar is bright red. "She's done her part. Surpassed my expectations, to be honest."

Uneasiness settles over me. My stomach drops, and I can't stop the shaking of my hands.

"Mr. Gaspar, with all due respect, how I discipline—"

"She's not yours anymore." His words are spoken low, with ease, but the heavy implications fill me with dread and all I want to do is run out. Kray is in the building along with Lindsey, waiting for me in the main lobby, with the excuse that we're heading to dinner right after. At once, I put my hand inside my pants pocket, and find the number *3* on the old prepaid phone Lindsey insists I carry with me now. "Isn't she?"

Because it's easier to find a number in button form than on a screen from inside a purse or pocket. And now, I see how right she is. I press and after fifteen seconds, hang up, and then again, following the same pattern.

"No. I guess not, my apologies." Dad's expression is cold, unaffected. He's speaking about me as if I were an item and not his child. "But for today, I need her cooperation in the exchange. That statue has a buyer, and we made an agreement to split the profit to appease Rigo's debt."

"I don't care about the profit and consider the debt canceled. She's already proved her worth." The man moves in his seat and a second later, another lamp is turned on. It illuminates him, bathing him in a soft yellow glow, which presents just enough of his profile for me to make out his features. He seems very familiar to me. *Where have I seen him?* "My plans are larger than the bullshit statue she's been carrying around for you. This was just a preview of what she's capable of, and my wife did more than satisfy my curiosity."

"Wife?" I ask, swallowing back the bile rising. This—he can't be serious.

No. No. No. No!

"Yes, princess. We're betrothed."

My reaction to that is instantaneous; I take the artifact out of my bag and slam it atop my father's desk, glaring at him. If the damned thing cracked, I have no clue nor do I care, but my ire is mounting and for the first time, I understand how Callum can kill without remorse.

And while I don't consider myself to be a violent person and choose to pacify and de-escalate always, right now that's all out the window when all I can taste is the bitter edge of betrayal. This is a hard pill to swallow, and had I brought my Glock, I would've shot my father.

Of that I have no doubt. Right between the eyes.

"I will not marry him."

"You don't have a choice!" Dad thunders. The tumbler with a few fingers' worth of amber liquid flies past my head. It shatters upon impact, the picture frame it hit breaking too. "This isn't up for negotiation, Aliana. You will marry Mr. Gaspar or else—"

"I'm already seeing someone."

"Who?" the man asks, voice ice cold.

Before I can respond, the door is opened, and Kray walks inside. He doesn't give either of them any attention, his sole focus on me, gun drawn. "You ready to go, Miss Rubens?"

"Who the fuck are you?" comes from the governor. That man is no longer my father.

Kray's eyes turn hard; he's now looking at my father. "Callum Jameson sends his regards."

That's it. That's all he says before ushering me out while I avoid the two heated gazes on me.

They remain quiet. My guard's words still hang heavy in the air.

Callum staked his claim.

"TELL ME AGAIN WHY I'M GOING WITH YOU TO LOOK AT BRIDESMAID dresses?" I ask London while her cousin snickers beside me. We've been to three stores today, and we haven't stopped for food. They literally drag me from bed, stuff me in clothes, and make me try on dresses while my best friend's newly found cousin picks one.

Mind you, I'm not in the wedding. I'll be a guest, not because she didn't ask me to be, but because they decided to keep the numbers very small; Mariah and Aurora for London, while Javier and Casper, even though my best friend doesn't know this tiny detail.

Not like she's shared info on him either.

"Because it's easier to be objective on someone else's body." London walks around me, studying the red dress I'm in. It's an empire waist with an off-the-shoulder neckline that ends just below the knee. Very form fitting and classy, but also plain. "I feel like we're getting close, but no dice yet. Can you try the eggplant one next, please?"

My stomach is eating itself; I'm annoyed with her, but she's too sweet to get mad at. Grumbling, I take off toward the changing room while they discuss something between them.

Reaching for the zipper on my right, I lower it and slip off the garment. The hanger is next, and I place everything neatly for the salesgirl when my phone rings with *his* tone. I'm quick to pick it up before they hear or ask, moving further back into the changing area.

This area is private; a large space where you normally have someone helping you change into their gowns, but with London's selection being less extravagant, I've been given free reign. Which works, because he's Facetiming me.

"Hello, love," he says the moment I answer, that grin I love in place. Callum looks a bit tired, and I know it has to do with the new business venture the Jamesons are taking on. The last few weeks have been busy for him with extensive travel from London to Spain to Chicago, the latter for me. "Having fun?"

"No," I pout, angling the camera so he can see how little I have on. I'm in a nude, strapless bra and tiny hipsters which leave my cheeks bare. "I'm hungry, sleepy, and ready to start the next season of our show."

That's another thing we've been doing since our time is limited at the moment—something that is wearing heavy on him and me.

I'm still here while he's home, because that's what London is to me now, and while he comes to see me as often as possible—at the least a day a week—I promised Aurora I wouldn't leave yet. Not until after London's wedding, since her mind is on Boston and her cousin will take over the Chicago office. At least, until Roe's brother is older, and the kid wants to take over.

To me, it sounds like she's avoiding.

She's dodging Casper and his calls. His every attempt at communication.

"Fuck, Venus. This is a cruel punishment."

"Would you prefer me taking the view away?"

"I'd rather saw my arm off than miss this."

"That's overdramatic."

He shrugs, not the least bit embarrassed. "I stand by my truth."

"You're too cute sometimes." Callum tries to argue, but I hold a hand up and he quiets down. *Huh, so that does work.* I've seen him do it before, and those around him tend to zip it when he does. "But I wanted to discuss our show. How deep are you into the fourth season?"

We've become addicted to a horror show based in America with storylines that seem to always intertwine with a previous season. It's addicting, and our thing. We try to watch an episode together every night it's possible, and two or three when he's here between my being bent over and displayed for him.

"It's good…isn't it? And I haven't watched any without you."

"Bloody brilliant, you smart lad." My British accent sucks, and a second later he's laughing so hard, Callum snorts. "I heard that."

My sing-song mocking makes him stop, fake glare in place now. "You heard nothing."

"Yes, I did. You snorted!"

"Prove it."

"Maybe I—"

"Who you talking to, chick," Aurora asks, and my eyes widen while Callum rolls his eyes. "You've been in here a while."

"Be right out. It's Giannis."

"Giannis?" Callum gives me an almost insulted expression.

"Since when are you so close to him?" Aurora taps her fingers on the door. "You two dating?"

"No."

"Okay…" she drags out the word while Callum tries hard not to laugh "…well, I just wanted to tell you that London needs to see the eggplant dress within the next few minutes. Malcolm's on his way to steal her away for a late lunch. And yes, before you ask, I know you're hungry and getting bitchy. I'll stuff you full the second we get out of here."

"You freaking better. Your treat, too."

"Deal, but hurry up." Her feet move away from the dressing room, the sound becoming fainter and fainter until I hear nothing at all.

Leaning against the wall, I let out a sigh. "That was close."

"Tell her the only stuffing you take is from my cock."

It's my turn to snort. "Seriously?"

"Yes. My cock and nothing else."

"So possessive," I hiss low, before blowing him a kiss. "Call you later?"

"Aye. Behave."

30

Aliana

ESTINY HAS A way of showing you it can't be tampered with. You will end right where you're meant to be, and I've never been more sure of this than I am now.

The traditional wedding march fills the church and guests stand, watching a beautiful woman walk toward her future, but they're not the ones I'm focused on.

No, right now I'm watching my best friend smile and shiver as a man with a familial resemblance to Callum mouths words I can't quite make out. Anyone with a pulse can feel the electricity that flows between them.

He's her person. Her lobster.

Stubborn woman. How could she try and fight that?

"They're being fresh," Callum chuckles from his seat beside mine just one pew behind Malcolm's closest family members. Another sign that fate is a persistent, all-knowing bitch. Without our knowledge, London sat us next to each other, and it's been a blessing and a curse. I'm happy, but keeping my true emotions hidden is nearly impossible when the man I love is currently running his pointer finger across my wrist, his touch gentle. He smells so good; I'm fighting every instinct in me to lean over and kiss him.

"My guess is they kissed and made up."

"Why do you say that, love?"

London walks past us, her eyes on the man waiting for her. Malcolm sees no one but his bride. It's there in the way he walks forward before she makes it to the end of the aisle and kisses her without shame or pause. Not caring for tradition or what the priest has to say, a man who's watching them with amusement and not rebuke.

"Because I caught the sight of a hickey on her neck right before she met my questioning stare, which she's avoiding. That, and the way she shivered when he kissed her hand before taking their respective places."

"Observant little thing."

"For years, watching is all I did."

"Not anymore."

Turning my head, I meet his warm eyes and nod. "I don't need to when you've brought me back to life."

The priest chooses that moment to start the ceremony, and I face forward once again. His sermon is about love and acceptance. About opening your heart and letting go of what ails you in order to welcome what heals.

His words resonate with me.

There's so much I want to do with my life, so much to see and enjoy, but to move forward, I need to let go. My leaving Chicago is inevitable, my being with Callum is destiny, but to move past the pain I've buried deep, I need to find closure.

I'm going to speak with my parents.

Something the man beside me will not be happy about, but I need it. Their lack of communication lately—since the day in Dad's office —while welcomed—has left me thinking. I've questioned so much.

Him. Her. And how a parent could not care or hurt those they brought into the world for personal gain?

I also miss my brothers. The most I've gotten out of the two in the last few months is a message here or there with a *hello* and *we're good.*

"You okay?" Callum whispers beside me, his breath tickling my neck, and I smile. Hold back a giggle. "That serious expression on your face doesn't sit right with me. You're too pretty to frown."

"I'm okay. Promise."

"Swear?"

"I do."

"Good, because I do too."

His words had their desired effect and I blush, warm heat with this incorrigible need to smile, and I do. Ignoring the world around us and the two people saying their vows, I look over and give in to my desires:

I kiss his chin and then lay my head on his shoulder while his arm wraps around my waist, pulling me in closer. Touching. Keeping me warm. *Now, I'm home.*

"MY GORGEOUS GIRL," CALLUM CROONS AS WE SWAY TO THE MUSIC a few hours later. Most of the guests are drunk, overfed, or heading home at this point. No one's paying us a lick of attention in our corner of the room.

Malcolm and London didn't stay long themselves, and Aurora never made it to the reception.

Now, it's just us while Malcolm's family says goodbye to those walking out of the reception hall inside of Chicago's most coveted hotel. I'm tired and could eat, but leaving Callum's arms isn't something I want to do, no matter how much my feet hurt in these heels or how tight my dress is.

No one can pull me away.

"You like?" Fishing for compliments never hurt anyone, and I give him a shy smile.

"Don't give me that bashful look." He spins me out, twirling me fast twice before pulling me back in. "You and I both know you look simply ravishing."

"Say that word again? Slowly this time."

His chuckle is warm against my temple. "I quite enjoy using my accent to tempt you."

"Tempt me how?"

"You feel like getting out of here?" Another turn, and this time when I come back into his embrace, I'm tipped back. He rights me, smirk on his lips. "We're overdue for another date."

"Hmmm." I purse my lips in contemplation, making the cocky man wait. Callum doesn't like that and pokes my side with his finger. It makes me laugh, the sound a little loud, and I blush. "You suck."

"Your answer, Miss Rubens."

"Yeah."

"Good girl." Callum all but drags me out of the room using a back entrance. It leads to a long hallway that holds back-up chairs and a secondary entrance for the kitchen staff before curving left. No one's here and we walk right through, following the signs that lead to different sections of the hotel that are for staff only.

The last door we encounter, though, this one says valet parking.

"You have a car here?" I ask, following him out into the cooler night air. This time of year is enjoyable, not too cold or warm out, but the nights can nip at you. Especially in my strapless, emerald bodycon dress with a little ruching at the waist. The length is modest at just below the knees, while the fit accentuates my every curve, which the man currently keeping a firm grip on my hand has been enjoying all evening.

"A rental." I shiver and Callum removes his jacket, draping it across my shoulders. "Better, or would you rather we stop at your place so you can change?"

"I'll be fine, but you might need to carry me or buy me flip flops."

"It will be my pleasure."

"Oh, I'm sure." My eyes look toward the entrance, and an idea comes to mind. "I'll be right back."

"Where are you going?" The two men working the valet area turn toward us, the older of the two looking to reprimand, but his co-worker saves him with an elbow to the side. "Wait for me. I'll go with you."

"No need, I'm just going to the restroom right quick. Give me five."

"Okay. I'll be here." Leaning over, he pecks my lips before turning to face the two men. "Here's the ticket. Heavy tip if it's back quickly."

The younger man jumps from his seat inside the small two-person kiosk. "Yes, sir."

I leave him there and head inside, rushing to the in-house mini-store and grabbing three things before Callum comes to investigate: hotel moniker on the joggers and shirt while the flip flops are plain black. Not the sexiest outfit, but it'll do in a crunch like this.

After paying, I rush to the bathroom not far from the reception desk and nearly rip my clothes off in my haste. It feels like heaven to take them off, especially the shoes, and I nearly shove the expensive garments in the bag the attendant gave me. There's a knock on the door while I'm shimmying into the bottoms, which becomes a little harder while I tug down the shirt.

"That man is so impatient." My hair's been down all evening in soft waves down my back and I open the small clutch with me tonight and dig through for a hair tie. "Bingo!"

Quickly, I tie my hair up, check for smudges in my simple makeup, and walk out. He's standing there when I exit, and the look on his face is comical. Callum does a double take, then narrows his eyes. From head to toe, I'm inspected as he reaches for the bag with my dress and shoes inside.

"How do you look even more beautiful like this?" Not the question I'm expecting, and I giggle because words fail me. The compliments and attention and the way he's always watching is enough to drive any woman mute, but for me, it's the lack of control of my impulses.

Right now, I want to kiss him stupid outside of the hotel bathroom, but can't. One kiss wouldn't be enough for me. With him, it never is.

"You ready?" I ask instead, trying to walk past him, but Callum isn't a man to be denied. And secretly, this thrills me. His grip on my arm isn't tight yet unyielding, and I find myself being pushed against the wall by a very amused man.

Lowering his face to mine, he pauses just a few inches from my mouth. "Did you really think I'd let you walk out of this hall without stealing a kiss?"

"We can't."

"Says who?" There's no playfulness now. This is a man determined. "Who the fuck is going to stop me from showing the woman I love how important she is to me? Who's the arsehole stupid enough to try?"

"No one."

"Correct." A little closer now, he skims across once. "I'm not hiding us. That's a disservice to you and our relationship, and I won't stand for it."

"Then why sneak out of the ballroom?" Up until this moment, I didn't realize this bothered me. Yeah, it's fun to rush through long corridors with a man unafraid of the devil himself, but walking out together would've been fun too. *Is it all on him, though? I've been watching myself all night and keeping things as innocent as possible.* "Sorry, that's not entirely on you either. I've been—"

"Aliana, I do what makes you feel comfortable. My claim on you has already been established; if someone knows or doesn't, that's irrelevant to me." This time I get a peck. Small, but it sets me ablaze with want. "That, and I didn't feel like talking to anyone. We'd still be doing the bloody goodbyes that never end with Mariah and Javier, or agreeing to head out somewhere because that woman can convince a monk to snort a line or two."

"Tell me about it. She convinced me to join her for a spa day next week."

"What's so bad about that?" He looks genuinely perplexed.

"I'm going for a Brazilian."

"What day?" And just like that, he turns boyish. Almost giddy. "I'll take the day off and fly in—"

"Let's go on our date, and if you behave, I'll tell you before bed."

"Fucking trouble," Callum grumbles before kissing me. One arm wrapped around my waist, the other now cradling my neck, he slants his mouth over mine in a needy and possessive kiss. I taste the whiskey he's been drinking with a hint of cigar from when Javier pulled him outside earlier tonight. I taste him, that uniqueness that makes me weak in the knees, my lips moving as eagerly against his onslaught.

This man owns me. Knows it.

"Do we need this date?" I nip his bottom lip harshly, and I love the way his eyes flash with fire, a warning I won't heed. There's something so sexy about a man who loses control and worships you until there's nothing left but a satiated body and a sleepy grin. "We could—"

Abruptly, he releases his hold on me before taking a step back toward the opposite wall. The lack of physical contact sucks; I don't like it and neither does Callum, as a second later he picks up my hand, sliding his thumb across my knuckles. "Spending this time with you is something I need, too. I miss you, Venus. I'm ready for you to come home, but I promised to be patient while you settle your affairs and now help Aurora."

Could he be any more perfect? Those words mean more than any gift or orgasm. He wants me. To just be with me, and this time, I'm the one who kisses him. It's quick and fast, my body pressing against his on the wall, but before his arms cage me in, I pull back.

"I'm ready to leave, too." I place a tiny kiss to his chin, and then Adam's apple. "This is just until London gets back, or Aurora decides that she's staying after all."

"Because they fixed their shit?" Voice hoarse and hair a little disheveled, he's the epitome of sex and the promise of depravity.

"Yes."

"Let's hope."

"Now, that date?"

"You cheeky little thing, you." Callum winks before turning to walk away, giving my hand still in his a small tug. I follow him out the small hallway and out to the quiet lobby where a guest or two still lingers, but we don't stop to talk to anyone. Instead, we make it to the car and after making sure I'm in, he walks to his side and slides in behind the wheel.

I don't know where we're going as he peels out.

I also find myself not caring.

As I study his profile in the dim lighting and the city zooms by my window, I realize something:

This is a man I'd follow to the ends of the earth. This goes beyond fun or love. We are much deeper than that. The tether that keeps us together vibrates between us; I can almost physically feel it, and it's not something I'm going to give up for anyone.

I need to tell Aurora. I need to move to London.

"Sweetheart," I hear his voice, but it's not coming from the side he slept on last night. No. This is a few inches from my face, and it's confirmed when he caresses my cheek. "I need you to wake up for a minute or two, please."

I whimper but do as he asks while pouting. A pout he nips at. "Where are you going?"

Callum is dressed, albeit casually, but it's late out. Then it dawns on me; this is business, and I sit up, almost knocking into his forehead. "Is everything okay?"

"It is, love. I'm just meeting with Casper and Aurora at a hotel nearby."

Shifting my eyes to my bedside clock, I take in the time and look back at him with a raised brow. "You do realize it's a little after two in the morning, right? Most people are sleeping at this time."

We came home about two hours ago after spending most of the night on a private yacht cruising slowly out of Navy Pier. Lake Michigan is cool at night most days, but today the slight chill was pleasant, especially when Callum kept me close. We sat at the back of the boat with a blanket and a pint of ice cream, talking and joking. Extravagant but simple. Perfect for us.

Best date to date, and I don't know how he'll ever top it.

No one around. No guards or interruptions.

I find myself liking his version of spoiling quite a bit.

"Not for a criminal." At his words, I snap out of my memory fog and glare. "Relax, tiger. I'm just stating a fact."

"Don't call yourself that." Accurate or not, I hate the title. I view him more as a loving man, my man who has a short leash on his temper when his family is wronged. When it comes to my safety.

"Aliana, the truth is the truth no matter how we disguise it." My answer to that is to flick his forehead hard, which he doesn't like. One minute he's daring me to do it again with his eyes, and the next, I'm on my back with his hands digging into my sides. He's tickling the hell out of me; knows my weakness and uses it against me without shame. "Say sorry."

"No." I kick, squirm, and bite his arms—he's unyielding. "Stop it!"

"Say sorry."

"You'll pay for this," I say, choking on a laugh when he finds my sweet spot. The area just above my hip bones are sensitive, the one place I laugh so hard I cry. "Oh fuck!"

"Say. Sorry."

"Sorry!"

"Good girl." Lowering his body fully on mine, he kisses the few tears that fell and then the tip of my nose and lastly, places a chaste one on my lips. "I'll be back by midday tomorrow to take you out for lunch and then, I want you to meet Casper." Before I can respond, he places a finger over my lips. "Just him, no Aurora as I'll let you handle that, but I want him to know about us and who you are to me. He's my cousin—brother—and we don't hide things from each other."

"Okay." I wasn't going to deny him. Not after his mini speech last night.

Callum is right.

My father knows, and I'm sure the rest of my family does as well.

There's no need to hide, nor am I ashamed of who he is. I'm actually proud.

It's time everyone else finds out, too.

"Thank you. I'll set that up during our meeting."

"And then you'll come back?"

"I will." Lifting the sheet covering my naked body, he bites his lips while those gem-colored eyes traverse my frame. Every curve. My tattoos. He watches me with hunger before dropping the bedsheet, standing, and digging his clenching hands inside the front pockets of his pants. "You have any plans of your own?"

"There might be a nice warm bath involved and a few naughty kisses, too."

"I'll be here." With one last heated look, he turns and leaves, but before crossing the threshold, he pauses and tilts his head. "I'm going to suggest you sleep in late and enjoy the quiet, because once I get back, your screams will fill every inch of this home while your come bathes my cock."

31

Aliana

A POUNDING ON my front door wakes me up God knows what time later. It's bright out, the high beams of light filtering through the side of my curtain and illuminating the room. The next thing I realize is that Callum isn't back, and an unsettled feeling crawls under my skin.

Another knock, louder this time.

"Who the hell could be…" I trail off, scrambling off the bed as the worst-case scenario plays out in my head. There's a small stack of loungewear on a chair in the corner, and I grab whatever is at the top before running out of the room. "I'm coming!"

This time the knocking is less loud, but still as persistent. "Hurry up."

I almost trip over the bag with my clothes. *How did that end up in here?* Not that I stop to pick it up or try to remember. I stumble-jog with a little jumping thrown in as I find my balance before throwing the door open. Giannis is there, hand poised to knock again and grinning.

What the hell?

"Who's hurt?" I ask, my hand shooting out to grab his shirt. "Where's Callum?"

"That man is more than fine, but busy at the moment. It's why I'm here." I've never gone from worry to annoyance so quick in my life. "Lose the grip, Ali. I really like this shirt, and so does Dwayne. He bought it for me."

"Why are you here?" Each word is spoken slowly while I release my hold and step back, hand on the doorknob so I can slam it in his face. "Why knock like that and scare a few years off my life?"

"Callum said you might be sleeping, so I wanted to make sure you heard."

Closing my eyes, I take in a deep breath and let it out slowly. *Choking him would be bad. He's been there for me.* Looking at him again, I nod and take it as that. He's an idiot sometimes. "Okay. And why are you here to wake me up?"

"Because your boy toy said to do so. We're getting a mani-pedi!"

Sweet man. *I bet this has to do with me hating the green on my toes to match my dress last night.*

"WHAT DO YOU THINK OF PURPLE FOR MY TOES?" GIANNIS ASKS TWO hours later, sipping on a coffee while the nail tech files his nails. "It's my favorite color."

"Depends on the shade, but I much prefer white on feet. I haven't seen a single person it doesn't look good on."

"True, but Dwayne likes bright colors."

"What about teal?"

"Teal could work." He's pensive for a moment, then takes out his phone and sends out a text. It chimes back within seconds, and Giannis's smile is sweet. The way his eyes brighten is adorable. "He approves, just asks that it's on the darker spectrum than pastel."

The lady doing his nails stops and looks at him. "I have the perfect shade. Just came in a few days ago."

"Perfect. I'd…"

The cell in my wristlet alerts me to a text message and I take it out, opening the app. It's from Callum, and I frown.

I'm sorry. Still with Casper. Impromptu business meeting with his father on a video call. ~Callum J.

I don't like it, but I'm not mad. He needs to talk to them and in the meantime, I'll spend a little time getting pretty for him.

Before I can tell him that, though, I get another text.

I miss you. I'd rather be taking that bath with you now than listening to these two talk. ~Callum J.

My fingers fly across the keyboard on the screen.

Raincheck for later, Mr. Jameson? And by the way, thank you for the lovely surprise. Although, if you ever send him to wake me up again, I will shoot you. ;) ~Venus

Three dots appear. Then pause. Appear again. And pause.

So violent, my Venus? I'm hurt. ~Callum J.

You will be if he ever pounds on my door like a maniac again. Idiot scared me half to death. ~Venus

Do you need me to scare him? I can make him pee his trouser's in penance. ~Callum J.

Laughter bubbles out, loud at that, and Giannis looks over at me with a cautious expression. More so when the more I look at him, the harder I laugh. There's no doubt in my mind that Callum would do it, scare the hell out of him, but I'm not *that* mean.

Not this time, but if he ever does it again… ~Venus

Noted. ~Callum J.

"Why do I get the feeling that my life's been threatened?" Giannis asks, leaning over to try and read the message thread. My response is to flick his nose. "Ouch! That stung."

"Then don't be nosy." The nail tech finishes massaging my feet and cleans the nail bed in prep for polish. She holds up two bottles:

one that is just stark white, while the other has a bit of gold glitter to it. "Always go with the sparkly."

"Good choice."

Turning my face toward Giannis, I raise a brow. "What's next on the agenda? Nails will be done in the next ten minutes, and I'm getting hungry."

"Lunch? There's that new gastro pub on South Port."

"Works for me. I'd kill for a burger and beer."

"Let's do it, then."

Heading to lunch with Giannis next. Want me to send something over? ~Venus

I watch the screen for a few minutes, but no reply comes through.

Unusual, but I don't pay much attention to it. He's with his family and they need to talk.

He'll get back to me the second he can.

Is everything okay? ~Venus

That's the last message I sent Callum around four in the morning, fifteen minutes before sleep pulled me under. We didn't talk again after our exchange while I was getting my nails done. Not so much as a smoke signal from him, and the more time passed, the worry grew.

And grew.

It grew to the point that I called Aurora under the pretense of returning her calls from the day before. Not that she gave me much to go on; Aurora's attention was on her guest, not us, and after a few minutes of stilted conversation, she promised to call in an hour or two.

She didn't. Hasn't.

So, I sent him another text. No answer.

Another one around ten at night. Nothing.

Watching my phone's screen became a necessity, and I did so, until I couldn't stave off my sleep. That's why I'm uncoordinated when my doorbell rings and the app chimes through the kitchen's hub and then my phone. The time right now is irrelevant to me, and as if in déjà vu, I once again scramble and rush to the door, not worrying about how I look.

All I want is to see him. To know he's okay before I punch him for scaring me like this.

However, the person on the other side is not someone I expected to see today.

I don't want to see him.

"What are you doing here?"

"Is that how you say hello to your father?" He's looking at me with disdain, something that makes him grimace as his face has been at the end of someone's fury. Black eye. Busted lip. His clothes are disheveled and he smells a bit, as if he forgot to put on deodorant and spent a few hours under the hot sun. "Well?"

"Why are you here?" My ponytail sometime during the night became undone, and I take the tie out and twist my shorter locks into a low bun. "We have nothing to say to each other."

"That's where you're wrong." Pushing past me, he enters my home and heads straight for the fridge. Inside he finds a frozen bag of peas and after removing his jacket and rolling up his dirty sleeves, he puts the cold vegetables against his face. "Fuck, this shit hurts."

"Again, why are you here?" My phone is on the counter, and I press number one this time, Callum's digits. Lindsey and Kray are out of town for a few days, taking advantage of Callum being here, to spend some time alone. Lowering the volume, I wait for the connect sign to come on, but nothing.

It never connects. As if he's out of service range.

What the hell is going on?

I try Giannis next. The same. No call goes through.

"If you're calling Mr. Jameson, he's busy at the moment."

"Busy?"

"Are you deaf now as well? What part are you not—"

"Get out."

Ignoring my request, Dad walks to my sofa and sits back, looking at me with humor in his eyes. "Tell me, hija. Why aren't you at work today?"

"That's not your concern."

"Are you ill?"

"Leave."

"Is that why you weren't there for Aurora? Your best friend?" The blood in my veins freezes at his words. Literally turns to ice. It's almost as if my body shuts down and time slows; I sit down in the nearest chair, hands shaking as panic seizes my body. "You don't know, do you? This is priceless."

"What do you—"

"Aurora's gone missing, Aliana. Taken right outside of the Conte House, and she's God knows where now. Not that I care." He shrugs before stretching his jaw, wincing a bit. Whoever did this to him got him good—I'd thank them if I could function. *Is this why Callum has gone missing? But why not tell me himself?* "Better for me if the little bitch and her new family are far from you. The Jamesons have cost me enough trouble with the Gaspar's boss."

"How can you be so cold?" Tears fall from my eyes and my chest aches, the pain intensifying. "You disgust me."

"I'd watch that mouth if I were you. The Gaspar men don't tolerate that in their women. Then again, maybe that's what you need. Someone to smack the rebellion out of you."

"Leave," I say, voice low and shaky. "Leave, and don't come back."

"Fine. Have it your way." My father stands and after tossing the soiled pack of peas on the floor by my feet, he grabs his jacket and slips it on. He fixes his lapel, buttons the front, and walks over with the calmness of a monk. For a moment or two, he stands there silently; I feel his angry gaze on me, but then two fingers appear in my line of sight and my face is tipped upward.

The asshole smiles down at me, happy in my misery.

"I wish you weren't my father."

"And yet, you're stuck." Those same two fingers tap my cheek hard. "You will marry Flavio Gaspar and save your family, Aliana Camila Rubens. You will not fight me on this. You will spread your legs when he wishes. And you will continue to steal what we decide."

"So that he doesn't kill you? What does he know that you don't want getting out?" I strain my head back in time and he misses, the slap meant for my face catching nothing but air. He tries again, but my front door slams open and Giannis rushes in with Dwayne in tow.

"I was just leaving."

"You do that, Mr. Rubens," Giannis steps between us, and I catch sight of a small line of stitches over his right eyebrow. There's also a wrap around his wrist. *Did someone come after him, too?* "Your driver is waiting outside."

"Listen to him. Leave." Dwayne takes a step closer to me as well. "It's the smart move, and you know it."

"Of course. I'll be on my way." Dad eyes Dwayne and rethinks his attempt to lean down and kiss my cheek. Any other time, it'd be funny to watch him bend and stand like a scared puppet, but I'm shaking hard in my seat, gripping each armrest tightly. "We'll be in touch, Aliana. Just remember what I said: you are a Rubens, and the weight of making amends lies on your shoulders alone."

The door closes after him a few seconds later. We remain quiet.

That is, until I get up and run to the bathroom, emptying the liquid in my stomach. I'm dry heaving so bad, crying, and the bitter taste of bile only makes it worse.

"Tell me it's a lie," I whimper, begging Giannis. "Tell me he's just a lying piece of garbage."

"I'm sorry, Ali." Giannis holds my hair back from my face with his uninjured hand. "We heard, and once the doctor gave me the okay, I came right over."

It took a while for the nausea to abate and my stomach to stop clenching as if still heaving, but it did, and I stand on shaky legs. He helps me a bit, and I walk over to the sink after flushing the toilet to brush my teeth.

"What happened to you?" I'm watching him through the mirror, my body leaning heavily on the cabinet. The tears won't stop. The tightness in my chest won't lessen any time soon.

Giannis chuckles a bit, rubbing the back of his neck with his other hand. "Small fender-bender. I'm fine."

"You sure?"

"Yes."

"Okay." I'm still a bit queasy but manage to get a grip on myself and walk out of the room. The living room is empty, Dwayne nowhere to be seen. "Where's—"

"Making sure your dad left."

"Thanks."

"She's going to be okay. They'll find her."

"They?" *Please tell me Casper and Callum know where she is.*

"The Jameson family," he whispers, pulling me into a tight hug. Tears fill my eyes, relief settling into my bones. "They know where she is, Ali. They'll bring her home."

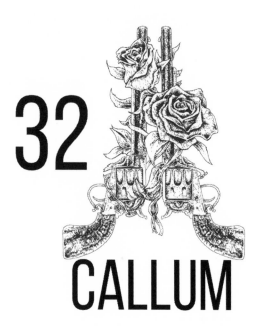

32

CALLUM

Seventy-two hours ago…

"ARE YOU SURE, Ezra?" I ask, reading the urgent email he sent me fifteen minutes ago. I'm still in the underground parking lot of the hotel where Casper and Aurora are staying; she knows where he stands, what he's offering, and Miss Cancio accepted with grace and a few terms of her own.

Did I give them shit? Yes.

But the woman has a quick wit, sassiness that reminds me of Aliana, and put me—and all the Jameson men—in our place. She'll do bloody well. Keep Casper on his toes.

"Boss, I'm sure." The clicking of a keyboard is heard in the background, several alerts pinging in different tones and ranges in volume. "The man's real name is Santis Gaspar and he's the youngest son of Cornelio Gaspar who's currently in ADX Florence serving a two-hundred-year sentence."

"Someone threw the book at the cunt." I'm going through each document with everything from passports, real and fake ID's, and then family photos dating as far back as the arseholes first birthday to as recent as a month ago.

"They did. Wanker's arrest was over tax evasion, but while inside, they pinned everything the city of Chicago could within the statute of limitations, from money laundering to the killing of two CPD officers, and then the added charge of distribution of heroin. This came on the heels of Governor Ruben's election. His prosecution of a known drug trafficker made him a man of the people and a champion for the city."

"And now they're getting paybacks from Rubens."

"Yes." Another email comes in and I open it, my ire growing the more I stare at the photo of Rubens celebrating with Gaspar and Martin. The date is from a few days after Aliana delivered the fucking statue and walked out shaking.

I've let this go on long enough.

I'm going to break each skull with that blasted fucking artifact.

An artifact I bought and will be getting a full refund for very soon.

"Does Casper know about Santis? Does Cancio know he has a rat in his organization?"

"No. I'm preparing the docs for Casper now."

"Send them to me and I'll forward it in the morning. He's busy at the moment."

"Will do." He doesn't say anything else, and I almost disconnect when he clears his throat. "There's one more thing, Callum. I was going to explain this to Casper, but you need to know as well. Santis has gone missing, two days now, and from my investigation into every soldier in that organization, he's close to Dominic."

"As in Cancio's right hand?"

"Correct." There's no bond with any of the other men, no drinking a pint after work or socializing. He talks to Dominic and no one else, the latter of which hired and promoted him to his current rank as head bodyguard for Aurora's father."

"Does he know them?"

"He's shown interest in one."

"Which one?" I grit my teeth, knowing the answer already. Dominic wants Aurora, and that leaves my Venus. "Who's your informant?"

"Pierro, sir. He's Cancio's driver, and both women like him."

. "And?"

"And he's confirmed that Santis makes Aliana uncomfortable."

"Thank you." Tossing my mobile on the seat next to me, I back out of the parking spot and then garage, taking a sharp turn and driving straight until I reach the interstate. "I fucking warned them."

THE STRIP CLUB IS EMPTY TONIGHT, NO CARS OUTSIDE OF THREE THAT occupy the spaces closest to the front door, and I park in front of it.

I have no backup with me. It won't be needed, and after grabbing my Ruger and extra magazine from the glove compartment, I put the latter inside of my trouser pocket.

I'm calm as I exit my vehicle and walk up to the door; a solid kick and it slams open, the wood damaging the plaster. Two men rush forward then, hands on their weapons, and they're dead before either can fully react.

A bullet to one head, the other to the neck.

"What the fuck is...Callum?" Flavio Gaspar's imbecilic second-in-command pales, his body moving backward. Probably remembering the damage inflicted the last time we met. "We didn't know you were in town. Flavio would've... *son of a bitch!*" His gun now lays on the dirty ground while blood drips from the wound on his wrist. "Why the hostility," he grits out, eyes darting behind him. There's movement back there, more than one person. "Let's talk this out. Whatever you're here for—"

"Open the curtain."

"This isn't a good time."

"You sure?" At his nod, I shoot him two more times. Thigh and shoulder; he'll bleed but won't die *yet*. "Is that still your answer?"

"No."

"Good boy." I point at the curtain. "Open it."

Whimpering, he does as I ask. The sound is pathetic, almost comical, but what I find as he pushes the fabric aside infuriates me. There are five women, no older than twenty and naked, some with a few bruises on their faces.

These are not their dancers from the other night.

With how they're being treated, I'd say forced prostitution, and I can't allow that.

"You sick fuck," I snarl, biting back my action for a moment when some of the girls scream in fear. Exhaling roughly, I lower my gun and then face them. "Grab your clothes, get dressed, and head outside. Please wait for me. My family will help you with whatever you may need."

"Why are you doing this?" One of them, a short blonde, asks. She's shaking. Her left eye is almost swollen shut. "We were tricked like this once before."

Before? The bloody fuck?

"How long have you been held against your will?"

"A month," she says, tears falling down her cheeks.

"Shut the fuck up, Jenna, or I'll—" The twat doesn't get to finish, not when the next bullet enters and exits through his hip. I'm sure the bone shattering has something to do with his scream of pain and the way he crumbles to the ground like a broken puppet.

"Threaten them again, and the next one will be on the tiny prick you try to pass for a cock."

"Callum, we can talk this out," he gasps, pain radiating across his features.

"No." Pulling out my mobile, I text Lindsey and Kray. They're off, but together, and I need them here fast.

Situation with women held against their will. Going to need

help with clean up and delivery to the Conte House. 3 dead and 5 innocents. ~ Callum J.

Kray is the first to respond.

Where? Medical attention? ~Kray

Gaspar strip club, and basic. They seem roughed up and are untrusting; I need Lindsey here to gain their trust. ~Callum J.

Flavio's right-hand man drags himself toward the blonde, more than likely seeking to use her as cover, but I walk over and place my boot on his chest. Press down hard enough that it hurts, and his wounds bleed profusely.

A text comes in, and I look down at my mobile.

Fifteen minutes from there now. OMW ~Kray

"I have someone coming that will help you," I keep my voice low and unthreatening. They still cower back, and I don't blame them. God knows what these arseholes have done to them. "Lindsey works for the Conte House—"

"I know that place." A brunette, tall and gangly, steps forward. "They helped my sister escape an abusive husband. You know them?"

"My girlfriend works there. Her name is Aliana."

"She's not your girlfriend. She belongs to…" You can't understand garbled speech when the person is choking on his own teeth.

"Aliana, I know her! She teaches and helps in the office."

"That's her."

"I trust you. Where do we go?"

"Grab clothes, yours or not, and cover up. They'll be here to help you soon." When she steps forward to go, the others follow with a look of pure relief but before they exit, I ask for a final favor. "Do not leave, but keep out of this area. Wait in the dressing room with the door locked if that makes you feel better, but stay away. This is a conversation you do not need to witness. Understood?"

"Yes," they answer in unison.

Before the last girl closes the door to the dancer's dressing room, I turn and meet the scared eyes of a man who has a few minutes left to live at best. "You want to know what the saddest part for you is?" He tries to answer my question, but instead spits out blood with fragments of teeth. His lips and gums are a bloody mess, the cuts very deep. "Don't hurt yourself, lad. I couldn't give a flying fuck if you want to know either way."

"P-please." *Pathetic.*

"I warned your boss. I made my demands very clear."

Another cough, his face etched with pain. "Don't."

"Flavio didn't listen, he didn't stay away from her, and now I'm going to show him just how deep my reach goes."

"Callum—"

"You're a lackey with no real worth. I'm going to kill you, and I still don't even know your name." Standing over him, I aim my gun at his head and empty every last bullet in the clip and then exchange the empty one for the full one. His head is unrecognizable, what's left is disgusting, and yet I empty that magazine in him too.

A real man doesn't hurt or force a woman. A real man doesn't follow a weak leader.

There's silence as I walk out of the strip club, spliff in hand and a cloud of weed smoke behind me. I'm a mess, and those women inside have seen enough horror to last a lifetime.

Kray and Lindsey pull up a few minutes later. They take one look at me and share an amused look.

"Disposal or a delivery?" Kray walks to the boot of his car, finger on the key fob.

"Freeze him. This is personal." I take in a deep drag and hold it, before letting the smoke exit through my nose. "As my second, you're going to need more men with you. Assert yourself."

He takes it for what it is. That was his interview and promotion. "Done."

"And the women?" Lindsey has some first-aid items in hand. "What of them?"

"Whatever they need, make it happen. I'll assume the cost." Pointing at one of the water bottles, she tosses it, and I catch.

"There's another stop I need to make tonight before going back to Aliana's. There's a rat, and I'm going to find him."

"Need help?" Kray offers.

"Not for this one."

Forty-eight hours ago…

WE'VE GONE FROM MIAMI TO CHICAGO AND NOW VEGAS IN LESS than twenty-four hours, and a few things are weighing heavy on my mind:

I didn't find Santis.

I didn't see this attack coming.

I didn't have time to call Aliana.

The latter one stings the worst. I'm not trying to ghost her, to avoid her, but right now Casper needs me, and I will do whatever it takes to help him save Aurora. For him. For my Venus.

Aurora is her best friend, and she has to be worried sick.

How could her father not realize his right hand's intentions? His lack of background checks on the people he employs is concerning. Lazy, if I'm being honest.

"I'll be home soon, love," I whisper lowly, not that anyone can hear as I shoot the lock and then kick the doors to the run-down wedding chapel open. They slam against the wall, yet no movement comes from the inside. Quietly, we make our way in, Casper at the front, and he pauses when the view of an older gentleman playing the organ comes into our line of sight.

There are people inside, some drinking cheap stout while others watch as if this were one of the soaps my aunt loved to watch when we were lads.

A woman begins to walk down the aisle, all but dragging Aurora behind her, and I want to shoot the cunt. This is her stepmother; a cow of a woman with no heart or conscience.

"Don't do this, Samantha. Let me go!"

"Shut the fuck up, brat. I should've had you disposed of years ago."

None of the people watching do a thing.

They will now.

Casper raises his gun and shoots the man pretending to be a preacher. He falls to the ground, a puddle of blood around him, and they all scatter like insects. They don't get far, and I take great pleasure in watching bullets descend on the crowd of nobodies as we pick them off one by one.

It almost reminds me of a video game I used to play in my teenage years.

To my right, the De Leon brothers take care of the organ player and the lady with fake flowers, while I shoot a tweaker in the neck. They came with us from Miami no questions asked, and I trust both with my life. Bodies fall all around me, blood staining my clothes, but it's one particular son of a bitch that catches my attention.

Amid chaos, Santis Gaspar tries to sneak out of the room. *Fucking twat. This is where he's been hiding.*

I don't aim to kill. Not this time.

Instead, I fire low, shattering both kneecaps and causing the arse to tumble. His head smashes into a tall mirror, and his body sags. He's knocked out cold, unmoving, and when Thiago raises his gun beside me to finish the job, I shake my head.

"He's mine." Yet I don't fire again. Instead, I plan. My mind goes through ways to get him back to Chicago for the time being, until I'm ready to deal with him.

"Did you forget how to shoot?"

"Oi, that's insulting." I chuckle, killing a man just to the left of Aurora's stepmum. "His is a long-term care treatment, and I need to fly his *live* body out of Vegas."

The man scratches his jaw, pursing his lips. "If you pick him up in Miami, I'll take him outside now and dump him in a trunk?"

"I owe you."

"Family never owes." He walks away then, and I turn my attention back to the old cunt now screaming, crying over someone who's dead on the floor while the idiot holding Aurora backs himself into a corner. They know they're fucked, and I watch, amused, when that moment of clarity hits.

Aurora's mother takes off running in a ridiculous pair of high heels, and the act alone is almost insulting. Almost, because the moment Ivan De Leon goes after her, she teeters.

A few stragglers attempt to crawl away, and while the others are occupied, I make quick work of those groaning while covering Thiago, who drags an unconscious Santis out the door. If Casper saw him, I'll explain later, but right now the son of a bitch is too valuable to kill.

The last body still twitching is that of a heavier set man who'd been drinking from a paper bag. Three bullets to the chest, and he's still complaining; one bullet to the head ends that. Then, those inside turn to watch my cousin as he walks toward his Gem and a shitting himself Dominic.

"Let her go."

"I'll kill her."

"No, you won't." His eyes meet Aurora's, and the bloody tosser smiles at his woman. "Close your eyes and walk toward the sound of my voice, sweetheart. Trust me, baby. Nothing will happen to you."

"He's got a gun to my back," she says lowly. A tremble to her voice.

"He'll die before a single bullet dislodges from his gun. They will all make sure of that."

"I'm right here, you piece of shit."

"Nico!" Samantha's screech fills the room; she's fighting Ivan's tight grip. He all but drags her back, clothes ripped and one shoe missing. "Baby, help!"

"Mom!" Dominic yells out, pulling the gun away from Aurora. Big mistake, because a second later, Aurora ducks just as we raise our guns and empty what's left bullet wise in his torso.

His body jolts with the onslaught, blood splattering across the room. He's lifeless when he hits the ground, disfigured and with a wailing mum as the only being to mourn him.

A woman who will spend the rest of her life replaying that image as a penance.

Dominic broke a sacred rule in our business: loyalty above all. You don't turn on the organization, your boss, and his family.

Aurora is in Casper's arms before I look over, talking to him lowly while the rest of us walk out and give them a moment. They'll come out when ready, and we'll burn the place down to the ground with the bodies inside. Fuck them all.

Thiago meets my gaze when I walk over to the car, and I accept a towel Ivan's holding out. "Are we good?"

"Yeah, we'll be heading back right away. I have my own woman to reclaim."

"If she lets you," his brother teases, but Thiago doesn't fall for the bait. His story with Luna is a bit complicated, but that's a mess of his own doing.

"I'll be by soon for a pickup. We'll be in touch."

"Dale, I got you." Thiago gives me a hug first and then Ivan, both standing back when my cousin and his girl walk out. They're smiling. Happy. And I find myself in a rush to head back to Chicago for the sweet girl I left behind.

To explain. To ask for forgiveness.

Not talking to her isn't something I can do again.

Not even for an emergency.

Present...

I knock on her door and wait. Not that it takes long as the padding of her feet rushing toward me is heard through the thick wood a few seconds before the object of my adoration all but yanks the door open.

Then she's there, and I'm breathing again, exhaling roughly as the heaviness of the last few days hits me in the chest.

One second, she's looking at me through teary eyes, a fist raised to her mouth, and in the next, my arms are full of my sweet girl. Aliana's shaking, her tears gutting me, but I understand she needs to let this out. It's been a rough few days.

"Is she?"

"Safe with Casper and very happy at the moment."

"Oh, thank God!"

"Please stop crying, sweetheart. It cuts to see you like this."

33

Aliana

"**P**LEASE STOP *crying, sweetheart. It cuts to see you like this.*"

That only makes me cry harder.

Between his disappearing act, my father, and constantly throwing up these last few days...I've been a hot mess. My panic is high and my tolerance for stress is at an all-time low. I'm tired and just not myself, but I know it's not because I'm pregnant. The test Giannis made me take came back negative, and a quick trip to the doctor confirmed it to be anxiety related.

"It's been a crappy few days, Callum." I sniff, burrowing my face in his neck and tightening the hold of my legs around his waist. "Very crappy."

"I'm sorry, Aliana. Truly, I am." He walks us over to the couch and sits with me wrapped around him. *I don't have plans to let go any time soon, either.* "Will you please look at me?"

With a small whine, I pull back and sit up. Meet his soft gaze. "Before you begin, I don't want specifics. No gruesome details, a gloss over works more than fine for me. All that matters is that you guys saved her and she's happy."

"Dominic—"

"Doesn't he work for Mr. Cancio?"

"Aye. Dirty fuck kidnapped Aurora with the help of her stepmum."

"Why?" *He's always been a bit creepy. Just like the other man.*

"Greed. Power. Corruption." His shoulder's shrug, but then again, in his world, all that is normal. "Which is why I'm taking you with me in two weeks. Aurora and London will be back by then, and we'll head home. For now, I'll be working from here and flying back every few days to oversee the progress on the Jameson Arms."

"You don't need to—"

"Yes, I do," he cuts me off before giving me a kiss. It's tender, so soft, and I melt against him. My clothing feels constrictive even though I'm just wearing one of his oversized shirts and some panties, something, he notices and confirms when he lifts the back and grips a cheek in each hand. "Fuck, baby girl. I shouldn't be trying to—"

It's my turn to cut him off, and I do by biting his chin. "I'm thankful you helped them, Callum. I can't be mad at that. Never that." Another nip, this one to his bottom lip. "I'm more upset by other things that happened while you were gone, things we'll talk about after."

"After?" He smirks, but I still see the lingering guilt in his eyes, and I hate it. As much as he dislikes my tears, it hurts to see him down. To me, he's a hero. End of. "What could we possibly do but talk right now?"

Rising myself slightly, I move my panties aside and show him my bare pussy. Just a small landing strip neatly trimmed above my clit. "You could be stretching me. I want to feel every inch of you buried deep."

"Are you sure?"

"Nothing makes more sense than reconnecting with you." It's the truth. The last few days were horrible, I have so much to tell him, but right now I need this. Need him.

"Want to go to your—"

"No. Right here." Reaching down, I undo the button of his jeans and lower the zipper. His hips lift and so do mine, and I hover over him, bending a bit at the waist to help him lower his pants. Cock hard and throbbing, Callum grips himself once he's out, pumping his hands twice while I push my panties aside. "I want you just like this."

"Then come sit on my cock, beautiful. Lower that warm cunt and squeeze me tight."

"My pleasure." Pushing his hand away, I replace it with mine and rub the head along my slit from clit to entrance and back again, twice, and then slip the first few inches inside. Just an inch or two, and then I circle my hips, letting him slip in and out a few times while watching his frustration mount.

His hands clench at his sides. His nostrils flare.

"Aliana," he warns, lifting his hips, but I follow and evade. *Not yet.* "Don't be cruel, love. I've missed you too much."

"You know I love you, Callum."

"Aye. Just like I breathe for you."

"Then I want you to know that I'm ready to start my life with you." Before he can respond, I drop my weight and take him in deep, body flush with his. At once he twitches, throbs, and I close my eyes to savor the moment. "I've missed this connection. I can't go so long without it."

"Never again. I promise," Callum grunts, meeting me thrust for slow thrust while his hands grip my asscheeks. Tight grip in each hand. We keep a steady rhythm, his touch controlling my movements while his cock drives in deep from beneath me. "This is my heaven. Where I find peace."

"I'm yours." Leaning my forehead against his, I stare into his eyes. Breathe in the delicious scent of his skin while those hands on my skin squeeze and push down harder, my body bouncing slightly. "Always yours."

"Mine." It's a growl. His chest rises and falls faster, as does mine, and I'm teetering on the edge. Almost there. "Let me feel you, beautiful. Fuck, just like that."

"Oh, my damn." Every inch of my body tingles; I'm shaking.

"Come." A command that Callum follows with a sharp smack to my right asscheek and I clench, muscles locking tight, and a cry leaves the back of my throat. I'm caught off guard by the sudden roll of pleasure, how quickly I heat for him, and I'm left gripping his shoulder and bouncing hard when he whispers my name. So low. So soft.

My name is on his tongue as he comes inside me.

Destroying me. It's not the first time he's done so, either. And yet, it doesn't stop me from seeking the feeling again and again.

Becoming a mother doesn't scare me.

Even if it's too soon. To be honest, I was disappointed at the negative result.

I want everything with him.

"DO WE REALLY NEED TO COME HERE?" I ASK CALLUM, STEPPING inside of an elevator I'm all too familiar with. We're a few floors from my father's office heading to speak to him, and to be honest, I'd rather the man beside me have done so by himself.

To say he's furious is an understatement.

He knows about the stunt my father pulled. He knows every word he said.

I'm also done with the games my family plays; always willing to threaten my brothers while risking my life and freedom.

"It is. Trust me." The elevator opens and we walk through, heading toward a closed door while ignoring his secretary and assistant. He has both; one is a doormat while the other is there to look pretty. One glare from him, though, and both women go mute. "Behind me, sweetheart. I need you to do as I ask and trust me."

"With my life." And when he barges in without knocking, I follow a few seconds later, closing the door so we're not interrupted. "Gentlemen. What a surprise."

"What's the meaning of this? Get the..." My father doesn't finish his sentence, eyes wide when Callum pulls out two large guns, one pointed at his head and the other at who my father called Gaspar. Both watch him with trepidation. Fear.

But it's the third occupant inside the room who I find amusing at the moment. Rigo Martin sits across from Gaspar, no gun aimed in his direction, and yet, he's shaking hard enough for his teeth to rattle. He's pale, looking between my father and the man across from him for help, and nothing like the boisterous, pompous jerk he usually is.

"Aliana, love?"

"Yes." Dad chokes at Callum's term of endearment. The severity of the situation is dawning on him.

"Do you want me to kill the governor? Say yes, and I'll pull the trigger right now." I don't answer right away. To be honest, I've wished so many times for someone to do just that. To end it all and release me from this burden. "His pathetic life is in your hands."

"Mi hija, answer him!" Dad yells, and it doesn't help his case. If anything, it annoys me. "How can you let him do this?"

"You don't get to speak to her." And while I decide, my boyfriend looks down at the phone in my hand and nods. "Toss it at the arse on the couch, please."

Once I do, the man with dark, leering eyes picks it up, grip tight. "This is all a big misunderstanding, Jameson. We're all friends here."

"Press play, Flavio. I warned you."

"Callum, I—"

"Press. Play."

"I know what you did. I don't need to—"

"Press play, or it'll be your brain matter the janitor peels from the ceiling. Your choice."

In this moment, I see the man everyone fears. The brutal killer and shrewd mob boss.

And yet, I feel no trepidation at his side. *Does that make me crazy? Or just as bad?*

Flavio, as Callum calls him, hits the button and a clip begins to play. The sound is off, for that I'm thankful, but his expression says it all. He's horrified. Looks a little sick. "I've seen enough."

"Have you?"

"Yes."

"Then I suggest you walk out and don't look back. Final warning." Flavio stands, dropping the old cell phone beside him, and walks toward the door. We step aside, my body covered by Callum's, but before Flavio can place a hand on the handle, the man beside me clears his throat. "I'm letting you walk out alive because Aliana's here—you owe your life to her, arsehole. However, you come within a thousand feet of her again and what I did to *him* will seem like a gentle pat on the back. Understood?"

"I do."

"Then go and give him a proper burial. He's been delivered to your home." Callum's message is there. He knows where Gaspar lives. The door closes after him, and we turn to look at my father and Rigo who sit as still as statues in opposites sides of the room.

Both guns are on my father, though.

"Your answer, Venus."

"As much as it would make my life easier, no. The answer is no," I say and Dad exhales roughly, shoulder slumping in relief. "But not out of love. That, I need to make sure you understand." My eyes are on the man I no longer see as a father. Not after how easily he threatens, hits, or sells me to save his own skin. Parents should protect and love, two things the man sitting behind a desk is incapable of. "I do this for the two boys you couldn't care less about. They deserve better than you, an absent father and a vain mother, but I can't in good conscience be the reason they bury a parent at such a young age."

"Aliana, you can't mean that. I've always been there." His indignation is almost amusing. His acting, though, leaves a lot to be desired. "You kids are my life."

"Bullshit, and we both know that." Callum walks over to the chairs across from my father and motions for me to sit. His guns are still out but lowered. "You don't give a bloody fuck about her well-being or happiness, and I can only imagine what your sons put up with. Which is why you're going to be doing a series of tasks to prove how unselfish you can be…isn't that right, Governor Rubens?"

"Yes." He swallows hard before picking up the pen beside a notepad.

"First, you will be sending both to study abroad. You have two choices: London or Sweden." My eyes widen, a smile curling at my lips. This beautiful man. *Christ, I love you.* Dad writes it down, his teeth gritting, but I'll give him brownie points for nodding. "Second, you will end whatever business dealings you have pending with the Gaspar family. I don't want them near you or the entire Ruben/Martin idiocy. And trust, I will find out if you do."

"Of course."

"And lastly…" Callum moves quickly. I don't see it coming until he slams the butt of the gun on my father's hand. He does this four times, and only stops because the unmistakable crunch of bone is heard. For his part, the governor bites down hard on his lip and keeps most sounds to a minimum—a low cry here or there while looking at me for help. No part of me wants to. This is his bed. "Lastly, you ever look at her wrong. Put your hands on her. Or use Aliana to do your dirty work again, and I will gut you like the spineless cunt you are. Nothing, and I mean not a bloody fucking thing, will stop me from ripping you open from neck to dick before throwing you in Lake Michigan and watching the fish pick you apart. Nod if you understand."

He does, and my boyfriend puts his guns away before grabbing my hand and leading me out of the room. I don't say anything. I don't look back either.

This is closure for me. I'm ready to start a new life.

We're almost to the door, though, when Callum stops to look at a scared Rigo. "Stay in your lane, Mr. Martin. I have eyes and ears everywhere, and I am everything you heard me to be."

THERE'S A CERTAIN BEAUTY IN LIFE WHEN YOU'RE HAPPY.

Things seem brighter. People appear nicer. And friendships morph and adjust, creating something special.

Like mine and Aurora's. It's been a few months since her kidnapping, eloping, and then taking over Boston with Casper by her side. They're domesticated now, living and working between Chicago and Boston, while plans evolve and their family grows.

For the first time, I can say that she's living and not just maintaining her mother's dream.

I've been to the grounds where Conte House #2 is being built in Boston, and the area is huge and will easily double the size of Chicago. This one will also have a few things that we don't have back home; the expansion of an on-site school for the elementary-aged-kids is one of them.

That, in and of itself, will help the anxiety mothers go through when their children are off to class. Older kids understand the situation and will defy the abuser's attempt to pull them out of school, while the younger one recognizes a parent or someone close to their mother and can be swayed with something as simple as candy.

We've seen it. It's sickening the lengths an abuser will go to in order to hurt someone.

Then, there's the original women's home. My second home.

I've spent so many years of my life working there, helping in the day-to-day planning, but my heart just isn't there anymore. London's is, though. She's such an amazing woman and has plans to expand the location, too, but I don't see myself in those plans. Not because they don't want me to be, but because the moment I felt secure in her reins, I asked for time off.

No return date. No plans to do so at the moment either.

I came to London, and I found *my* home.

This is where I live and breathe, especially, with my brothers nearby at a school a short car ride from Callum's penthouse in the city, where we stay most days.

For their part, my parents have left us alone. No news is the best news in my opinion.

"Miss, your order is ready," an older lady, who has a crush on Callum, taps the counter and I smile. Beside me, Lindsey snickers; she finds the stink eye I'm getting hilarious. *I need a new guard.* "Do hurry with those, ma'am. Mr. Jameson is very particular about his afternoon cuppa."

"Of course. Right away." Grabbing my items, I keep a straight face until we step outside and then I lose it. Laugh so hard that it starts a domino effect we can't stop. I laugh, she laughs, and it goes round and round until a throat clears behind me.

When I turn around, a sickening feeling turns my stomach.

"Hello, prima."

"Jorge, what are you doing here?" Beside me Lindsey moves slightly, the glint of her gun visible, but I shake my head when a group of kids who appear to be on a field trip walk by with some nuns. "Please leave."

"I can't do that." He shows his own piece, a heavy caliber revolver. "You're coming with me. You both are."

"No. We're not," Lindsey hisses, but then stumbles a bit. My head turns and I notice Alicia for the first time. In her hand is a syringe, the end dripping with some kind of liquid. But when my guard loses strength in her legs, she's caught by two other people. These men I've never seen before, but worst of all, the way they crowd around us makes it hard for anyone to notice what's happening.

They hold her up while I turn horrified eyes at Jorge. "What do you want? What did you inject her with?"

He shrugs uncaringly. "Your mother simply wants to have a word, and she'll live. A mild sedative never hurt anyone. Besides, your brothers survived it. You all will."

"My brothers? What the…you *bastard*!"

The pinch was sudden; I didn't pay attention to Alicia's movements. She smiles at me as the sedative begins to work, my legs feeling weak first and then my tongue is heavy while black dots fill my vision. "He is a *bastard*, Aliana. You've always been too stupid to realize what was happening right under your nose."

"What's that…?"

34

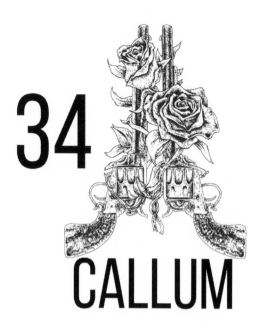

CALLUM

NINETY DAYS. THREE MONTHS.

That's how long my Venus has been missing, and no one can find a single trace of Aliana. It's as if the ground has swallowed her, hiding all remnants of her existence, and those around me are paying for the volatile ramifications of my failure. Because this is on me.

She was in my city. My motherfucking country.

Then, there's the disappearance of her guard, brothers, and the rest of that sack-of-shit family. *I should've killed them all, even if it meant she'd be angry at me.* That's where I dodged up. I take full responsibility for not chopping the head off the snake before burning the nest with the other members inside.

"Callum, I think I found something. Or better yet—someone," Ezra says from the other side of my office inside the pub. He's been here since she was taken, working tirelessly to find her, but all leads so far have been dead ends. "This is Jorge Rubens, is it not?"

My eyes shift to the man on the screen and sure enough, that's

one of the arseholes. *I'm just missing Rubens, Martin, and Gaspar.*
"Where is he?"

Before Ezra can answer, Giannis comes to stand beside me. I look over and find his eyes narrowed and lips in a thin line. "I know exactly where he is."

"You do?"

"Yup." His head tilts, studying the screen. "That's their grand-mother's home in Fornells. That son of a bitch has been in Spain this whole time." He's angry. Has been furious since she disappeared. And I understand him. I feel the same gnawing guilt.

This sense of responsibility because she was there to pick up a drink for me before we could meet up with him. The three wanted to visit some shops in the area and I volunteered to accompany them, be the added protection because a repeat of what happened to my aunt isn't something I can live with.

And yet, to me this is worse.

I don't know how she is.

If she's hurt.

"How soon can we be there?" Kray pushes off the wall. He's kept a solid grip on his emotions for now, but I do pity the bloke that receives the brunt of it once he unleashes.

"In two hours." Ezra moves the mouse, clicking on another webpage. This one is a database; he's running Aliana's picture through it. "I'll have everything ready to go and will call you with any news."

"Thanks, mate." I give his shoulder a squeeze and look at the others. Archie, Kray, Dwayne, and Giannis await my orders. "You have five minutes to grab whatever you need; the vault is open."

FORNELLS IS BEAUTIFUL, A QUAINT VILLAGE IN A BAY NORTH OF THE Balearic Island of Menorca, Spain. The population is small.

Everyone knows everyone. And this couldn't be more apparent when we disembark the boat chartered to bring us over.

The locals stare.

They murmur.

Yet, it's a small boy no older than eleven that approaches when we make it to the village center. He's sweaty and is missing a few teeth, but I appreciate his bravado. "Are you here to take the idiot home?"

The others laugh at his description of who I'm certain is Jorge Rubens.

"That depends on the idiota?" I ask, and his eyes narrow. Behind him, a worried man—by resemblance, I deduce he's the father—walks over.

"Forgive my son. Lino can be too outspoken at times."

"Nothing to forgive. The bloke he's referring to *is* a pest." At my words, his shoulders relax a bit. "Now, can you please point us in his direction. We need to clean him up and get him home. His mother is worried sick."

"Of course." He's not buying it, and he's a smart man for doing so. "I'll take you to my family's small bar."

"Gracias."

"De nada. Just take him and don't let him come back," the boy interjects, and I laugh for the first time in months.

"You're something else, kid."

"That's what my mama says, too." Lino begins to walk toward a small building not far from where we stand, but before he steps inside, he motions for us to follow.

No one else in town says anything. They watch us. Untrusting.

"Keep your eyes open, and any member of the family is to be taken in."

"Yes, sir," all four answer, voice low. If Lino's father heard my instructions, he pretends otherwise, and we walk inside the establishment to find quite a scene.

Jorge Rubens is here and drunk off his arse.

He's stumbling, trying to find rhythm in a flamenco beat playing in the background and doing a piss poor job. There are bottles occupying three of the eight tables inside, all empty and some broken from being slammed down too hard. Then, there's what looks to be vomit on the floor in various spots.

It's a disgusting sight.

"Hello, Jorge." At the sound of my voice, he freezes and his face whips around toward me. It's almost funny how quickly he sobers up a bit, face paling when he takes in the others behind me. "You've created quite the problem for yourself? Yes?"

"Jameson, what are—"

"Silence." The two other patrons leave the bar while I turn my head to Lino and his father. "Please take your family and go. I will pay you for the damages incurred, but this won't be gentle."

The father swallows hard, his eyes flicking between me and the nuisance. "Understood."

Lino, though, has other plans and tries to resist when his dad ushers him out. "But, Papa!"

"Listen to your dad, kid. Help him take care of your mum." At the mention of his mum, his chest puffs out and he nods. Takes off in the direction of the back, while I move my attention back to the scum pissing on himself. "Get him a change of clothes and on the boat. We have somewhere to be before sundown."

"Hijo de puta!" Jorge screams. The boiling hot water dripping from his naked torso has taken most of his skin off, the top layer anyway. He's in pain. Bleeding in some parts. "Please. No mas…I can't take…*fuck*! I'll talk."

"Mate, you really suck at this whole torture thing." Those standing against the wall inside the pub back in London all chuckle. We've been at this for ten minutes now; we allowed him a nice nap since returning, but the man makes this too easy for his position on floor. "You're supposed to let me ask the question first."

"I know where Aliana and her brothers are."

"I'm sure you do."

"Isn't that what you want?"

"It is." I hold a hand out, and Archie places my whip at the center of my palm. Its weight feels good. This weapon is an extension of me, and I let the leather unfurl and crack it once against the cold concrete. I press the button to release the blades, and the audible click sends a shiver through Jorge. "But I need to know the full story before I pass judgment."

"She's in Nicaragua. So is the woman, Lindsey, and the boys." Jorge licks his cracked lips. "They're not hurt, but that's because Aliana will be stealing something very valuable in three days." *Three days. Day after Valentine's Day.* Instead of celebrating with me, they'll be putting her life at risk for their personal gain. *I won't allow that.* "That's what kept them safe, for now. They need her compliant, and my mother—"

"Your mother is dead," Giannis interrupts, his lips curled up in disgust. Normally, I'd shoot someone for doing what he just did, but he has permission to do so if the wanker is lying. "You forget I went to the funeral."

"That woman wasn't my mother."

"Then who the fuck is…" Giannis trails off and his eyes widen. The look on his face is almost comical. *Almost*, because I'm clueing into what he's hinting at and it's sickening. "You mean to tell me Ada Rubens is your mother?"

"She is. She also killed Aliana's father, and he's not her first victim."

"Governor Rubens?" He nods at my question. "What else has she done? Why is she holding Aliana and her siblings?" You have to be one mentally fucked individual to hurt your own kid. Then a thought occurs. "Is she even their mother?"

Because at this point, nothing would surprise me.

"She is."

"But?"

"But she loves money and her freedom more. That's why she killed my father all those years ago, the governor's ambitions were similar to hers. However," he coughs, then rubs at the skin of his chest which is a mistake. His hiss is loud. "Fucking shit."

"However, what?"

Jorge's face is pinched tight with pain. "She does have a weakness."

"Which is?"

"Rigo Martin."

Rigo's son is in the room, and the look on his face says it all. There's hurt and betrayal, but more than that, I see hatred and a thirst for vengeance that rivals my own.

"I want every last detail of your mum's plan, Jorge." Flicking my wrist forward, I strike across his blistered chest twice and then watch the skin part where the blade sliced through. He screams, snot and tears mixing together at the bow of his upper lip before sliding lower. *Disgusting.* "I want her location, and that of your wife, because I know she's involved, too."

"Yes." A whimper.

"You will also call your mum and tell her you're taking a holiday somewhere you've always wanted to visit."

"Yes."

"And Jorge..." bloodshot pupils stare back at me, the pain on his features prominent "...I'm going to thank you ahead of time for your cooperation. Now, please try and relax. It's going to be a long day."

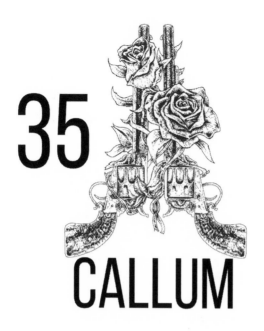

35

CALLUM

I'M OUTSIDE THE penthouse door, leaning against a wall, when Casper steps out. My eyes are on my cell, reading my last text exchange with Aliana three months ago. It was a silly argument over a TV show character's death, and she'd been pissed by my nonchalance. But that's one of the things I love about her; she's passionate in every aspect of her life, even something as mundane as a television series. "Took you long enough, mate."

"You consider this late?" At his reply, my eyes snap to his. His are on my mobile, trying to catch a glimpse of the photo of her flipping me off, but before he can make her out, I pocket the device. He'll know soon enough. The world will.

I never wanted to hide us but did so because Aliana wasn't ready.

And when she was taken, Casper was busy. Our conversations have been stilted at best, but I understand more than anyone what the safety of the woman you love means to you. He dismantled and rebuilt the Boston syndicate, eliminating every single threat to the

Cancio name, and then handed their heads to Aurora and her father on a silver platter.

I can't fault him for that.

"I can always head back inside and slip beneath the covers and violate—"

"Shut it," I snap, a shudder of disgust running through me. *Disgusting arse.* "Aurora's like a sister, you wanker. I don't need to hear that shit."

"Noted." Casper's chuckle grates on my nerves, but I've missed the condescending sound just as much. *Aliana has made me soft.* He checks his pocket, taking account of all placements, and then adjusts the custom gun holsters I got him last Christmas. "Lead the way."

"You told her where to meet up with your dad in case of...?"

"Gem knows everything." There are no secrets between them; she's aware in the same capacity Aliana will be. A way of thinking we share.

Nodding, I turn toward the elevator and press the down button before pulling out a small remote. I toss it at him. "This is for the cameras on this floor. You have them blocked, no?"

He takes it, turning the fob in his hand. "The hotel's security is circulating the feed from last night; I paid them handsomely for their discretion and compliance. Inside, though, my own devices are on. Everything is being recorded."

A snort escapes me at that. "Did this compliance come with a threat attached?"

"Would I be me if it didn't?"

"Touché." Tilting my head at the device, I send him a meaningful look. This is part of the *just in case* precautions. "That will send you a direct feed of this door. Add it to the app dashboard that Ezra set up on your mobile... it's my Valentine's gift to you."

"Very thoughtful, *love.*"

"Piss off." The elevator signals its arrival, and I flip him off before stepping inside the now open doors. We're heading toward the parking level where my men wait inside of a black Range Rover with dark windows.

Once inside the vehicles, no one talks. Casper's attaching the new security system to his app while I go over every detail Jorge shared before taking his last painful breath. Because I beat him— brought him to the brink of death multiple times in the last seventy-two hours, only to start all over again.

He bled for his sins. He told me something very interesting about the item they want Aliana to steal.

Countries have secrets.

Many countries pay handsomely to hide them on foreign soil in hopes of no one ever finding proof of their dirty deeds. The United Kingdom and Spain are two of those countries; interchanging classified information to avoid anarchy amongst their people.

There's money involved in that. A lot of it.

Power too.

The drive to the port isn't long, and when it comes into view, I hand Casper a small stack of papers. My driver passes the parking lot and drives straight through; he knows where to go, while the others stay alert. These are men my cousin isn't too familiar with; the other Collado brothers being two of them.

Contract killers from Spain I've hired on a long-term basis, something they were pleased with since Mauro is my weapons supplier. We're keeping it all in the family. And with them, once a contract is signed, nothing will break it.

"Read it and tell me what you see," I say, my tone leaving no room for jokes at the moment. Right now, he's not my cousin. I'm in charge.

Nothing will fuck up a job more than lack of focus.

"Okay." His eyes scan the top sheet with the artifact's picture and estimated worth in both legal avenues and the black market. The numbers are high. Ostentatiously, which could mean one of two things: others know what's hidden inside, or it's a set up by Interpol.

The second sheet holds the schematic, weight, number of people working the dock tonight, and the container ship's number. Then, he flips to the last and his brows furrow. I know what he's looking at—it's a picture of the thief. My Aliana.

They show a thin person wearing all black with a demon's mask covering her face. However, there are two things you can't hide from me; the brown hair even if the length is off—and the small tattoo she got while in London of a black whip on her wrist.

It's her idea of a corny joke. She holds the whip in our relationship.

Funny thing is, she does. That woman owns me.

The next picture is of a man I don't recognize, and he's not a part of their family either. He's either someone they know in Nicaragua or was brought in to do a job. These images came from a small memory drive on Jorge's keys Giannis went through and saved what was important, before demanding to know what they'd done to her. *He's grown on me, to say the least.*

What came out of Jorge's mouth next is why I lost one of my favorite hunting knives that day. I drove the blade so hard into his skull that the handle broke and we had to bring in a butcher to remove it.

"Two different people here. A couple?"

"Possibly." *No.* My jaw clenches, leg shaking. He knows my tells. "Don't give me that look, Casper. I need your help to confirm my suspicions."

"Okay. You know the risks attached to your request."

"I can't let her get hurt." Once those six words are out, I know they change everything. He'll do for me what I did for him. "I'm asking as your best mate. If she's involved...if she's *really* here today, I need to get her the fuck out."

"Done." Papers down, he holds up both hands. "The right one means in and out without incident. The left is we tear the bloody place apart and walk out with everything, and this time it includes the artifact they are here to steal."

"This one depends."

"On the *why*?"

"On what it means to her." If she wants me to break it into a million pieces, I'll do so happily. If she wants to live dangerously by my side, I'll marry her tomorrow. "You in?"

"I'd never let you go in alone, wanker." The car stops behind a stack of old containers for shipping overseas—the area seems empty, devoid of security, but we know better. Casper spots a flashlight skimming along the ground; he rolls down his window and aims in their direction. "Ours, or not?"

A low whistle rends the air, and I snort. "Ours. It's Archie."

"He's a good lad."

"A little psychotic too." All doors open and we step out. The smell of salt in the air is crisp, as is the wind coming off the water.

Archie stops before us, hands full of uniforms similar to what he's wearing. "Good to see you, Mr. Jameson." Casper shakes his hand while I take a port overall for myself. These are customary for all employees working the unloading zone. "It's a busy night and all hands are on deck—bobbies and every other department they could swing this way. Bloody bastards are watching every entry point for movement, but they missed this section due to it not being used and the museum's director wanting them to surround the piece until it's inside the armored car waiting to transfer."

"How many in total out there?" my cousin asks, slipping on his own uniform.

"About fifty, and twenty of them work for us. Those handling are all under payroll." Archie looks at his watch and then back at me. "You two will walk toward the armored truck, slide your ID, and pretend to go to the bathroom to clean up afterward."

"We have our change in the truck?" I'm smearing mechanic's grease across my face, making sure to look dingy before handing over the tub to Casper. Our hands are filthy now and our faces have enough to dissuade others from looking our way, especially when we put on hats with the company's logo.

"Yes, sir. Everything is there."

"Good job, mate." Turning to look at the brothers, I give them a pointed look. There can be no fuckups here. If Aliana gets hurt because of someone's stupidity, their families will pay. "Everyone knows where to meet after. Be there by five, or we come looking. No one will be left behind. Understood?"

"Yes."

"Go on."

"We are taking the truck?" Casper claps me on the shoulder. He knows I'm worried. Knows how this feels.

Nothing will make this right until I have her in my arms again.

"Yes."

"You're banking on her being inside."

Not a question, but I nod anyway. "She's smart. Way smarter than me, and I know that stealing this from beneath the watchful eyes of Scotland Yard and Interpol won't be easy, but sneaking onto an isolated truck isn't impossible. We know this. They'll watch and track all movement while outside, but once inside behind a locked door, they always become sloppy."

"Underneath the truck?"

"Or above."

"We'll help her, bro. You know I'm here for you."

I'm not the biggest sentimental bloke with my family, but in that moment, I turn and give my cousin a quick hug. It catches him off guard, but he squeezes me just as hard before we pull apart. "Thank you, and I apologize ahead of time. It'll all make sense soon, and I understand now your reaction when it came to Aurora. I wouldn't hesitate to kill for her, and if shit goes south, I'll give my life for hers."

"It won't come to that. Trust me."

We bump fists, and then it's all work. No more jokes. No talking.

We walk toward our destination while the commotion on the dock grows in crescendo. Dock workers yell out, and heavy machinery is being used to lift the crate. Every employee is watching that wooden box as if it were the holy grail while ignoring the two men who don't belong there.

Shouts to be careful fill the night's sky.

Loud noises follow as machinery lowers and then opens it.

And all while Casper slides in the keycard through the reader, making sure to avoid touching anything. He uses a handkerchief to open the door, and just before we step through, there's a loud cheer from the unloading zone.

The metal door closes, and all noises cease, especially the low whining noise from the cameras as they move to follow our movement. We don't look up while I press the scrambler to fuck with the signal, making it impossible for photo detection to play a part in the case when it's discovered we have it.

The truck is right where Archie said it would be, and we open the cab to find our bulletproof vests and jackets, the holster that these drivers wear, and two badges. Each has a fake name, company IDs, and a pack of gum in mine that Casper raises an eyebrow to.

"It's her favorite candy and trust me, she'll freak out. I thought it might make her smile."

Changing takes seconds, and I jump into the cabin and grab the set of keys along with the lock from the glovebox. I switch the originals to ours before coming back to where I wait.

After a minute, we hear a small thump and low curse. The noise is easily hidden behind the commotions the loading crew makes and the orders being shouted out by the museum director.

"Where are the men driving the decoy?" she suddenly yells out, and the Collado brothers walk forward, changed and with a set of papers in hand. They are dressed like us, and the older of the two makes eye contact through the side mirror as dock employees secure and lock up the artifact. "You two need to split up at the designated intersection. The maps are in the truck."

"Yes, ma'am," they answer in unison.

"Thank you, gentlemen." There's a hint of a fluster in her voice. It's softer and husky.

"Of course." This time it's the younger of the two who answers, amusement coloring his tone while from my view, his brother's eyes become hard. *The hell?* Within minutes, two other engines roar to life and Casper turns the ignition, waiting for the signal to back out and go.

"You okay?" he asks, his face holding concern. My knee bounces and my jaw ticks.

"Two of them.," is all I can manage through gritting teeth, my eyes on the live feed from inside. Again, two figures. The male and the female; she's doing all the work, though. Prying the container open with a crowbar to make sure they're in the right truck. "They came in from the top, and their hope is to be out before we leave. There's a beam above the truck they could climb out onto, and then escape through a window just below the roof line."

"Electrical?"

"They haven't noticed it yet." As soon as I say this, the man moves to open the exit latch they used to get in and quickly snatches his hand back. All movement stops then for a moment, shock on their faces before they begin to communicate lowly. They're murmuring to themselves while she waves her hand in a frantic motion.

Bang. Bang. Bang.

"Seatbelt, and keep your eyes down." Casper pulls back and out, following the instructions on the pre-set GPS they provided. We're heading toward the A13 and we'll deviate paths at the second round-about, where the Collado brothers will go to a warehouse twenty minutes out and dump these trucks there before blowing each up.

No evidence left behind.

The direction has us driving the main road that connects east and central London, but we'll disappear at Limehouse Link Tunnel. That's where our connection will cease and so will all the cameras in this area, not one being able to tail our direction.

And that's what we do until reaching an open field out in the middle of nowhere.

That's as long as I can take it, and the second Casper puts the truck in park, I'm rushing toward the back. There are no houses here. No witnesses. My hands shake as I input the code on my lock, and when it beeps, I all but yank the entire thing off its hinges in my rush to see her.

It's been fucking months.

Brutal and agonizing days where I thought she might be dead.

The doors bang open, and inside two people stand with fear in their eyes. But it's hers I'm focused on, the pure relief that pours out of her slim body and she sways—grips onto the wooden box to right herself at the sight of me.

"Aliana, come here." My tone is gravelly. I'm at my limit of patience. "Baby, please."

"Callum?" The worry at once evaporates, and she breathes out a heavy exhale. The man beside her calms too, as if he knows who we are but is playing a dangerous game of pretend. His clock is ticking. "What are you doing here?"

"Come." Not that I wait. Before the last syllable passes through my lips, I'm in the truck and have her in my arms. *Home. She is home.* Our lips meet, her desperation near the same as mine while my hands wander and explore, from the back of her head down to her shoulders and then sides, where I pause. I touch her stomach and a heavy breath leaves me, my eyes cloud with tears. "Venus?"

"I'm three months, I think. We've been hiding it best we could, but my mother...she—"

"It's okay. I'm here now."

"She's my little cousin." At the sound of the other man's voice, I whip my head to the side and glare. He shrinks back, pretending to be defenseless. "I couldn't leave her alone in this."

"The fuck did you just say? Her cousin?"

"Yes." He runs a nervous hand across the back of his neck. "I'm on her mother's side."

"Is it true, Aliana?"

"No." Venus's voice is shaky. "He's my handler."

"And who the fuck orchestrated this?"

Casper raises his gun and points it at the git. He pales, shaking his head, hands up in the air.

"Callum, please. I just need to—"

"Who, Venus. Tell me, baby."

"I can't." My face turns to her, and the tears I see there kill me. "It makes it real."

"Your mum?" Keeping my movement slow, I pull her against me once again. I sway us a little while she lets out a sob, her tiny pregnant body shaking. "Is what Jorge said true? She killed him in front of you?"

"Yes." Aliana swallows hard, and I'm proud of her for trying to calm herself. The stress she's been under is something I will never forgive myself for. "After they took us, I woke up tied to a chair across from him. He was beaten, a little bloody, and by those he considered friends and family. Those he protected above me."

"Can you give me names?"

"I can tell you where they're all at."

"Good girl." I kiss the crown of her head. "They won't get away with this."

"It was Rigo, Gaspar, and my mother. Jorge and his wife were also there; they took us, but the latter is dead."

"Jorge's wife is dead?" Just to make sure I heard right.

"Yes." Aliana pulls back just far enough for me to meet her sad eyes. "She'd been sleeping with my father for over a year. Jorge pulled the trigger while my mother egged him on, calling him all kinds of names until he snapped and grabbed a knife, stabbing her to death a few feet from me."

"Oh, sweetheart." *Fuck*, she should never have seen something like that. Not her. Never her. "Jorge is dead, by the way."

"Good riddance. My cousin was a pig." *She doesn't know.* And for now, we'll keep it that way. The less stress, the better. "By the way, it was my mom that put this all together. Her and Rigo, who is also her lover, and I'm disgusted by the level of trash my family has become, and all for greed. They needed the money from that sale to disappear, while Gaspar wants me. They attempted to kill two birds with one stone."

"I'm sorry, love. I never wanted something like this for you."

"I know and I don't blame you. Y-you came for me," she cries lowly, her bottom lip trembling as she speaks. "I've been so scared. She kept threatening us and—"

"Baby, where are your brothers and Lindsey? There's a second team waiting to take off and grab them."

"Just Lindsey is with them. But why my brothers?" she poses the last as a question. *I'm missing something here.* "What about them? She told me they were in a new school...it was one of the agreements we made."

"Not here in London. Where are they?"

"They let me pick between Nicaragua or Sweden. I chose Sweden with the hope you'd find them first since that was one of the choices you gave my father."

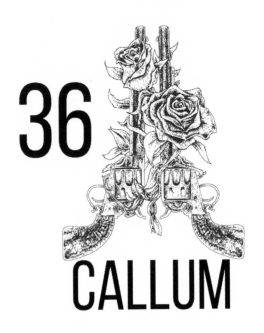

36

CALLUM

I CAN FEEL Casper's eyes on the side of my head, but right now an explanation will have to wait. There are more pressing matters to deal with than my relationship status, and after all my men regrouped at the meet up, we detoured to a small building near Heathrow.

The place is isolated.

As if the owner closed shop recently and just left everything as is.

Exiting the car, I turn to look at Aliana. "I'm going to need you to—"

"If anyone is going to shoot her, it will be me." My little firecracker is back. It took us thirty minutes into the drive for her to go from weepy to fuming and every other emotion in between. And I'm proud of her, but right now, that baby inside her belly comes first. "Sweetheart, please. I'll drag her to the car if you want, but I need you safe."

"I'm the safest next to you."

"She's right." A female voice comes from our left, and Aliana's eyes fill with tears once more. "You will protect her like no one else will."

"Roe Roe, I'm—"

"Shut it." My eyes narrow at her tone, but I relax when I see the smile on her face. "So, he's dirty-joke dude?"

"Yeah. Just like one-night stand turned into a solo wedding?"

"Touché."

"Are we okay, then?"

"I don't know." Aurora turns an icy glare on me. "Do you love her, Callum? Plan to spoil her while also accepting that once every few months, we will be having a sleepover?"

It's hard, but I manage to keep my lips from twitching. "Aye."

"Then I see no reason why we can't get this show on the road. Let's get a move on."

My cousin chuckles at my perplexed expression. "Is she always this bossy?"

"Pretty much. From my understanding, they both are."

"Nice."

"Callum, can we get a move on?"

"Yes, dear." Aliana exits the large SUV, but before she takes a step forward, I'm kissing her again. Passionate and quick, enough to steal the breath from her chest. "Are you sure you want to come?"

"Please."

"Then give me your hand, love. You're a Jameson now, and we don't hide or cower."

"Aye," comes from the other two.

Giannis is a few feet away, smiling wide when we approach with a quiet Kray and Dwayne beside him. They have their weapons drawn, but I spot a smaller Glock at Martin's hip. At my questioning stare, he shrugs sheepishly and hands it to Aliana. "Just in case."

"Thank you," she breathes out before stepping away from me and then hugging all three men; Kray nods to whatever she whispers. All

I'm able to catch is Lindsey's name, and I can't blame the man for the gratitude shining in his eyes.

She's his and has been missing just as long.

He already has orders to take a holiday as soon as we're done here.

"Ada Rubens is Aliana's kill. No one touches her, but she is not to escape. Is that understood?" Everyone taps their chest once in unison and then we're moving, walking toward our respective posts. Archie and the Collado brothers will maintain the back while Giannis and Dwayne cover the sides, and the rest walk inside as if strolling through an open garden.

They don't notice us at first. A grave mistake.

The man they hired to control my Venus is tossed at their feet with a clean slice across his neck. The gaping wound is large and gruesome, his body still warm, and the last of his blood trickles to the floor, creating the smallest of puddles. It's almost cute.

"Henri!" Ada screams, her eyes widening at the corpse. The others follow suit, and yet it's the older two of the trio that fail to look up. Gaspar is slowly trying to move away from them. *They truly fail at being criminals.* "What the hell is going on?"

"Hello, other," Aliana says from beside me, and Rigo's head snaps up a second before Ada Rubens's. "How have you been?"

"Mamita, I've been so worried." The tears begin, fake as the pearls around her neck. "How could you do this to your family? You killed my husband and now...now..." She pauses, a sob catching in her throat. I'm bored by her already. "How could you hurt me so? After everything I've done...fuck!" Ada's scream is loud, a painful wail, and it's because of the bullet to her right foot.

From experience, I know that stings.

"Tell the truth, or the next one will be to your face." Aliana's voice is devoid of all emotions. Her grip is firm, and I'm proud of her. "It's time for you to come clean. No more bullshit."

"I don't know..." My girl shoots past her head and Ada shakes, almost falls if not for Rigo keeping her upright. "Stop shooting!"

"The truth, carajo!" A tear slips down her cheek, but she's quick to wipe it away before retaking her stance. Her aim is now on her mum's chest. "Tell them how you blame me for not wanting to marry the man slowly moving away from you. Tell them how you forced me to watch you unload a gun on my dad's body, all the while saying I drove you to it. Tell them how you planned to make me abort this pregnancy before disappearing with the money to a private island while Gaspar made me his whore."

Never have I wanted to strangle someone so much in my life. To literally deprive them of oxygen while their body shuts down and eyes bulge out of their head.

I take a step forward, my intent clear, but Casper and Aurora grab my arm, the latter of which shakes her head and mouths *her kill*.

"Go on, Mother. Show your true colors."

"We were never meant to be parents, Aliana. That was our biggest downfall."

"Agreed."

My eyes shift to Kray when the oldest of the Collado brothers enters the building. I give them both the signal and they move quickly, one darting to the back where Lindsey is watching us from an office behind the three wankers. She's awake, but tied up, and I know Aliana will be happy once Kray gets her out of here.

"Callum, please!" Flavio's painful yell catches Rigo and Ada's attention. They watch as Collado lifts Gaspar off the floor and walks over to a large, dirty sliding glass door. "I'll disappear. I won't touch her!"

"Boss?" Collado asks, and I nod. Not a second later, Gaspar goes through the side exit and then doesn't move. He lies unconscious, small cuts littering his arms and face. Giannis is also there and while Rigo looks relieved, his son's face holds so much ire. "Do we take him to the car?"

"Not yet."

"As you wish, boss."

"Giannis?"

"Yes." He knows what I'm going to ask. I'm giving him the same courtesy as Aliana; Malcolm will just have to deal with it. Their kids get first right to claim.

"You or me."

"You." Rigo's son swallows hard; he looks at his father one last time and then turns his back.

"Son, you can't—"

"Silence." Everyone but my queen adheres to the command, her stony expression crumbling a bit. "I can handle them both. You don't have anything to prove."

"But I do. No more nightmares," she whispers, sad eyes glittering with tears she fights back. "She threatened our baby, Callum. A defenseless child."

"I know."

"Her daughter's child."

"I'll follow your lead, then."

"Thank you." Tilting her face up for a kiss, I give her one before aiming at Rigo's head. "Together, beautiful."

"Aye." A unanimous vote from every member of our family. Not the two pieces of shit crying and whimpering.

"You're our kids. You can't sentence us to death!"

"Stop this insanity. We can pay you!"

"Please, give us a chance to change."

"I don't forgive you, Ada." Her mother sobs louder—bangs on her chest as if in pain, while her daughter just sighs. "You're scum, worse than, and I hope you rot in hell for your crimes. Please know that I'll live my life to the fullest and become everything you never were: successful and loved. Fuck you."

She fires a second before I do, and we don't stop until the two bodies on the ground no longer move. They're not breathing, both with eyes wide open and blood pouring from their mouths, the multiple gunshot wounds visible on various parts of their body.

The first sob comes from Giannis. I know this is hard, but when Aliana walks over and they embrace, he crumbles. They both do, and we give them a moment. No matter how shitty both sets were, they are blood. It will always sting a little bit.

"So, Aliana?"

"I never hid it, Casper. You just didn't bloody pay attention."

My cousin scratches his jaw, lips thinning. "I'll blame my wife for the lack of awareness, and I extend a sincere apology."

"Oi, cut that shit out before she hears you."

"It would be just my luck, too."

"However, you can do me a favor to make up for the inconvenience…"

"Breathing or unconscious?" Casper asks; he knows me well. He's also no longer laughing but watching the small woman who's my world. My family. *Mine.* "I want him alive and delivered to the property in Dorset. His next job in this life is to be Zeus's snack."

"You and that large cat."

"I warned him, cousin. Told him he'd become my tiger's catnip." Aurora looks at us with a weird fascination, but I'll introduce her to my pets another day. When they're not hungry. "Come out to the property before heading home. It's a literal mini zoo."

Her eyes bug out. "You're serious?"

"Aye." I leave her with her thoughts on the subject and pick up Aliana, giving Dwayne room to step in as well. They'll be fine; it'll be rough for now, but what matters is that they're free. No more worrying. No more threats.

"It's over."

"You okay, sweet girl?" I ask, pushing her hair back from her face. She's lost a little weight since she's been gone, but the slight baby bump is unmistakable against my lower abdomen. *My baby.* "What can I do for you?"

"A burger and fries with a large cherry Coke?" For some reason, that cracks me up. Dear God, this woman is insanely beautiful. "I'm starving, Callum. It's been quite a busy few months."

"Then why the tears? I know this was—"

She places a delicate finger over my lips. "I'm not upset she's dead or traumatized by being the one to take her life. Not in the least. She's never been a mother to me. We never had that kind of connection. And before you ask, my father lands in the same category."

"And the crying?"

"Hormones, Mr. Jameson. I'm tired and hungry."

"Then let me get you out of here and fed." The emotions hit me hard then. The months without her, the constant worry, and I close my eyes while hugging her close. *I could've lost them both without ever knowing about the baby.* "I need you to know that I love you beyond all measure, Aliana. More than my own life."

"I love you, too. I've missed you." Her eyes tear up again, and she huffs at herself. It's cute. "This hormonal crap is going to be a pain."

I chuckle. "What can I do to make it better?"

"Never let me go," she whispers against my lips, kissing me once again, and I forget the world around us. Nothing matters but the treasures in my arms, clinging to me just as desperately as I hold her.

I'll never stop chasing her.

I'll never stop loving her.

Aliana Camila Rubens was born to be mine.

Aliana

Six months later

I STAND TO the side and watch with pride as Callum cuts his palm and let's a few drops of blood fall into a crystal chalice his uncle is holding. My eyes are riveted by him, watch every move he makes, and my heart fills with so much happiness as I take in the people inside the room bowing their heads.

My Callum.

My savior.

Their boss.

Closed fists bang on chests once and he follows suit, his gem-colored eyes flicking to me. But then again, he's always seeking me out. Even inside the same room, he needs me nearby.

Come, he mouths, and his father places a hand at the center of my back to help me up the walkway and then the small staircase which lead to him. The platform isn't large, but it's secure, and I have my own vows to make.

And while not as official and sacred as his, it's important for the wife of the boss to pledge her loyalty.

I'm his.

Today. Tomorrow. Always.

"Don't be nervous, little one. We're not like other families, and the women aren't shunned," his father whispers, tone affectionate and sweet. But then again, he's been like that since I came to live here.

One look at me, and I was claimed by the same parents that failed him. Weird, in a way, but the arse is having too much fun watching them fawn over me. He also gets a kick out of saying I'm the reason he's not the product of a broken home.

The two bickering old people have united with me as their goal.

Or better yet, to be the kind of grandparents that our child deserves.

"Easy for you to say, Abuelo." I'm out of breath already, but being nine months pregnant does that to a woman. "I'm the size of a whale, and everything makes me feel like a hundred-year-old chain-smoker."

My father-in-law bites back a laugh. "Would you prefer to be carried?"

"You wouldn't?" I turn to look at him, eyes narrowed. "I'll tell on you so—"

"He wouldn't what?" Callum asks from the bottom of the stage, his eyes dancing with mirth. "Carry you in front of all these people? You know the answer to that, Venus."

"Don't you dare!"

"My apologies, your majesty." And then, I let out a low squeal that makes those closest to the stage chuckle. Not at me per se, but how often I get caught in this type of situation. The moment he sets me down, though, I smack his arm and walk over to Uncle Jameson. He's another softie. "Get your nephew to leave me alone."

"You heard her."

"I did." Callum's tone holds no remorse. "Are you ready, love?"

"Yes."

He takes my hand in his, and together we face the men and women who work for the Jameson family. My family. Giannis and Dwayne are a part of that group now, as is Kray and Lindsey, who stand a few steps from the stage and to the left of Mariah and Casper.

Everyone is smiling. Happy for us.

"You will lay your life to protect her."

"Aye."

"You will respect her as you do me."

"Aye."

"I will never forsake my family. We are one blood."

"One blood." The last unanimous chant is loud, and it almost drowns out the music coming from the other room where politicians, heads of countries, and a few generals mingle and drink, unaware of what's happening within this room. We're celebrating more than just his blood oath, but the grand opening of Jameson Arms.

Don't let a country at war fool you. They all rub elbows in one way or another.

"My Venus," Callum's voice is reverent. So low no one else can hear, but I do.

"I love you, Mr. Jameson." However, the smile turns into a frown when I gasp a minute later.

"Aliana, baby?"

"Callum, I think…" I feel wet, not a lot, but like I had one of those accidents all pregnant women have. You sneeze or laugh at the wrong time and things happen down there. "Callum, I think my water is about to break."

"Are you sure?"

"Yes."

"Out," his voice booms, and everyone but our family leaves. They're crowding us now, worried, but Aurora meets my gaze, and she gets it. Gentle hands cup my face, thumbs rubbing across my cheek. "Are you in pain?"

"Not yet, but I feel off. Some pressure, but our doctor said that's normal." Callum's mom stands to our left, her hand massaging my lower back where I'm most uncomfortable, and I shoot her a small smile. "Thank you."

"I'm so excited, Aliana. My heart is racing!"

"Mum, let me get her to a seat. We need a—"

"Casper, honey. Don't just stand there. Please bring the car around the back."

"Gem, what're you—"

"I swear to God, if my best friend has our niece or nephew here because of you, I will smite you." At his wife's words, he nods dumbly but then jumps into action, rushing out of the room with all the men in this family on his heels. "Well, that lit a match under them. Pussies."

I'm surrounded by crazy people. I laugh at that, full-on giggles, but it quickly turns into a grimace as wetness rushes down my leg and feet. *So gross.* "Yeah, that was definitely my water breaking. I'm going to need a change of clothes."

"We have some in the car."

"Which one?" I ask, but Callum just shrugs and mouths *all of them.*

"You're that prepared?" Carefully, he picks me up, not caring about his clothes, and walks us down the stairs and across the room to a side exit. "When did you even have time to do all this?"

"While you sleep."

While I sleep. It's things like this that make me a believer in the possibility of a long and happy life with the person you love. Because only someone who cares will plan while you're asleep to make life easier. They'll sacrifice their rest and comforts so that when the moment comes, you never go without.

This man loves me for me.

With the good, bad, and ugly. Through sickness and health.

He holds me when I cry.

He understood my need to never discuss my family again,

including Jorge being my brother and not the cousin I was led to believe all my life.

He respects, loves, and protects.

Callum is why I'm not afraid to become a mother. To take this step, because I know no matter what life throws our way, he'd never allow what happened to me to happen to our children.

He's caring and loving and so patient.

My brothers already lean on him. Look up to him.

And when its time to push a few hours later, it's his eyes I focus on. All I see and understand is his hand in mine, fingers intertwined, while my body handles the rest. The entire delivery lasts a few hours; there was one moment where my blood pressure was high and a concern, but then she cried, and I lost my heart to the Jameson charm all over again.

Paisley Camila Jameson
Sex: Female
Weight: 6lbs 9oz
Height: 19 inches

CALLUM

One year later…

"**A**RE YOU SURE about this?" Malcolm asks, sitting back while watching the scene in front of him unfold. But then again, so is every other man I consider to be family. We're congregated atop a large deck with a table at the center just a few steps from me, but for this occasion, we stand. The veranda is all that separates us from falling into the den of my two favorite pets: one has lived with me since he was a cub, while the other I took in when the original owner couldn't keep up with its care.

My Hera and Zeus.

They're large and hungry.

Vicious and loyal.

To me. Only me.

And I treat them as if they are my babies, more so than the other animals that reside on my more than two-hundred-acre lot. There are various snakes, both poisonous and constrictors, while I also keep a few wolves. However, my Siberian tigers are who we watch today.

For over a year, I've babysat Flavio and Santis. Kept them in the same room, provided food and entertainment, while giving them a false sense of security that today won't be their downfall.

I never lied, but the more you make your prey wait, the easier it is to strike when the time comes. Complacency is a truly vile behavior, makes a person vulnerable—weak—but I did warn them.

A day. A week. Twelve months to the date.

None of that mattered in the long run, because they were always set to die.

The puppet master just hadn't chosen the *when.*

"Aye." Bringing the glass to my lips, I take a sip of my gift. The De Leon family has bought into the liquor industry, taking over a distillery in Cuba known for world-renowned rum. The amber glow alone is sexy while the taste is smoky with subtle tones of fresh pear and coconut, and while I'm not a rum drinker, this one I'm a fan of. "The information given to Aliana is accurate, and those are the codes that lead to their underground vault. One for each bank. Ezra verified it all, and he's never wrong."

"What you propose could change everything, my brother." Thiago smirks, and I know he's in. We've talked about this; Luna and Aliana have become close since our last trip to Miami, both women bonding over their growing up Latina. "The way we operate, live—how the world moves."

"The world." Malcolm shakes his head, but he's smiling. Santis and Flavio have been brought out to the enclosed space; they're sweating and complaining—waving their arms around and frowning. *They're still blind to their reality.* "We would be above the law."

"Yes. We would." My eyes look over to Casper, and he nods. He wants to make the move. "Aliana's father wasn't fully aware of either artifact's worth. The jade statue in Brazil, that one holds a heavy price tag, yes, but etched at the bottom is a set of numbers that belong to that government's missiles. Then, there's the vase in

London. That beauty is the only way in and out of the underground vault, the same one where Spain and the United Kingdom have their secrets and crimes stashed away deep underneath their largest bank. We are talking about war, civilian, and every worldwide transgression committed, which isn't public knowledge between the two."

Javier chuckles, fixing his cufflinks. "It's a good start, but the US will hold some leverage. Our hit has to have ramifications for them as well."

"That's the beauty of it." A whistle rends the air then, and we all turn our heads. My animal's handler holds a large red flag high above his head, and I pick up the matching one, waving it twice. He knows to exit swiftly, and he does, backing away slowly so as to not startle my pets. "With treaties come favors. With alliances come expectations, and the US has skeletons in both closets."

Malcolm raises his glass, his eyes ahead while the others follow suit. "To immunity."

"Aye." Every family present agrees. This would change the world's dynamic, our stronghold in every bloody thing a government does or prosecutes.

Flavio and Santis look at the keeper, then at us and wave back.

Somehow, they've come to think we're friends.

We're not. They're nothing more than overgrown catnip.

And while they watch me, walking a little closer to the high, above-ground terrace we stand on, the keeper walks out and locks the exit. A whirring sound fills the air, a loud rattling of metal, and then white and orange paws come into our line of sight.

The Gaspar siblings startle and take a few steps back. They scream, nothing of what they say making sense, and it won't matter for long anyways.

Zeus and Hera stalk their prey slowly, lowering their bodies to the ground and inching forward. The Gaspar siblings freeze, but their eyes are on me, on the megaphone in my hand that Casper was so kind as to grab from the table.

It clicks on, an annoying whine that settles into a low static until

I speak. "I warned you." Their heads shake, bodies moving closer to the enclosure's gate. "You had multiple opportunities to walk away, to stay clean, but you didn't listen. Here you will reap what you sow —just like your cunt of a father who aligned himself with people he shouldn't have—interfering with my family and the Boston organization."

Their family name will end here.

You don't make moves against this family.

You touch one—you bloody deal with all.

Flavio is angry, but scared. Santis is close to pissing himself, and yet, he's saying something I can't make out. He could be blessing or cursing me, I have no clue, nor do I give a bloody fuck.

However, the noises he's making Hera doesn't like, and hisses. Her nails dig into the ground, but both cats haven't lunged yet. These animals are hunters by nature; they wait and wait until the right opportunity arises. Or in this case, fucks up.

"I slit his throat." They both swallow hard at that, hands clenching. "Now, I'm going to make this fun. I'll have the keeper unlock the door and give you thirty seconds to make it out. You win, you walk out. You lose, my pets will pick their teeth with your bones."

I don't wait for their agreement and give the okay to unlock.

"Go."

Eyeing my tigers, they move a few steps and Hera remains low while Zeus rises midway, poised, yet he makes no move to attack. At the ten-second mark, though, both brothers turn around and run, pushing their bodies as far as they can, but it takes three full strides from each cat to reach them.

They pounce, forcing the men to the ground while locking their jaws at the back of their necks, shaking them from side to side. Horrified screams reach me, and I'm impressed by how far the sound travels when a true panic-induced cry for help is unleashed.

Zeus tosses Flavio aside like a rag doll, his body bouncing a bit on the ground, before pinning his chest with a front paw. Blood and spit dribble from the animal's muzzle and onto his prey, the latter of which is pushing with all his might but the beast remains unmovable.

For her part, Hera is already enjoying a chunk of flesh, taken from the still-alive idiot. It's from his leg, the thigh area to be precise.

Yet, this is nothing compared to what they deserve.

Yes, Flavio wanted to wed my Venus, but she would've become property of the family and would've been used as such. They spoke about it a week after their capture, unaware of Ezra recording this conversation. Back then, they had hope. Thought their organization —father—would come to save them, and they made plans.

The brothers wanted to share her. Lend her out. And eventually, when she'd become older and loose—their words—they'd whore her out to their seedier clientele with no limits to their depravity.

For that, I could never forgive them.

I'm being merciful by letting my pets feed on their rotten flesh.

Which they do. Piece by piece.

An alarm beeps from my mobile and I put my glass down, walking away without looking back, the others slightly behind me. I'm fixing my jacket and tie as I go. The stupid handkerchief on my breast pocket looks a little wonky, and I hope Aliana doesn't notice or she just might kill me at my own wedding.

Guests are beginning to shuffle in, each of the fifty chairs filling fast while Casper takes his place beside me. Our brothers find their seats in the first row on the bride's side, their wives all wearing cheesy grins while Luna smirks, camera poised to shoot.

They want my honest reaction to seeing my bride photographed.

I understand why a minute later when the traditional wedding march begins to play and my Venus pauses at the other end of the aisle. Everything stops for me. The air in my chest ceases to exist while the world fades away until she's all that's left.

My Aliana. My wife. Mine.

She smiles at me, and my heart beats inside my chest with the cadence of a war drum.

She takes her first step, and I'm able to breathe again.

She places her hand in mine a few seconds later, and I'm home.

Everything starts and ends with her.

Aliana Camila Jameson is the future I don't deserve but will fight every day to keep.

THE END.

Turn the page for news on the next Beautiful Sinner #6

THE BEAUTIFUL SINNER #6

Coming 2022!!!

That's right, my loves. We are going back to Miami, and it is time for Ivan to claim his woman. Who is she? Do you remember?

I left clues in Mine…

Keep up to date on News and add it to Goodreads!

https://www.goodreads.com/book/show/58858828-beautiful-sinner-series-6

BEAUTIFUL SINNER SERIES

ABOUT THE AUTHOR

Elena M. Reyes was born and raised in Miami, Florida. She is the epitome of a Floridian and if she could live in her beloved flip-flops, she would.

As a small child, she was always intrigued with all forms of art— whether it was dancing to island rhythms, or painting with any medium she could get her hands on. Her first taste of writing came to her during her fifth-grade year when her class was prompted to participate in the D. A. R. E. Program and write an essay on what they'd learned.

Her passion for reading over the years has amassed her with hours of pleasure. It wasn't until she stumbled upon fanfiction that her thirst to write overtook her world. She now resides in Central Florida with her husband and son, spending all her down time letting her creativity flow and characters grow.

Email: Reyes139ff@gmail.com

Find My Books Here:
https://www.bookbub.com/authors/elena-m-reyes

Elena's Marked Girls.
Come join the naughty fun.
Link: https://www.facebook.com/groups/1710869452526025/

Newsletter:
http://bit.ly/2nHJxTI

facebook.com/ElenaMReyesAuthor

twitter.com/ElenaMReyes

instagram.com/elenar139

bookbub.com/authors/elena-m-reyes

ALSO, BY ELENA M. REYES

SERIES:

FATE'S BITE SERIES
LITTLE LIES
LITTLE MATE
HALF TRUTHS {COMING 2022)
OMISSION {TBD}

SERIES:
BEAUTIFUL SINNER SERIES
Each book is a standalone.
Now Live!
SIN (#1)
COVET (#2)
MINE (#3)
YOURS (#4)
RISQUE #5
Beautiful Sinner Spin-Off
CORRUPT

(Marked Series)
Marking Her #1
Marking Him #2
Scars #2.5
Marked #3

(I Saw You)
I Saw You
I Love You #1.5

(Teasing Hands) Re-Released

Made in the USA
Middletown, DE
19 April 2023

29145866R00203